Title Page

Bilhah, Mother of Solace

Women of the Covenant, Volume 7

Angelique Conger

Published by Southwest of Zion Publishing, 2026.

Copyrights

Book Cover by Dar Albert

BILHAH, MOTHER OF SOLACE

First edition. May 5, 2026.

ISBN: 978-1946550859

Written by Angelique Conger.

Table of Contents

Given Away

Mama called to me. "Bilhah. Come, eat before your brothers take it all."

I delayed, in no hurry to get my food before my brothers Avdon, Melik, or Agos could grab the last flatbread.

The argument between Papa and Mama had ended with his leaving the day before.

I scooped watery stew onto the last crust and chewed on the bread which tasted like sawdust. Mama had little more to give us.

After the fifth day, no more stew filled the pot. Did my tears come from missing Papa or the food he brought to our cooking pot?

How could you leave us? Why have you not returned? I am so hungry.

Mama left to heal others each day, and often at night, usually taking me with her, even though I was only eight when she started taking me. We went when needed. "You must learn," she whispered when she woke me late at night. I worked hard to learn all I could. My brothers cared for our younger sister, two-year-old Nissa, grumbling about doing 'women's work.'

One morning Mama brought home a mutton leg to add to our stewpot. My brothers ate as if it would fill our pot forever. It was soon gone.

She took me with her more often after Papa left. I helped care for women giving birth, men with gory injuries that turned my stomach, children who fell into fires, and many other illnesses. I learned to treat them with patience and gentleness as Mama did. Although I did not like the horrors of healing, I was proud of my efforts and all I learned.

I returned too tired to cry for Papa. Yet my heart cried for him. We needed his help. Mama could not provide enough for all of us. My stomach always hurt.

Jehovah, why did Papa leave us? Help Mama get us enough food.

One day, Mama left with Avdon and did not come back with him.

"Mama," I asked the next day as we walked to visit an injured patient, "where is Avdon? I do not miss his teasing, but where is he?"

She waved her hand. "He works for a man, herding his sheep. He is old enough to work."

Never come home? Avdon protects me. Who will protect me now?

Sadness and loss overwhelmed me.

"Will he not come home at night?" I asked.

I glanced up to see her brush a tear away. "No. He serves his master."

I bit my lip. *Avdon serves a man here in Harran. Why? Papa said we would never become servants of another. He told me he was proud of me learning and becoming independent.*

After that, we left Nissa with my grandmama when we went to heal others. Melek and Agos could not care for one so young. Tears leaked onto Nissa's dark hair as I pulled her close to me when we took her to our grandmother. Would Mama leave her with Grandmama?

I feared more when in the next days, Melek and Agos disappeared, also becoming servants to others. I did not miss the food eaten by my brothers or their fighting. I did miss their gentle teasing and their warmth when I needed their love.

Will Mama *give me and Nissa away as well?*

One morning, two weeks after Avdon disappeared, Mama took me to care for a boy with an injured leg. As we worked to bandage his leg, her face became grim. I asked why, but she only shook her head. After working a short time longer, she led me home, refusing to answer my questions. We stopped by Grandmama's for Nissa.

Mama must not plan to heal anyone else today.

At home, with crisp, brusque words, Mama sent me to wash and change into a clean dress. She then inspected me, ensuring I had washed the blood and sickness away.

“Bring your other clean dress and sleeping robe,” she ordered. "We are going out."

“Where are we going?” I asked, wrapping the clothing into a bundle.

Mama only shook her head and wrapped a scarf around Nissa and tied it over her shoulder.

“Come,” she said.

I followed, asking no more questions. Mama had drilled into me the need to stay quiet. She knew more than me.

It was early, not yet midday. Fear filled my heart, and I trembled. *Where would she take me? Will she give me away too? She would not. I help her heal. But where is she taking me?*

When we passed the road to Grandmama's home, Mama went another way. At last, we reached a large brown house with the usual beehive-shaped roof. I searched my memory, trying to remember the owner. Mother had brought me once when I was six. Now I had much more experience. Perhaps someone in this home needed our services as a healer. But who lived here? Why would we bring Nissa?

She wouldn't give Nissa away! Would she?

At last, the name sprang into my memory with fear. Laban.

I shuddered. I had heard rumors about the mistreatment of servants by Laban and his sons. *Mama will not leave me here! She would not! Would she? Perhaps for only a day or two. I can help someone and then return home.*

Mama called out the usual greeting, "Peace," and we waited at the red-colored reed door covering. I expected a manservant. But Laban answered. I stared up at a tall, burly man with graying hair and beard, dressed impeccably in a light green tunic topped with a darker green robe.

I sucked in a breath. Laban scared me.

Before he could speak, Mama pushed me forward. With pain in her voice, she cried, "You said you owe me a debt. I can no longer care for my children. Pay your debt to me. Take Bilhah. Feed and clothe her as your maidservant."

I stood frozen, my eyes wide in disbelief, no longer seeing Laban or his home. I saw only emptiness. No Papa. No brothers. No Mama nor Nissa. "Why, Mama? I help you with your healing."

As if she did not hear me, she said, "Obey Laban. He is your master now."

Chills ran down my spine. *She would leave me here? Had she not heard the rumors? Was there not another home she could take me to?*

She pushed me forward. I stumbled into Laban, who stopped my fall.

"I only take her because you helped Avagail give birth." Laban turned his stare from Mama to me. "Did you teach her your skills?"

"As much as I could teach a child of ten."

Much more than that. I learned many things from you, Mama. I could help you if you let me!

But the words would not leave my mouth.

She turned and marched away, never looking back, with Nissa still clinging to her.

Will Mama give Nissa to another? Jehovah, please. Let her not do such a thing.

I swallowed my tears. Laban would not see my pain. How little I understood the world of adults, only the grief of the past months. I now belonged to Laban. *Jehovah, bless me! What will happen to me?*

"Do not stand there gawking. Follow me," Laban snapped. He turned and walked into the cool darkness of the house, his back straight. I could not depend on him to love me.

I followed him, struggling to remember something good about Laban and his wife.

Avagail stomped her foot on her soft blue rug when Laban brought me to her.

A tall, angular woman scowled at me. I wondered if she ever smiled. She had piled her dark hair back on top of her head, making her look stern.

"What am I to do with this ... this scrawny little girl?"

"What do you always do with a maidservant? She can cook and clean, and her mother taught her about healing." Laban's voice lost its coldness as he all but begged his wife to accept me.

"Maidservant?" Avagail growled. "Why would I take on this little girl," she ground out the word 'girl,' "to be my maidservant?"

I can do more than you think. I am a healer. If you do not want me, I will go back to Mama. I would have run, but Laban stood between me and the entrance.

"She will learn. I took her in payment."

Avagail harrumphed. "No doubt her lazy father left town owing you money."

Laban grimaced and my heart froze. *Is that what happened to Papa?*

"Eila —"

"Eila, the healer?" Avagail asked. Her frown softened.

"Yes, the healer. Bilhah worked beside her mother."

Laban's Home

Laban nudged me toward Avagail as she stood and turned on her heel. "Come. Did you bring anything?"

"Only a dress and a robe." I held the bundle of clothing up to her retreating back, then scurried after her. I did not want her to be angry with me already.

Avagail strode down the hall to the stairs. Without looking back, she clumped into the darkness of the chambers below. I shuddered and followed behind her. A small, uncovered opening high above us provided dim light.

An earthy smell of stone filled my nostrils, not the musty smell I expected. Avagail must have required regular cleaning here. We walked down the ever-darkening hallway on uneven, rough stones until she pushed open a thin cloth leading to a small chamber. "You can leave your things here. Zilpah will have to make space for you."

Dismay filled me as I stared at the small straw-filled pallet on the floor against the wall, covered neatly with a yellow blanket . Hooks on the opposite side held this Zilpah's clothing.

Am I *to stay here in this small space? I should have brought my blanket.*

"Set your clothing there," Avagail ordered.

I gazed past her at a small wooden stool, already filled with Zilpah's possessions. I gulped and set my small bundle beside hers.

Avagail jerked her head toward the hall. "We have work to do. People need to eat."

I trailed behind her, allowing the cloth divider to fall across the open space. We marched back down the dark hallway. Avagail strode onward. I tagged close behind. A hardness lurked beneath her feminine exterior. I did not want to cause it to emerge.

We entered the kitchen where an older maidservant raked the coals in the fire, preparing to add the dung we burned. An open hearth lay in the center of the floor, as it had in Mama's house. A tannur had been sunk in the courtyard just outside the kitchen door.

I glanced up at the smoke hole at the top of the house, allowing smoke to escape. The sun stood before its apex. Time to prepare the evening meal. Avagail left me in the care of the older maidservant, Ada, who handed me a pail of tubers and a knife. I peeled and cut them into a copper pot filled with water.

Unfamiliar noise surrounded me. I counted six maidservants chattering as they worked. I peeled and listened. The older girls ignored me. I did not mind.

"She is a pretty little thing," one commented, uncaring of who listened. "Problem is, she knows it."

Who are they speaking of? Not me. I am not pretty, and I know it.

"It will cause her problems," another said.

"Have you ever seen a pretty little girl who does not have problems?" the first asked.

Avagail entered the kitchen. The chatter ended.

Gossips. They do not speak of me, or they would not end their gossip. I searched my memory. They must speak of Avagail'sdaughter. What will they say about me when I am not here?

Mama had delivered Avagail's children. The last two were daughters. The oldest, Leah, who must be twelve now, had beautiful eyes. Sadly, scars covered her face and body from an illness while she was two. At the same time, they waited for another child to be born. Mama had tended to her until Avagail called her away to help deliver the baby.

In the time it took Mama to deliver Rachel, the illness had settled into Leah's face. Mama gave the servants a lotion, but they refused to help, fearing they would catch her illness. They left the tiny girl alone until the sores began to heal. Only then did they return to smooth the lotion on her face too late, leaving scars to cover her face.

Mama could not care for Leah. She hurried home to give birth to me.

Ada took the pot and set it over the fire. "You did well. What is your name?"

"Bilhah."

"Is your mother not Eila?" she gazed into my face. "I remember seeing you with her when she came to help heal one of the boys."

"Yes," I mumbled, my face heating.

"Why are you not with her helping Norit give birth?"

The short, pudgy cook brushed a loose lock of hair off her face. *She likes the food she cooks. But I like her. Her voice is kind, and her smile is cheerful.*

"Mama brought me here this morning. Says she can no longer care for me." My lip trembled, but I refused to share my pain. *Why did Mama leave me here?*

The woman nodded. "It does not surprise me. Eila works hard, but it is a struggle with five children."

"She took my brothers to other men." I bit my lip, fighting back my tears. "What now?"

"It is hard for your mother," she crooned and handed me a stack of plates. "Go with Shiri to set these on the table." She turned. "Shiri. Show Bilhah where to set the plates for the evening meal."

Between the two of us, we prepared the table with fine dishes, silver, and linen for the family.

"Will we eat?" I asked over the grumbling of my stomach.

"After the family eats. We eat last before cleaning the dishes." A few years older than me and pretty, Shiri could become a friend.

"Do you live here, too?" I asked.

Shiri shook her head. "No. Mother comes each night for me and brings me back in the morning. Your mother is not coming?"

I shook my head and fought back the tears once more. *Why could Mama not have done this little thing?*

"Sorry." She put her arms around me briefly. "This is not a bad place to live."

***

Ada introduced me to a tall, slender girl, Zilpah, as they prepared to serve the family. She smiled at me, then hurried away.

Ada grabbed my arm and kept me back. "Watch this time," she said. "You need to know what Avagail demands of us. You can join the others tomorrow."

I watched from the doorway. Laban and Avagail had three sons and two daughters. The sons were older, old enough to marry. I gazed at the daughters, naming them. Rachel, the one my age, and Leah, two years older than us. I did not see her scars from a distance. The brothers sat near and on either side of Laban. The sisters sat on either side of Avagail. Serving them did not seem a demanding job, but I waited and watched. Certainly, something must make it difficult.

The oldest son, about nineteen, stretched his hand out and touched Shiri's leg. She flinched, but said nothing as she served him and moved on to a daughter.

I shuddered. *Could I ignore such touching? Would they expect me to accept this and more?*

"You take a wife soon, Gera," Laban said. "Have you spoken with Ilan about when you can marry his daughter?"

The offending son turned to his father. "Ilan demands a bride price."

"It is expected. How much?"

Gera chewed on his beard. "Silver and sheep."

"How much silver and how many sheep?" Laban set his hands on the table and leaned forward.

"Two silvers, thirty ewes, three rams ... and a home for us to live in. He will not allow Devora to live here. He says too many live here already."

Avagail harrumphed. "A wife has no say. She lives with the mother of her husband."

"You want another woman to help you?" another son asked.

"Is that not what all mothers desire?" the oldest daughter said. Leah. I saw her scars.

"Always room for more help," Avagail said with a covetous grin.

"Which is why I accepted the new maidservant," Laban said. He turned to Gera. "Have you bargained with him?"

Gera licked his lips. "I have a flock, but if I give that many to Ilan, I will have few left."

"And silver?"

"I have the silver. Mother helped. But where will we live?"

"Father's uncle lives in a tent," the younger sister said. A grin filled her face. Rachel?

Gera gasped. "Devora living in a tent?"

"It would be a home." Her saucy reply filled the room.

I want a home where I will be safe. A tent is better than no home.

Gera shook his head and growled. "I have looked everywhere. There is an empty house I think I can bargain for ..." his voice drifted away.

"What is the problem with it?" Laban asked, tilting his head to the side and staring into Gera's eyes. He twitched a finger at Zilpah.

She stepped forward and filled his glass with more wine.

Ada pulled me back into the kitchen. "Do you see the maids standing back near the wall, not noticing anything until someone signals a need for more?"

"Yes." I bobbed my head. "Gera touched Shiri's leg. Will he touch me?"

Ada growled. "Laban has warned Gera about that. For now, I will keep you in the kitchen. But soon you will be big enough to help serve. Avagail will question why I keep you away. You are small enough Gera may not be enticed by you. Perhaps he will have a wife by the time you grow big enough I can no longer keep you in the kitchen."

"And live elsewhere," I murmured.

"You listened to their conversation?" Ada asked, her eyebrows lifting almost to her hair.

"What else do I do? Everyone stood still, doing nothing, until Zilpah refilled Laban's cup."

"Do not repeat what you hear at the table." She frowned at me.

"Yes, Ada."

"May Jehovah take Gera and his bride to another home," Ada grumbled. "Now go back to watch. We will bring in more food."

***

After the servants ate, Zilpah, Shiri, and I helped Ada clean the kitchen. I had dried many copper pots and colorful dishes, but many more waited.

Ada handed me a clean, dry towel. "Zilpah, you and Bilhah can help Shiri with the dishes. You should know, Avagail put her in your chamber."

Zilpah's long dark hair hung in a braid down her back. Her dark eyes matched her hair. She stood a head taller than me, probably a little more than two years older than my ten.

"My chamber?" Zilpah pressed her lips together. "It is small."

"You have no choice," Ada said.

"I have little," I said. "Just my dress and sleeping robe."

Zilpah's mouth twisted . "You are not big. I suppose you can fit in with me. It could be worse. You could be fat."

I drew back, looking down and touching my belly. "Me? Fat?"

Zilpah giggled. "No, you are not fat."

What could I say? *She seems like a cheerful person. Perhaps she teases like my brothers did.* A sudden longing for my brothers tugged at my heart.

Shiri set another dish on the drying towel and giggled. "You will never be fat."

"The mistress will provide you with more dresses," Ada said. "She likes us to be dressed alike."

I had noticed everyone wore a soft green, the color of sage. Ada's dress had stripes. Both Zilpah's and Shiri's had subtle flowers.

I nodded and set a dry plate on the stack.

Zilpah took a wet plate. "My pallet is cold in the winter. It will be more comfortable with someone to keep me warm. Even in the summer, the temperature does not change enough to notice down there." She smiled. "Welcome, Bilhah."

I grinned. "I will help with that."

"Good. Our chamber is not beneath the kitchen and receives little heat. Yours will help me sleep."

I lost myself in thought, imagining what it must be like to have a friend to share with. Mama did not give me time to be with other girls. This would be different.

"How old are you?" Zilpah asked, interrupting me.

"Ten."

"I am thirteen and a woman," she said, lifting her chin.

"Do not be haughty about that," Ada said, tilting her head to the side and staring at Zilpah. "You have had only one experience with the woman's flow. Wait a year. You will not be so proud."

Zilpah dropped her eyes. "Yes, Ada." She looked at me. "Be grateful you are not yet a woman."

"Why?"

"It is a bloody mess, and when you are a woman, men want to touch you where they should not," Shiri said.

"Ugh," I made a face. "I saw Gera touch your leg."

Shiri shuddered. "Thankfully, that was all he touched."

"You dare not say much, especially when the man lives here." Zilpah glanced toward the front of the house.

Did she fear Gera, Laban, or Avagail?

"No, Avagail does not like to know," Ada said.

We changed the subject and chattered together until the kitchen was clean. At a tap at the outside door, Shiri opened it and waved goodbye to us.

"Her mother ..." Zilpah said.

"I know. She told me. Why do you stay here?"

"Ada found me alone in the market after our home burned." Zilpah spoke with little emotion.

I sucked in a sharp breath. "Mama expected Laban to take me because she helped Avagail give birth." I said with a shrug. "She says she cannot care for us any longer. I do not understand why he still owed her. She gave my brothers and me away. Only my little sister remains. I do not know if she will keep her." I swallowed my sudden tears.

Zilpah touched my shoulder. "I hope she keeps your sister."

I rolled my lips in. "Me too. I wish ..." I rubbed my stomach, trying to soothe away the hurt. "I wish she had kept me too. I helped her..."

Ada hugged me close, reminding me of my grandmama's love for me. Perhaps Ada would love me as Mama had. "Your mama loves you. She did what was best for you. We will be your family now."

I nodded, refusing to allow tears to slide down my face. It felt good to be among women who cared for me. Perhaps they would become my family, and I could survive here, even find some happiness.

When we finished, Zilpah led me to our chamber.

"We cannot always light the lamp, so learn the way. Touch the walls."

Zilpah walked behind me and directed me as I felt my way.

"Turn right," she said.

I turned, touched a door, and pushed it open.

"We are given a small amount of oil each month," Zilpah said, striking the flint to light the lamp wick. "Usually, I light this in the cooking fire."

I blinked to adjust to the light, though it was not much. "Easier there than using a flint here," I murmured.

"Much." Zilpah moved around, picking up her possessions. "You can have this trunk for your possessions," she said, pointing to a small trunk.

"My possessions?" I choked. "My old dress and my night robe."

"You will have more clothes later," Zilpah said. "Avagail sounds gruff, but she is generous with her maids."

Our door opened and Avagail stepped in with a larger oil lamp lighting our little chamber. "I cannot have you wearing that dress, Bilhah."

"It is my best dress," I murmured.

"Perhaps, but it is not appropriate. This may be large. Do you sew? Can you fix it?" She handed me a sage green dress with small flowers, made from a rough wool, similar to the wool Mama dressed me in.

I wanted to set my hands on my hips and exclaim my abilities, but my hands were now full and Mama had taught me not to talk back to my elders. I had sewn clothing and bodies beside Mama. I held the dress in front of me. Much too big. I lowered my eyes. "Yes. I sew. If Zilpah helps, I can work on it tonight."

"Good," Avagail said. "Zilpah, help her." She turned back to me. "Wear this tomorrow morning."

My eyes widened. It had been a long day. "It will take most of the night. And our oil —"

"If you use it all, you will be in the dark. Only enough to fill your lamp once is allowed each month." Avagail turned and left, closing the door behind her.

Our tiny lamp hardly lit the chamber.

"I will help you fix it," Zilpah said.

Her warm smile helped soothe my concerns.

***

In our rush, we did not trim the seams, and my new dress rubbed uncomfortably at my sides and under my arms. They made me itch.

"You will want to let the seams out when you grow," Zilpah counseled as we mounted the stairs. "This dress is big now, but you will grow."

I had no time to do anything else but grow.

Ada nodded with approval when Zilpah and I entered the kitchen, rubbing our eyes.

"She gave you last night to make that dress fit?" Ada asked. I expected surprise, but she expressed none.

"Yes," Zilpah answered for me. "And our lamp guttered out as we finished."

"Not much sleep, then?" Ada asked.

We shook our heads, too tired to answer.

"I will keep the two of you away from the fire today. However, you must learn to be alert even when you do not sleep. I will not always be here to protect you."

I rested my head on my hand as I sat at the kitchen table and scooped my morning grains into my mouth, giving me warmth and hopefully enough energy to lift my head.

Ada touched my shoulder. "You will do fine. Pay attention. I will try to give you a break to rest later today. Avagail tests her new maids this way. You should plait your braids again, however. They look unkempt."

That is why she expressed no surprise. She expected this from Avagail.

I nodded and braided my dark brown hair on either side of my head, as Mama had always braided it.

Ada assigned me to dust the furniture downstairs. "But do not go into Laban's office. He fears the maids will mix up his papers."

"Perhaps he thinks he has something secret," Zilpah said with a yawn. She had undone the braid down her back and rebraided it in the time I braided one braid. I still had one to plait as she hurried from the kitchen.

Ada shrugged. "Dust everything downstairs. Do not miss any surfaces and do not drop or break anything. You do not want to know what happens to one who breaks Avagail's trinkets."

I shuddered. I had not seen her temper, and I did not want to.

I yawned many times, but soon the focus on not dropping expensive decorative plates, gold-rimmed urns, and the other heavy objects I dusted woke me. Among the heaviest objects were idol statues of local gods.

Why idols? Laban and his household worshipped *Jehovah, did they not? Jehovah would not approve* of Avagail *placing these idols where all can see.*

I thought about it throughout the day. How could Laban expect protection from Jehovah if he worshiped idol gods?

When Abram and Sarai fled Harran, Grandmama had continued to worship Jehovah, teaching her daughters and warning them to keep the name private, for the priests of Libnah and Elkenah would choose them as sacrifices if they knew, as they tried to sacrifice Jacob.

Perhaps Avagail and Laban considered it less dangerous to scatter images of the gods around the house for others to see? I could not do such a thing, but what did I know? I was only ten.

When I finished, I reported back to Ada. "What now?"

"Clean your chamber. While there, sleep. Someone will wake you in an hour," Ada said.

"Are you certain?"

"Avagail is shopping and will not return for another few hours. I will have you working before she returns. Now, go. You are wasting your hour."

I rushed down the stairs, holding onto the wall to keep from stumbling. The little windows lit my way, but I closed my eyes, trying to remember. I needed to know how to reach our chamber in the dark.

I pushed open the door. Everything we had left on the floor or draped on the stool lay folded on the trunk. Zilpah slept on the pallet.

She looked up at me with sleepy eyes. "Rest while we can."

I expected the excitement of working in a new house to keep me awake. It did not. I yawned twice. I remember nothing else.

***

Zilpah touched me. "You must wake up. Avagail returned early and is not happy."

Confusion darkened my mind as I struggled awake. "Avagail? Not happy?"

"She did not purchase the saffron she wanted. Shiri says they were also out of the silk she wants for Gera's betrothal rite. We must rush to the kitchen."

Sleep fell from my eyes, and I leapt from the pallet and pulled my dress over my head. I tied the sash at my waist as I loped up the stairs. Before entering the kitchen, I pushed my braids over my shoulder, hoping they still looked presentable.

Four other maids scurried around the kitchen, looking busy as I entered. I strode to the fire, where Ada handed me a spoon. "Stir this," she said as she stepped away.

"Is the midday meal prepared?" Avagail asked, storming into the kitchen.

"It is, and the evening meal is cooking," Ada answered.

"I expected you to waste time while I was gone," Avagail said with a growl.

"No. We complete our assignments whether you are here or gone."

"The downstairs tables were dusted?" Avagail sank into a chair at the kitchen table.

"Bilhah dusted them," Ada said, dishing up a bowl of soup from the pot I stirred. "Get the mistress a spoon," she whispered.

I hurried to the basket of spoons, grabbed one, and laid it next to the bowl in front of Avagail. I dipped my head and backed away.

"You dusted the downstairs?" she asked.

I stepped forward. "I did. Some things on the tables are heavy, but I did not drop any."

Avagail's gaze turned from her soup to me. "You dropped nothing? Not even the heaviest idol?"

"None of them. I wondered ..." I stopped speaking, fearing her response.

Her eyebrows lifted. "You wondered? What did you wonder?"

"I mean no disrespect," I said in a low voice. "I thought you worshipped Jehovah."

Ada warned me with a glance, but it was too late.

"And you wonder about our idols?" Avagail's voice turned syrupy sweet.

I nodded. "Mama taught me about Jehovah ..."

Avagail blew out a breath. "You know Jehovah?"

I nodded.

"And you heard the priests tried to sacrifice Abram?"

I nodded once more. "Grandmama was a little girl in Ur. She was there."

Avagail shook her head. "I hear that was a terrible time. I was not yet born, but Terah was there. He told us of the rumble that filled the city. He thought his home would fall. He was Abram's father, you know."

I shook my head. "I did not know."

I did, but Avagail did not need to know *that.*

"He came here with Abram and Sarai, but they moved on after some years. Terah's other son, Nahor, and his family joined him here later. Our family has been here since then."

"That must have been frightening," I whispered.

"Yes, Nahor and Bethuel agreed to keep images of the idol gods out for others to see. They hoped to confuse the priests and keep their attention away from our family and our home."

"That makes sense," I said. "Has it worked?"

"It has so far. No one has come to take us to be sacrificed." Avagail turned away from me and spooned soup into her mouth.

I stepped away, glad she had not slapped me for my impertinence.

Ada signaled for me to help wash the dishes. I sighed as my hands sank beneath the water. I did not mind washing the dishes. It kept my hands busy while I observed the others.

Avagail continued to grumble about the missing saffron. "Gera will want a special meal for Devora. They will celebrate their betrothal next week. I told the spice seller to save the best for me. He promised to have some in three days. If he does not, I do not know what I will do."

The maids circled around her, offering sweets and support.

"I am certain he will have saffron before next week," Ada said. "If Yubal said he would have it, only a disaster will prevent it."

Avagail leaned back in her seat and accepted the sweets with a sigh.

I will have to learn the art of calming my mistress.

Soon Avagail rose and left the kitchen, mumbling about needing to rest before bringing her girls down to teach them about the kitchen.

Leah and Rachel were at the evening meal the night before. I missed seeing them that morning. I supposed someone took food to them in their chambers. It must be nice to have maidservants to wait on you.

Ada put me to work scraping the skins from vegetables once more. I did not mind. I could work and observe.

"You know, you will not stay in the kitchen all the time," Zilpah said, coming to sit beside me.

"I know. I dusted earlier." I kept scraping the vegetables.

She nodded. "Yes, but you will be assigned to Rachel soon."

I glanced up at Zilpah before returning to scraping. "Why?"

"You were given the dress of a personal maidservant. Look at the dresses of the other maids."

I looked more closely at the other dresses. Three were different — Zilpah's, Shiri's, and mine. The others had plain sage green dresses tied at the waist. None had the ties at the shoulder like mine. Ours looked nicer than the others.

Did Avagail plan to assign me to Rachel? How would that affect me? Could I do it without causing Avagail to complain? Why could I not be home with Mama and Nissa? Would I ever have a safe family again?

Personal Maid

Later that day, I turned from my assignment when Alma, a maidservant cutting vegetables, cried out in pain. She gripped her finger, but blood dripped through her hand.

"Bilhah," Ada cried. "Can you help with that?"

"I need a clean cloth," I called as I hurried to Alma's side.

Alma whimpered in pain and held up her hand. Blood dripped on the table.

"What happened?" I murmured as I took her hand in mine.

Alma did not release her grip on the injured hand. "Knife slipped."

"Where did it cut you?"

She lifted a finger, showing a gash on the tip. "I cut off the tip of my finger."

My stomach gurgled, but because of Mama's training, the injury did not make me sick. I needed to apply pressure to stop the bleeding. I glanced at the table where she was cutting the vegetables. "I do not see it here. Let me look."

When I examined her finger closer, Alma had not lost the tip of her finger. It bled down her arm. I stopped the bleeding, cleaned it with herb-infused water, and spread honey on it before bandaging it. I then gave her herbal tea to prevent further illness.

She lifted her eyebrows in question, but drank the remedy.

After bandaging Alma's injury, I returned to preparing food. A young boy came into the kitchen. I thought little of it, not yet knowing boys and men seldom entered Avagail's kitchen. The other girls stared and tittered at him. Red climbed up his neck and onto his face. Still, he walked over to Ada and whispered to her.

"Now?" Ada asked.

The boy nodded.

"Bilhah. The mistress needs you. Go with this boy."

"Me?" I asked. "Why would she need me?"

"How would I know?" Ada waved her spoon. "Wash the blood from your cheek and go with this boy."

I used the last clean cloth and the now-cool herb-infused water to wash my face and hands.

"Is that better?" I held up my hands.

Ada inspected me. "Much. Now, go with the boy. Do not keep Mistress Avagail waiting."

I followed the messenger up the stairs and to the door at the end of the hall. He rapped on it and shoved it open at Avagail's call, before running off.

"Well?" Avagail growled. "Are you coming in?"

I sucked in a breath and entered, allowing the beads to fall behind me. The chamber held soft, cushioned seats and a small wooden desk and chair with papers in neat piles.

Avagail inspected me, her eyes roaming from the top of my head to the tip of my toes, peeping out from beneath the dress I had taken in the night before.

"No slippers?" She asked.

"Mama had no money for slippers." I had never worn slippers.

She shook her head and grimaced. "Why do they expect me to provide everything?" she mumbled. "You will have to live without slippers for a day or two. Have you any service experience?"

"I just bandaged Alma's cut finger. It was bad, but it could have been worse. Mama taught me about healing, and I helped her bring a child into the world this week."

Avagail drew her eyebrows together. "Who is your mother again?"

"Eila, the healer."

"Yes, yes, now I remember. And she could not care for you any longer?" Her voice rose a bit before she stopped to swallow. "I would expect she could easily care for her family as a healer."

"She could before my father left us. She then had too many mouths to feed."

Avagail quirked her eyebrow up. "How many children are there?"

"I have three brothers and a sister. I am the second oldest." Sharing about my family squeezed my heart tight. I missed my family. Why —?

"Your father kept her busy with children." She tapped the side of her face near her nose. "You can be useful with your healer training. How old are you?"

"Ten. Mama took me with her since I was four."

Avagail continued to tap her face. "Perhaps you can be taught. Or you can clean the night pots." She looked up at me. "You know how to obey?"

"Yes, mistress." I did not want to be assigned to clean the filthy night pots.

She stared at me a bit longer, then stood. "Come with me."

***

Avagail led me along the hallway to another chamber, and a girl my age with golden-brown eyes matching the lighter color of her hair looked up. Like many girls I knew, the light and dark streaks in her hair made her more beautiful. However, the ends of her hair stuck out of the braids hanging from either side of her head.

Her eyes and face resembled Avagail. This was the younger, saucy girl from dinner the night before. This must be the girl Mama helped to birth before giving birth to me. If so, she was one day older than me.

"Mother?" the girl asked.

"Rachel." Avagail waved toward me. "It is time you had a maidservant. This is Bilhah. She is here to serve you."

Rachel's face twisted in thought before she smiled. "Like Zilpah helps Leah?"

"Yes." Avagail turned to me. "You are to be here early each morning to help Rachel brush and braid her hair and dress her each morning. You will also help her dress for the evening meal and prepare her for sleep at night. If she has other needs, you are to be available to help her."

"Does that mean I do not have to learn how to clean?" Rachel asked.

"No. You and Bilhah will clean together. She will teach you. Her mother did not permit her to avoid work, as I have. You are ten, Rachel. No longer a child. Time to grow up." Avagail glanced at me. "Get to know each other. Bilhah, maybe you can fix those braids. And then, do not stay here. Ada has chores for you in the kitchen. Both of you."

Rachel flinched, then whined, "Me? Mother?"

"You must know how to run a house. You will be responsible for your own home someday. Perhaps even in the home of your husband's mother. Time to learn. Be in the kitchen in half an hour." Avagail kissed Rachel on the forehead, then left the chamber.

Rachel poked her tongue out at Avagail's retreating back.

I stared with bulging eyes in shock at her disrespect.

Rachel stared at me. "Do you not poke your tongue out at your mother?"

"Never. Not when I lived with her. I cannot now. She gave me to your father."

"She left you here? Will you ever see her again?"

I shrugged. I hope to one day. Maybe I will find her at the market or the well.

Rachel pouted and stared at me. "How old are you?"

"Ten."

"I am ten as well."

I grinned. "My mama helped your mother give birth to you, then she went home to give birth to me. We are almost the exact same age."

"Almost twins," she clapped her hands. "But you are my maid. I can tell you what to do." She rolled her eyes, then laughed.

"Your mama told me to work on your hair." I glanced around the chamber. "Sit at your dressing table. I will see what I can do. I used to braid my little sister's hair." I bit my lip as sudden tears filled my eyes.

"You miss her?" Rachel sat on the stool in front of her dressing table and stared up at my reflection in her polished bronze mirror.

"I do. I miss my mother and my sister — not so much my brothers."

Rachel perched on the stool, and I picked up her brush.

"You have brothers, too? Are they as mean as my brothers?" she asked.

While we shared stories, I brushed her hair. "I have not seen your brothers much, so I do not know how mean your brothers are. Only my brother, Avdon, is older than me. The others are younger. They did not like Mama taking me with her to learn how to heal. I helped heal her patients."

"You are a healer?" Rachel squealed.

I braided one side of her hair. "These ends do not want to stay in your braid. I was learning about healing. But Mama brought me here before I learned all I need to know. I bandaged a cut finger this afternoon."

Why did Mama bring me here? I could have helped her?

Rachel's hair ends refused to smooth into her braid. *What can I do to keep the ends in her braid?*

Lotion sat in a jar on the table. I took the lid off and sniffed it. "Nice." I dipped a tiny bit out of the jar and rubbed it into my hands.

Rachel stamped her foot. "That is mine. Not yours."

“I know.” I ran my hands through her hair. “This should keep your ends where they belong.” I braided it once more. The ends stayed put.

“Oh! How did you know to do that?”

“Mama,” I murmured as I brushed the other half of her hair and smoothed a dab of lotion into it. The hair stayed in her braid.

“We should go to the kitchen now.” I tied the braid. “I do not want your mother to be angry with me.”

“How could she be angry? My braids look much better.” She spun around on the stool and threw her arms around me. “We are going to be friends.”

Friends between a girl and her maid? Can that be? Will such a friendship take the place of Mama and Nissa? I miss them. I hope she becomes my friend.

***

Rachel raced down the stairs with me following behind. I passed her as we entered the kitchen panting and giggling. Ada glanced up at us, frowning.

“Do you have any sense about you, girl?” she growled.

Then Rachel stepped past me. “Mother told me I was to help you in the kitchen.”

Ada smoothed her face. “She said you would come. You girls can wash the dishes.”

Rachel stared at me. I led her to the cleaning table.

“I will wash. You can dry.” I handed Rachel a cloth for drying.

She stared at the cloth dangling from her fingers. “What do I do with this?”

“Wipe the dishes dry after I wash them.”

I washed the dishes and set them in the hot rinse water. Rachel picked them out with the tips of her fingers and set them on the towel before drying them. I tittered. “You need to grab those dishes with more than the tips of your fingers. You do not want to drop them."

"But that water is hot," Rachel complained.

I showed her how to grab the dishes out of the hot water. We laughed and talked as we worked.

I washed the last dish as Avagail entered the kitchen. "Where is Rachel?"

"Over here, Mother," she called as she set the dry dish on the stack of clean dishes.

"What have you done?" her mother asked.

"Ada assigned Bilhah and me to wash those dishes," Rachel laughed. "We are almost finished."

Avagail drew her eyebrows together. "You are working."

"It was fun," Rachel gushed.

Avagail's eyebrows shot up. "Fun? I did not expect to hear those words."

Rachel's shoulder twitched. "I had fun with Bilhah."

Avagail's eyes moved from Rachel to me. "You made it fun?"

"We giggled a lot," My face burned.

Avagail nodded. "Good. Rachel will join you again tomorrow morning."

I grinned at Rachel, but her face fell.

"I thought it would only be today." Her lower lip slipped out in a pout.

I would never have argued with my mother.

"No, Rachel. You will learn how to clean everything. You must know how to manage your own home. This is just the beginning."

"Mother!" Rachel cried.

The next morning, Rachel joined in dusting furniture in the halls upstairs.

"Be careful," I warned as she lifted a heavy decorative plate off a table. "Those break."

She set it on the floor before responding. "I know. I knocked one off the table in my chamber. It shattered. Pieces went everywhere." Her arms flailed in demonstration.

"Watch out!" I cried as her hand swung near an urn.

She pulled her hands and arms close and hugged herself. "Mother would not be happy if I broke that urn. Grandmother Milcah purchased it with the gold Abraham's servant gave her when he came for Rebekah."

"Rebekah? Abraham?" I lifted the urn and set it on the floor before dusting the table.

"She is Father's sister. Abraham was Abram. Jehovah changed his name. He sent a servant to bring her back to marry Isaac, his son."

"But Abraham had to be ancient." I could not understand how his son would marry Laban's sister.

"Father says he was over a hundred when Isaac was born." Rachel dusted a table as she spoke. "I do not know if he still lives. Few people live that long anymore."

"Mama's grandmother was old, over a hundred when she died. Mama told me that few live that long." I grunted with the weight of the urn and set it back in place. "Mama's grandmother was a little girl when she and her mother watched the priests try to sacrifice Abram. Mama says she spoke of her fear until the day she died."

Rachel stared at me. "I did not know your family knew Abram."

I ran my dusting cloth over the front and legs of the table. "Mama's grandmother came to Harran as a servant with Sarai. She married a man from here and did not leave when Sarai and Abram left. Many times, Mama moaned about Grandmama and her family staying here in Harran."

Rachel stepped close. "You are here because Jehovah wanted you here. If your grandmama had gone to Canaan with Sarai, how would you be here to become my maidservant? I needed to know you."

My eyes widened. "You needed to know me?"

"Yes, I feel it." She placed a hand over her heart. "I needed a friend. You are my friend."

Friend? Mama gave me to Rachel's father because she could no longer care for me. He owns me as a servant. How can I be her friend? Rachel has never suffered hunger or want. She will never become someone's maidservant because her parents could no longer feed her. She will never know family separation as I do.

I turned toward her. "It is nice to be your friend." *But I must always remember you are my mistress and I am your maidservant.*

***

We worked together most days after that, as Leah worked with Zilpah, although neither girl joined us on laundry days. Avagail and her daughters never came to help wash clothing.

One day as we maids worked together, Zilpah lifted a dress from the water. "Leah says her mother does not want them to risk burning their hands in the hot water."

"Rachel would fall into the fire," one maid teased.

"No," I pushed the apron I washed into the hot water. "Rachel is careful when we work together. She would not fall into the fire."

"But her mother fears she would do something to her beautiful face," another maid laughed. "They want to marry her off to some wealthy man. Leah's scars will prevent her from marrying a wealthy man. She will be lucky to marry at all."

How can a maid become so hateful and snobbish?

"Leah's scars are healing," Zilpah cried. "A man will be blessed to marry her. She is a kind and gentle girl."

"Unlike Rachel," the maid said.

Her words hurt. My face warmed more than my hands grabbing clothing from the boiling water. "Rachel is kind to me."

"But we have seen her." Zilpah shook out the dress. "She complains about the chores her mother sets her to do."

"But she does them," I argued.

"And you go behind her to ensure they are done correctly," Shiri pointed at me. "We have all seen it. You cannot deny it. Rachel works, but she never completes the assignment."

I opened my mouth to argue, but Zilpah nudged me. "We see it, Bilhah. You cannot argue for her. Not among us."

"She is good to me," I plunged the apron in the hot water. "She is learning to work. She has not been required to work before."

The others tittered. I did not reply. I knew Rachel tried her best. She only complained when others were around. I believed she did because they expected it.

I had often entered Rachel's chamber to help her, finding her reading scrolls from her father's library. She loved to read. Mama taught me to read so I could write the directions for making the cures she made. I missed reading and writing, although I seldom had the opportunity.

Some days, Rachel would ask me to sit beside her as she read to me. I dared not take long reading with her, fearing her mother would find me lounging beside her daughter rather than serving her.

I asked Rachel to read to me as I brushed and braided her hair. She loved thinking she was better than me. I do not think she knew I could read the words over her shoulder.

However, I had to admit the other maids were more right than I wanted to admit. Rachel did not want to do anything that would make her look less than beautiful, and she was happy to shrug off work early and let me finish. She often stamped her foot and complained about her mother's requirements.

I hoped that would change as she grew. Her mother would insist. Until then, I accepted the responsibility of teaching her.

Ada learned of my ability to read and write and asked me to write for her. I appreciated the opportunity to practice. Zilpah had been writing for her for a few years, and suggested I help sometimes when she was busy.

At Ada's insistence, I filled a basket with healing supplies and left it in the corner of the kitchen where I could readily retrieve it. I kept packets of herbs and clean bandages in the pocket I wore over my shoulder to have them available when needed.

Ada purchased a packet of needles for me to stitch injuries, along with lengths of the thread Mama used in multiple thicknesses, to sew those injuries requiring more attention.

Whenever Ada or Avagail called in another healer, I helped, becoming more confident in my healing abilities. They called on experienced healers less often as time went by, choosing to use my healing abilities.

In the years I served in Laban's home, I never saw Mama. I wondered if she had left Harran. I prayed she had not died. I missed her. Did she give Nissa away?

Lion Attack

All of Rachel's brothers married in the following years and moved to the other side of Harran away from us. We maids cheered in private, no longer needing to fear their unwanted touching or other advances.

Laban could no longer depend on his sons to take the flocks to the well to drink. Herders opened the well only once a day to water the flocks. Laban had dug the well, but if one of his sons did not join the herders, others would drive the sheep away.

To resolve the problem, Laban assigned Leah and Rachel to go with the herders. They were thirteen and fifteen. They took turns after their father went with them the first week. Rachel did not want to go, but her father gave her no choice. Stomping and arguing did not help. Leah never complained, but she never complained about anything around others.

Rachel asked Leah to take her turn almost every time. Sometimes Leah gave in. Rachel seldom took Leah's turn unless Leah was sick, which did not happen often.

"Why do you fight your father?" I asked her one day a few months after Laban had assigned her the job.

"The sheep are smelly and dirty." Her face twisted in disgust.

"But you wash it all off when you return." I said. "And you have men who will protect you. Perhaps one will admit an interest in you."

Rachel shuddered. "Herders? I have little need to know them."

"But they protect you from the other herders and wild animals. You should not act as if they are terrible. You may need them sometime."

She shook her head in disbelief. I could do little more than help her clean off the smell.

One day when Rachel was nearing fifteen, she returned shaken and quivering.

"What happened?" Avagail unexpectedly greeted her at the door. She seldom met the girls at the door after watering the flocks.

I stood behind Avagail, waiting to help Rachel clean off the sheep's smell.

"A ... A lion ..."

Avagail threw her arms around Rachel. "Are you injured?"

"No ... no. The sheep surrounded me, and Iben fought the lion off." Rachel shuddered, and tears dripped onto her mother's shoulder.

When Avagail was certain of her daughter's safety, she walked with Rachel to her chamber, signaling for me to follow. I helped wash away her tears and mud.

Avagail did not ask about Iben's safety or the sheep. Did she not care?

Rachel soon calmed enough to enthuse about the lion. "It was big, Mother. You should have seen him! His fur is tawny yellow with a black mane. I hope Iben's arrow did not hurt him."

"I will talk to your father. You are too young to be facing lions," Avagail put her fists on her hips.

"No, Mother," Rachel looked up at Avagail. "It frightened me, but Iben and the other herders fought him off. I will go again."

"But not tomorrow," Avagail said.

"No, tomorrow is Leah's turn. Has she seen a lion yet?"

Her mother shook her head. "If either of you sees another lion, someone else will take the flocks to the well." She examined Rachel again to ensure she had no injuries before leaving us.

"Are you sorry the herders accompany you to the well now?" I pulled a clean dress from the peg.

"No, Bilhah. The lion frightened me, but I have never been so excited. I will go again."

She lifted her arms so I could pull her dress over her head. Narrow red scratches marked a leg.

"Did you not say the lion did not reach you?" I asked.

"Yes. The herders kept him from me."

"How did you get these scratches? It looks like the lion caught you with his claw."

Rachel twisted to see the back of her leg. "I do not see it."

"Here and here." I ran a finger across the scratches. "These are not deep, but he scratched you."

Rachel shivered once more. "He got that close to me?"

"He must have." I poured water from her urn into a bowl, pulled a packet of herbs from my pocket, and dumped it into the water. "I will clean them."

Rachel lay across her sleeping pallet while I cleaned the scratches, covered them with honey, and bandaged her leg.

"The herders saved you if they drove the lion away." I was unsure if I wanted to be as close to a lion as Rachel had been. I shuddered at the thought.

"They did. If they had not, the lion would have hurt me worse."

"Do not forget to thank Iben and the other herders," I pulled the clean dress over her head.

"And the sheep," Rachel said. "They stayed between me and the lion."

"How will you thank the sheep?" I tied the sash behind her back.

"I thanked the men today and the sheep. I dropped to my knees and hugged the sheep, one by one, as they came up to me. They are big, friendly animals." She thought a bit, then said, "I will give them hugs every day. They are my friends now."

"Although they smell and make you dirty?" I grinned.

"They are wonderful animals, and I wash." She hummed as she thought. "I will be there early for my next turn to take them to the well. I will not argue about being there."

After she was clean, bandaged, and dressed, we bounced down the stairs together.

"Ada," Rachel said as we entered the kitchen. "Can we make something special to give the herders when I go with them the next time?"

Ada's dark eyebrows lifted and she glanced at me.

"They prevented a lion from attacking her today," I said with a shrug.

"Iben and the other herders fought him off," Rachel gushed. "I need something special to thank them. Can we make something together?"

"I can make —" Ada started.

"No. I want to help. It should be from me," Rachel leaned forward, holding her hand in the air in front of her.

Ada nodded. "Come early tomorrow. Is it not Leah's turn to take the flocks to the well?"

Rachel grabbed a carrot from the pile a maid cleaned and munched on it. "Yes. Tomorrow is Leah's turn. I will be early. Do you know what we will make?"

"Let me think about it and look in the cool closet and see what is available. I will have something to make tomorrow." Ada turned to me. "You can help, Bilhah. It is time the two of you learned to cook."

I ducked my head. "Yes, Ada."

We worked together in the kitchen, chatting about the lion and what Ada would have us help cook the next morning, until time for Rachel to get ready for the evening meal.

The next morning, Ada supervised Rachel and me in the making of sweet cakes with figs. When we filled the basket for the herders, Rachel set it near the door where she could take it with her the next morning.

Then we made more to serve to the family for the evening meal.

"The family will be surprised when I tell them I made the cakes," Rachel trilled. "These taste good." She took a bite from one.

"Do not eat any more," Ada said, "or there will not be enough for everyone."

Rachel swallowed her cake. "Mother and Father will be proud of me."

I nodded. "You did well."

"You helped," she said. "I could not have done this without your help."

"And Ada's," I added.

"Thank you for your help, Ada." Rachel smiled.

Only Rachel, Leah, and their father and mother ate together.

"These cakes taste wonderful," Laban licked the stickiness from his lips. "Who do we have to thank for them?"

"Rachel," I murmured from my place by the wall. "She made these."

"Rachel?" Avagail asked. "When did you learn to bake sweet cakes?"

"Today," Rachel grinned, proud of her cooking. "I needed something to thank the herders tomorrow for protecting me against the lion. Ada taught Bilhah and me how to make these."

"A lion?" Leah gasped. "Iben mentioned a lion. I did not believe him."

"He tried to get me, but Iben and the sheep protected me. I will give cakes to the herders tomorrow."

Her parents laughed and congratulated Rachel. I grinned.

Leah grimaced. Perhaps she would not take Rachel's turn as often if lions were involved.

Everyone stared at Rachel as she all but skipped out the door with her basket of cakes early the next day to meet with the herders.

"What happened to Rachel?" a maid asked.

"A lion tried to attack the flocks on the way to the well when Rachel last led them." I continued washing the pots.

"And she is happy to lead them again?" Her brows crunched together.

I lifted a shoulder. "The sheep surrounded her, and the herders fought off the lion. She is grateful. She is taking the herders a treat to thank them."

The women in the kitchen stared at each other. "She has changed," one said, with wide eyes.

"An attacking lion will do that." Ada shuddered.

The lion attack had changed Rachel. Although she slipped back into her old habits of pleading with Leah to take her turn to go with the sheep, she never complained about stinking sheep or the herders again.

***

In the following months, Rachel continued to beg Leah to take her turn with the sheep. When I asked her about it, she shrugged me off. "I have better things to do."

Better things? Like lingering nearby when Laban invited men to meet Leah?

After the first time Rachel listened in to her father and a young man outside the sitting area, she came to the kitchen in tears.

"Father growled at me. He thinks he must find a man who will marry Leah before he finds one for me. He fears if he does not, she will never find a man who will have her."

"Leah is beautiful," I said. "Those men are blind if they do not see it."

"Even with scars on her face, she is beautiful," Rachel agreed. "But Father does not agree. He told me to stay away when he is entertaining young men unless he calls for me."

Rachel did not stay away. She listened to her father talk to the young men with Leah, often stepping inside. The young men would not consider Leah after they saw Rachel.

"Those men are fools," she would say. "Leah is beautiful. She will make a wonderful wife."

I would nod. "Leah is smarter than they are. They probably recognize it in her."

Rachel set her hands on her hips. "You do not know what you are talking about, Bilhah."

I knew.

Rachel continued to beg Leah to take the flocks to the well for her, but Leah refused more often as time passed. Her refusals did not stop Rachel from trying.

Jacob

Later that year, while we were still fifteen, Rachel tried to convince Leah to take her turn with the flocks yet again, not knowing this day would change all our lives. I suspect she later became grateful to Leah for her refusal to trade turns, although she will never admit it.

Avagail had called all the maids to help deep clean the kitchen. When a room required deep cleaning, Avagail joined to ensure we cleaned it to her requirements. I thought Rachel would rather go with the sheep than spend the time cleaning the kitchen. I would have.

I ducked my head and did as I was told until Rachel squealed from her father's office. "Father, I met a handsome man."

I glanced at the other maids who shook their heads. It was not the first outburst coming from Rachel. I continued cleaning and almost missed Laban taking his guards out to find this "handsome man." Perhaps Rachel's "handsome man" was more than a stranger.

I would like a handsome man to be interested in me. I would like to see Avdon, Nissa, and the others. I miss Mama.

We continued cleaning until the men clattered past the kitchen door on their return.

Avagail dropped her cleaning cloth into the pot of warm soapy water and dried her hands. "I will go see about this 'handsome man.'" Her eyes fell on me and Shiri. "Get started on the cold closet while I am gone."

I groaned. We had not cleaned the cold closet for a few weeks. It would be nasty. Shiri shrugged.

We emptied the closet and dumped spoiled food into a pail for the animals. Since Avagail had left the kitchen, we could gossip in excitement.

"Why do you think Laban went off with his guard?" Shiri asked from inside the cold closet.

"To meet Rachel's handsome man, of course," Ada replied from within another closet.

"How handsome do you think he really is?" Alma's cleaning cloth dangled from her hand.

"She is young. Who knows?" Ada's sharp glance encouraged Alma to clean once more. "We have work to do."

"He could be handsome," another maid said.

Leah and Zilpah soon joined us in cleaning the cold closet. We had almost finished the nasty job when Avagail came back.

"Who is this stranger?" Leah dumped nasty food into the pot.

Avagail's answer was terse. "Rebekah's son, your father's nephew."

Laban had become wealthy with the treasure Abraham's servant gave them for Rebekah. He had many flocks of sheep until he divided them among his sons. Now his ewes no longer gave as many lambs, and his flocks had dwindled. He had spent much of the wealth that came from his sister. Perhaps he desired the bride price he would gain from marrying off Leah?

Rachel would not be happy when Laban invited this son of Rebekah to marry Leah. I would prepare for her cries and comfort her.

"Bilhah," Avagail barked.

My attention snapped back.

"Since Rachel is still dreaming in her chamber and has not yet returned, go to Laban's study and show the stranger to his chamber. Give him the last one on the left, the one Gera occupied."

Me? She would send me? I wiped my hands and made my way to Laban's office before Avagail could change her mind. She should have sent Zilpah or Leah. Not me. I was still the youngest maidservant. I did not complain. I was ready to leave the stench of the cold closet.

I tapped on Laban's office door and entered at his call.

"Mistress Avagail sent me." I glanced at the stranger sitting across from Laban. Even in dusty travel clothing, his virtue and grace shone through. Deep blue eyes gazed from beneath dark, thick eyelashes. A smile softened his rugged face. He could not hide his broad shoulders under his simple traveling clothing. I sighed.

No wonder Rachel gushed about a handsome man.

Laban interrupted my examination of the man. "Bilhah will show you to your chamber, Jacob. We will meet for a meal before sunset. I will send a servant to show you the way."

Jacob glanced around. "This is not a large house, but I will appreciate a guide. I rarely stay inside buildings."

You do not stay in buildings? Where do you live?

I dropped my eyes to the floor. *I am a maidservant. I have no need to know.*

"I will send a guide." Laban allowed a grimace to flit across his face. "Until then, Avagail will send hot water to your chamber."

Jacob glanced down at himself and sniffed. "A bath would be nice. I will smell better when I meet your daughter again."

"My *daughters*. Remember, I have *two* for you to choose from."

"Yes," Jacob grinned. "Your two daughters. Too bad Esau did not come with me."

You have a brother? Does he look as good as you do?

"He may yet come." Laban rubbed his beard.

"He may," Jacob replied. His face did not show any hope of that.

A brother could marry the sister *not chosen by Jacob, or he could cause problems between the sisters.*

"Bilhah," Laban said. "Show Jacob to his chamber."

Jacob picked up his pack and slung it across his shoulder.

I ducked my head to Laban, then turned to Jacob. "If you would follow me, sir."

Jacob's soft chuckle followed behind me. "Sir? I suppose I am now."

I led him to the chamber Avagail had instructed me to give him.

"What is Rachel like?" he asked as we climbed the stairs.

"She is a good mistress and my friend," I answered.

"Does she treat you well?" Kindness filled his deep voice.

"I am her personal maid. She confides in me."

"Does she take her father's flocks to the well every day?"

"No, Rachel and Leah take turns."

"At her age?"

"Her father considers her old enough."

We reached the top of the stairs and walked toward his chamber.

"She is a beautiful woman," he murmured, then sighed. "What flower does she prefer?"

I smiled, then my eyebrows squished together while I thought about it. "It is hard to tell. Rachel brings many flowers into her chamber. If I had to choose one, I would guess she loves the desert rose."

"Will she be at the evening meal?"

"The family eats together. You will see her there."

We neared his chamber. Menservants left as we entered.

"Ah, they brought water already," Jacob said. "It has been days since I had enough water to bathe." He glanced at me. "And I probably smell like it, too."

I ducked my head and grinned. "Probably."

Jacob dropped his pack on a chair near the door and began to strip off his robe, exposing his muscled arms.

"I, uh, I should go. Someone will come for you when it is time to eat."

Jacob glanced at my red face. "I am sorry. I should have waited before undressing."

"Perhaps, sir," I stuttered. "I will leave you to your bath."

Rachel's family was large. I missed mine. Would I ever have a family I could love? One I could hug and visit often? I could only hope.

***

Rachel had joined the others in the kitchen when I returned, answering questions about Jacob. I stood outside the door, listening, wondering how Rachel would describe him.

"He is taller than any of our herders. Taller than Father, even." She paused to inhale before continuing. "He is strong. He cannot hide his muscles beneath his clothing."

No, he *cannot hide his muscles.*

"His eyes?" Leah asked. "What color are his eyes?"

Rachel paused as if trying to remember. She liked to be dramatic. *How could anyone forget his eyes?*

"Blue," she whispered. "Blue with a fringe of dark lashes." She sighed. "His light brown hair and beard are unkempt and dirty from his travels."

"He will clean and brush those," Leah said.

I stepped into the chamber. "His eyes are deep blue and so kind. And he is strong."

Rachel frowned at me. "He is a handsome man with a rugged face."

"A handsome man in our home," Shiri dropped her cleaning rag into the water pot. "How did he find us?"

Rachel shrugged, unwilling to share what she knew.

"Why would he come all the way from Canaan to Harran?" I closed my eyes, remembering his muscles. What would have brought him so far?

"Did you not ask him?" Zilpah lifted her brows in question.

I lifted my cleaning cloth from the dish of soapy water. "I directed him to his chamber as Avagail instructed. He looked tired and in need of a bath." I glanced at the pot of water heating over the fire. "Oh good. More hot water for him if he needs it."

Rachel stared at me. I could see she wanted to stamp her foot. "He is a handsome man with a rugged face," she tossing her braid over her shoulder.

We gossiped about Jacob until Avagail hushed us. "You have other work to do," she said. "Shiri, you and Bilhah clean the floor while Ada works on the evening meal. We have a guest. Everyone should wash and change into a clean dress, then come back here to help with the meal."

My day to be chosen by Avagail. I did not mind leading Jacob to his chamber, but cleaning the floor, too?

"Leah, Rachel. Come with me." Avagail nodded to Ada. "The menservants will come for more bathwater."

Ada glanced at the water cauldron. "Yes, Mistress. There is enough."

Without a word, Shiri and I swept the dirt out the kitchen door before bending to wash away the dirt that we did not sweep up.

When we finished, Shiri bounced down the stairs behind me. She kept spare dresses in Zipah and my chamber for days when we deep-cleaned the kitchen.

Zilpah brushed past us in the passage, then stopped and turned to me. "Is he as handsome as Rachel says?"

I nodded. "He is. But I fear he will cause us problems."

"Problems?" Zilpah's eyebrows lifted. "How can one man cause us problems?"

I ran my fingers over my braid, realizing I would need to rebraid my hair. "I sense there will be problems for Laban's daughters."

"Sad," Zilpah said. "Leah deserves some happiness, not more problems."

Zilpah's braid swung against her back as she turned to climb the stairs. "You should hurry. Rachel will be waiting for your help."

"I know. But she knows I had to clean the floor first."

Shiri had already washed when I entered my chamber. I grabbed a cloth and washed away the sweat on my body, then dressed as fast as I could. Shiri tied my tie. "Go. I can tie mine. You need to hurry upstairs to help Rachel. She needs you."

"Thanks, Shiri." I rushed from the chamber.

Smitten

Rachel's best dress lay on her bed, ready for her to wear to dinner. The dark red pattern woven into it would enhance her beauty. Not all young women would look beautiful in that shade of red. With Rachel's warm coloring and golden brown eyes, she could wear vivid colors.

She maintained an uncharacteristic silence as I pulled the dress over her head, then brushed her hair. I chattered on about Jacob.

"Jacob is kind and handsome," I said.

Rachel sighed and sat without speaking.

Something happened.

I talked about taking Jacob to his room and the bulk of his muscles. "Jacob is a fine man." I sought to elicit her thoughts.

She gazed into my face through her mirror. "A fine man. Did you learn anything more about him as you took him to his room?"

"He is interested in *you*, Mistress Rachel. He wanted to know more about you. Only you, not anyone else."

"Only me?" She lifted her eyebrows. "Nothing about Leah?"

My stomach hardened. "I do not tell untruths. He spoke only of you."

Rachel closed her eyes. "What did he ask?"

"Do you water the flocks every day, and how old you are."

"Old enough." Rachel frowned.

"I did not share. Do you want your hair braided or left down for dinner? Oh, then he asked the strangest thing."

"Leave my hair down tonight. What strange question?"

I brushed her hair until it shone. "He wanted to know which flower you preferred."

"Flower?" Rachel's eyes widened. "What did you tell him?"

I lifted a shoulder. "I told him it is hard to tell. You bring many flowers to your room. I told him your favorite may be the desert rose."

She turned toward the vase of desert roses next to her bed. "I love many flowers, but I think the desert rose is my favorite. You are sure he did not ask which flower is Leah's favorite?"

"Why would he? Jacob has only met you. Not Leah."

She moistened her lips. "That is right. He has not met her yet."

I nodded and finished brushing her hair.

"Beautiful." I stepped back. "You are ready to meet Jacob again."

"Will he be impressed?" Rachel asked, with an uncharacteristic wistfulness. "Will he look at me rather than Leah?"

"Impressed?" I crunched my eyebrows together. "Yes."

"I need a tichel to cover my hair like Leah does." Rachel pointed to the tichel on her sleeping pallet.

I pinned it in her hair. "You can pull it across your face if you want to look demure." I pulled it over her face.

"I am always demure," Rachel replied in mock anger.

I grinned. "Are you?"

"No, but it would be an interesting look. Does Jacob like demure women?"

"I do not know about demure. He likes you. Is that not enough?" I shrugged. "Perhaps you should be yourself." The meal bell echoed through the house. "Beautiful as always, and dinner is ready."

I followed her out, then hurried down the servant's stairs in the back. Ada would need my help, especially with Jacob here.

"There you are," Ada sighed. "We are extra busy tonight."

"Rachel took longer to dress tonight." I lifted a pot of soup to carry into the eating area at Ada's signal.

"That must be going around," Ada said. "Zilpah arrived just before you."

"Leah asked for extra attention tonight." Zilpah tossed me a knowing look as she lifted another dish of food.

During the meal, we stood waiting for someone to signal they required more food or drink. *Would Jacob touch us as Laban's sons had?* Thankfully, he kept his hands to himself.

As the family ate, Rachel seemed lost in her thoughts, even when Jacob asked if she went to water the sheep every day. When she did not answer, I stifled my urge to step forward and poke her.

Instead, Leah nudged her in her ribs. "Did you hear Jacob's question?"

Rachel pulled her veil across her face.

Frustrated, I let out my breath because I needed to return to the kitchen for another platter of food, and missed Rachel's answer. Although I heard the family's laughter, I could do nothing to help her.

When I returned, Jacob was talking. "Mother tells me I held fast to Esau's heel during our birth. I wanted to be first, but he was in my way."

I have never heard of such a thing. I wonder if Mama has. Jacob mentioned his twin! Too bad his twin did not come too.

The family ended their meal and left for the sitting area.

"We must eat and clean up the meal," Ada reminded us. "I know we are tired, but Avagail insists on a clean kitchen and will return to inspect it."

I squelched a groan.

Later, Rachel quivered with excitement as I helped prepare her for bed.

"Jacob sat by me. He took my hand in his when Father looked another way." She talked more than she had earlier as I helped her change. "I think he likes me."

"I told you he did." I pulled a sleeping robe over her head.

"Yes, we sat close on the long seat. Of course, Leah sat on Jacob's other side. I wanted to scream, but Mother would have sent me away if I had."

"Is that seat wide enough for three?" I took the brush from her dressing table and brushed her hair.

"We were pushed close together." She giggled again. "Father could say little about us touching." She closed her eyes and spoke in an airy, dreamy voice. "I hope Jacob asks me to marry him."

"After someone marries Leah?"

Rachel's eyes popped open. "Bilhah. Must you destroy my dreams?"

"Mistress Rachel, you know your mother gave me that responsibility." I stared at her until she laughed.

"Mother would do that."

I nodded and joined in her laughter. Avagail had given me specific instructions to remind her of her place in the family and that Laban expected Leah to marry first. They expected me to help Rachel remember that. I guess that made me a dream destroyer.

As Rachel's laughter slowed, she stared at my reflection. "Do not always follow those instructions. I am old enough to make my own decisions."

***

Jacob went with Rachel and Leah to water the flocks. Because Rachel had taken her turn the day before, Leah went with him the first day . Unusual for Rachel, she fidgeted while Leah was with Jacob. Her feet tapped, and she stared out the window often, as if that would bring Leah home faster.

I shook my head. Leah would come when they finished watering the flocks. She would take as long as she needed, as she always had.

That day Rachel cleaned the hall while I folded the clothing I had washed the morning before with the other maids.

As I passed Rachel with a stack of folded laundry in my arms, I glanced out the window to see what Rachel stared at. Leah dawdled toward home from watering the flocks, though without her usual firm stride. She seemed to look at the trees and flowers with a slight smile on her face.

"Do you think Jacob will choose Leah?" I asked.

Rachel turned toward me with clenched fists and a raised foot. Did she mean to kick me or would she just stamp it? I expected her to scream and stepped back from her. With a shake of her head, she huffed out a breath and smoothed the frustration from her face, and said in with a false sweetness I had learned to be wary of, "He may choose whomever he desires," and moved to the next table as if dusting was all she had to think about.

"I do not blame you. I have dreamed of having Jacob as my husband." I walked toward the cupboard where the linens belonged.

Rachel spun on her heel to face me. "You too?"

Although I did not respond, my hot cheeks belied my dream.

"What about that man has affected all the women of this house?" she mumbled, bending to clean the table.

"We all desire marriage. He is the best man to come into our lives. We are smitten," I sighed as I passed her.

My dream of Jacob the night before had awakened in me a desire to marry. Sadly, he would not look in my direction. Not as a lowly maidservant. But I hoped some man would someday. Would Laban allow me to marry? I belonged to him.

I tried not to let the thought sadden me. I hoped Laban would permit his young maidservants husbands and families.

When I entered Rachel's room to help her dress for dinner, a small bouquet of desert roses sat on her dressing table. She perched at her dressing table, staring at them.

"Where did the desert roses come from? I did not see you go gather more."

"I did not pick them," she said in a dreamy voice. "I have been busy."

Desert roses. The flower I told Jacob she liked showed up on her dressing table.

"Shall I put these in a vase?" I asked.

She nodded. I dumped older, dry flowers out of the vase and set the new bouquet in it, adding water. "Jacob must like you," I said, setting them on the back corner of her dressing table.

"Mmm. I hope so."

"He has excellent taste in flowers." I wanted to know how she truly felt about Jacob. Would I need to calm her desires as Avagail demanded??

"I hope he sees me as beautiful as these flowers," Rachel mused. Her face glowed.

"He plainly cares for you. Why else would he bring you such beautiful flowers?"

"Perhaps." Her wistful face showed more than she wanted me to know.

And, like you, Rachel, I hope a man will ask for my hand in marriage. I felt the same goofy expression fill my face that filled hers.

***

Life continued. Rachel stopped complaining about going to the well, cheerfully taking her turn until Jacob convinced Laban he no longer needed his daughters to accompany him. Between lions that roared near the city at night and men who wanted to steal the sheep, it was no longer safe. Rachel grumbled about her father taking away her opportunity to spend time with Jacob. But that did not last.

One night about two weeks after Rachel and Leah stopped going with Jacob to the well, I walked with Rachel to the well. Each of us carried buckets of water. "Do you think Jacob will ask you to marry him?" I asked.

"I want him to ask Father for permission to marry me." She had a far-off look.

"You know your father expects to have Leah married first." Avagail expected me to remind her. I knew it would cause my friend heartbreak if Jacob did ask for Leah's hand.

Rachel closed her eyes and took a deep breath. "I know. But I think Jacob cares about me. I hope he will insist."

"Some within the household have taken notice," I cleared my throat.

She sighed. "I cannot stop the maids from talking. They have as long as I can remember. They envy me. I am beautiful and the daughter of Laban."

Pride would not serve her in this, but Rachel's beauty had caused the maids to gossip since before I came. "The gossip may stop if you spoke to them more as you talk to me. Be friendlier. They do not know you like I do."

She stopped and stared at me. "I have never had a friend. Just Leah, and she makes me feel sad when I look at her."

I startled back from her. "Am I not your friend? And why would you feel sad for Leah?"

"Her scars. I am responsible for them."

"What?" I snorted.

"When Leah lay sick in the bed with the rash raising on her body, your mama left Leah to help Mother bring me into the world." She kicked at a clump of grass.

"The maids were to help Leah. It is not your fault they refused to enter her room," I cried.

"They feared her disease."

"With reason, but Leah was only two. Mama told me about that time. People died of that disease."

"Because my birth took your mother away from helping Leah, and the servants assigned to care for Leah refused to help her,"

Rachel continued. "and refused to give her the healing teas your mama left. They refused to smooth the salves and lotions on her to help soothe the blisters." Her face sagged. "Well, they did not offer them until it was too late. And, well ... I am the reason for all of it."

No, I am the reason Mama did not return. But I will not take the blame for Leah's scars. "That is not your fault." My braids bounced against my cheeks as I vigorously shook my head. "Mama was distraught when she learned the servants had refused to help Leah. But she could have done nothing else. She had to go home to give birth to me."

"Oh, right. We are almost twins." She grinned for a moment, then frowned again. "But Father is not finding a husband for Leah. How will I ever marry?" We walked on toward home.

I chewed on my lip. "I do not know, but I trust Jehovah will make it possible for you to marry."

"Jehovah. Father speaks of him. We attend worship services occasionally. Would Jehovah help me?"

"Mama taught me Jehovah loves us and will help with our righteous desires. He will not make me beautiful like you. That is not righteous to ask such a thing. But your desire for a husband is righteous."

"Does Jehovah care who I marry?"

"That I do not know, Rachel. But I know Jehovah expects you to desire a righteous husband. A desire for a husband is normal and necessary."

As is mine.

"Could he convince Jacob to want to marry me and for Father to agree?"

I nodded. "Jehovah loves you. He will help you if Jacob is right for you."

"I believe he is."

"Remember to pray. Ask Jehovah tonight."

"Can I pray?"

"Yes."

"Will you pray with me?" She stepped to the side of the path and knelt.

"Here?"

"I need Jehovah's help."

I knelt beside her and raised my hands, joining her in prayer.

Jehovah heard Rachel's prayers, for the next evening Laban announced Jacob's request to marry Rachel to the family. As I went to help Rachel prepare for bed that night, I heard Leah's soft sobs from within her chamber.

However, Rachel bubbled with excitement in her chamber. She danced around nonstop, making it difficult to help her undress.

"You were right, Bilhah," she giggled. "Jehovah loves me. He helped Jacob convince Father to allow him to marry me. Father did not insist he marry Leah instead." She stopped spinning. The bright joy fell and her smile became a pout. "But he insisted Jacob give him seven years of work as a bride price for me. I do not know how, but Jacob agreed."

I gasped. "Seven years!" What was Laban thinking? Was this his selfish way to get free labor, since Jacob did not bring the chests of gold and jewels Abram's servant brought for Rebekah? Or did Laban hope Jacob would give up hope and never fulfill the contract and accept Leah instead?

Rachel plopped onto her dressing table stool. "Yes. Seven years." She stroked her lower lip as if considering the extreme conditions Laban had set. "I hope Father changes his mind and allows us to marry sooner. "If not, the years will pass and eventually Jacob will be mine." She hugged herself and laughed, joy filling her once more.

I joined in her laughter. Jehovah loved her.

Does Jehovah love me? Will there ever be a man for me to marry and love? Will Jehovah open the way for me to have a family? How long will I have to wait? What can I do?

Avdon

Who will love and marry me? I considered the men of the city as I walked from Laban's home to the well. All I saw were rough, harsh men who became easily enraged or who taunted women. Nothing like Jacob. I wanted none of those men to become my husband.

Laban had assigned me to walk behind Jacob and Rachel when they walked together in the evening, to ensure they conducted themselves with honor. I appreciated the way Jacob treated Rachel with kindness, bringing her flowers, talking with her, their heads together. Each evening I followed them at a discreet distance, observing their love grow. Their growing love left me wanting a man like Jacob to come and take me away. She brushed his hair from his eyes and stared into them, leaning forward for a kiss. He kissed her so tenderly, there was no way to say they did not love each other.

I waited for a man to appear as Jacob had. I doubted it would ever happen. Laban would never allow me to leave his service. He seldom let maidservants go. Still, as I walked behind Jacob and Rachel each day, I dreamed a man would see me and consider me for his wife.

One spring day, more than three years after Jacob entered our lives, a young herder suddenly burst into the kitchen. He struggled to speak after rushing for help.

"Healer," he panted. "We need ... the ... healer. Injured ... bleeding."

Ada turned to me. "Bilhah, get your healing basket. The herders need you."

I darted to the corner and grabbed my basket, glancing in to ensure all my supplies remained within. With a nod, I scurried to the young man. "Show me who is injured." I was not just a maidservant, but a healer.

He turned on his heels and rushed from the kitchen with me behind. We raced to the sheep paddocks where some sheep had been sheared. Others stood bleating in the heat, awaiting their turn to have their heavy wool removed.

Inside a pen, a knot of men huddled in a tight circle. The young man pushed the others aside. "The healer is here. Let her through."

Men moved, allowing me to follow the messenger to the center, where three men knelt on the ground, pressing a bloodied sash around a man's leg, clearly applying pressure and trying to stop the bleeding.

I dropped to my knees beside them, setting my basket beside me. "What happened?"

The man writhed in pain. Blood soaked the dirt around him and his sash.

"The shearing knife slipped," one man announced.

"How bad is the injury?" I moved the bloody sash to see.

"Bad," a man whispered.

The herder moaned, and blood oozed from the gash, pumping wildly when I removed the bloody sash. I tied it above his wound, slowing the flow of blood to a trickle. Mama had done that with severe injuries.

"What is his name?"

"Yitzchak," a herder said.

"We will help you, Yitzchak," I murmured. "Pray to your god, as I pray to mine."

I spoke a low, fast prayer, asking Jehovah to bless my hands to help this man. When I finished, I asked. "Is there water to wash away the blood so I may better see his injury?"

A man poured water from his drinking gourd onto a linen cloth and handed it to me. I glanced up to take it from him. Blood rushed to my head. I knew those eyes, that face.

My brother, Avdon, nodded.

I gave him a quick smile. *Later. I will speak with him later.*

Taking a deep breath before accepting his cloth, I washed away the blood. His injury was long and deep. I cleaned the wound and stitched it closed, all the while telling the shepherd what I was doing. Some men left the circle.

I remembered the first severe wound I had seen Mama close. My stomach had quivered and my hands had shaken, but I did not leave, nor did I lose my meal. That was when Mama took me with her on all her visits. I think I was four. She taught me much in the next six short years.

Now I held Yitzchak's life in my hands as I struggled to close the wound and save his life.

When at last I removed the sash above the wound, I watched and prayed. Only a little blood seeped from between my stitches. *Thank you, Jehovah.*

"I need Yitzchak moved to his home. Is it near?" I glanced up, seeking an answer from the men who still surrounded me.

"He lives in the servants' quarters," Avdon waved in that direction. "We will carry him there."

Yitzchak slept because of pain and loss of blood. Avdon and three other herders gently lifted him and carried him away. I followed, thinking about what I still needed to do. *He needs something to heal him from* the inside *as much as I need to cleanse that wound. Honey will protect it and help stop the bleeding. I hope they have hot water.*

Avdon and the other herders set Yitzchak on a hard pallet in a long room filled with twenty or more pallets. *This is where the herders live? Sparse. My room with Zilpah is more comfortable.*

"I need a bowl of hot water." I pulled a stool close to the pallet and sat on it.

Avdon hurried away. In my basket, I found a packet of herbs I had prepared for injuries like this. When Avdon returned with the bowl of hot water, I dumped the packet in and stirred with a clean cloth.

I cleansed the wound thoroughly, covered it with honey, and bandaged it, then made a herbal drink. Yitzchak awoke, and I lifted his head and helped him drink. "You lost too much blood. You need to drink water to replenish your blood. Stay off the leg until I come and tell you it is safe to move again. Moving will cause the wound to seep. You must give it time to heal completely."

As I gathered my supplies, I glanced up. Only Avdon waited beside me. "Is he your friend?"

Avdon nodded.

"Check his leg often. If you see red streaking above the wound, come get me. Yitzchak will need to drink the herb water I am leaving morning, midday, and evening. Can you help him?"

"Yitzchak would do that for me." Avdon gazed at his friend. "I will do it for him."

I stood. "Come get me if he gets worse."

Avdon walked with me to the door of the servants' quarters. "Thank you, Bilhah," he said at the door. "If you had not come so quickly, I fear Yitzchak would not have lived."

"Who wrapped the wound with the sash? That helped him to live."

"I did. My sash was all I had. I remember Mama stopping the bleeding like that."

I nodded. "I do as well." I inhaled a sharp breath. "I miss her and I missed you."

"I missed you too, sister. I see you with Rachel sometimes. Since you cannot be with Mama, I am happy you are here near me." He put an arm around me and gave me a brief hug.

"Now that I know you are here, I can rest. I have missed you and our family." I lingered on the step, not wanting to leave my brother. He had grown, as I had. His tall, sturdy frame and his long, curly hair reminded me of Papa. A pang of resentment toward Papa surged through me. I shook it off. I could do nothing about him now.

"Will they miss you in the house?" Avdon asked.

I glanced up at the sun. It had moved farther than I expected. "They will. I must go. I will have to change."

"You are a mess. Perhaps you need a tunic or an apron to cover your clothing when you work as a healer?"

"Probably. I will have to find something."

Avdon touched my face with a tenderness I had not felt for many long years. I swallowed the tears that threatened to fall and hurried to the kitchen and my other duties.

***

When Jacob offered his yearly sacrifice at the edge of Laban's fields, as he did every year to thank Jehovah for bringing him to Harran and Rachel, I spoke with Avdon about our lives.

"Have you seen Mama?" he would ask each year.

I would shake my head. "No. Have you?"

"I glimpsed her along the path near here one day years ago," he said the first year we met after Yitzchak's injury.

After that, he would drop his head. "No. I have not seen her. I fear for her."

"Would Papa ..."

Each time, "I do not know. I sometimes see Melek and Agos from a distance. They serve another man."

I chewed on my lip. "Have you seen Nissa?"

He usually shook his head. But after Jacob's sixth yearly sacrifice, he grinned. "I spoke to both Melek and Agos last month. They serve the same man, Warda."

"The merchant selling fabrics?"

"Yes, him. They rode ahead of a wagon filled with cloth, taking it to a buyer."

"Together? Warda must trust them."

"They were happy, proud to be given the responsibility. I did not speak to them long, for they had a long journey ahead of them."

I sighed. "But you have not heard of or seen Nissa?"

He shook his head and kicked at the dirt.

Rachel's home

I watched Rachel and Jacob struggle, always showing their love for each other, as they waited for their seven years to pass so they could marry. Sometimes, when I went to the garden, Jacob would stop and visit. Over time, little by little, I shared with him the trials of my childhood. He listened with grace, never suggesting I had done anything wrong.

"I miss Mama and Nissa," I often said.

"You would. I miss my mother and father." He would respond, then chuckle. "Sometimes I miss Esau. More than I like to admit."

In these brief conversations, my fondness for him grew. He could have been my older cousin. I trusted him.

One evening after walking with Jacob in their fourth year of waiting, Rachel sat on her stool and stared."Father is cruel. Yet Jacob will not take me with him from Harran. He is too honorable. Father should allow us to marry now."

"Your father wants to ensure he gets his bride price for you." I brushed her hair as I did every night.

"He is a greedy man. Have you not seen how Jacob is increasing Father's herds? He fears Jacob will not work as hard if we are allowed to marry."

My hand stopped. "Jacob would not do that. Would he?"

"No, but Father expects Jacob to act as he would. Father will find a way to keep Jacob working. Watch. You will see."

I struggled to believe Laban had become that selfish. How could he? No, he appreciated Jacob's work.

"We have almost three years." Rachel slumped in her seat. "Why does he have to be like this? I need to convince Father to let us marry earlier. I will be an old woman before he allows us to marry."

"Old woman," I guffawed. "You are only nineteen. Your day will come sooner than you expect."

Rachel turned in her seat. “How will I give children to Jacob if I must wait?”

“How will you have children if you do not?” I bit my lip. “I should not have said that. It is not my place to tell you what to do.”

“No, it is not your place, but you are correct.” Rachel pursed her lips. “I do not desire children before we wed. I doubt Father would handle that well.”

I nodded. *Laban would not treat them well if she did something like that. He would not treat me well if I allowed it to happen and did not prevent it. He would send me away. No one would take me in to serve them. But as a healer, I could live as a free woman. Mama does.*

I shuddered at the thought.

Thankfully, Jacob continued to be prudent. He would take Rachel into his arms and kiss her each evening. I saw Rachel’s yearning for more, but he would step back and murmur soft words to her. In those actions, I grew to love him too.

Through those years of waiting, messengers came looking for me when injured herders required healing. Most of the time, the herder had cut himself, although not as badly as Yitzchak had. I always brought the leather apron Avdon had made for me to protect my clothing.

***

Rachel and Jacob walked along the lane many times in those seven years while they waited for the payment of the bride price.

One evening in the sixth year, I heard Jacob exclaim, “I will not live in your father’s home after we marry."

“Where will we live?” Rachel asked as they walked.

In my heart, I knew all would be well. Jehovah would help them find a home.

They discussed the problem often and sometimes passionately, but could not resolve their differences.

Then, near the end of the seventh year, we passed an empty home down the lane, a few homes from Laban. Jacob stopped and stared at it.

The house, like all the others in Harran, had a conical roof made of mud. The thick adobe walls would keep the interior cool during the hottest months. But the leather skin used as a door had blown away in the wind. The few bushes looked dead.

Who knew what the inside looked like. No one had lived in it for years. Mice and vermin may have made their homes in it. I shuddered at the thought. But who owned that home? I pondered the question as we returned to Laban's home.

Later, while I helped Rachel prepare for bed, Rachel explained.

"Jacob believes we can live in the house down the lane. He plans to ask the herders about it tomorrow. Someone will know why it is empty."

She stepped out of her dress and I pulled her nightdress over her head. "That old house? I believe Sufi and Gaitha lived there until a few years ago."

"Sufi and Gaitha? I remember them. They were kind to me. Mother took us to visit them when Leah and I were young. Gaitha always told such fun stories and gave us honey treats." She slipped into her robe and tied the sash before sitting on the stool in front of her dressing table.

I untied her braid. "The grounds need work. Will the inside need as much work? Perhaps it is unlivable."

Rachel leaned back and closed her eyes, enjoying my brushing. "We have time to clean it before Jacob and I move in."

"True." I hoped it would work for them. Rachel and Jacob deserved good things.

"Jacob will know more about the house soon. I need to ensure I have enough linens, pillows, and other items needed to make my home comfortable. I cannot believe it. I will have a home away from Mother soon." She sighed and smiled, her eyes still closed.

"Did you believe this would happen when Jacob first came into your life?" I asked as I finished.

"Seven years ago? No." She hugged herself. "A home of my own."

Where will I go when she marries Jacob? I serve Rachel, though perhaps not after the marriage. I belong to Laban, not Rachel. What will he do with me? Will he let me leave and become a healer in the city? If only I could have a family away from Avagail and Laban.

I fought off my concerns and smiled. "Jehovah blesses you. You will love having a home of your own."

"I will, though I sometimes wondered if it would happen." Rachel opened her eyes and stood. "Father still insists Leah needs to marry first. I do not trust him. I wish Jacob's twin brother Esau had come. Then Leah would have a husband too."

I set the brush on Rachel's dressing table. "That would help Leah."

"And I would not need to worry about trusting Father."

"I do not think he can stop your marriage to Jacob. Can he?"

Rachel stretched. "He will try something to ensure Leah marries first. He says his honor is at risk. 'Leah must marry first. It is tradition.' How can he demand it?" She tossed her hands out as if she were throwing his words away. "It is evident he does not want Leah here forever. I think he fears she will become a burden."

I shook my head. "Leah will never be a burden."

"Father will think she is."

"What will you do?"

Rachel clenched her fists. "What can I do? Father has continued to seek a man for her, but men do not see her beauty beneath the scars."

"It is in Jehovah's hands. Trust Him." I trusted Jehovah. I hoped to convince her to do the same.

"Yes," she murmured, sounding uncertain. "Trust Jehovah? I can do that."

As she got into bed, I went to the door. "Sleep well."

Trust Jehovah. Good advice for Rachel. Will it work for me? Who will see me as a woman to marry? I seldom leave Laban's home to meet other men. And where will I find a man who worships Jehovah? I sighed. *Trust Jehovah. It is my only hope. If not, I can continue to heal.*

Jacob made an agreement with the homeowners who lived across the city. Many times over the next weeks, Avagail led the maidservants to clean until we had it ready to live in. My fears were realized. Vermin had moved in, making nests in almost every chamber of the house.

In the evenings, Jacob and some other men cleared away the overgrowth of trees and bushes, cutting them back until they looked like they would live. The home was ready to occupy a month before the seven years of Jacob's required service. I joined Rachel, Leah, and the other maidservants in placing linens, rugs, dishes, pots, and other household items in Rachel's soon-to-be new home.

Rachel and Leah squabbled about where to place rugs and pillows. However, Rachel reminded Leah that the home was hers, and she would put her possessions where she wanted. Uncharacteristically, Leah scowled and mumbled something I could not understand.

"Leah has dreamed this house would be hers for years," Zilpah whispered to me. "It is hard for her to accept that Jacob and Rachel will live here."

"How did she expect to live here without a husband?"

"She hoped a man would marry her before Rachel and Jacob wed. She struggles still, knowing she will not."

I glanced at Leah. No wonder she acted irritable and argued with Rachel about where to put things.

Three days before the planned wedding, Rachel and I took her red wedding blanket to the house and spread it across the bed.

"This will be mine." Rachel spun in the sleeping chamber. "Jacob and I will lie here, uniting as one. Jehovah will bless us with many children. I trust Him. He has blessed me with Jacob and this home."

Seventh Sacrifice

The day arrived at last. As he had each of the last six years before, our small group of worshippers joined Jacob to celebrate the sacrifice ending his service to Laban. As usual, on the edge of Laban's field, Jacob led a willing, pure, young ram up the ramp and followed the exacting rite his father had taught him. As Jehovah's portion burned, Jacob offered a prayer of thanksgiving for Jehovah's blessings, especially that he would soon marry Rachel.

Rachel glowed. Jacob would soon be her husband. They would marry in two days. Although happiness for her filled me, a sadness darkened the edges of my joy. I had also dreamed of marrying, but I was now twenty-two. My advanced age would make it harder to find a man interested in marrying me. How would I marry?

At the outdoor feast, where we celebrated the sacrifice together, I helped serve the line of believers who joined us. The fragrance of cooking lamb filled the air. Laban always gave an old ewe or ram to add to the part of the ram Jacob sacrificed for the feast we held after the sacrifice. Women from our small congregation provided the rest of the meal.

Laban's face twisted when others congratulated Jacob. He sat slumped in his seat, probably considering ways to cause sorrow for Rachel and Jacob. But what more could he do?

Avdon sat alone under a tree with his food. I took a plate and sat beside him. "Good day, Avdon."

He glanced up, surprise filling his face. "Oh, Bilhah. I did not see you earlier."

"I have supported Rachel today. She is excited"

"She would be," Avdon said. "Is she not to be married soon?"

"In two days. We will be kept busy during those two days. I am grateful for a day to rest before all that happens."

He laughed. "She will work you."

"Have you seen Mama?" I asked.

"I rarely get to town. She does not come out to the meadow where I herd the flocks. Have you seen her?"

I set my spoon on my plate and gazed at the grass. "I do not leave Laban's home often, except to follow behind Rachel and Jacob on their evening walks. Mama does not come this way if she still lives in Harran. I have never seen her since she brought me here."

"I pray she still lives." His eyes lifted upward before falling back to his plate. "Papa is a wicked man."

I gasped. "Do you think so? What do you remember of Papa?"

He rubbed the back of his neck. "He tried to hurt her before he left us. People think he left because he found another woman. That is not what happened. Mama threatened to report him to the city guard if he did not leave. Since she had healed the child of the captain of the guard, he knew she could fulfill her threat and he had to leave."

"That was the captain of the guard? I helped her with his son."

"I think she spoke with him about Papa, for Papa growled and cursed him and Mama as he stuffed his clothing into a pack before he left."

"I was not there that day."

"You were helping Mama."

We sat for a short time without talking. I remembered those days before and after Papa left. I had loved the way he treated me. But I still felt the hurt of his abrupt departure and the destruction of our family. Avdon was right. Papa was a wicked man.

Avdon broke the silence. "Will you go with Rachel to her new home?"

I sighed. I still had no answer. "I do not know. Neither Avagail nor Laban has said anything to me. I suppose I will stay in the kitchen working."

"Will Laban expect Jacob to hire maidservants for Rachel?"

I shook my head.

"Laban would expect Jacob to hire his own servants. He is cheap."

"Avagail will not want to train new maidservants if some of us go with Rachel." I bit my lip. *Would Laban send another girl or me?* "I have spent the last twelve years in this household as Rachel's maidservant. Perhaps Laban will have mercy on Rachel and send me with her. But ..." I pleated the hem of my skirt.

"You do not want to go with Rachel?" Avdon asked.

"I hoped a man would consider me as his wife."

"You belong to Laban," Avdon murmured, "as I do. I fear there is no hope for either of us to have a happy family again."

Zilpah and Yitzchak strolled past. I grinned, hoping for good things for her.

"Do you have hopes for a wife and children?"

"I hope to one day. I walk with Alma many evenings now, when she slips out after cleaning the kitchen. Avagail does not know she leaves. We have spoken of marriage, but will Laban allow it?" He glanced toward the serving line and grinned at Alma.

"When did you start walking together?"

He thought back. "It has been about three months since we started repairing Jacob's house. I walked back with Alma that first day. We have spent many evenings together since then."

"You told her I am your sister? I would not want her to be unhappy because I am talking with you."

"Alma knows. I told her long ago. It surprises me she did not speak to you."

"We have not worked together since we cleaned Rachel's home."

"I see. That must be why she did not tell you."

"She is quiet." I had always liked Alma, since the day I stitched her finger. She had not joined in the gossiping about Rachel with the other maids. Avdon would be happy with Alma if Laban allowed their marriage.

"Her quietness draws me to her. After being with the other herders and their chatter all day, her calm warms me."

"I hope Laban allows you to marry her." I stared at my hands. "I would like a man like you to walk with me and ask me to marry him."

"It will happen," Avdon set a hand on my arm. "Trust Jehovah."

"Those are the words I gave to Rachel." Could I believe them for myself? I waited so long. How much longer must I wait?

"And words you should depend on for your own joy."

I must believe him. "Have you seen Nissa?"

He looked at his lap, his body caving in on itself. "Agos did."

"Is she well?"

"Melek saw her on the last feast day of Muloch."

I shivered. *The dreadful god who demanded sacrifices of children and virgins.*

"Is she well?" I asked again, afraid of his answer.

"Melek said no." Avdon drooped farther as he stirred up the dust with his foot.

"No! Not a ..." I could not finish the thought. They could not have sacrificed my little sister.

"Yes."

Avdon lifted his head and gazed at me with sorrowful eyes. He wiped my tears. "She is with Jehovah, no longer part of this wicked world. We should rejoice." His words were certain, but they were more of a question.

I gulped back more tears and nodded. "She is safe with Jehovah." This was my only comfort. I had to trust Jehovah. How could Papa have destroyed our family? What happened that those priests of Melek took Nissa? It had to have been Papa's fault. He forced the destruction of our family. Because of him, I no longer knew Avdon or my other brothers. I had not learned more about healing from

Mama. I missed her. I missed our family. Avdon was right. Papa was a wicked man.

Avdon gave me a hug before I had to return to my responsibilities at the serving table. "Remember, Bilhah," he whispered. "Trust Jehovah."

I was blessed to have a brother who listened to Mama when we were young. He was a much better man than Papa would ever be.

I found Jacob later in the meadow. Rachel had left him to get something. I knew I could trust this man who obeyed Jehovah, who treated me like a cousin. "I just learned the priests sacrificed Nissa to Muloch." I swallowed the lump in my throat. "Can she still be safe with Jehovah after dying like that?"

His face softened. "I am sorry, Bilhah. I know how much you loved her. Did your mother teach her about Jehovah?"

I nodded. "She taught my brothers and me. Certainly, she taught Nissa as well."

He took my hands in his. "She will be blessed. Jehovah loves his children. He will hold her in his hands." His gentle voice filled me as his tender blue eyes gazed into mine. I could trust this righteous man.

Rachel came to stand beside Jacob, concern for me filling her eyes.

I fought back my sorrow. This was a day to rejoice. Soon Rachel and Jacob would become husband and wife.

"Do not fear for your sister," he continued. "Remember what your mother taught and trust Jehovah."

Sadness filled me. Nissa was so little when Mama left me with Laban. Her sweet smile had filled me with joy. I remembered her slight weight as I carried her on my hip, the warmth of her tiny body, and her kisses on my face.

Laban's Deceit

The morning of Rachel's wedding, the noise of activity filled the kitchen when I entered after helping Rachel dress.

Ada threw me a grin as I entered, as filled with joy as the rest of us. "I did not expect you to come this morning. I thought Rachel would need your assistance."

"She asked me to return soon. I knew you would be busy this morning and in need of an extra person."

"Thank you, Bilhah, for coming to the kitchen. I appreciate you."

After preparing some honeyed dates for the wedding feast, I returned to Rachel's room. Open trunks and baskets spread across the floor of her room. Some were half-filled. Others waited for Rachel's possessions.

"What do you need me to do now?" I asked.

She waved her hands around. She covered her nervousness with a grin. "I need to pack my clothing for the men to carry to my new home later this afternoon. I need to ensure my dress and jewels are ready for the rite. I am so excited!" Almost out of breath, she spun in circles, as she did so often.

I grinned and waited for her to calm.

When she finally sat on her dressing table stool, I looked around. "Are these all the trunks to fill?"

"Father said I may take these trunks. I hope they are enough for my dresses and other possessions not already packed."

Three trunks stood open near her bed.

"Shall we begin with your dresses? You will need the dress for tomorrow left out, and a dress for the day after your marriage set on top."

Rachel had spent months spinning the fabric for her dress and tichel. After stitching them, she embroidered a beautiful design on them. She had everything prepared for this day.

We had gone through her dresses three times in the past week, deciding which of her dresses to take to wear in the first days after the marriage.

We spent the late morning and early afternoon packing her possessions and giggling about her marriage in happy busyness. By midafternoon, I left to help in the kitchen once more, still unsure of how Avagail would use my services once Rachel left her home. Probably put me to work in the kitchen. I still dreamed she would let me serve others as a healer.

Near the time for the wedding feast, Laban sent his messenger to fetch me.

"You called for me, Master Laban?" I asked as I entered his office.

He sat behind his desk, spinning his quill pen between his fingers. He nodded. "There has been a change of plans. Rachel will not go to her new home tonight. Her wedding will take place next week." His frown seemed to deepen.

Did I hear him right? "What about the wedding feast we are so busy preparing?" I stammered.

"There will still be a feast and wedding tonight. However, Jacob will not receive Rachel as his wife. He will marry Leah."

I gasped. "Leah? What will Jacob think?" I swayed where I stood. *Why? I expected you to do something, but not this terrible.*

"After he overcomes his anger with me, he will see I gave him a bargain — both of my beautiful daughters." Laban grinned like the cat in the kitchen who ate the cream.

"What do you want me to do?" I asked, swallowing my horror.

"Go help Rachel. She will need your support. Keep her quiet and in her room until tomorrow. The other maids do not need to know what is happening. After the wedding and after Rachel sleeps, you may return to your chamber." He handed me a folded note. "Give this to Tuval. He stands at her door to keep her from warning Jacob. He will need this to allow you into Rachel's room. Do not let Rachel warn Jacob of this. Do not warn him for her. If you do, I will send you away. If I did that, no one would dare hire you to work in their home."

My chin trembled as I took the note from him.

At Rachel's door, Tuval opened the note and read it twice before he pushed the door open for me. I entered to find Rachel sitting at her dressing table, her face blotchy from tears.

I rushed to her. "Oh, Rachel." I fell to my knees in front of her. "Your father sent me."

"Did he tell you what he is doing?" she demanded.

I nodded, unable to speak. Instead, I poured water into a bowl and added herbs to soothe her face.

"He will cover her face so Jacob thinks he is marrying me. Father thinks Jacob will not know until tomorrow, when it is too late." She kicked the dressing table's leg. "He says I can marry Jacob next week. Will he return for me after Father's horrible tricks?"

I grabbed the table before anything fell off and handed the damp, herb-filled cloth to her. "This will help you feel better. You do not want Jacob to see you with a blotchy face."

"If he sees me again. Ever. What will I do if he refuses to marry me after Father's deceit? After they ... after it is too late?" Her sobs increased. "How could Father do this to us? Jacob loves me, not Leah. It proves how horrible he can be."

I dabbed the cloth against her face.

"Why would he do this to me? I feared he might do this, but why would he wait until our wedding day?" Tears flowed down her cheeks without stopping.

I continued to dab her face. What else could I do? "I do not know. You said you did not trust him. Did you say anything to Jacob before now to warn him?"

Rachel chewed on her lip. "I did. He laughed at me. What will he do tonight when Father gives Leah to him? Will he argue and insist on receiving the woman he worked seven years for? What will I do if he does not?"

I shook my head. "I do not know. Let me brush your hair. It will soothe you. Perhaps we can think of something."

"Father will not allow me out of my chamber. I tried. Tuval is there to keep me in. He shuttered and locked my window."

Rachel pushed my hand away. "You can go tell Jacob what is happening," she cried.

"I cannot. Your father warned me against it. If I warn Jacob, Laban will put me out of his house and ensure no one else will hire me. I will be homeless and alone." I gulped back the tears. "Oh, Rachel. I cannot do it."

"Father is exceedingly heartless. He would send you away. But you could work as a healer. You would not be left alone. Please go find Jacob. Tell him what Father is doing."

I shook my head."You are wrong. He is too powerful. He would destroy my opportunities to serve others as a healer. We must obey him." I coaxed her onto the stool and took out her braids.

I hummed a tune Mama sang to me when I was little and needed to relax. It did not calm Rachel. "Father said Jacob could marry me in a week, if he would work another seven years."

"Another seven years!" I cried. "How can your father expect that of him?"

Rachel kicked her foot, narrowly missing my leg. "He said Jacob will do it if he loves me." She turned her anguished face to me. "He loves me, but does he love me enough?"

"Oh yes. Jacob loves you. He will work another seven years for you." I hoped he would. I saw the love in his eyes when they walked together. What would we do if he refused Laban in his hot anger? He left his home when his brother threatened him.

"I pray you are right. What right does Father have to insist that Jacob marry Leah instead of me?"

"He is your father. That means he can do anything."

"Even if he says we may marry in a week, it is little consolation."

Scraping echoed in the chamber on the other side of the wall. Leah's chamber. "Leah is preparing to be Jacob's wife," Rachel whimpered, more tears filling her eyes. "She is preparing to move into my home." She pounded on the wall between the chambers, then stomped to the door and pushed. It would not open. She banged on the door.

Before Tuval could open it, I gently grasped her shoulders to pull her away. "Stay quiet, or Tuval will take me away. Your father will not allow me to stay, and you will be left alone."

Rachel put a hand over her mouth and nodded as her sobs continued. "I do not want that."

I encouraged her to sit on her sleeping pallet and dampened another cloth. "Your father is giving Leah a week with her husband before Jacob marries you. Laban will give you the same time alone with Jacob before he is required to return to the flocks."

"Do you believe he will? Oh, Bilhah. I pray you are right. I cannot change my father or his awful plan. Please, let it work." She ducked her head and heaved deep breaths.

I stroked her arm, knowing it sometimes aided in calming her.

Eventually, she stopped crying and washed her face. The red did not lessen. "I cannot change this. I can only accept it. I must. I must."

I sat on the floor, listening to the noises of preparations for the feast through the closed window. Trunks scraped across the floor in Leah's chamber while Rachel's sat half-filled and forgotten.

I prepared a cup of tea for Rachel and gave it to her. She sipped it as we listened to the noise in Leah's chamber.

Someone, probably Zilpah, must be helping Leah prepare for her unexpected wedding. Would Laban expect Jacob to provide a maidservant, or would he ensure Leah had one? If Laban sent one, who would he give to Leah? Perhaps Zilpah. It would make sense.

"She is going to my home. Leah will replace my possessions with hers." Rachel covered her face with her hands.

I removed the cup, not wanting her to throw it at me. I stroked her hair, hoping she would not cry in rage again. We did not need Tuval to come in. "She may move a few, but you can work it out when the two of you are there together," I said.

"Together!" she screeched. "She will be married to Jacob first. The house will be hers, not mine," Rachel batted my hand from her head.

She turned and threw herself onto her pallet and buried her face in her pillow. I wanted to embrace her, soothe her fears, but I feared it would cause another angry reaction.

Rachel closed her eyes. Soon the tea worked. She slept.

The activity in Leah's room increased. I thanked Jehovah that Rachel slept.

When Rachel awoke, the feast had already started in the courtyard. Men laughed and chatted as they ate, celebrating Jacob's coming marriage rite.

Rachel unsteadily strode to the window and placed her ear against the shutter. She stood there for a long time, not speaking, her eyes staring at the floor.

The chamber darkened when the sun dropped behind the mountains. The scrape of Leah's door opened. Moving feet whispered past Rachel's door.

Rachel turned as the footsteps slowed near her door, then moved on. She rolled her lips, and a low growl rumbled in her throat.

I cautiously watched Rachel's face, waiting to see if I needed to stop another bout of banging on the door and walls. *How did Leah accept the news? She could not be happy about this marriage.*

Defeated, Rachel leaned against the window. Muted noises of the celebration entered her room. She reached out to me. "Hold my hand, Bilhah. I cannot do this alone."

I held her hand as the voices outside quieted. *Laban must be giving Leah to Jacob as his wife. Although they were similar in size, how did Jacob not know Leah stood in front of him instead of Rachel? How did Laban deceive him?*

"Next week he will be your husband," I whispered.

"Next week," she murmured. "Jacob loves me."

After the men cheered the marriage and the noise diminished, Rachel crawled onto her pallet and dragged the blanket over her head. It took time, but her breathing slowed and she slept.

I opened the door, expecting to meet Tuval, but he was gone. I crept through the house to my chamber, hoping to share Rachel's plight with Zilpah.

All signs of Zilpah were gone. Did she go with Leah?

I laid my head on the pillow and slept, although the events of the day worried my sleep. Why did wicked fathers ruin lives?

***

I woke early as usual and hurried to check on Rachel and help her dress. When I entered the room, she pulled her blanket over her head.

"Do you not want to get up?" I asked.

"No. Why would I want to get out of bed?" Her blankets muffled her voice. "Today was to be the first day with my new husband. Instead, he spent last night with Leah. He will give her a child before he gives me one. He did not fight for me last night. He did not insist on marrying me first."

"You know he did not know of Laban's deception. You will be with him next week."

Pounding on the kitchen door caused Rachel to sit up. "Is that Jacob?"

Jacob would confront Laban's deceit.

"Laban! What have you done to me?" Jacob shouted from outside Laban's study door.

"It is," I whispered.

"He is not happy." Rachel pulled a robe over her sleeping dress and strode toward the door.

Laban's voice rose to join Jacob's. "It is the law of the land."

Law? It is a custom.

Rachel huffed out a breath and stepped closer to the door, her hand reaching for the latch.

I hurried to block her exit. "You are not going downstairs like that," I said.

Laban shouted, "... can have Rachel in a week, *if* you agree to serve me another seven years."

"Why can I not go?" She turned in a rage. "Jacob, the man I love, the man who should be *my* husband, is downstairs."

"Your hair. You are not properly dressed." I pushed myself between her and the door, trying to close it before she could leave.

"And? He will see me undressed with tangled hair after we marry, so why not now?"

Jacob's voice echoed through the house. "I served you seven years already. You cheated me. I agreed to work for Rachel, not Leah."

Laban's voice softened. "You can still have Rachel. You will only ..." The office door clicked shut, silencing their voices.

"Next week," I soothed, doing all I could to calm her. "Your father said next week." I held the door and stood between it and Rachel.

"I should be married to him now."

"But you are not." I took a deep breath and worked to soften my voice. "Next week ..."

She stomped her foot. "Jacob should be mine. That house should be mine." She stomped again. "Another seven years? He told me we could marry next week, Bilhah. He said next week."

"He may require another bride price for you. But he cannot force you to wait another seven years. Your father is not that cruel." I wanted to believe he would not expect them to wait.

"Is he not?" Rachel pushed at the door. "He forced me to sit here while he married my ugly sister to the man who loves me."

"Ugly sister?" My voice roughened. "Leah is not ugly. Her scars are hardly noticeable."

"Then why would no man marry her?"

I shook my head. I had no answer.

"Help me dress." She spun from the door.

"Where are you going?" I asked as I found a dress we had not tucked into her trunk.

"I want to talk to Jacob."

I frowned as I helped her dress and brush her hair.

"You do not approve?" she asked.

"It is not for me to approve or not."

She grumbled as she left her chamber and pounded down the stairs.

I straightened the mess of her half-filled trunks and baskets before I went down the stairs to help Ada and the others prepare the morning meal. On the way down, I passed Rachel stomping up the stairs.

"Shall I bring you a tray?" I asked.

"No," Rachel said in a terse voice, before pounding up the rest of the way.

She is hurting. Laban has gone too far. This week will be miserable for her and me. I hope Jacob comes back for her.

***

Ada glanced up at me, her eyes wide, when I entered the kitchen. "When you did not return yesterday, I thought Laban had given you to Rachel as her maidservant, and you had left with her last night."

The other maidservants gathered to listen.

I shook my head. "No. I did not go with Rachel last night."

"Why then would Laban call you to his office yesterday?"

"He sent me to help Rachel." I would not share Rachel's sorrow. They would learn and start gossiping soon enough.

"Where is Zilpah? Why did Jacob come in shouting at Laban?" I asked.

"Laban called Zilpah to his office soon after he called for you," Ada stirred the grains. "We were forced to serve the wedding feast without either of you."

"Zilpah did not return either?" I asked.

Ada shook her head. "Why were you both gone?"

I swallowed the tears threatening to drench my face. I did not know if they were tears of grief for Rachel or anger at Laban. "Laban had other plans last night. He gave Leah to Jacob, not Rachel."

Ada's eyebrows crunched together. "Did Zilpah go with Leah?"

I tied on an apron. "Leah married Jacob last night. That is all I know. Zilpah's possessions are gone. I suppose she went with Leah."

"How could Laban do that to Jacob and Rachel?" Shiri asked.

"I do not understand it," I scooped food into a serving bowl. "Laban has always insisted it is law his eldest daughter should be married first."

"That is not law. It is custom," Alma blurted.

I shrugged, still fighting to control my tears. "I know. But Laban insisted."

"And Jacob agreed?" Alma shuddered. "Why would he do that?"

"Would he have come here shouting at Laban if he had agreed?" Ada asked.

"He was deceived," I said.

The maidservants chattered until Ada clapped her hands. "You have things to do. The master and mistress will want their morning meal soon."

The others scattered.

"Will I be two maidservants short then, Bilhah?" Ada asked.

I shrugged. "You are short one maidservant for now. I do not know what Avagail will do with me."

"He will send you with Rachel. You have served her since you came here. When will you and Rachel leave?"

"*If* he sends me with her." I mused. "Laban gave Leah and Jacob a week alone together."

Only Laban and Avagail waited for their morning meal.

"Where is Rachel?" Laban asked.

Avagail turned. "Bilhah, where is Rachel?"

I stepped forward. "In her chamber, as you commanded."

You saw her this morning. She passed me on the stairs. But I will not contradict you.

"That was last night," Laban growled. "She is free to leave her chamber now. Go tell her to come down."

I ducked my head in assent. *If her anger is as hot as when she went upstairs, she will not come.*

I tapped on Rachel's door and pushed it open.

She sat on her dressing stool, staring out the window. "Your father requests your presence at the morning meal."

"He has no right to request anything of me," she said stiffly, not turning toward me.

"What do I tell your father?" I asked.

"Tell him I am not hungry."

I lifted my eyebrows. Rachel always ate in the morning.

"But bring me a tray after he leaves."

I shook my head. "I knew you would want food."

I returned to the eating area. Laban had eaten most of the food on his plate. He looked up. "Where is Rachel?"

"She is not hungry."

"Do I care?" he asked. "I sent for my daughter."

"She is angry," I whispered.

Red raced from his chest to his hairline. He pounded a fist on the table. "She is still my daughter, and she will come to the table when I require it."

I ducked my head. "I will tell her."

"Tell her I expect her to join us immediately, or I will send Tuval to drag her down," he shouted as I left the room.

He would send Tuval for her.

I hurried up the stairs and opened the door to Rachel's chamber without knocking. "Your father will send Tuval to drag you down if you do not join him," I cried.

"Tuval?" Rachel turned from the window. She swallowed. "I have no choice about my life until next week, when Jacob marries me. After that, Laban will have no control over my actions." She shoved her hair back off her face.

"Do you want me to brush your hair first?" I asked.

"I do not have time." She opened the door, rushed down the stairs, and slipped into her seat. I followed.

"It is past time for you to join us," Laban rumbled.

"I am not hungry," Rachel replied, refusing to look at him.

"That does not matter," Laban grumbled. "You are expected to join us for meals unless you are ill."

She glanced at her mother. "I am ill."

"You are here. Stay with us." Avagail picked up her spoon and dipped into the grains, as though her daughter had no reason to be upset.

I stood in my usual place, ready to serve, hoping Laban and Avagail's words would not hurt Rachel worse.

"Jacob was not happy with my trade," Laban tried to sound sad, but his chin jutted out and he cocked his head to the side. "Everyone in the house must have heard his roar."

"Do you blame him?" Rachel asked, setting her jaw.

I heard him. He had every right to shout at you.

Laban shrugged. "Perhaps not, but my oldest daughter had to marry first."

"Why?" Rachel demanded.

"You know the law," he said.

"The law," she sneered. "Law, custom, or your desire? You did not believe you would find a husband for Leah, so you stole my husband."

"Rachel," Avagail's low voice was filled with warning.

She always agrees with Laban. She should help her daughter for once.

"He worked seven years for me," Rachel said with little penitence.

"How did Jacob respond when you informed him of your new requirement?" Avagail asked.

Rachel's head jerked. "Do you expect us to wait another seven years?"

She is making an excellent point.

"I told you last night." He turned to Avagail. "He roared again. But afterwards, he dropped his head into his hands. 'You know I love Rachel. I will do anything to be her husband.'"

I held my breath, waiting to see if he would betray Rachel once more. She sat still.

"I told him he could marry you, Rachel, if he covenanted to work the extra seven years for you."

Her eyes flicked toward what was now Jacob and Leah's home. "Can he trust you? Can I trust you?"

I do not trust Laban. He has betrayed Jacob and Rachel.

Laban looked down his nose at his daughter. "You know I am trustworthy. After he has given Leah a week — as an honorable husband, he can claim you."

"You covenanted with him seven years ago — and gave him Leah. How can we trust you?"

With a growl, Laban forced his hand to stay on the table. "I am honorable. Is Jacob? Will he come for you?"

It surprised me he did not lift it to her. He was angry enough and had hit his sons.

Rachel lifted her chin. "He will come. Will you allow him to marry me at the end of the week?" She stared at Laban.

"I told him to come back after his week with Leah. Then he can marry you."

Uncertainty flickered across Rachel's face before she sighed. "He will come."

I hope he comes. He has to come, or Rachel will never be the same.

"Plan on it," Avagail whispered. "He loves you."

As if Avagail cares.

Zilpah's Loss

A week later, I trod down the stairs after helping Rachel prepare for her wedding to work with Ada in the kitchen. My thoughts were as heavy as my steps. I still did not know what would happen to me. Would Laban send me with Rachel as he had sent Zilpah? I wanted to go. I did not want to stay in Laban and Avagail's home.

Avdon had reminded me to trust Jehovah. *Jehovah! I need your help now.*

As I passed Laban's open office door, he beckoned me to enter. When I walked out, Jehovah had answered my prayer. I was to go with Rachel!

After I helped her prepare for her wedding, I bounded down the stairs to gather my possessions into a small basket. I took two dresses Avagail had given me. When Rachel provided me with new dresses, I would return them.

I slipped out the kitchen door and hurried to Jacob's home in the dark. Jacob led Rachel into the house as I neared. Did I take that long, or did Laban cheat Rachel out of a wedding feast?

Standing in the dark, I waited until they entered, then followed and found Zilpah and Leah sitting in the dark so Rachel would not notice their presence. As if she would notice. She would only see Jacob.

I rose early each morning to take Rachel and Jacob their morning meal, leaving it on the floor beside their door, rapping on their door, and hurrying away. They did not need me to interrupt their happiness. As I turned to plod down the stairs the first morning, the door opened. I grinned. The empty tray sat on the floor later that morning when I returned for it.

We did not see Rachel and Jacob during their week together. In the mornings, we saw the remnants of their foraging in the kitchen.

Each evening, I left out food Rachel could easily prepare to support her.

Leah asked to have her loom brought from Laban's house. It gave her something to do during the week, as she did not want to think about her sister and her husband. Laban sent Rachel's loom as well.

I found unexpected freedom after my years of restricted service to Rachel. What was I to do? The house was clean. Zilpah and Leah helped me prepare the meals. There was no clothing to wash yet. I had only two dresses, and nothing to mend. The days loomed in front of me.

The first day, I stayed close to serve Rachel if she needed it.

She did not. Jacob was all she wanted, night and day.

On the second day, flowers beckoned me, and I gathered bunches and set them in small urns throughout the house. Their fragrance filled the air with pungent sweetness. Then I lay in the grass and watched the clouds drift by, seeing shapes in them. Though I thought of climbing a tree, I could not. It stood outside the window where Rachel and Jacob hid away. It would never do to have them think I was spying.

Avdon found me outside picking berries on the third day. "Ada told me I would find you at this house. I need your help now! " His face was flushed from his run to find me.

I jumped up. "What help do you need? What happened?"

"A herder fell down a hill. He hit his head on a rock and will not awaken. Can you leave here to help?"

Glancing at the house, I shook my head. "Rachel is busy with Jacob. She will never know I am gone." Running into the kitchen with my basket of berries, I set it on the table, grabbed my healing supply basket, and rushed out to Avdon. "Take me to your herder."

Thinking he would lead me to the hill where the herder fell, it surprised me when he took me to the servants' quarters and led me inside. Three men stood around a pallet. They moved back as we entered.

Yitzchak! No! A sudden coldness filled me to the center. "You did not say who was hurt." I jabbed Avdon in the ribs with my elbow. "You know Zilpah and he are friends?"

He shrugged. "They were together after the last sacrifice. I have not seen Zilpah since then."

Squatting next to Yitzchak, I touched his wrist, seeking his heartbeat. "Did you know Laban married Leah to Jacob before he allowed him to marry Rachel?"

The men around us murmured words of surprise.

"Why would he do that?" Avdon asked.

I lifted Yitzchak's eyelids. The centers did not shrink in the light as they should, and one was bigger than the other. He stared without seeing. Not good. "I suspect he believed no man would have her ... because of her scars."

The men grumbled.

"She is a beauty. Any of us would have married her if we had been acceptable to Laban," Avdon said.

"That is the problem." I touched Yitzchak's face. "Who is acceptable to Laban? No heat." I examined his head, touching every part. An enormous lump marked the point where his head hit the rock. "That would do it."

"Avdon, can you and your men move him onto his side?"

"Why?" Avdon asked as he and the others knelt next to the injured man and rolled him.

"He hurt his head. Did he hurt himself somewhere else in his fall? If I only treated the head and he has broken bones or bruises elsewhere, those injuries will not heal."

"That makes sense." A herder helped turn Yitzchak. "He tumbled a distance before hitting the rock."

Nodding as I allowed my fingers to probe along his back. "Can you lift his tunic so I can see?"

"You are a woman, a single woman." Another herder recoiled and bounced his gaze to Avdon's face for confirmation.

"And the only one here who can help our friend." Avdon waved a hand to dismiss the herder's concern. "Bilhah is a healer, not a woman seeking to see a man's nakedness. Take your scarf off and cover him if that will make you feel better."

I breathed out my concern as the herder covered Yitzchak. I did not desire to see Yitzchak or any man naked before I married.

As I suspected, he had bruises on his back, arms, and legs. He had protected his stomach from injury somehow. As I prodded his bruises, Yitzchak moaned. He probably had broken ribs. I could do little for his ribs, but I could help his head.

"Can someone get me water?" I opened my basket of supplies.

"Hot or cold?" the concerned herder asked.

"Cold for his head, warm for the rest of him."

He walked away, grumbling about women. I chuckled under my breath. He was right. We did some strange things.

While waiting for the water, I examined his arms and legs. He had bruises, but no broken bones. *One less thing to worry about. How would Mama care for an injury like this?*

I opened my basket and considered the herb packets, withdrawing two. One to clean the bruises and bumps, the other to make a remedy to help him heal from the inside. A bump on the head could be dangerous.

When the herder returned with water, I dipped a cloth into the cold water and laid it on the bump on Yitzchak's head. I prepared tea from the contents of the other packet in the hot water, then prepared a wash to clean his bruises, and cleaned them with more warm water. Last, I washed his head and the bumps there, covering the big bump on the back of his head with a fresh, cold cloth.

When I looked into Yitzchak's eyes once more, one eye still did not shrink as it should, causing me to shudder.

I hope he heals. This injury is serious.

By then, the remedy had steeped and cooled enough to swallow. "Lift his head, please?" I asked Avdon.

Avdon lifted Yitzchak's head with care while I put the cup to his lips. As the moisture touched his lips, his tongue flicked out, tasting it. He shuddered.

"Wait. This needs honey." I dug into my basket for the small pot of honey. I dripped a bit in, stirred it with a finger, and set the cup to Yitzchak's lips again. This time after tasting, he swallowed half of the cup.

"He will need more of this later. Who will care for him?"

"I am his brother," the herder who had been concerned about me seeing his naked body, said.

"Give him the other half this evening. Let me know when he wakes. If he does not wake by dark, come get me. I will come check on him later."

Yitzchak's brother nodded. "I will stay with him if you can watch the flocks without my help." He glanced at Avdon.

Avdon set his hand on the man's shoulder. "We need you to be with Yitzchak, Tam. We will manage," : He turned to the other men, "but we need you other men back with the flocks."

The other two men set a hand on Yitzchak's heart, then stood and left.

After checking my basket to ensure I had left nothing behind, I stood.

"I will walk you back," Avdon said.

We strode in silence until almost to the kitchen door. Avdon stopped and touched my arm. "Are they treating you well at this new house?"

"So far. Jacob and Rachel rarely emerge from their love nest." I shrugged. "Since Leah stays busy weaving, probably to escape thoughts of her new husband with another bride, I have little to do. Zilpah helps her, leaving me free. That is why you found me picking berries."

"Let me know if they mistreat you." He stared into my eyes.

I raised my eyebrows.

"Send me a message if Rachel or Jacob hurts you."

"What can you do if they do?" I shook my head. "I doubt Jacob will mistreat me. He is a good man and is busy with his two wives."

"I would not like two women," Avdon made a sour face.

"Not taking them so close together." I shuddered.

"I will do what I can to help if you need it." Avdon set a hand on my shoulder. "I am Laban's servant, as you were until this week."

I looked into his eyes. "I will let you know."

Avdon kissed me on the cheek. "Be certain you do." He turned and strode back toward the hill where the flocks grazed.

I watched him leave, grateful to have one member of my family close and caring. Still ...

***

When I entered the kitchen, Zilpah sat at the table cutting the green tops off the berries. "I heard you bring these in, but before I could come ask about them, you were gone."

"Avdon came for me. A herder fell and hurt his head."

"A herder?" She did not stop cleaning the berries. "Who?"

I lowered myself onto a chair across from her and traced the wood grain. "The herder, Yitzchak."

The knife rattled from her hands onto the table. "Yitzchak? What happened?"

I took her hands in mine. "He fell down the hill. I do not know why. His head is hurt bad, and he has not woken since the injury."

"Still? Even after you went to help him?" Her eyes plead for a different answer.

"Still. The injury is serious. His brother is with him."

She bit her lip. "I should ... I should go to him."

"You know we are not allowed in their quarters. You can go with me when I return to check on him, if Leah agrees."

"Leah. Surely she will agree." She stood to find Leah.

Grabbing her hand, I pulled her back to her seat. "He sleeps now. There is nothing you can do for him. There was little I could do." My stomach hurt at her pain.

"Will he live? Will he heal?"

I stared at the table. "I hope so."

"Bilhah, tell me he will heal! Tell me he will live." Zilpah's voice rose in fear.

"He is in Jehovah's hands." I dropped her hands and searched for another wood grain to follow with my finger. "I have done all I can do. Mama did not have time to teach me everything. I have had little practice with head injuries, especially injuries this bad."

"He must heal." Zilpah stood, panic filling her voice. "What will I do if he does not?"

Remembering the words she had used to calm me earlier, I repeated them for her. "He will heal if Jehovah allows. Certainly, he will."

She wiped her eyes with her apron. "I shall pray for him." She walked away, leaving me with the berries.

I did all I knew to help Yitzchak. I had not received enough training to heal a severe head injury.

Throughout the day and the next, although I tried everything I knew, and some things I only hoped would help, he did not awaken.

Zilpah went with me each time I went to the servants' quarters on Laban's land. She sat and whispered soft things to Yitzchak, begging him to awaken.

On the third day, Tam shouted as we entered, "Go away! You can do nothing for him! Your healing balms bring only death!"

"Death?" I pushed past him. Zilpah followed behind me. Yitzchak lay on his pallet, his eyes open, staring, and his mouth open. Bending my face close to his, I hoped to feel his breath.

None. I touched his neck. No heartbeat.

"I told you," Tam said, his voice filled with grief. "He is gone."

I bowed my head and shook my head. "I did all I knew to do."

"It was not enough," Tam cried.

Tears filled my eyes as I turned and ran.

When Zilpah found me, her eyes red from grief and tears, she had little to say. "It was Jehovah's will."

"You cared for him," I sobbed. "And I allowed him to die. What more could I have done?"

"Nothing." She put her arms around me. "Jehovah needed Yitzchak. He was not for me."

"If not him," I said through my tears, "who? Who will marry you? Who will marry me?"

"I do not know." Zilpah rubbed my back in small circles. "Jehovah will provide."

Jehovah will provide. How can she trust Him after losing so much? Who will trust me to heal them after this? *What will my life be like?*

We never spoke of Yitzchak again.

But one evening Zilpah brushed my hair before sleeping. "Bilhah, you do not have to be perfect at everything."

I became still."I am not. I make many mistakes."

"But you try. It is not necessary."

I considered her words. "Perhaps if I am, Rachel and Jacob will not send me away."

"Why would they send you away?"

I shook my head. "Mama did."

Zilpah wrapped her arms around me from behind. "Rachel will not send you away. She needs you. You are safe."

Surprise

Rachel enticed Jacob to her sleeping pallet every night after he returned from tending the flocks. Leah frowned when he cheerfully climbed the stairs to spend the night with Rachel. Only when Rachel's womanly time came did Leah manage to slip ahead of her sister and invite their husband to sleep with her.

"Jacob is my husband. He wanted me. He should spend every night with me," Rachel grumbled. "Why must I suffer this indignity?"

"You know why?" I helped her undress. "It is the way of women. Without it, you cannot conceive."

"But Leah takes advantage. She takes Jacob to her pallet when I am unable."

"She is married to him as well."

"She should not be. Father deceived Jacob." Rachel's voice rose in frustration.

"Perhaps she should not, but it is as it is. Leah is also his wife."

"Jacob loves me!"

"And he must give time to his first wife, whether or not he loves her."

Rachel considered this. "Yes. He must spend time with her. But only during my moon time."

A little more than four months after their marriages, a messenger came.

"The ewes lamb," the messenger said. "Jacob is helping them give birth. He will stay with them until they have all given birth."

"Tell Jacob I will miss him," Rachel stepped forward.

"Yes, mistress. I will tell him," the messenger nodded.

Leah entered the kitchen as he left. "Did I hear Jacob's name?"

"A herder brought a message from him." Zilpah dished grains into a bowl for her mistress.

"He must stay with the flocks. The ewes are lambing." Rachel sat at the table.

Leah joined her. "I expected this sooner. The ewes are late this year."

"Babies come when they will." I scooped food into a bowl for Rachel. "Mama taught me. I helped her deliver babies before I came here."

"Your mama helps mothers give birth?" Leah leaned on her elbow.

I straightened my back. "She did. I enjoyed helping her."

"Your mother should have kept you." Rachel glanced my way. "But then you would not be here with me." Her gaze settled on me with a softening of her eyes around the edges.

"Mama tried, but even as a healer, she could not provide for us." I swallowed.

"You said she trained you to help in childbirth?" Leah asked.

"Yes. I helped. I can deliver a child if no problems arise. I was but ten years old when she left me, and when I last helped deliver children, so there is much I did not learn."

I glanced at Zilpah. *I could not save Yitzchak. I did not have enough training.*

I turned my gaze back to Leah. "Do you know someone who needs a midwife?"

Rachel turned to stare at Leah.

"Perhaps," Leah murmured.

"You have changed," Rachel said. "What is different about you?"

Leah's hand touched her stomach. *She carries a child!*

"Can you not tell?" Leah asked.

"No! Tell me you are not carrying Jacob's child," Rachel said with a gasp.

How could Rachel not expect this to happen because it did not happen to her?

"I can tell you I am not, but it would not change the truth. My son will be in about five months." A small smile graced Leah's face.

"So soon?" Rachel blanched as she counted back. "You conceived during your first week with Jacob? How ..."

It happens. Mama spoke of it. Avdon came within the first year after Mama married Papa.

"Does Jacob know?" Rachel demanded.

Leah lifted her chin. "How can I keep it from him? I am available to him when you are not. You keep Jacob from me except for a few nights with him each month. He noticed I was with child early because of his experience with ewes."

Rachel looked away. "I wanted the first child," she whispered.

You love Jacob, *and he loves you. His children should be yours.*

Leah bowed her head and murmured. "Jehovah blessed me in my grief."

Zilpah stepped away from the table. I joined her.

"Your grief?" Rachel cried. "What grief? You spent time with *my* husband before I could. What do you have to grieve over?" Rachel fingered her bowl. Would she throw it at Leah?

Leah's head lifted, her face filled with humility. "My *husband* hates me. My *husband* loves another. My sister. What greater grief can a wife have?"

I squelched a gasp.

Rachel clenched her fist. She dropped her head and whispered. "No children for me yet. Father caused this. I pray Jehovah allows me to have a child soon."

And for maidservants, no husband and no hope for children.

***

About a month later, I walked into Rachel's room concerned when she had not come for the morning meal. She lay on her sleeping pallet, kicking her feet and pounding on her pillow.

"Rachel," I cried. "Are you unwell?"

"It is not fair," she cried, kicking the pallet with each word. "It should be me! I should be with child. Not Leah."

"I agree. It does not seem fair."

"I have prayed, begged Jehovah for understanding. No answer comes." She rolled over and stared at me.

I dampened a cloth.

Her lips pressed together in a slight grimace. "Perhaps I prayed for the wrong thing."

"What should you pray for if not a child?" I wiped tears from her face.

"Perhaps I should pray for Leah and her child. I should pray for their health. It would cause Jacob pain if anything should happen to either of them."

I handed her the cloth, saying nothing.

"Yes," Rachel continued. "I need to pray for Leah. Maybe that will influence Jehovah to open my womb and allow me to have children."

Would that work? It sounded selfish to me.

I prayed for Jehovah to bless her with a child.

***

One cool morning, about six months after Rachel's marriage, Zilpah and I washed clothing together while Leah and Rachel wove inside. We enjoyed this time away from them when we could speak openly together. But today would be different. The sorrow was too great to ignore.

"This has been a difficult time," Zilpah said. "Especially for Jacob with two wives when he expected only one. Can you imagine the challenges we would have if both our mistresses carried children?"

"It may be easier for us." I rinsed a dress. "Rachel yearns for a child. Perhaps she would be less self-centered if she had children to care for?"

Zilpah lifted an eyebrow, too busy scrubbing to do more. "You can say that about Rachel?"

I breathed out a deep breath. "Life has not been easy since she learned of Leah's coming child." I shook out the dress and draped it across a shrub.

Zilpah snorted. "Laban still makes life difficult for all of us."

I grabbed the wooden paddle to drag out another dress. "It is easier for you and me. We are not alone here with only our mistress and her husband as we could be. I could have all the responsibility for cooking, cleaning, and caring for Rachel. It is much better that we are here together."

Zilpah draped another dress over a bush. "Jacob would have needed to find his own servants to help his wives. He still may need to do that. How can he have the means or the time to find others to help us when all his time is spent herding Laban's flocks?"

We shook our heads and moaned together.

"How does Laban expect to have grandchildren when he keeps Jacob so busy?" I muttered.

"He will have one soon," Zilpah said. "Leah is healthy, and her babe grows. He kicks her often."

"He?" I asked, turning to stare at her.

"This is as clean as I can get it." Zilpah focused on a stain. "What woman expecting her first child does not think she will bear a son?"

"The women at the well chatter about coming children. They all think they carry a son."

Zilpah rinsed the tunic and draped it over a bush. "I once dreamed of children ..." Her voice drifted off.

"Until Yitzchak?"

She nodded. "Where will I meet another man interested in me?"

I sighed. "You were blessed to have him. I have never had a man interested in me." I busied myself washing another dress. Moisture filled my eyes, making it difficult to see. I brushed it away with the back of my hand.

"Perhaps Jacob will find men for us?" Zilpah's voice filled with hope.

"He could, but then he would have to find more women to serve as maidservants for his wives."

"Will we never have sons of our own?" Zilpah asked. "Will we never have daughters?"

I turned to gaze at her. A tear slipped past my control and slid down my face. "It is in Jacob's hands."

"And Jehovah's."

***

Since Mama left me as a child, when I went to the market and passed the stalls, I searched for Mama. If she returned, she would sell her healing remedies there. I had almost given up hope of finding her in Harran, when one day I glanced into a stall and stuttered to a stop. A woman stood wearily in the back of the stall. My heart leapt to my throat, and tears dripped down my face.

"Mama?" I whispered. "It's me, Bilhah."

She lifted her head and stared at me. She had aged. Her hair had grayed and wrinkles marred her beautiful face. Life had not been easy for her.

I swallowed the lump as I moved closer.

Mama moved to the barrier separating her from me. Leaning across it, she lifted her hand to touch my face. "Is it really Bilhah?"

"It is, Mama. I serve Rachel. I use the skills you taught me as a healer. Avdon comes for me to heal Laban's herders when one is injured. I have only lost one." I bit my lip, hoping she would understand the loss. "I did not learn how to help a serious head injury." I dropped my head.

"You help the injured?" She gazed into my face with interest.

"I learned from you, Mama."

Mama lifted the board between us and stepped through into my arms. She cried my name as she embraced me. "Bilhah, oh, Bilhah. I watched for you since I returned to Harran. I feared Laban had sold you away."

"I have watched for you since Zilpah and I moved from Laban's house to Jacob's."

Her eyebrows lowered. "Why did both you and Zilpah move to Jacob's household?"

I shared the story.

"And now, Leah will have a child in a few weeks. She expects me to help her. But it has been many years since I helped deliver a child. The last was when I assisted you. Will you come help me when her time comes? I could use your skills and support."

"You know I will, Bilhah. I would like to be there to help Leah's child come."

I hugged her once again. "Thank you."

Why did you leave me with Laban? I could have helped you. I wanted to ask, but the words would not pass my lips.

Still, I returned home with my basket of food and a gigantic smile.

A Son

One morning, six weeks after I found Mama, Zilpah ran into Rachel's chamber as I helped her prepare for the day. "I apologize, Rachel," she cried. "But Leah needs Bilhah now."

"Is the child coming?" I asked, dropping Rachel's dress over her head.

"She is in much pain. She rolls on her pallet with cramps. If it is not the child, something is terribly wrong," Zilpah pulled on her hair.

I tied Rachel's sash in a bow at her waist. "I will help her. Bring my basket of healing supplies up and send a boy for my mama or another healer. I have not helped a woman give birth to a child in many years. If there are problems, I will need help."

"Does your mama read?" Zilpah asked.

I nodded, thinking of the supplies I would need.

Zilpah sat at Rachel's desk, writing a note to my mama.

"How can I help?" Rachel ran a hand through the hair I would not have time to brush.

"Fill a pot with water and set it to boil. We will need lots of hot, clean water." I hurried from the chamber and rushed to Leah's chamber.

I found her curled in a ball on her sleeping pallet, moaning. "I am here to help you." I touched her leg and encouraged her to lie back and work to relax some so I could examine her. "It will not be long." I said, after checking how close the baby was coming.

I prayed for Jehovah's help and that the boy would find Mama. I needed her help. It had been years. Did I remember everything I should do?

She nodded, panting from the pain. Sweat had drenched her face, along with the tears of fear. Her hands clenched at her stomach, pressing in to ease the hurt.

Zilpah slipped into the chamber with my healing supplies. I nodded to her. "Dampen a cloth and wipe her forehead."

She sat beside Leah and wiped her face, soothing her through the squeezing pains.

The door opened and closed. I looked up to see Mama. I wanted to throw my arms around her and sob.

"How is she doing?" Mama asked.

"She struggles, but the child is properly settled and will arrive soon."

Mama examined Leah, then patted her leg. "You are doing well. It will not be long."

"He is taking too long," Leah moaned. "Will he be born safely?"

"Mama is here. She will bring your son into the world safely." I patted her leg. I learned much from Mama that day.

Leah struggled to push her son out much longer than I expected. Zilpah wiped away more sweat than I thought possible. Leah's hands clenched the stool handles. As the head appeared, the sound of feet pounded up the stairs.

Jacob pushed the door open, only just keeping it from slamming against the wall. "Is my son here yet?"

"Your son?" Mama asked, her eyebrows lifted high.

"This is my first child. Surely Jehovah will give me a son."

"And if this child is a girl?" Mama asked.

Jacob showed no repentance for his outburst. "She will be loved." He squatted next to Leah. "What can I do to help?" His brow softened, and he gazed steadily into her eyes.

"Hold my hand," Leah whispered.

Zilpah allowed Jacob to take her place and moved away to help Mama and me.

Shortly after Jacob's entrance, Mama guided my hands and showed me how to deliver the child. "A boy!" I announced to a delighted Jacob.

As I wrapped their son in a soft blanket and handed him to Zilpah to clean out his throat and encouraged him to breathe, Leah sighed weakly. Even in her exhaustion, her face glowed with the joy of having a son. "A son! Jacob, we have a son." She sagged on the birthing stool, still clinging to the handles.

I heard the sweet sound of the child crying. This boy child would live.

Mama had tied the cord in two places and invited Jacob to separate the child from his mother.

He sliced through the cord with the sharp knife Mama handed him, then moved back to Leah's side and kissed her cheek.

Mama encouraged her to push once more to expel the afterbirth, then wrapped it in a rag and set it aside before we and Jacob helped Leah move to the pallet.

Zilpah gave Leah her child, and Mama taught her how to help the baby suckle while Zilpah and I gathered the bloody towels and cleaned the floor.

I heard the sweet sound of the child suckling. We had succeeded, this boy would live.

Mama checked Leah once more, picked up the bundle of the afterbirth, and ushered Zilpah and me out of the chamber, saying, "This little family needs some time alone."

***

"You did well." Mama and I walked down the stairs. "Now we need to bury this afterbirth."

"Thank you for your guidance. I did not know if there would be problems, and it has been many years ..."

She gave instructions to help me keep Leah and her son stay healthy. As we walked through the kitchen, I picked up a small spade and nodded at Rachel, sitting alone in the kitchen.

"Her child is here?" Rachel fought back her tears.

"A son," Mama said.

"I am sorry, Rachel." I touched her arm as I passed her with the spade. "I know how much you wanted the first son. Perhaps you will have the next one?"

"If Jehovah is willing." Rachel slumped in her seat.

Mama and I left the kitchen.

“How is Rachel?” Mama led me toward the trees in the back.

“Not happy that Laban forced her man to marry her sister first.” We stopped beneath a tree, and I stooped to dig a small hole.

“She let me in when I arrived," Mama said. "Their two marriages are much spoken of among the women in the market. And that Leah would have a child born so soon after her marriage —“ Mama raised her eyebrows.

“Rachel tried to keep her far from their husband.” I dropped my eyes. “It did not help.”

“There is contention between them?” Mama squatted beside me and dropped the bundle of afterbirth into the hole.

“Some. Perhaps it will ease when Rachel has a child.”

Mama’s eyes widened. “She is with child too? Jacob must be a happy husband.”

“No, not yet, but it will help everyone when she does.”

I covered the bundle with dirt, and we stood together under the tree.

“Oh, Mama,” I cried. “It is good to work with you again. It has been so long. Avdon and I have worried about you. Where have you been?”

She leaned back, stretching. “I left Harran shortly after bringing you here. I feared your papa would take Nissa.”

I rubbed my back. “We feared he might have taken your life.”

“He tried.” Mama shook her head. “That is one reason I left after making certain you and your brothers were safe.”

I pushed dirt over the bundle and looked up at her. *I wish you* had *explained that to me before taking me to Laban. Ten was old enough to understand your concern, and Avdon was older. You did not tell* him *either.* "What about Nissa? Where did you leave her?"

Mama didn't speak for a long time. We stood over the little pile of dirt and stared at each other. Tears filled her eyes.

"Mama?" I cried.

"I do not know," she murmured.

"You don't know what?" I wanted to shake her and shout. *I needed to know if she had given my sister to the priests of Muloch.*

"Men took her in the night almost a year ago. They warned me not to shout or they would kill us."

"Men? What men?" I wanted to scream, but I did not want to disturb Leah and Jacob.

Mama dropped her chin to her chest. "I do not know. No one has shared with me where she is. No one would help me search for her. No one could help me bring her back. I came home to Harran hoping your father could help me find her."

"When?"

"When, what? When did they take her? When did I return?"

I fought tears and frustration. "Yes?"

"They took her almost eleven months ago in Damascus."

I sucked a hissing breath through my teeth.

"I know. It is not a safe place for women, but I could hide from your father there. I returned only five months ago. I needed his help. He has connections with the Ziaeddin." She bit the inside of her lip. "Nissa is a beautiful young woman, as are you, Bilhah." She brushed the hair back from my face. "I pray she is with a good man who will care for her, a man better than your father."

Could I tell her? How could I not?

I hugged her. "I missed you, Mama. Agos and Melek saw her ... at the feast of Muloch."

Mother gasped. "Does she ... she ... live?"

I bit my lip and shook my head.

"No!" In Mama's anguish, tears suddenly dripped from her chin.

I nodded in understanding. It hurt as much to tell her as it hurt when Avdon shared the news with me.

She fell into my arms, and we wept together.

At last, we separated. "Come find me again." Mama wiped the tears from my face. "You and Avdon."

"We will if we can get away." I tried to smile, but could not push a smile past my heartache.

"I must return. Remember what I told you to do for Leah. She will need your care over the next week."

"I will. Must you leave?"

She nodded and hugged me again before leaving, her body collapsing on itself, with slumping arms hanging and slumping shoulders. Can she recover from Nissa's loss — and as a sacrifice?

In a small corner of my heart, I resented Mama. Her responsibility was to keep Nissa safe. If Jehovah ever blesses me with children, I will keep them safe. I sighed. That is not entirely fair. Mama did her best. She did not have a man in Damascus to protect her and Nissa. Oh, Jehovah, bless me to have someone who cares enough to keep his family safe.

***

"How are Leah and her child?" Rachel asked when I returned to the house, wiping tears from my eyes.

"She and her son are healthy." I poured hot water over my hands and washed them.

"Leah has a son, then?" Her pinched face showed her stress of waiting for news.

"She does. Jacob is with them."

"I saw him come in. He did not notice me." Her fingers tapped on the tabletop.

"Focused on reaching Leah before the babe came, I suspect." I dried my hands. "Will you go see them? He will welcome you."

"Will they allow me?" She bit her lip.

"I do not know why not. You are the babe's aunt. You have reason to rejoice with them." I grabbed a chunk of bread from the meal the night before. "Did you eat?"

Rachel nodded. "I heated some soup from last night while heating the water you needed. Perhaps Jacob and Rachel would like some soup? They must be hungry."

"I am certain they will. Leah worked hard today. They will appreciate soup." I glanced toward the upstairs chamber at a sound. "I apologize. I must go check on her ..."

"Go," Rachel said. "I will bring food."

I felt a fluttery feeling in my stomach. Rachel had not carried food up the stairs in many years. "You can do that?"

She huffed. "Yes. Go."

Suggestion

After Reuben's birth, I asked Mama to give me remedies that would help Rachel conceive a child. Each month, Mama gave me a nasty tincture or other bitter remedy to offer Rachel. But each month, her monthly moon time returned, and I suffered from her anger, as she cried and kicked, sometimes striking me.

Rachel could not stop Jacob from giving his time to Leah and Reuben, as Jacob insisted on helping Leah with him. However, as soon as she could, Rachel enticed him back — one night, then another, and another, until he spent all his nights with her. But each evening the four of them spent time together, with Rachel gritting her teeth. She did not enjoy sharing Jacob with Reuben and Leah.

Jacob's annual sacrificial offering, soon after the birth, included thanking Jehovah for his son and wives. I watched Rachel and Avagail sitting together with their heads close, fearing devious plans.

What advice would Avagail give? She and Laban have *caused too many problems. How could they not* have foreseen *the problems it would cause?*

One afternoon, Rachel stomped her foot. "Why must Jacob spend so much time with Leah's family every evening?" She plunked onto her desk chair to watch me remake her sleeping pallet.

I shook a blanket over the pallet. "Reuben is his son," I said, surprise filling my voice. "He loves the boy."

"Must he love him with Leah always nearby?" Her unexpected snarl caused me to glance at her.

I clamped my mouth shut. How could I respond to that without angering my mistress? The blanket settled across her pallet, and I bent to smooth the wrinkles.

"They share the boy, I know," Rachel continued. "But must he spend every evening with them?" She stared pointedly at me, demanding a response.

I shrugged a shoulder and ducked my head. "I suppose parents believe they must spend time together with their children." *I would want to ...*

"I suppose they must." Rachel huffed out a breath and leaned back in her chair. "But I dislike spending every evening with them."

"I suppose ..." I drew out my words, thinking about the next one and how Rachel would respond. "You could ... perhaps ... stay in your chamber ... and not join them."

"What?" she shrieked. "Give Leah time alone with my husband?"

"He is her husband too," I murmured. I picked up another blanket to spread over her pallet.

Rachel stamped her foot again. "Because Father insisted. It makes me angry to think of it."

I closed my mouth, keeping my thoughts to myself. *Jacob accepted her as his wife. He could have set her aside when Laban deceived him. If he had, would you still love him?*

She huffed a breath out through her nose. "Leah could have refused to go along with Father's plan."

I lifted my eyebrows as I stood from smoothing the second blanket. "Could she? You agreed to his plan."

She leapt to her feet, her clenched fists in the air. "I had no choice. He threatened me."

I set Rachel's pillows back on her pallet. "I doubt Leah had any more choice than you. Your father is rather persuasive. Have you ever seen anyone go against Laban?"

She snorted. "You are not the first to say that about him."

"And I will not be the last." I smoothed the pillows and stretched my back. "Laban has a way of insisting his way is the only way. Look what he has done to Jacob, forcing seven more years of work."

Rachel leaned back and pouted. "Yes, Father's plotting makes life difficult for all of us."

I nodded. "He thinks he will get his way every time."

Rachel started a litany of all the things her father had done to hurt Jacob. I had heard them before and had chores to do before Jacob returned from work, and I needed to have food ready for the family.

"Your father has done much to keep Jacob busy working for him. I apologize, but I must leave. I must prepare our evening meal, and Zilpah is caring for Reuben."

***

Four months after the sacrifice, Leah did not join us for our morning meal. "Where is Leah?" Rachel asked when Zilpah brought Reuben with her to the table.

Zilpah lifted her shoulder. "She is not well this morning."

Rachel lifted her eyebrows, but asked no more questions.

When we separated to complete our chores, I took my basket of healing supplies and went to see about Leah's sickness.

As I opened her chamber door, Leah retched into the night jar near her sleeping pallet.

I dampened a cloth and cleaned her face and mouth. I touched her forehead. "You do not burn. What makes you so ill?"

"Can you not guess?" Leah asked as she leaned back on her pillows.

"Did you eat something to make you ill?" I asked as I searched through my basket for something to help her stomach, unwilling to suggest the true cause.

Leah grinned. "No. I carry another child."

I jerked up. "Another child? Already?"

She placed her hand on her stomach. "Yes."

"But Reuben is not yet weaned!"

"Does that matter?"

I leaned over my basket once more and finally found the mint leaf. "This should help with your nausea."

Leah took the leaf and popped it in her mouth and chewed it. "Ah. That helps my stomach already."

I found more and left them on the table beside her sleeping pallet. "Hopefully, you will feel like leaving your pallet soon."

But she did not. She struggled with the nausea a few more weeks. I went to Mama asking for suggestions. She mixed a tincture, teaching me about it as she mixed, and promised it would settle Leah's stomach.

"Remember, she needs to eat. Give her soup filled with shredded meat and vegetables."

"If she can keep it down."

"A little at a time," Mama reminded me. "Too much will make it worse. Be sure it is mostly broth at first. You can give her a thicker version as she heals."

Between the soup and the remedy, one morning Leah rejoined the family.

Although Rachel welcomed Leah back, Rachel soon disappeared. I took a dusting cloth and went upstairs to dust the table in the hall. As I neared her chamber, I heard her stomping back and forth across the space, crying out her frustrations to Jehovah.

I lifted an urn and dusted the table beneath it, then cleaned the urn on the inside and out. I lingered outside Rachel's chamber, waiting for her anger to subside.

I had dusted everything in the hall and stood with my cloth in my hand before her pallet creaked.

At last, I sighed. *She settles. I can go to her soon.*

I wiped nonexistent dust from the wall along both sides before I dared open her door. I slipped into the chamber. "What happened?" I closed the cloth door behind me. "I heard your cries from the hall. Are you unwell?"

Rachel lay face down on her bed, the red wedding blanket crumpled beneath her. She turned her tear-stained face toward me. I wanted to embrace her and let her know I felt her pain. Sometimes she accepted my caring touch with grace and gratitude. More often lately, she screeched at me. I refrained from touching her.

She gazed at me for a long moment before she rolled over and stood with her arms outstretched.

I embraced her, allowing her tears to soak my dress.

"You must be desolate," I murmured.

"I am," she whimpered. "Why? Why always Leah?" After a short time, she subsided into soft sobs and sniffles.

When her tears ended, I asked, "What will you do?"

She lifted her head. "What can I do?"

I wiped tears from her face.

"My body refuses to accept Jacob's seed." Her hands shook. "None of your treatments help. My prayers have not helped. What can I do?"

I chewed on my lip, wondering what she would do. "I tried almost everything Mama and other healers suggested. I had hoped an herb would open your womb."

"Mother suggests —" She broke off and stared at her feet, biting back the words.

What did Avagail suggest? Do I want to know?

Words slipped from me, unwanted and unbidden. "What does your mother suggest?" I held my breath. I knew this would change our lives. Would she listen to her mother?

"Mother suggested I do as Sarah did."

My forehead creased as I brought my eyebrows together.

Rachel continued. "Sarah is not the first or the last woman who could not conceive. Others have done what she did."

My mind raced, trying to understand what solution Sarah had found. "Sarah? What did Sarah do?"

"Sarah, the wife of Abraham." Rachel sat at her dressing table. "Would you brush my hair while we talk? It soothes me and helps me order my thoughts."

And she would not have to look me in the eye yet could watch my reaction in the mirror.

I undid her braids and brushed her hair, all the while trying to determine how Rachel could imitate Sarah. After a few strokes of the brush through her long hair, she breathed out a heavy sigh.

"Sarah gave her maidservant to Abraham. She substituted Hagar's womb for hers. Hagar's son became the son of Abraham and Sarah."

My hands stopped moving the brush through her hair mid-stroke. *No! She would not!* I stared at the back of her head, fearing to look in the mirror and see if her stare was earnest.

She continued, slowing her words as she considered them. "I do not suggest I am prepared to give you to Jacob. I do not know if I could bear for Jacob to give you a son when I cannot."

No! Rachel! You would not! I do not want Jacob to father my children. I want a husband who loves only me. I want a home of my own. And how could I withstand your jealousy? You will want to control my children. *You will claim them. No!*

With trembling hands that could almost no longer hold the brush, I sucked in a deep breath and lifted my eyes to meet hers in the mirror. "I do not want your husband."

Her anger flared. She spoke in a tight voice. "Jacob is a kind man."

"I know," I said, interrupting her. "But he is your husband. Yours and Leah's. I have always wanted ..." My voice drifted off. Rachel's eyes flashed angrily at me through the mirror.

"Jacob is a good man," I said before she could shout at me. "He treats you and Leah well. He is a kind father and treats Reuben with love. But you forget. I want a man of my own."

"You are my maidservant. Father gave you to me," Rachel lifted the volume of her voice.

"I know," I whispered. "How can I ever forget it?"

Her voice hardened. "If I choose to give you to Jacob, you will have no choice."

My stomach churned as I nodded. Unless Rachel conceived soon, she would give me to Jacob. She had spoken the words. She would not go back. I could no longer hope Jacob would find me a husband.

Throughout the rest of the day, thoughts spun through my mind. How did this happen? Why would Jehovah allow it to happen to me? I had been obedient, keeping myself pure for a husband. I wanted to be a wife, not a concubine, not a surrogate for Rachel. *Oh, Jehovah! Why? Is there a reason for this? If so, I cannot see it. Please, please, open Rachel's womb. Do not allow her to force this on me!*

***

By fall, Rachel had not repeated her suggestion that my womb take the place of hers and give her children. I prayed every night that Jehovah would open her womb and prevent her from doing this terrible thing. The thought concerned me, never letting me go.

Then in the fall, we spent a morning harvesting. The others picked the vegetables from our garden, while I cut leaves from my herbs.

Leah tried to hide the cramping that showed her child would soon come. While Zilpah and I carried the vegetables to the storage room below the house, Rachel cleaned her hands and disappeared into the weaving chamber.

Leah trudged up the stairs to her chamber, with Reuben working to climb the stairs with his short little legs. He had only walked in the past months, and stairs were still too tall for him.

Zilpah helped me put away the squash before she said, “I should go see how Leah is doing. She was more uncomfortable than usual this morning.”

I nodded. “I suspect her child will join us today. Let me know when she is ready for me.”

Zilpah had not gone long before she hurried back down the stairs, her face white and her hands trembling. “Leah needs you now. Her child is coming.”

“Bring hot water up after you and send a messenger to Jacob.”

“She said to come quickly,” Zilpah warned me, fear filling her voice.

I nodded as I grabbed my supply basket and rushed up the stairs to see to her needs.

Reuben sat beside Leah, patting her stomach and chattering in his baby talk.

“I expected you would need me today," I held my breath, trying to calm myself. "Zilpah will bring some hot water soon. How are you feeling?”

“This babe is ready to come into the world.” She grabbed her stomach and groaned.

Zilpah soon came with the hot water and took Reuben away.

“I will help you bring this child into the world,” I murmured. “There is no time to call for my mama. I fear the baby will not wait much longer.”

“*He* will not wait,“ Leah corrected.

“Yes, he is coming fast,” I agreed.

This child was in a hurry, slipping from his mother faster and easier than Reuben had. "Another boy!" I announced. "You were right again."

After she expelled the afterbirth from within her body and I cleaned her, I helped her back to her pallet. She lay panting from the effort of delivering her child. I handed her the swaddled bundle of a baby boy. "Congratulations."

Footsteps pounded through the kitchen. "Who forgot to tell me about my son's birth?" Jacob roared.

I glanced at Leah and shrugged. "Not my responsibility. Your son kept me too busy."

"He knows now," Leah said with a slight grin.

Jacob burst into the chamber, his frown rapidly becoming a beaming smile. He strode over to kneel next to Leah and their young son.

He stretched his hand to touch the baby when I asked, "Did you wash your hands? Or do you still have the stench —"

Before I could complete the question, he muttered something and left the chamber, running down the stairs.

"He could have washed here," I said. "But he needs to control his voice."

"Jacob is a proud papa," she murmured.

I was cleaning the towels and the mess from the floor when Jacob returned, slamming the door open. Both Leah and I warned him with a shush.

He blushed as he sat on a stool next to Leah, cooing to the child. "What will you name this one?"

"Simeon."

"A fine name for a son," he said.

I picked up the bloody cloths and the bundle of afterbirth and walked to the door.

"Where is Reuben?" Leah asked.

"I will ask Zilpah to bring him up. I am leaving now. Enjoy your new babe," I said as I opened the door.

"And ask Rachel to come meet Simeon," Jacob said.

I nodded and left them alone.

When I had completed the other necessary chores, I searched for Rachel. I found her in the dark weaving chamber, unmoving.

"Leah and Jacob would like you to come meet their new son."

Rachel shuddered. "Perhaps it is time to speak again of your carrying a child for me."

My blood ran cold.

Rachel rose from her stool and climbed the stairs.

***

Rachel withdrew after Simeon's birth, although she tried to keep her grief from the others. I understood her sorrow. I doubted she was aware of mine.

One evening she whimpered as I helped her prepare for sleep after Jacob kissed her goodnight and left her for Leah's chamber. "I will never give Jacob a son. Jehovah has sealed my womb." She inhaled and sighed. "Leah is not to blame for my barrenness. Perhaps if I were more obedient, He will open it."

"What more do you need to do?" I asked, hoping to keep our discussion on Jehovah giving her a child. She had worked to be obedient, especially in the years since meeting Jacob. I pulled her green nightgown over her head.

"I must repent of my jealousy," she whispered.

"Jealousy?" I lifted my eyebrows.

I knew, but I could never say such things.

"I must repent of the jealousy I feel toward Leah and her children." She sat on the dressing-table stool and dropped her head into her hands.

I massaged her neck. What could I say to keep her thoughts away from me? Eventually, I spoke. "I do not know your heart. Only you and Jehovah know your heart." I picked up the brush and brushed my mistress's hair.

Rachel stared into her mirror, mute for some time. When she spoke, she said, "Only I can know my heart. Only Jehovah and me."

As brushing her hair soothed her, I continued.

"Jehovah will open my womb when it is right. I must trust him. I trust him. How can I not?" Her whisper was almost a whimper.

"Trust Jehovah," I said. "He is the only one who can help you."

And the only one who can help me.

How Could She?

Because of his growing family, Jacob hired more servants, including Amina, who came to serve as a nurse for the children. The extra support was a blessing, giving me more time to assist Rachel and more time to care for the injured and sick.

I stayed busy, hoping once more that Rachel had forgotten her suggestion. Jacob already had two wives . He would not want me as his concubine.

Since she had planted the possibility within my soul, I grew more aware of Jacob — the way he touched Rachel and Leah, his kind words, his gentleness. He loved his sons and wrestled with them on the floor until they giggled. I could not ask for a better father for my children.

But I wanted a man to love only *me*. Jacob divided his time and love between two other women already. When would he have time for me?

Though I tried to stop them, Jacob filled my thoughts. Would he be gentle with me? Would I conceive when Rachel could not? Could I share my children with her? She made it sound as if I would have no say about my children. Would we find ourselves entwined in jealousy and hatred rather than the love we now shared? Could I have another woman's children?

It did not surprise me when one morning Rachel cleared her throat as I braided her hair . "I will give you to Jacob as his concubine at our next Sabbath meeting."

I held my face still as I completed the braid. I did not reply.

"You have nothing to say?" Rachel asked.

I pinned the braid around her head. "Do I have a choice?" I swallowed the lump in my throat. Why now? What caused her to decide?

Her eyes fixed on mine in the mirror. "No."

I wanted to run away screaming my rejection. As I had no choice, I spoke quietly, "You warned me. I hoped you would not make this decision. As you said, I have no choice."

Her eyes bore into mine. "No. You have no choice in this. I have not conceived a child. Bilhah, do you not understand my challenge? Jehovah has closed my womb. I cannot live without children." Unshed tears welled up in her eyes.

Mine pricked the back of my eyelids. I would not allow them to fall. Not now. She would not share my pain. I had feared this conversation since she first spoke of it. Now it was happening. How? "You will claim my children as yours."

"Your children will be my children." She wiped her tears, gazing into my eyes, hoping for my ready acceptance.

How can I give her acceptance? She has taken away everything I ever dreamed of. I will have no husband and no children of my own. Only seconds. The substitute. I must give everything I have long desired to Rachel.

Could I escape? Find Mama?

A chill ran down my back.

No. Obedience is the first law. I will obey. I have no other choice.

"You told me I would substitute my womb for yours." I focused on pinning her last braid. "I will share my child with you."

I swallowed my sorrow and cleared away my ugly thoughts, but I could not smile. "I have until the Sabbath?"

"Yes. Wear your best dress."

I stepped back as she stood. "Which of my dresses do you consider best?"

Rachel closed her eyes, considering. "You have that newer cream-colored dress, the one you embroidered tan flowers on. Your dark blue belt looks beautiful with it."

I loved that dress once, but it is old now. My new blue dress with white flowers embroidered on it fits better.

I nodded. "Yes, that is a nice dress."

"You prefer another?" Rachel asked, turning toward me.

I wanted to scream, 'No, I do not want to participate in this. I want a man of my own.How can you talk about the dress I am to wear when my life is caving in?' Instead of sharing my grief, I answered, "No. The cream dress is lovely. I will be certain that it is clean before then."

"You have only two days. I hope it is clean already."

I brushed my braid back over my shoulder. "I will make certain it is clean."

Clothing? Not now! All I want to do is go to my chamber and sob. I will wear whatever she desires, as long as she lets me leave.

I gave myself a little shake. "Do you need anything else for now?"

"Not now. You have things to do."

I bobbed my head and left her room.

I stood outside her closed door and leaned against it, allowing frustrated tears to fall, washing away all my hopes. I had dreamed of a man of my own, one who would love only me and who wanted to give me children who would love me. I would never have a man of my own. My longing for a home with my husband and children was gone. No man would see me as desirable. I would not be available if he did. Every hope and dream was gone. All I had left for myself was my healing. Would she take that away too?

The door to Leah's son's room opened, and Amina shooed Reuben out. I leaned closer to the door, praying she and Reuben would not turn around and see me.

"It is a beautiful day," Amina said to Reuben. "After we eat, we are going outside."

Reuben cheered and hurried toward the stairs, with the nursemaid following. I waited until they had bounced down the stairs before stepping away from Rachel's door to follow them sedately. I wiped tears from my face with my linen square and took slow, deep breaths, hoping the traces of my disappointment would lighten before I met anyone who would question them. I would not share this news.

***

I kept to myself after Rachel's announcement, not wanting to share my grief.

On the Sabbath, as we walked toward the small sanctuary, Zilpah grabbed my arm. "Are you unwell? You have stayed to yourself for the last two days."

I nodded, not wanting the tears to flow again. If Rachel followed through, I did not want a red and spotted face. It was hard enough to walk with the others after two nights filled with dreams that woke me shivering with fright.

In my dreams, I stood beside Rachel in the sanctuary as she placed my hand in Jacob's. He stared at me, disgust and horror filling his face, before he threw my hand at Rachel and stomped out of the sanctuary.

He refused me! In his anger with Rachel, he refused to take me as his concubine. Does he not know this is not my idea? I desire a man of my own, not a man whose heart belongs to two others? How can he refuse me? Did Rachel not warn him?

I had wrapped my blankets around me as I sat on my pallet, thinking. *Rachel will not do this if Jacob does not agree. He will not refuse to take me.*

I had lain back, chanting the thought. 'Jacob knows. He will not refuse to take me.'

The dream returned many times over the two nights.

Zilpah had approached me once as I leaned against the wall in a corner, tears dripping down my face.

"What is wrong?" she had asked.

I waved her away. How could I tell her? "I cannot say. I must not say." *I pray there is nothing to fear.*

"What has Rachel done this time?" she asked, setting her hand on my arm.

I shook my head and swallowed the tears.

Zilpah had embraced me, allowing my fears to water her shoulder.

"I am here for you, whatever problem you face."

I choked on my tears. After a time, I lifted my head and dried my eyes. "Perhaps this is nothing."

Zilpah lifted her eyebrows. "Perhaps it is something."

I swallowed.

"If it is something, I am by your side," Zilpah had murmured as one of the new maidservants, Nita, passed us in the hall.

Now we walked together toward the sanctuary, and I still could not share with my friend.

"You have not worn that dress to Sabbath for some time," she said.

I glanced down at the cream-colored dress. "Rachel recommended I wear it today."

Her eyebrows rose. I did not like to stand out among the others, and this fancier dress would cause that.

"I would have worn a different dress, but Rachel insisted."

I had said too much, and lapsed into silence, praying Zilpah would understand and leave me to my fearful thoughts.

She took my hand and gripped it, not letting go.

I glanced at her with a tight smile, then looked away, not wanting to share anymore.

We sat behind Leah and her sons as usual. Zilpah often helped to contain them when the boys lost interest in the teacher.

I could not sit still and heard little of the sermon. I squirmed in my seat, seeking to find a comfortable position. Then one foot bounced without my permission. I forced it still, and the other jiggled up and down.

I closed my eyes, focusing on stillness, praying for Rachel to change her mind.

A small, comforting voice entered my thoughts. *'Obey your mistress as I have commanded. I am pleased with you. Do not fear. Jacob will accept you. I will give you sons who will love you and lead nations. I gave Rachel the right to choose or* to believe. *Her belief is not your concern. Your belief is accepted. Trust Me.'* The message filled my soul with light, stilling my concerns. Jehovah accepted my trust in Him. That was more important than anything else. I did not understand what would happen for me, but I trusted Jehovah. I would obey Him.

I opened my eyes and glanced around for anyone who would whisper such words to my soul. No one near me could have.

Jehovah? I will obey you.

'I know your thoughts? Trust Me.'

My body stilled. I kept my head bowed and waited, accepting what would happen.

Too soon, our teacher ended his sermon. As he did most Sabbaths, he called up those needing prayers or to make announcements.

The chair ahead of me scraped the floor, raking my nerves. I glanced up to see Rachel striding forward.

Is it time?

Rachel shuffled to the low podium. "You may remember Sarah, Abraham's wife, could not have children for many long years. Only after she thought it too late, did she conceive Isaac."

She is doing it. I clung to Jehovah's words of peace.

"To give Abraham a child," Rachel continued, "Sarah gave him her maidservant, Hagar, as a concubine to bear children. She gave them a son, Ishmael."

Rachel flicked her hand toward me. Even as I tried to miss her beckoning, I could not. I slumped and shuffled forward to stand next to her. I felt waves of her frustration at my sluggish delay. When I arrived, she took my hand, then gestured for Jacob to join us.

How can she order him like this? He must love her.

Jacob straightened his back and walked forward to stand next to Rachel. She took his hand in hers, now holding both our hands.

I kept my eyes down, not wanting to see the stares from those in the congregation.

"As of today," Rachel said, "I give my handmaid, Bilhah, to Jacob as his concubine to bear my children. Any children Bilhah gives Jacob will become mine as well."

She did it. She claims me and my children.

She set my clammy hand in his. "Jacob, I give you my maidservant as your concubine. Will you have her?"

I glanced up to see a plea pass from Rachel to him.

I half expected him to deny her, but his voice was strong and confident. "I will."

She turned to me. "Will you, Bilhah, give yourself to Jacob as his concubine and become the mother of my children?"

I took a breath. *Only because Jehovah commands it!* "I will."

Rachel stepped back, leaving my hand in Jacob's. "I present Jacob and Bilhah."

With that, Jacob led me down the steps and up the aisle to the sanctuary door.

As I passed, I could not avoid the sorrow in Zilpah's eyes.

Jacob opened the door and led me outside.

***

Jacob walked beside me, leading me down the track away from the sanctuary.

"Where are we going?" I asked. His hand gripped mine, not allowing me to fall behind or stop walking.

"I have a place for us," he said.

I nodded and followed.

We walked through busy streets. Men and women, both free and slave, hurried through the lanes. Few in Harran celebrated the Sabbath.

I dreaded passing near the market. Mama would be in her small booth. I did not want to tell her about Jacob. Not yet. I sighed my relief as he turned down a lane before we reached her booth.

He gripped my hand, finally slowing as we neared the edge of town, far from home and Rachel.

Jacob turned to me with the kindness I had learned in the past years to expect from him. "I did not want a concubine," he said, speaking to me at last.

"I did not want to be a concubine," I said.

"Rachel insisted," we said at the same time.

He stared at me, then laughed.

"Rachel is stubbornly insistent," he added, pulling me along the lane.

I nodded. "Since I first met her when we were little."

"We should have expected this," he murmured.

"She spoke of it months ago. I had hoped she would forget. I wanted you to find a man for me to marry."

"Women deserve men who love them. Men deserve to be loved by their women." Red crept up his neck. "We want one person to care for us."

"And now you have three," I whispered.

He slowed his steps. "Are you angry?"

I shook my head. "Not now. It is too late for that. But I was. Were you?" Could I share the sacred whisperings that came from Jehovah?

"I learned long ago that anger does not resolve difficulties. Here we are." He gestured toward a tent in a small copse of trees. It stood alone. No other houses or tents were nearby.

I lifted an eyebrow. "A tent?"

"It is safe and quiet. No one will disturb us here." He lifted the door flap, holding it open for me to enter.

I ducked inside, curious. I had never been in a tent, nor did I expect to be. Though small, Jacob had furnished it with thick rugs, a sleeping pallet, and a small table with two stools.

He pulled meat rolls from the basket on the table. "You must be hungry."

Their aroma caused my stomach to gurgle. My ears heated.

He set the meat rolls on a small plate and pushed it toward me. "Eat."

I sat on a stool while he retrieved a jug of wine from the basket and two cups, filling them, while I bit into the roll.

"These are good. Where did you get them?"

Jacob grinned and handed me a cup. "I made them. My mother taught me to cook. I often cook when we are out for long hours with the flocks. Drink."

I sipped the wine, then finished the meat roll while Jacob ate one. "This food is delicious."

"I knew you would be hungry. You did not eat this morning."

I swallowed the food. "I was too nervous."

"And you are not now?"

I glanced at the neat pallet with the blankets spread across it, and bit my lip. I would never have a marriage blanket now.

I swallowed the sudden lump in my throat. "Yes," I whispered. "I am still nervous." Should I tell him of Jehovah's promise?

He nodded toward the cup. "Sip a little more of the wine. It will help your nerves."

I sipped from the cup but did not finish it, watching Jacob. He picked up a knife and cut the flatbread.

When I leaned back after eating three meat rolls, Jacob leaned forward. "I am sorry Rachel insisted on this. I know you wanted a husband. But if I must take a concubine, I am happy it is you." His deep voice rumbled as his gentle smile warmed my heart. I had seen him smile at Rachel like this in the early days of their courtship, a gentle, hesitant smile, seeking understanding. His blue eyes expressed hope. Hope for what? That I would agree?

I set my hand on my chest. "Me? Why?"

"I have watched your quiet cheerfulness, encouraging Rachel to find joy in her life. I know how difficult she has been since Leah ..." His voice drifted off.

"Gave birth to Reuben?"

He nodded.

"And then Simeon." I grimaced. "Rachel has struggled in many ways."

"And now she gave you to me."

I chewed on my lip. "I am hers to command. Laban gave me to her."

"As though a man can own another," Jacob growled.

I stared. I had never heard him express an opinion about his wives' maidservants before.

Jacob shook his head. "I cannot change what her father did. I agreed to take you as my concubine, as Rachel requested." He pulled me from my stool onto his lap. "May I kiss you?"

I nodded and closed my eyes. No one had kissed me since Mama kissed me before taking me to Laban's door. How would it feel for a man to kiss me?

His lips found mine, softly brushing across them, hesitant, questioning. I responded, and his lips hardened, becoming more insistent until he lifted me into his arms and carried me to the pallet.

"Do not be afraid," he whispered. "I will not hurt you."

***

Darkness filled the tent when we woke later. Jacob moved his leg off me and rose from the pallet. He pulled his tunic over his head and dug into the basket once more. After he lit a lamp and put it on the table, he came to the pallet and kissed me once more.

"I am not sorry anymore that Rachel insisted I take you as my concubine. Are you?"

I ducked my head. "Not if I can look forward to more of this." I pulled my dress on, keeping my back to him, not wanting him to see the red filling my face.

"It will not happen every night. I have two other women to love and care for. You will receive my attention in your turn. Remember, however, you are a concubine, not a wife."

My smile faded. "I know. I will never be a wife." I sat at the table.

He leaned across the table to kiss me, but I leaned away from his kiss.

His eyebrows rose.

"I am Rachel's broodmare. When I conceive a child, you will forget me. She will insist."

"If she does, she has not thought this through. Although you are not my wife, I made a commitment to you." He ran his hand through his hair. "I feared this and took it to Jehovah. I did not want a concubine. I have enough problems with Rachel and Leah."

"Did Jehovah respond to your query?" Curiosity tempered my sorrow.

Jacob nodded. "He told me to do as Rachel demanded. She will receive children in her turn, but not yet. Jehovah told me to take you and treat you well, for you will enlarge my family. Many years ago, Jehovah promised me, as he promised my grandfather, Abraham. I will have a large posterity. You are to help me enlarge that posterity."

I gasped. “I learned this today. I am part of Jehovah’s plan. I heard His whisper.”

In the lamplight, his eyes sparkled. “I am not surprised. You have worshiped Him since you were a child.” He gazed at me earnestly. "I am blessed."

My eyes widened. He had approved of me. My dreams were all false! Jacob accepted me and is happy I am his concubine.

His face softened and he smiled. “Jehovah knows each of us on this earth, especially His daughters who worship Him. And as you are part of my household, He has greater knowledge of you.”

“I am to help increase your posterity. After my nightmares of the past three days, it is good to know this is right for us. It makes me happy.”

"I am as well." Jacob dug in the basket once more and withdrew bread and slices of meat. “You will conceive and give me children. I worry about Rachel. She forced this on us, even as she struggles with jealousy of Leah. Be prepared. She will claim your children.” He handed me the meat he had layered on the bread. “But you have become part of my family. You will always be the mother of your children, regardless of Rachel's claim.”

I thought about Rachel as I ate the food Jacob gave me. What was she doing? Did she know Jehovah accepted her actions?

“Do not worry about Rachel,” Jacob said.

How does he know I am?

“She can prepare herself to sleep for a few days.”

"A few days?" That surprised me. “How many days will we stay here?” The basket did not look big enough to hold food for more than one day.

“I gave Rachel and Leah seven days alone.” He bit his lip. “Laban knows I am with a concubine,” he glanced up at me. “But he will expect me to return to his flocks soon. I am sorry you are not one of his daughters. I would give you the same seven days. As it is, we can only be together three days."

I shuddered. "I am grateful I am not."

Jacob smiled wistfully and ran a finger along my face. "I am as well. He would demand seven more years from me." He laughed, happier. "Come with me." He stood, took my hand, and led me into the night.

We sat a distance from the tent as he pointed into the sky. "Look."

I glanced up and sucked in a sharp breath. The full moon hung close to the earth, lighting the night, reminding me of Jehovah's many creations, miracles all. Stars sparkled in the black sky. Although I had gone outside after dark many times, I had usually hurried back inside without gazing up. I do not remember ever seeing the moon so big or so low.

We lay back to stare up at the stars.

A star flew like a bird across the others.

"What is that?" I asked, pointing.

"Jehovah sends His approval."

He kissed me and I returned it. I would gladly accept his seed.

Before Jacob escorted me back home, I knew our time together had been successful. Our child settled into my womb. For now, I would not even share the news with Jacob. I would not share this secret until my body betrayed me. I would protect this child as my mother had not protected me. For now, I would enjoy our time alone.

Neither Wife nor Maidservant

Jacob woke me early on the third morning. "I must take the animals to the hills today."

I sighed. "Must we return?"

"We must. I have responsibilities to my household and to Laban." He opened the food basket we had eaten from while in our hideaway. "Besides, we are out of food." He shrugged. "Zilpah will have food for us when we return."

He brushed my hair as he had each morning and helped tie my dress before opening the flap for me to step out.

The world felt different. Brighter. Happier. We had to return to Rachel and Leah. But I would cherish the three days we had spent alone, three days of learning to care for each other.

When Rachel lashed out in jealousy, as she was certain to do, I had these days to remember, knowing she had given me a gift I had not expected nor wanted.

"I am grateful to Rachel for giving me to you," I said as Jacob took my hand and led me along cool paths through the dark early morning. These same paths would burn our feet after the sun had heated them. Dew glistened on the leaves of the plants. I will never forget the joy of that early morning.

He kissed my hand. "And I am grateful she did as well. Life will not be easy for you. No woman should be required to become a concubine. You have been gracious and kind to Rachel and me. I will always treat you well. I will always care for you."

"As you treat Leah well?" I asked.

He turned and gazed into my eyes. "As I treat Leah well. Rachel is and always will be my first love. But I have space in my heart to love Leah and now you. Rachel believes she controls me. She does not. I do nothing without asking Jehovah. Some things she demands are actions I planned anyway. I let her believe what she wants."

He bent close to my ear. “Do not tell her. It is our secret.” We strode through the still streets as dawn pierced the dark. "You will give me children. I look forward to that day."

My breath caught in my throat. Did he know? “If your seed settles in my womb.”

“As it has. I will continue to come to you in your turn, although I know already you carry my child.”

“How can you know?” I asked as we turned a corner.

“Jehovah tells me. I know. You will give me a son.”

“A son?” I asked.

“Yes, you will bear me a son. Rachel will claim him as hers. Let her.” Jacob gripped my hand in his. “Rachel will not be happy, though she will rave on about how you provided her with the son she could not. Deep within her soul, she mourns for the children Jehovah will not allow her to have yet. She will forget to claim your sons when hers come.”

“When will she have sons?” Hope filled my heart. When Rachel had sons, she would forget to claim mine.

“When Jehovah allows it.”

We walked together, deep in our own thoughts until we turned a corner and saw our home down the lane.

“Thank you for your kindness, Jacob,” I said, struggling to push the words around the sudden lump in my throat.

“You are welcome, Bilhah.” He grinned at me. “I have enjoyed getting to know you in every way.”

My face heated at the memory of our knowing.

“Your life will be different now. Do not allow Rachel to push you around too much. You carry our child.”

“Do not tell her yet, please.” Sudden fear caused my limbs to tremble.

"No. This is yours to tell. I will keep your secret until you are ready." The squeeze of his hand helped me to stop trembling. "Or until your body gives you away."

"Leah's always did," I said with a little laugh.

We turned up the path to the house and walked to the kitchen door. Before opening the door, Jacob kissed me.

That kiss helped me through the challenges of the rest of the day.

***

As we entered the kitchen, Zilpah turned from preparing the morning meal and smiled.

Jacob kissed me on the cheek before releasing my hand, whispering, "Stay strong."

I smiled at him.

"You will need to move to a chamber upstairs, now that you are my concubine," he added.

I lowered my eyebrows. "I like my chamber."

"Although it is a nice enough chamber, if I remember right, your status has changed." He winked at me. "It will not be fair to the other maids to hear us together," he cleared his throat, "at night."

Now Zilpah's face burned.

I giggled. "I suppose that would not be kind. Which chamber do you recommend?"

Jacob scratched his chin in thought. "The chamber across from the boys?"

I nodded, thinking about the chamber layout on that floor. "That will work. Zilpah, will you help me move later?"

"You know I will," she said. "I will miss having you close."

She set the food on the table and swept her hand toward it in an invitation to sit. "Eat while you can."

As we sat together, Jacob's leg pressed against mine, and he turned to me and grinned.

After he left to care for the animals, I gave Zilpah a hug. "It is good to be home."

"Where have you been? Where did Jacob take you?" she asked.

A smile filled my face. "He took me to the other side of Harran, outside the city, to a small tent. We stayed there all the time."

"A tent?"

"He grew up in tents. He said he felt at home for the first time since coming to Harran." I brushed my hair away from my face. "I need to braid my hair."

As I turned to do that, Zilpah asked, "Will you have Rachel's child?"

My hand strayed to my stomach almost on its own, protecting my tiny son. I glanced over my shoulder. "The child will be mine."

"Rachel will not agree."

"She will claim him. But my children will be mine. Not hers," I repeated, as much for me as for Zilpah.

I hurried to my small chamber and brushed my hair, surprised at how much it soothed me, as it soothed Rachel when I brushed hers. *Rachel will claim my children, but I know, I will always know, this child, and any others I* have, *will be mine. I will protect them.*

I twisted my hair into a braid, then returned to the kitchen where I went about my usual early morning chores with Zilpah. Later, she helped me gather my possessions and carry the baskets up to the chamber Jacob had suggested. In the hall, outside the door to my new chamber, I glanced toward Rachel's. *How will she react to this?*

As we carried my possessions into my new chamber, she stepped from her chamber. Teary blotches covered her face. "What are you doing?" Her foot tapped against the floor, demanding an answer.

I no longer had anything to fear from her rages. She changed my position in the house. "Jacob gave me instructions to move to this floor. He suggested this chamber, since my position has changed."

She stepped close. "He wants you here?" Her voice rose and she flung an arm toward her chamber. "This close to me? Does he not know that assigning chambers is the right of the woman of the house?"

Leah had stepped from her chamber and now came closer. "What is going on?"

Rachel turned on Leah. "Jacob assigned this chamber to Bilhah without asking me!"

Leah lowered her eyebrows. "I am the first wife. It is my right to make chamber assignments." She stared at her sister until Rachel dropped her eyes with a grumble.

I sucked in a breath. "Jacob suggested this one would be a safe distance from both you and Rachel. He told me to move in here." I waved toward the contested chamber.

Leah gazed up and down the hall as if measuring the distance. "This chamber makes sense. It is a good distance from mine and yours." She glanced at Rachel. "We cannot expect Jacob to go to the maid's quarters to be with his concubine. *You* changed Bilhah's status. You should have thought of this. Jacob is right. This is a suitable chamber for her."

Rachel stuttered something I could not understand, then turned on her slippered heel and returned to her chamber.

As Rachel's door slammed, Leah turned to me. "Do you need anything?"

I shrugged. "Not that I know of now. I brought my few belongings." I waved at my baskets in the doorway. "Zilpah helped me."

Leah nodded. "Excellent. When you finish unpacking, perhaps you would join me in the sitting area. I have mending to do and could use your help."

I glanced toward Rachel's closed door. "If Rachel needs —"

"Rachel has a new maidservant. Nita. Your position has changed. While we mend, we can discuss the differences and your additional responsibilities. Now, you and Zilpah put your possessions away, then come find me in the sitting area."

As we emptied my baskets, Zilpah bobbed a small curtsy to me. "I will miss having you near me." She swallowed tears.

"Do not do that!" I exclaimed. "We are still sisters. We have spent too many years together to let that change."

"But it did when Rachel gave you to Jacob last Sabbath."

Would I also lose my best friend and sister because of Rachel's decision? I could not live with that. My position changed, but I would always love Zilpah. "I will not lose you."

"I will still be here for you, just not in the chamber next to yours." She waved around the chamber, larger than my small cell below, then turned to put my clothing into a trunk.

"I will still come visit you," I said, fighting back my own tears.

"Yes, when you are not busy." She closed the trunk and peered into the empty baskets. "That is everything. Come tell me how your life has changed when you can." She gathered up my baskets and stored them beneath the pegs of my closet.

I threw my arms around her and held her close, whispering through my tears. "I did not choose this. I wanted a man of my own, not Rachel's man. What could I do? She owns me."

She clung to me, patting my back. "Nothing different than what you did. You had no choice in this."

We separated, and I dug through the bag across my shoulder for a clean cloth to wipe my tears. Zilpah found hers faster and handed it to me while she wiped away her tears with her hands.

"We are still sisters." My fierceness almost surprised me. "We will not become sisters like *them*." I nodded toward Rachel's chamber, then toward Leah's.

"No, Bilhah," Zilpah replied with equal determination. "We will be kinder, more considerate sisters than them."

We walked out of my new chamber together, parting only as she turned toward the kitchen and I strode to the sitting area and Leah's new instructions.

How else has my life changed? What will Leah tell me? Oh, Jehovah, help me avoid acting like Rachel. I am not like her. Help me remember.

***

I considered the possible changes to my life as Jacob's concubine? Perhaps an end to dishes and laundry, although I would continue to wash my private clothing. What else?

In the sitting area, I sat down on a comfortable chair. I would soon learn.

I chose a tunic from Leah's mending basket. Whose was this? Reuben's?

We mended in comfortable silence until Leah sucked in a deep breath. "This is a big change for you. Did you expect a new chamber and different responsibilities?"

I jerked up my head. "No. I thought only of that first night, wondered what would happen, but I had no idea." I shifted in my chair and held Reuben's tunic up, hiding my face so Leah could not see it color. I did not want to speak about that.

Leah's soft laugh surprised me. "I remember my dismay when Father insisted I marry Jacob. All I could think of was the first night with Jacob. Mother had shared nothing about *that*."

"You? Really?"

"I believe every virtuous woman struggles with the first marriage night."

We giggled until Leah added, "You are a normal woman. Do not think you are different in that."

I set the tunic on my lap. "It helps to know. You said we have things to discuss ... about my changed status?"

She shifted in her seat. "I was thinking about it. How do you think things will change for you?"

"My living space has changed. I expected Rachel to be unhappy, but not as angry as she was today. I suspect she did not think about how this would change our lives any more than I did."

Leah grunted. "She often forgets to think things through."

"I want to continue as the healer in our home. Who else will be available to deliver your children?" I glanced at her stomach and grinned.

"I had the same thought. You have a gift. You do not want to give it up, and I," she touched her stomach, "will need your services again in the next months."

I leaned forward, my hand hovering over her stomach, then sat back. "Thank you. I do not want to give up my healing gifts."

"And I could not take that from you. Do you have any other thoughts?" She leaned back and picked up her mending.

I appreciated the time to think more about my desires. "Dishes and washing clothing," came out with little more thought. I picked up Reuben's tunic and jabbed my needle into a seam.

"No. You will not do either of those again. We have maidservants enough for that." She nodded her head. "You need a maidservant assigned to you."

My eyes widened as I stared at her. "For me? I am the maidservant."

"You *were* the maidservant. Now you are a concubine, Jacob's concubine."

"I know how to dress and care for myself," I argued.

"I too know how to do those things. However, to support Jacob's image and status, we accept help from others. We do our part. When we return to Canaan with him, he will be a prince or a king. We, his wives—"

A prince or king? I cleared my throat to respond, but Leah continued. "And concubines must give up pride and accept help. I will assign Orna to be your maidservant."

"Orna is young."

"As you were when you came to Father's house and became Rachel's maidservant. You can train her."

As I thought about her words, I completed my repair on Reuben's tunic. "Orna will do fine. Thank you for thinking of me. When will you give her the assignment?" I tied a knot, cut the thread, and held up the tunic. "Reuben can wear this again." I shook it out before folding and setting it aside.

Leah grinned. "I suspect Simeon will fit into it better than Reuben. Both boys are growing fast."

I tilted my head. "Yes. This tunic will fit Simeon better than Reuben."

"I will assign Orna before our evening meal. All the maidservants will be in the kitchen then."

She went through a list of changes to my life, including joining Rachel, herself, her sons, and Jacob in the evenings in the sitting area, supervising some chores rather than doing them, and many others. I had no complaints about anything she suggested. I had been happy in my place as a maidservant, but the changes were many. Would I remember them all?

"I am unsure about giving you space in the weaving chamber," Leah said.

"No. I would rather stay busy as a healer than learn to weave. Rachel would not want to share her space with me anyway." I shook my head. "I never learned to weave. Maybe later."

"Perhaps later. I would not want to press Rachel any farther than we must."

"She has enough changes in her life," I said, my head still shaking.

Leah cleared her throat.

Now what? The next change must be delicate.

"You know I claim Jacob's nights when Rachel suffers from her womanly moon time."

"I will not conflict with you," I said, feeling my ears warm. "My moon time coincides with Rachel's and has for many years."

Leah nodded. "I suspected. Thankfully, I do not. Otherwise, I would never have time with Jacob, nor have my sons. It will be a problem for you, however, since she expects you to give her children."

"Certainly she understands that and the need to share Jacob with me. If she does not, I will never give her children." *I should not have to say this. But this was Rachel.*

Leah nodded. "We need to discuss this with her."

"And if she refuses to join us?" I asked.

"This topic is much too important for you and her."

I cleared my throat and pulled at the neck of my dress.

"You are his official concubine," Leah continued, "given to Jacob by his wife, Rachel. You have the right to spend nights with Jacob. I hope she understands," Leah said.

***

With everything else settled, Leah asked me to find Rachel. I knew where she would be.

"I know it is not something you want to do," Leah leaned forward. "But we need to counsel together." Her hands fluttered over her stomach.

I rose and stretched. "What shall I tell Rachel?"

"Tell her we have some things to discuss. Life has changed for us. She needs to join this discussion." She shifted.

I slumped and walked to the door.

"And remember, you are no longer a maidservant. Rachel changed that when she gave you to Jacob."

I lifted my head and straightened my spine. I glanced back at Leah. "Yes. Rachel changed my life. I should thank her."

I found her in the weaving chamber. "Here you are," I said, stepping in.

Rachel glanced up at me. "I am often here at this time of day."

"Yes, you are." I cleared my throat. "I thought you might still be in your chamber."

"Did you think I hid there while you were gone?" Her harshness forced me to take a step back.

I swallowed and bravely stepped closer. "I know you well enough."

Rachel took a deep breath and let it out. "I hid while you were gone. No more."

"Good." *Now how to say this?* I chewed on my lip, remembering Leah's words. "Leah asks that you join us in a discussion."

"I will not come at her command. I am Jacob's first wife by choice."

I nodded. We had often discussed her beliefs about this. "Choice has nothing to do with this. Leah is his first wife, since she married Jacob first."

I saw her frustration rising, but, as Leah reminded me, I was no longer the meek maidservant. I stood tall and stared at her.

"We need to discuss the changes in our relationship with Jacob," I said with a nod. "We need to discuss some household matters with you as well."

She snorted.

I chewed on my lip. "I thank you for giving me to your beloved husband. My life is better already as Jacob's concubine. I have a larger chamber, fewer menial duties, and more rights, especially with Jacob."

Rachel stared at me and swallowed, breathing deeply. "I will join you when I complete this row." She waved toward her weaving.

I inhaled, thinking to say more, but decided against it, closed my mouth, and left.

As I returned to the sitting area, I giggled. It felt wonderful to be free of her demands. I walked in, holding my stomach, giggling.

Leah raised her eyebrows.

I giggled even more.

At last, she asked, "Why the giggles?"

Between my giggles, I shared my exchange with Rachel. "She did not want to come to your call. She is Jacob's first wife by choice."

I lifted a hand as she tried to protest. "I reminded her that choice has little say in this. I told her the purpose of our chat, as you suggested, and she became quiet."

Leah stared.

"Then I thanked her for giving me to her beloved husband."

Leah giggled with me, and our giggles continued to make it hard to speak. I bent over, my laughter overwhelming me. "Rachel had no retort. She could say nothing to that, except she will join us presently. I do not think she expected me to change so much in such a short time."

We sipped water to stop the giggles, and I settled into my seat, taking out another tunic to mend. Rachel would not like to find us laughing.

Rachel took her time. I suspect she finished more than one row of her blanket before coming, just to show Leah she would not come when she called. When she entered, she acted as if it were her choice to join us, looking around and pretending to be surprised to find Leah and me waiting for her.

Leah glanced at me, warning me to stifle my giggles.

Rachel sat stiffly on a chair as far from Leah and me as she could, refusing to relax. She looked ready to leap out of her chair at any moment.

Leah leaned back and set her mending aside, while I put mine back in her basket. I leaned back, not as relaxed as Leah, but much more than Rachel.

"You asked me to come visit with you?" Rachel asked.

I could see she wanted to say something else, but she did not.

Leah tilted her head toward Rachel. "Yes. Now that Bilhah is Jacob's concubine and installed in her new chamber, we discussed her changed role in our home. Orna will become her maidservant."

Rachel pinched her lips together. "Her maidservant?" she cried. "Bilhah is *my* maidservant."

Leah showed no response to Rachel's frustration. "When you gave Bilhah to be Jacob's concubine, you changed her status. She may still be your maidservant in name, but she will no longer serve you as she has since she came to our father's home."

Rachel rolled her lips inward. *Will this not ruin our* friendship?

Leah continued. "Nita will continue to care for your daily needs. Orna will help Bilhah. When we travel to Canaan, we must help show how mighty Jacob has become. A maidservant for Bilhah will increase his stature."

I held myself still. I did not like being the object of their discussion. My thumbs moved in circles around each other.

Rachel glanced at me, then relaxed, leaning back in her seat. "That makes sense. But that is no reason to call me here. Why did you need me?"

Leah glanced at me and inhaled deeply. We hoped she could discuss the difficult subject.

"You gave Bilhah to Jacob."

Rachel's head bounced in agreement.

"As his concubine, she has a right to equal time with our husband at night."

Rachel bounced forward again. "Not equal!"

Leah lifted her eyebrows.

"Bilhah is a concubine, not a wife," Rachel insisted.

"And even the first wife is not allowed fair time with her husband," Leah murmured.

My chest tightened. I did not want to be part of this argument.

Rachel flinched. "Jacob wanted me."

Leah spoke as though Rachel had not spoken. "You want Bilhah to give you children. She must have time with our husband for his seed to settle in her womb. You must allow her time with him at night."

More than the three we spent together. She does not need to know of my child, tiny as he is.

"She can take your time while I suffer from my monthly moon time." Rachel flapped a hand toward me.

"No, Rachel," I said, breaking my silence. "I cannot. We suffer from moon times on the same days. You would not know, but we do."

I suspected she knew, but offered her an opportunity to save her dignity.

"Yes," Rachel said. "That will not help you give me children. I will take the first two weeks after my moon time. Jacob can go to Bilhah's chamber for a few days in the week after, then return to me. Then, he can go to Leah during the week of our moon time." She settled in her seat. "Jacob loves me. He will be in my chamber more than either of yours."

I ducked my head. "I may take Jacob to my chamber for the rest of the week, then?"

"No!" Rachel's shout echoed through the house. "He has already spent three days with you."

Leah cleared her throat, warning her sister. "Should we not allow Jacob to choose when to share our chambers? Let him sleep where he chooses each night?"

I grinned, thinking he might spend more time with me.

Rachel huffed out a breath. "He would spend all his nights with me."

"Unless you remember how much you desire children and send him to my chamber," I murmured.

Rachel's body stiffened, then she pointed her finger at me. "I will remember. You will conceive a child for me."

"If Jehovah is willing," I whispered.

Rachel stared at me as if I had grown another head. Then she rose, breathed in and out twice, and then grimaced. "Yes, if Jehovah is willing." She swept from the area, but I saw tears welling behind her eyes.

She stomped up the stairs to her chamber.

"That went better than I expected," Leah said.

I widened my eyes. "Better than expected?" Then I remembered how Rachel often responded to confrontations. "Yes," I agreed. "This was better than it could have been."

Overcoming Hurt

Zilpah led Orna to my chamber that night. I invited them in and welcomed Orna. Zilpah stood in the doorway, rocking back and forth on her feet.

"Thank you for showing her the way, Zilpah." I did not know how to act. All this was new to me. I tossed her a smile and turned back to Orna.

"You will do well, Orna," Zilpah said. "I must return to my duties." She left and closed the door behind her.

I hoped we would continue to be friends, but when I saw her again, she turned away from me. What had I done wrong?

I found Zilpah three days later, working alone in the upstairs hall outside the linen closet, organizing the linens. I had often dusted the tables and decorations in this hall.

"I thought I would find you here," I said. "We have been friends and sisters for many years. When you stop talking, I know we have a problem. Why are you ignoring me? Why do you never look my way?"

"You made it plain when I took Orna to you. You are better than me. You no longer desire to be my friend, my heart sister." She swallowed hard, fighting back tears as I often had, and bit her lower lip, returning to folding linens.

I moved in front of her, forcing her to look at me. "I am new to this. I have always been the maidservant, never had a maid. I did not know how to welcome you. Please forgive me for my awkward ways."

She grimaced. "You showed me my place. I am a maidservant. You are not."

I gulped. *Had I put her in her place? Had I not accepted her completely? I never wanted to hurt my heart sister!* "No longer a maidservant, but not a wife. I am somewhere in between."

Zilpah stared at me with the tablecloth she folded hanging from her hand. "No reason to treat me as the enemy."

"Have I treated you poorly?"

"You ignored me. It hurt." She pressed her fist to her lips, her head hanging low.

I touched her arm. "Not because I wanted to hurt you. You have been my friend since —"

She flinched away. "Since I helped you take in that first dress. But how do I help you now?" Anguish filled her voice.

I swayed on my feet. "How do I act as a concubine?" My breath caught in my chest. If I did not know, how would Zilpah?

"I do not know, but do not treat me like a stranger or a kitchen maid." Tears leaked from her eyes as she turned back to the linen closet.

With a heavy sigh, I reached toward her. "Zilpah, I am here to apologize. I know I hurt you. I did not know how to behave in front of Orna." I touched her shoulder, turning her toward me. Tears welled up in my eyes. unheeded.

Zilpah grabbed a napkin and wiped away my tears. "Rachel does not need to see you crying."

I sniffed. "I cry easier now than I did when you cradled me those first nights after Mama left me at Laban's house."

"You were a crybaby."

I ducked my head. "I was, but I kept my grief hidden until nighttime when we were alone."

"You did," she said with a grin. "Are you hiding it any better now?"

I shook my head. "I can if you will continue to be my friend. I have no one. I am neither a servant nor a mistress."

Zilpah's face crumpled. With such a kind heart, I could not have had a better friend. Perhaps she would still be my friend.

"Cannot Orna be your friend?" Zilpah suggested.

I barked a soft laugh. "Orna is a little girl. What does she know about my problems? I cannot burden her."

"You will burst if you do not share them with someone," she said. She knew me too well.

"I have always shared with you. You were there at night to help me try to understand Rachel, before and after we moved to Jacob's house. I had only to slip into your chamber to visit late at night. You always had the answer for my problems."

She brightened. "You can still come to my chamber." She folded the tablecloth she held and folded it, piling it on the shelf. "How will I know when you need me or when it is safe to come to your chamber? How will I know if Jacob is with you? You could hang a tablecloth on your door to let me know it is safe for me to come."

I giggled, then frowned. "A bit obvious. Besides, Rachel will always claim more than her share of Jacob's time."

"How can she do that when she wants you to give her a child? Does she not know how that happens?" Sarcasm filled her voice. She shook out another tablecloth and folded it.

I sighed. "She knows how it happens. She has never liked sharing." I pulled a tablecloth from the stack and folded it.

"Folding is my responsibility," Zilpah growled.

"Yes, and I am directing you." I waggled my eyebrows at her.

We giggled.

Zilpah returned to my grief. "If she wants you to give her a child, she must do things she does not enjoy." She grabbed another tablecloth and folded it.

"Rachel will always struggle with sharing her man. She has always been the youngest, and her family gave her everything she wanted, except marrying Jacob first."

Zilpah licked her lips. "I hope she grows up soon."

I barked a short laugh again. "Do not plan on that."

We discussed solutions and planned a signal I could give to invite her to my chamber. I would sweep my hair back, then bring my finger to my lips. Both were natural movements, but not ones I often did. Zilpah would nod her head to let me know she understood.

That evening during the meal, I felt her watching me. But I did not give her the signal. Jacob had whispered he would come to my room. I did not want to embarrass Zilpah or Jacob.

As was becoming usual after the meal, we spent a comfortable evening together as a family. I moved to sit across from Jacob, so Rachel and Leah could sit next to him, but he pulled me down to sit next to him. Rachel sat on the other side of him, and Leah settled across from us. The children played on the floor, often coming to share with their father who gave him his full attention.

After the children went to their chamber to sleep, Jacob went to Leah's room, then Rachel's, to say goodnight.

***

My door opened and Jacob sat on my pallet in the dark. He kissed my lips.

"Why did you come to me?" I asked.

"You must give Rachel a child." He kissed me once more.

"But —"

"She does not know," he said, setting a finger on my lips. "You know. I know. But she does not. It is too early for her to know. I am with you tonight because I choose it."

"And Rachel did not complain?"

Jacob leaned back to stare into my eyes. "I am the man of the house. I am responsible for my own choices. I have allowed her to think she is in control. That will change."

Will it? Will you avoid her jealous rages? Will you give in when she whines? I sighed. *For now, you are with me.*

We lay together, then Jacob drifted into sleep, his arm draped across my body. I never thought I would experience a man loving me. I had wanted a man of my own, but Jacob filled me. Would another man love me as he does? How could I have argued against this? If only he comes to me often. Sleep finally overtook me.

"What are you doing here, Jacob?" Rachel's shout jerked me awake. "You were to return to my sleeping pallet tonight!"

I grabbed the blanket to cover my nakedness. The moonlight through the small window brightened my chamber enough to see.

Jacob moved, now awake, but unaccountably did not respond to Rachel's shrill threats. He pulled me closer to him.

"You are my husband." Rachel's high pitch screech grew. "You are intended to spend your nights with me." She stepped closer to my sleeping pallet, her arm waving wildly.

Jacob increased the pressure of his embrace and kissed my lips once more before sliding his arm from beneath me and rolling over to face Rachel.

"You hold me that way," Rachel shrieked. "What right does she have for you to caress her?"

How could Jacob love this screaming woman?

He sat on the edge of the pallet and pulled his tunic over his body. "You gave me the right to caress and love her, Rachel." It amazed me to hear his calm voice.

I shivered at the loss of his warmth beside me. With her rage, how could our connection survive? Would Rachel permit me to continue to be his concubine? Could she end it as easily as she started it? No! She cannot. Jehovah gave me to Jacob, and Jacob accepted me. It is too late to change this.

"You gave her to be my concubine. This is how it works," he continued to ignore her rage.

Wrapping her arms around her body, Rachel tapped a foot. Did I hear a sob?

I stayed still, staring at them in the dark.

Rachel stepped around Jacob, coming closer to me.

Before she could spew any more hate, Jacob took Rachel's hand. "Do not fear, Bilhah," he said. "You did nothing wrong."

He led my mistress into the hall, closing the door behind him.

I lay shivering on my pallet, listening to Rachel's door open and close. *Should I put my nightdress on now? Will he return to me?*

I chose to wait.

Simeon cried out, and the door to their chamber opened. Rachel's cries had probably awakened the children. More possibly, everyone in the house lay awake, wondering at her cries. Jacob would not like that. Nor would Leah.

Rachel's door opened and closed again. Jacob spoke softly to his sons and closed the door to their chamber. I could hear no more.

Will he sleep in their chamber with them? No, he leaves them. Will he return to me?

He strode past my door and down the hall. Leah's door opened and closed. He would spend the rest of the night with her.

After that, I could not sleep. I rose and pulled on my nightdress and a night robe. I opened and closed my door as quietly as I could, then tiptoed down the stairs to Zilpah's room. She had invited me to come whenever I needed, and I needed someone to talk with, someone who could understand my sorrows. I hoped she could help me make sense of this change in my life.

She slept, her face softened from the stresses of the day. Perhaps Rachel's screams had not filtered down this far. Perhaps the other servants had not heard either. If they had, it would embarrass me. I did not want to wake Zilpah, so I lay on her pallet beside her.

She opened an eye. "Nightmare?"

"No worse," I whispered.

"What is worse than a nightmare?" she mumbled.

I could not hold back the fear and frustration of my night. "Rachel came in and screamed at Jacob and me."

"How horrible for you." Zilpah put her arms around me.

Her understanding calmed me. I shared what had happened.

When I finished, she sighed. "Rachel does not share well, as we both know."

I stared at Zilpah for a long moment, then laughed, covering my mouth to keep the sound from waking the other maidservants. "No," I said between my gales of laughter. "Rachel does not share well. I do not think she ever learned that skill." The release of my stress overcame my sorrow.

"It will be tough for her if she does not learn soon," Zilpah said, brushing my hair off my face. "She chose to add you to the women sharing her man."

I sat up. "I tried to tell her that problems would arise. She insisted I do as she commanded and become Jacob's concubine. She thought we could work out our time with Jacob. Leah spent a long time with Rachel and me discussing this. I thought Rachel understood." I sniffed. "I guess she forgot already."

"She did not forget. She has manipulated Jacob since their marriage. Why would she not expect him to do as she wanted tonight?"

"Jacob told me he lets her believe she controls him. Tonight proved she does not. He went to spend the night with Leah. I appreciated his calm kindness."

"Rachel needs to remember it was her choice. She has to share better."

I threw my hands in the air. "Perhaps she will — someday."

Zilpah groaned. "Someday? Someday is not soon enough. I hope Jacob tells her who is in charge. And it is not Rachel."

"I hope so too. Perhaps he told her tonight." I wiped my face and blew my nose. "I must return to my chamber. I liked it better when it was next to yours."

"I miss you," Zilpah whispered.

"And I miss you. I do not fit in anywhere anymore. I am not a wife, nor am I a maidservant. I am lost somewhere between." I stood to leave.

She rose from her pallet and hugged me before I left.

I softly trudged up the stairs to my new chamber. I loved Jacob's caring and thoughtfulness. He told Rachel he loved me tonight when he said, 'You gave me the right to caress and love her, Rachel." *Love her? Does he love me or just my body? Do I love him?* I wrinkled my forehead in contemplation as I returned to my sleeping pallet.

***

Jacob never revealed my secret to the others. No one recognized my condition until after Rachel learned Leah carried a third child.

One day, Rachel returned to the house in tears. She had confronted Leah about yet another child coming to Leah when they met in the garden. What would she do when she learned of mine?

I survived the early weeks without the misery of nausea. However, about two weeks after Rachel learned of Leah's child, the nausea hit me one morning as I awoke.

Orna came in to help me dress, but I could do little more than retch and spew the little food left in my stomach into the night jar.

Although she was young, Orna tried to help me, wiping my sweaty face with a cool cloth and speaking kind words. In the weeks she had served me, I found her to be gentle and willing to serve.

I crawled from my pallet to the healing basket in the corner and dug through it, looking for mint leaves. I found them at the bottom. "Add these to hot water and prepare me a tea," I said. "It should help me."

After she left, I crept back to my pallet, easing onto it, hoping not to bring on more nausea. I prayed it would not last long and turned away from the light of the window.

The tea helped, but not enough. I continued to retch. I eased back on the pallet and prayed the mint tea would relieve the misery in my stomach.

Rachel soon came to my chamber acting concerned. "Orna says you have a sick stomach. Did the tea help?"

I turned to gaze at her. "Some. I cannot do my chores today."

She knelt next to me and touched my forehead. "You are not hot."

I shook my head, amazed she would ask about my health. "I am not sick in that way."

"You carry our child?" Excitement and concern warred within her expression.

How can she focus her concerns on my giving her a child while I am sick?

"I carry Jacob's child."

She patted my hand. "Rest. You should be well soon."

I closed my eyes, fighting off the need to retch. "You would not know," I murmured under my breath.

I knew the words were unfair, but my roiling stomach did not care. Moving faster than my sick stomach liked, I pushed Rachel aside so I could retch once more in the night pot.

From that day on, I kept mint in my pocket for when the nausea caused me the greatest problems.

***

My child did not treat me as well as Leah's children had treated her. I kept mint leaves in my mouth much of the time until after the sixth month, although I did not allow my coming child to slow me down. I had responsibilities in the house. I continued to serve as a healer for Jacob's servants, and Leah insisted on my joining the family every evening after our evening meal.

Rachel's solicitous attitude did little to help cover my hurt when she claimed my coming child. I swallowed the pain. Expressing it would not help anything. Jacob had told me my children would know me as their mother. I was determined to make that happen.

Leah and Rachel spent many hours in the weaving chamber, making blankets and fabric to dress our babies. Leah also gave me time, reviewing my responsibilities, helping me understand my status, and alleviating my loneliness.

One day as we shared our morning meal, Rachel said, a snarl filling her voice, "Bilhah, get me another bowl of grains. This is cold. How could you give me cold food?"

"Your grains are cold? I am sorry." I turned and summoned Nita. "Your mistress needs your attention."

Nita grabbed the bowl of grains and hurried to the pot hanging over the fire.

I inhaled deeply, then turned to Rachel. "I am not your maidservant anymore. You no longer have a right to make demands of me."

I stared at her until she ducked her head.

I glanced over at Leah, who nodded her approval.

Leah and I soon shared experiences with our coming children. I knew how to deliver babies, and she knew about carrying them. Two weeks after her child moved within her womb, I sat with Rachel and Leah mending.

I cried out, "What is that? I feel something."

"A little tickle of movement?" Leah asked.

I nodded and stared at her in astonishment, my hand protecting my unborn child. "A little flutter."

"You feel him move." Leah smiled at me in a knowing way.

Wonder filled me. His movement verified his reality. The love for my unborn son I had felt since I knew of his presence grew within me.

Rachel scooted closer, her hand floating above my stomach. "May I?"

I nodded.

Her hand settled over the tiny movements.

"There!" I cried. "Do you feel that?"

Her eyes closed, and she brought her eyebrows together. Then she removed her hand. "I feel nothing."

"The babe is still too tiny," Leah said. "Bilhah is only sensing his movements now. Give him time to grow. Soon you can feel him move."

Rachel smiled. Her happiness reminded me of the days before her marriage, before Laban tricked her into becoming the second wife. Before she became a barren wife.

Births

A few months later, Zilpah ran down the stairs, calling for me. "Help! Leah needs you."

"Is it her time?" I asked.

Zilpah nodded, and I waddled up to Leah's chamber as fast as my baby-filled body would allow. "Bring boiling water," I called behind me.

Before entering Leah's chamber, I set my hand on my swollen stomach. "It is not your turn yet, little one," I murmured. "You can wait until your brother comes. Then you can come."

After a kick to let me know he heard, my child seemed to curl within me, sleeping. I turned to Leah's needs.

Jacob must have received the message, for he came running, staying by Leah's side, helping her concentrate on breathing through the pains, as I went about the tasks necessary to help the child come from her body. After a few hours, with Zilpah's help, Leah's third son, Levi, was born, red and screaming, but healthy.

After she returned to her pallet, Jacob lay beside her. With their newborn son nursing at her breast, Leah looked up to thank me.

I shared a grief with Leah. The father of our children had not asked for us to be his companions. He had not turned us away, but he loved another woman.

***

In my ninth month carrying my child, Jacob spent the night with me more often. One night after brushing my hair, he put his hands on my head.

"Why do you do that?" I asked.

"I wish to give you a blessing of peace and comfort," he said.

"Does this mean the baby will come soon?" I stared into his eyes through the mirror.

"Soon," Jacob said, patting my shoulders. "You move slower. The child will come soon."

"I hope so. I am ready to see my toes and walk faster once more."

He laughed. "It will happen." He kissed my cheek. "Sooner than you expect."

He placed his hands on my head and called on Jehovah to bless me and the child, that the birthing would be easy and the child would be born without difficulty, strong and healthy. He shared his and Jehovah's love for me.

Reverence for Jehovah filled me, knowing He would do these things because my righteous husband had asked. Love for Jacob and Jehovah filled my soul. I would deliver this child safely.

After he said amen, Jacob leaned down to kiss me tenderly. He then knelt beside me and placed his hands on my stomach, seeking to feel our son's movements. The babe kicked Jacob's hand, then stilled.

"He moves less now, but he had to say hello to his papa." I grinned up at Jacob.

"He will come soon. Be ready."

Leah had spoken of Jacob's blessings. She was right about the power and comfort they brought. I stopped fearing the coming birth.

Three nights later, Rachel begged Jacob to sleep with her. "Do not come tonight, little son," he said, kissing my stomach and then my lips.

In the night, a pain ripped through my stomach, waking me. I had never felt intense pain rend me like that. I rubbed my stomach, easing the pain.

When nothing more happened, I drifted back to sleep. Soon after, another pain tore at me.

What is this? Why the pain?

When the third cramping pain rippled across my stomach, I understood. My body was preparing to bring my child into this world.

I rubbed my stomach. Would Rachel allow me to name my child? I considered names, hoping Rachel would not name him. Sleep did not return. I pushed myself off the pallet and waddled to the window.

A full moon shone down on me, brightening my chamber. I sat in a chair and watched the shadows change as clouds floated across the moon. Often, the shadows darkened my face as pain filled me.

The pain increased, coming more often and harder. I slid to my knees, begging Jehovah to bless me and my child with a safe birth. I did not want to cry out for help. There was still time for someone to get Zilpah. I had trained her for this.

The sun rose and the pain attacked more often. I would need Zilpah's help before much longer. But not yet. I could wait for Orna to come wake me.

Sun brightened my chamber, and Jacob walked down the hall to herd Laban's sheep. I half-hoped he would stop to see how I was doing, but he had continued down the stairs and outside.

Orna's voice rang out with cheer. "Good morning, Bilhah. Oh, you are up."

I bit my lip as pain burned across me. "You are late. Where have you been?" I asked when I could speak again.

Her beautiful cheeks colored. "I thought Jacob spent the night with you. I did not want to intrude."

"Jacob spent the night with Rachel." I groaned through another pain.

"What is happening? You look unwell," she said.

"No? It is not usual for a woman giving birth to look wonderful." I heard the grating sarcasm in my voice. I had to remember she had not been around a woman giving birth before.

"Giving birth? What do I do?"

"Go get Zilpah. Tell her I need her."

Orna ran from my chamber.

I struggled to my feet, bending over with the staggering pain. My birthing water splashed at my feet. It would not be long now.

Will the training I gave Zilpah be enough? Will she remember what to do for me? I prayed she would remember and help me. It would do no good to call for Mama. She could no longer walk the streets of the city that had taken and sacrificed Nissa and had left shortly after I became Jacob's concubine..

By the time Zilpah entered, the pains followed one after the other, with little space between, losing me to the pain. The child wanted to come soon.

"Orna ... found you," I gasped. "Do you remember what to do?"

"Yes." She bit her lip.

She took over, remembering the things I taught her and helping me give birth. Orna stood back at first.

Zilpah growled at her. "Orna, I cannot do this alone. I need your help."

They came to me and assisted me to the birthing stool.

Interest drew Orna closer, and she helped without complaint.

I sucked in to breathe through the pain. "The child ... comes."

Zilpah concentrated on delivering the baby while I pushed him out. Eventually, she spoke the words I had waited to hear. "You have a son."

A son to love me when Jacob forgets about me. My son will not. I should have called out to Jacob to sit with me. Would he have come to help me as he helped Leah? Should I have asked Rachel to come? No. This child and this experience is mine. She probably still sleeps *anyway.*

I listened for his cry. When at last I heard it, I sighed. "He lives."

"He does!" Zilpah laughed and lifted him for me to see. His red face did not surprise me. Other babies were red. But he was larger than I expected. No wonder it hurt.

When Zilpah helped me to my sleeping pallet, and Orna handed my son to me to nurse, Zilpah had completed all the steps I had drilled into her.

"Thank you," I said, touching her hand.

"You taught me." She stared at me with her dark, loving eyes. Her wavy hair had escaped her braids. She sagged from the effort of helping me.

She and Orna cleaned the fluids that had missed the towels and gathered the afterbirth into a rag, preparing to leave me alone.

Zilpah touched me.

I opened my eyes.

"You are blessed. What will you name your son?"

I shrugged. "Rachel will name him."

Before Zilpah could respond, my door opened and Rachel flew in. "Why did no one call me?" She glared at Zilpah.

"Did you want to be part of Bilhah's pain?" Zilpah grimaced. "Besides, Bilhah gave me only enough time to catch the child. I had no time to send for you or anyone else."

Rachel's face softened and she smiled as if she had not just shouted at us. "We have a child. Is it a son?"

I nodded, unable to speak. I knew she would claim my child, but so soon?

Rachel sat in the chair Orna had vacated only moments before.

"May I hold him?" She leaned close.

"You should let her finish feeding him." Zilpah's irritation with Rachel leaked into her voice.

"Oh," Rachel said, leaning back a bit.

I swallowed. "What will you name him?"

Rachel blinked.

"He is your child as well as mine. What will you name him?" I asked again.

Rachel shook herself. "Jehovah has judged me, and yet he heard my plea. He has given me a son. His name shall be Dan."

Not the name I chose, but a solid *name.*

I brushed my finger across the babe's face. "Dan. Do you like that name?"

He continued to suckle. I gazed into his little face, looking as much like me as Jacob. Dark blue eyes sat above Dan's small nose. Would they stay blue like Jacob's or darken like mine? I wanted him to look like me, not like Rachel. Her eyes were golden.

I unwrapped his fingers and counted five on each hand. I would have to wait until later to count his toes.

"I will return," Zilpah said. "Will you stay with her, Rachel?"

Rachel nodded. "Send a message to Jacob."

"I will do that," Zilpah said.

***

Rachel sat beside me as Dan fed. I drowsed, sleepy from the effort of his delivery.

When he released and lay asleep in my arms, she leaned forward and stared at him.

"He is a beautiful child," she murmured.

I glanced from Dan to Rachel. "He is beautiful." I lifted him slightly. "I am exhausted from his birth. Will you take him?"

She smiled and stood to take him from my arms. They felt empty. *He is so young, and I miss him already. How do I love him so much so soon after his birth? Will she take him to her chambers when he is older? Will she try to claim him as her son and leave me childless? Jehovah forbid!*

Dan sighed and settled into her arms. Her smile softened.

I closed my eyes against the ongoing pain. I knew my body would continue to expel the blood and tissue. I did not expect the pain, however. I inhaled slowly and set my hand on my stomach, rubbing it, hoping to avoid notice. I did not want Rachel to see my pain.

I drifted off to sleep, aware of Rachel cooing to my son. Her words hurt almost as much as my womb.

"Bilhah," she said.

I kept my eyes closed, not wanting to awaken or talk with her yet.

"Jacob will love Dan," she whispered. "I hope he does not shout at me because I kept him away from this."

Was it deliberate, *or did you not know how close I was? It would not surprise me if it* were *deliberate. You desire his attention. Yet, I never heard him shout. And Zilpah and Orna helped* me. *We brought my child into the world.*

I love the name Dan. Jehovah blessed me as he blessed Rachel with this child.

I drifted into a deeper sleep.

I roused when Zilpah came in to examine me. She changed the wad of cloth and carefully massaged my stomach, urging the blood and tissue to expel.

I lifted my lips in a soft smile of gratitude, but kept my eyes closed.

Not long after, Jacob lumbered up the stairs, each foot a heavy staccato announcement of his coming.

When he strode into my chamber, Zilpah stopped him. "Did you wash your hands?"

I heard a swish as he lifted his hands and quieter steps as he hurried to my bed. He knelt and took my hands in his.

"Praise Jehovah. We have a baby son," he murmured next to my ear.

Zilpah must have warned him that Dan still slept.

I opened my dark eyes and gazed into his blue ones. "We do."

Zilpah waved farewell and left my chamber. I focused on Jacob.

He bent and kissed me on the forehead. "You did well. I am sorry I was not here to help you. I did not know."

Despite my exhaustion, I found the energy to smile. "How would you know?"

"You could have sent someone for me."

"No," I murmured. "You were with Rachel. She thought she needed you more than me."

His hands clasped mine tighter. "You needed me. You could have stopped me before I left the house." He let go with one hand and brushed back a lock of hair from my face.

"I knew what to expect." I sighed. "I survived."

"You did well, but I wanted to be here with you." His gaze held mine.

I wanted him here with me, but old habits of letting Rachel have her way are difficult to break, for me or Jacob. I could have called out when he passed my door, but I did not know if he wanted to be with me for Dan's birth. I should have called.

Rachel sighed from behind Jacob. She stood beside the window after laying Dan in his basket.

Jacob kept his focus on me. 'I love you,' he mouthed, his voice loud enough for only me to hear. Grateful, I was not ready for Rachel to know this yet.

I smiled and returned his words in the same voice.

Dan made a small sound in his basket. Jacob gently gathered him into his arms, then paced around the chamber, cooing and singing to his newest son.

After a bit, Rachel cleared her throat. "Sit here."

Jacob smiled at her. "Is he not beautiful?"

"You make beautiful children," she replied.

"What did you name our son, dear Bilhah?" Jacob asked.

Rachel frowned.

"Rachel named him Dan," I said.

Jacob's eyes widened. "Rachel named him?" He lowered his eyes, staring hard at Rachel.

"Bilhah is a surrogate for me. She gave me a child. As mine, it is my right to name him," Rachel said in an intense voice.

"Your right? This child, this son, is mine and Bilhah's child. We will discuss this later." Jacob's soft voice carried a warning.

I did not want the stress to affect Dan. "It is her right to name the child. She gave me to you to give her a child. Our child is also hers." I bit the inside of my lip, pushing the tears back. I would not cry today.

He touched Dan's face with his large finger, dark from working in the sun. "Dan. You are a beautiful baby boy. Grow big and healthy. Your brothers need you to join them."

Rachel gazed over his shoulder. "We are blessed."

Was I included in that we?

Leah tiptoed into the chamber. "May I see the baby? I left Simeon and Levi sleeping."

With a smile, Jacob set the babe in her arms.

She bounced him gently and gazed into his face. "Mama Leah loves you, little one," she sang. "What is your name?" She glanced at me.

"Dan," Jacob said. "Rachel named him Dan."

Leah cocked an eyebrow, looking at Rachel.

"A blessing to our family," Leah sang. "Grow big. Levi needs a brother to play with."

Mama Leah. I like that. Dan should consider each of Jacob's wives as his mother.

I smiled at Leah and then turned to Rachel. "I like when Leah calls herself Mama Leah. She honors me. Although we share Dan, will you honor me and allow our son to call you Mother Rachel?"

She bit the inside of her cheek, seeming to struggle with her emotions. At last, she bobbed her head. "It will honor me. Jehovah has blessed Dan with three mothers — you, Leah, and me."

Leah grinned. "Yes, I like that too. My sons will call you Mother Rachel," she turned to me, "and you are Mother Bilhah. Expect them to use the new names soon."

Burn

The days went by faster than I wanted. I stayed in my chambers during the first days to keep him close. I snuggled him close, sang songs to him, and cherished my time alone. I took time to recuperate, keeping the others away as long as I could. Mostly, I wanted to keep Rachel's grasping hands away from my child. I feared she would take him and keep him from me.

After the first weeks, Leah would not let me escape family meals or our evening gathering in the sitting room. Nor could I refuse Rachel's desire to hold and care for Dan when we were together. She mothered him, and I fought to smile, for inside my stomach twisted into knots. "Dan is my child, not Rachel's," I repeated over and over in my mind. I could not complain, for I was the strong one.

Each evening, Rachel lifted Dan from his basket after eating, whether he slept or kicked his feet waiting for me. Singing to Dan and playing little games, she carried him from our eating space to the sitting area.

I followed, carrying his basket and longing for Dan to be only mine. I swallowed my complaints. I would not have a son if not for her. I could not become a burden on her or on Jacob. He may find a reason to send me away and keep Dan with Rachel.

I envied Leah. Rachel had not given her sons attention until after she gave me to Jacob. Only after I gave birth to Dan did she pay heed to Leah's sons. Perhaps having my son as hers woke up her maternal feelings.

Now, my son became hers until he cried for food. Each time his hunger brought him back to me, I thanked Jehovah. Rachel could not take this from me. Every time I fed him, I snuggled him close, singing to him about how much I, his real Mama, loved him. Rachel could mother him, but Dan would know I am his Mama.

I returned to my chores in the house, bringing Dan with me in his basket. Rachel sometimes came looking for me. "You are busy. Dan needs to stretch and grow. I will take him to the weaving room where he can lie on the floor," she said.

How could I deny her the privilege of my child? I wanted to, but other words came from within me. "That is good of you," I said. "He will enjoy looking at all the pretty colored yarn."

As he grew, he needed my milk less, giving Rachel more time with him before he cried in hunger. I missed him, but he was still mine at night. I continued to sing him songs to remind him I was his mother.

Levi loved Dan. The two boys grew together, often sharing the same basket while Leah and I worked in the same places. Levi progressed only weeks ahead of Dan. Four boys filled our home with noise and laughter. After a time, Mother Rachel learned to laugh and play with them.

Months later, I recognized Leah's glow. She would have another child. How would Rachel accept a fourth child? Perhaps this time would be less difficult, since she had Dan to dote on and love.

When she first learned Leah had another child coming, Rachel did not become angry. She retreated to her chamber for the afternoon to mourn, but rejoined us before Jacob returned from the animals that evening. She did not ask for Dan, and when I walked to my chamber, I heard her soft cries. I did not enter this time. Rachel had become Nita's responsibility. For that, I was grateful.

Many days over the next weeks, Rachel retreated to her chamber for part of the afternoon before returning with a red-splotched face from her tears. She would sweep Dan into her arms and hold him close until he shrugged out of her arms to toddle off to play with his brothers.

One morning when Dan and Levi were about one, I was dressing Dan in my chamber when I heard a faint scream, followed by feet pounding up the stairs.

I grabbed my half-dressed Dan and opened my door as Zilpah reached it. Her dark face had lost all color, and her lips and chin trembled so much she stuttered out her request. "Bilhah, we ... need you ... to come to the kitchen now."

"Why?"

"Levi fell into the fire and burned his hand. We need your help."

I gasped.

Rachel stepped from her chamber. "How could that happen? Did you not protect him from the fire?"

Zilpah glanced toward Rachel, then back to me. "We were preparing the meal. Levi played with Reuben and Simeon. He needs your help now. Please come."

Rachel strode toward us, taking Dan from my arms. "Go. I will care for Dan."

"His other clothes are on my pallet," I said and raced behind Zilpah toward the kitchen. Dan squalled behind me. A small part of my heart cheered. Dan wanted me, not Rachel.

We slid into the kitchen.

Leah held Levi in her lap, holding his hand in a bowl of water. His scream tore at my heart. I had never heard a baby cry like that.

"Good for you, Leah, to have his hand in water."

"Zilpah gave me the cold water for his hand," Leah said. "Will it heal?" She lifted his little fist from the water, then when his scream echoed throughout the room, she quickly dunked it back into the water.

Poor little Levi cried so hard his face turned blue before he gasped for a breath.

I took Levi's and held it under the water, while I gently uncurled it. When I saw the burn on his palm, I sucked in a sharp breath.

"What?" Leah asked, fear filling her voice.

I shook my head. "His burn is bad."

"He fell into the coals before I could get to him." She snuffed back tears.

"I understand. Babies move fast." I swished Levi's little palm in the cool water.

His screaming dropped to a wail.

"Mother Bilhah will help you stop hurting," Reuben said.

I had helped heal Reuben's cuts and bruises many times over the years.

I considered how to heal a burn. The usual remedies would not resolve this deep burn. What would? Aloe? Honey? Calendula? None alone. Perhaps all of them together.

"Keep his hand in that water," I said. "I will get some aloe."

I stepped out the kitchen door, bending beside the door to cut a thick aloe leaf oozing with sap then returned to Levi.

"This will help your burn heal, Levi," I said, lifting his hand out of the water.

His cries once more became screams. "Do not fear, little one. This will help your pain. It will not hurt."

I dabbed his hand dry and dripped the oozing sap across the burn on his palm. It shone an ugly, fiery red.

Leah and Zilpah cried about how they should have watched the little boy. I ignored them. I focused on Levi's burn.

The sticky sap covered the burn, and Levi hiccuped. His crying slowed. Eventually, only little whimpers bubbled from him.

"The aloe helps cool the pain," I said. "He should feel better soon."

I hope. I have never worked to heal a burn as bad as this. I would send for Mama to help if she hadn't left Harran. Please, Jehovah. Give me the means to stop his pain and prevent damage to his hand.

"Will it leave a scar?" Leah asked.

I could not lie. "Perhaps a little one. But I will do all I can to prevent it." I dripped more aloe over the burn. "I will have to apply a honey mixture soon. I do not want his hand to scar closed."

Leah gasped. So did Rachel, as she brought Dan in.

"Levi," Dan whined.

Rachel set him on the chair beside Levi.

"Levi hurt?" Dan asked.

Levi lifted his tear-stained face. "Dan."

Dan hugged his brother and held his uninjured hand while I mixed and then smoothed a honey salve into Levi's burned hand. I wrapped a loose bandage around it, holding it open so it would not scar closed. I could not permit such devastating injury to destroy his life.

"I would not bandage a burn, but Levi is a baby. I do not want him to eat the healing mixture," I said.

"Will it make him sick?" Rachel asked.

"No." I allowed my face to twist at the memory of the taste of aloe. "I doubt he will eat much. It tastes nasty."

I shuddered, remembering the taste. Rachel and Leah shuddered as well.

"I will examine it again soon," I said, bending to kiss my son and Leah's on their cheeks. "I will do all I can to prevent a scarred and damaged hand."

"Please do your best. Jehovah bless him. I do not want him damaged like me." A sob escaped from Leah.

"He will not be damaged. Nor are you," I said.

"Jehovah will not allow Levi's hand to scar," Rachel said, running her fingers through Dan's and then Levi's hair.

"What will Jacob say?" Leah whimpered. "I allowed my son to fall into the fire."

"He will understand," I said. *I hope he understands. Babies move so fast. Leah could not have stopped him. I pray, Jehovah, prevent his hand from scarring closed. Help me know what is best for Levi.*

***

Many times during the day, I examined Levi's hand and alternated between covering the burn with aloe and a mixture of honey, calendula, and other herbs from my garden. Each time I wrapped it, ensuring his hand would lie flat.

While Levi whimpered at my ministrations, Dan sat with him, consoling his brother. When I finished, Dan brought blocks from the basket and built a tower. Soon, Levi joined him, stacking blocks with his unburned hand.

In the hours before Jacob returned, Levi's hand healed faster than I expected, but the fiery redness and blisters continued to blaze across his palm.

Leah offered to smooth the salve into his hand and bandage it, but I needed to ensure the salve reached every little crack.

"Tomorrow, maybe," I said. "But watch him. If sickness invades his burn, it will race up his arm. If you see streaks of red running up his arm like this," I ran a soft finger from his bandage toward his elbow, "get me fast! He will need extra help."

I answered Leah's questions and ensured she understood before I turned to mending.

That evening, my stomach tightened. What would Jacob say? I sat at the table with Levi in my lap smoothing salve into it, when Jacob came in. He stood next to Rachel and stared at Levi's blistered hand.

He slipped into the seat beside me and nodded. "What happened to Levi?" He pulled the little boy onto his lap.

I glanced at Leah, who chewed on her lip, fighting back her tears.

"He stumbled into the fire this morning. His hand landed in the hot coals," she said.

Jacob gasped. "Were you not watching the baby?"

Leah winced.

"I tried to stop him," Reuben cried, giant tears sliding down his face.

Leah put an arm around her oldest son. "Reuben did his best to keep Levi safe." She hugged him. "It is not your fault. Levi moves quickly. You tried."

"I tried," Reuben whimpered.

"We all tried, but Levi was fast," Zilpah added. "I grabbed him out of the fire as soon as I reached him."

"Babies are fast," Jacob agreed. He looked at me. "Will he lose the use of his hand?"

All the women in the kitchen sucked in a breath.

"It is early. I will do all I can to prevent it." I picked up the bandaging material and wrapped Levi's hand once more. "There you go, Levi. You are a brave boy."

"Levi better?" Dan asked.

"Not yet," I said. "But he will heal."

"If Jehovah is willing," Jacob stood. He set his big hands on Levi's little head and prayed for the child's hand to heal without scarring, and that I would know how to help.

Tears dripped down Leah's face when Jacob finished his prayer. "Will Jehovah honor your prayer?"

"If you trust and believe Him, Jehovah will bless our child." He lifted the child from my lap into his mother's arms. Levi sighed and snuggled into her, then giggled at Dan.

"Shall we bless this food now?" Jacob asked.

Levi struggled with pain for two days, but eventually the burn healed faster than I expected. A week after the burn, the family gathered for our evening meal. "I do not understand." I shook my head. "I am grateful for it, but Levi's hand should not have healed as much or as well as it has already. Burns take much longer to heal."

"Is it nearly healed?" Jacob asked.

I nodded. "He plays as if nothing happened to him. The line of scarring is pink and no longer blistered."

Jacob took Levi's hand in his, turning it over and tracing the lines of the scar. He closed and opened the hand several times. "The scar does not affect the use of his hand. Jehovah blessed your hands as you worked to heal his, Bilhah."

I smiled. "Little children do heal faster than older people. Mama told me about that. I helped other children heal before she brought me to Laban. But I never saw a child with a burn as bad as Levi's heal as well or as fast."

"Because Jehovah answered our prayers and blessed him," Leah said.

"Jehovah loves little children," Jacob said. "He has healed our little Levi. Jehovah has plans for him. Let us give Him thanks."

We knelt and offered thanks to Jehovah.

I continued to smooth the salve into his hand for another month to ensure all signs of scarring had disappeared.

Six Sons

Soon after Levi's injury, Leah carried another child, and life became busier for me. Leah's unborn child did not treat her well, and she struggled. She had not suffered from nausea much with her first three sons. This time, however, it affected her as if all the accumulated missing sickness had returned at once.

I examined her more often with this child than I had with the first three. She used mint every day. Other problems beset her that had not bothered her before.

I missed Mama. Her knowledge would have helped me with Leah's problems. But she left Harran. Anguish brought about by my loss threatened to overwhelm me each time I thought about her. I had little teaching and not enough experience.

It helped the agitation of her loss when I recognized the sensation of a child settling in my womb once more as Dan neared his first-year celebration. Before I missed my moon time that month, Jacob whispered his confirmation that another child would soon come when he came to my room. We lay on my pallet. The moonlight filtered through my window, brightening his curly brown beard in the dark.

"You carry another child." His whispered voice tickled my ear. I was grateful he had slipped away from Rachel to be with me.

"I do?" I knew he recognized a child settled in my womb early with Dan, but did not expect him to be aware of this one so soon, and I wanted to withhold the information from others yet. I especially did not want to share with Rachel. This child would remain mine alone for as long as I could.

"You do. Jehovah whispered the news to me."

I ducked my head. How can Jehovah know one so small as me? "I experienced the sensation of a child settling in my womb last week, but I struggle to trust it."

"You have not missed —"

"No. It is too early."

"Are you happy?" he asked, leaning close to kiss me.

"I am. I am happy to give you another child."

"But not willing to share another child with Rachel." He kissed my cheeks, then my eyelids.

"What woman is willing to give her children to another?" I waved my hands in the air. "I know women who choose to give away their children, women who prefer not to have children." I sucked in a deep breath through my teeth. "I am not one of them."

"That makes me care for you even more." Jacob grinned. "I am blessed by Jehovah. He blessed me with you and your children. He promised Grandfather Abraham a multitude of children, a large posterity. I pray that promise will continue. If so, I will soon have six children."

"And if it does not," I teased, "you will still have six children."

"And none from Rachel yet. How many will I have after she gives me children?"

I tossed my pillow at him. "You will have many children. Jehovah loves you."

"Does He?" All laughter left him, and he became thoughtful. "I pray He does and always will."

"How can He not? You obey His commandments. He speaks to you."

"But did I earn the blessing from Father? Did I steal the birthright from Esau? Did I cheat Father when he gave me his blessing?"

I slid my arms around him, desiring to comfort him. His brother, Esau, had come to him hungry and willingly gave away his birthright for food. "How can Jehovah not love you? You desire to serve Him in every way and work hard to obey His commandments."

Jacob kissed me, causing my pulse to race and making me feel safe as I only did with him. He would not desert me.

"You are good for me, Bilhah."

"Do you love me even a little?" I whispered.

"How can I not? You gave me Dan and allowed Rachel to name him without complaint. Now, you give me another child. But even more, I love how you give yourself to others beyond what any others would. You always seek to understand the trials of others. And I love how your brown eyes glisten when I am with you. Yes. I love you."

Not as much as you love Rachel. I do not expect that.

"I am grateful for your love," I whispered.

He kissed my eyes again. "And I am grateful for yours."

***

I waited to share my tidings of another child with the others until nausea again made it impossible to keep my news hidden. Before telling even Zilpah, I decided I must share with Rachel. I needed to keep her happy with me. I needed the peace of her acceptance to continue within our home. More importantly, I needed Jacob to stay happy with me.

I pushed her door open after Nita walked down the hall after helping Rachel dress one morning.

She stood staring out her window. "Did you forget something, Nita?"

"No, Rachel," I said. "I am not Nita, and I forgot nothing."

Rachel spun away from the window. "Bilhah! You have not come to visit me for a long time, not since —."

"You had Nita to help you dress —"

"I miss you. I treasured the special friendship between us. Nita cannot tame my hair as you did."

"I too appreciated our friendship ..."

"Until I separated us." I almost believed Rachel frowned at the loss of our friendship.

"You did what you believed you had to do."

"Can we be friends again? Nita treats me well, but there is no closeness between us. I find myself more alone than ever." Her lower lip protruded.

"Yes. We will always be friends," I murmured.

Rachel threw her arms around me.

"I have news for you," I whispered, fighting back the nausea.

"News?" The strength of her embrace lessened. "Something I will like?"

"I believe you will like this."

She let me go and stepped back. "What do you have to share with me?" She tipped her head to the side and blinked.

"I am with child again."

Her eyes widened, and her smile matched the width of her eyes. "Another child?" She bounced on her feet.

I nodded, then reached into my pocket for another mint leaf.

"I will help care for Dan if you need me to."

"I know you will. Dan loves you." I expected this to hurt more, but Dan knew me as his mama. I no longer feared she would steal all his love. Because she had shared her love with Leah's sons, and Dan insisted on playing with his brothers, she claimed Dan less than she had when he was young.

"And I love him." Rachel sat on the chair next to her window. "How soon will this child come?"

"In a little more than six months. It will be a while," I said.

Later that morning, I found Zilpah alone.

"I want to tell you before I tell the others," I said.

She turned away from the table she dusted. "You carry another child?"

"How did you guess?"

"What else would you share with me before you share with the others?" She giggled.

I joined her in giggling. "Lots, but you are correct."

She grabbed me and spun me around. I grabbed a mint leaf to chew from my pocket.

"Nausea again?"

I nodded.

Zilpah stilled and leaned closer to me. "When will your child come?"

"About six months. I will need your help once more."

"You have it always. Have you told Rachel?"

Tightness filled my chest. "Yes. This morning. She is excited. She is probably searching for names for the child already."

We giggled together again.

***

Three months later, Jacob woke me to help Leah give birth to Judah.

When Judah was three months old, cramps once again warned me of the impending birth of my child. They had started early in the morning. Jacob had spent the night with me each night for the past week. He wanted to stay with me that morning, but I sent him off to work with the animals.

"It will take many hours before these become strong enough to push this son out."

He wrapped his arms around me and kissed me. "Do not forget to send a messenger for me early. Do not wait until the last minute. I want to be here."

"I do not understand why."

He lifted my chin with a finger. "I am here to support you. Accept it."

I chewed on a lip. It was so hard to trust, even as I knew he would not leave me. "Come back after midday. I should be closer by then."

"You are certain?" He frowned at me.

"He will not come before then. You have work to do."

"Nothing is more important than you. I will stay close."

Dan went with me to the garden to cut herbs when my water broke, splashing my legs. I dropped my shears into the basket, picked it up, and took Dan's hand. "We must go in."

"Wanna play dirt," he whined.

"I know, son," I crooned. "But your new brother has decided it is time, and we need to send a messenger to Papa."

As we passed through the kitchen, Zilpah saw my face twisted in pain.

"Baby?" Her eyes widened.

I could only nod.

"Leah, Amina, someone come get Dan!" she shouted. She grabbed me by the arm. "Leave your herbs here. I will help you up the stairs to your chamber." She pulled the basket from my grip and led me toward the stairs.

Leah ran toward us from the weaving chamber. "Is it ... Your baby is coming. I will take Dan. He can play with Levi and the others."

"Send ... someone ... for ... Jacob," I panted.

"Reuben can get him." Leah's confidence settled me.

Zilpah urged me onward. With Dan safe with his brothers, I willingly followed her, stopping once on the stairs as a harsh cramp rippled across my stomach.

Zilpah had me undressed and on the birthing stool when Jacob bounced up the stairs.

"I knew this child would come sooner than you thought." He gripped my hand, letting me squeeze it with my cramps. He stayed with me, holding my hand, wiping away the sweat from my face, and murmuring his love and support.

How had I denied myself this support during Dan's birth? He knows all the right things to say and do to help me.

He moved behind to support me during the final stage of pushing, whispering in my ear, "You can do this. You are strong."

His tenderness comforted me. *I can do this. He trusts me.*

The child pushed his way out of my body sooner than I expected, and with less pain than Dan. *I will not push Jacob away if there is another child.*

His embrace from behind warmed me.

"I love you, Bilhah," he whispered.

“You have another son,” Zilpah said.

"Another son. You have blessed me, Bilhah. You did so well. I am proud of you.” Joy filled his voice.

I could only smile, too tired to speak.

After they helped me back to my sleeping pallet, Orna put my little son, wrapped in a new soft blanket, in my arms to feed.

My babe fussed until I helped him, then happy slurping sounds caused Jacob to laugh.

“Will you allow Rachel to name this child?” Zilpah asked.

"No!" Jacob flinched. "He is your son. It is your right to name him."

“She has a claim on him, as she has a claim on Dan. It is her right to name him." *I would rather name him, but I know she will have found the best name for this son. A name is a small thing. I am his Mama.*

“Can you have Rachel bring Dan up to meet his brother?”

Zilpah grimaced. “Dan needs to meet his brother, but ...”

“But she made it possible for me to be with Jacob.” I glanced at him and gave him a tired smile.

“And I am grateful,” he said.

“I will tell her to bring Dan,” Zilpah said, and left my chamber.

Our son finished eating, and Jacob took him from me, dancing slowly around the chamber, singing a soft cradlesong, one he told me earlier his mama had sung to him.

Rachel brought Dan in, as Zilpah returned.

"Be careful," Zilpah warned Dan. "Your mother still hurts."

My little son hurried to my side, and I pulled him onto the pallet beside me. Dan threw his arms around my neck for a hug.

"Do you see your brother?" I asked.

Jacob squatted and held the babe for Dan to see.

I turned to Rachel. "What will you name this son?"

Rachel took a deep breath, closed her eyes, and then smiled. "With great struggle have I wrestled with my sister, and have prevailed. His name is Naphtali."

Struggled with your sister? This is not a competition. And I did all the work.

Rather than say such words, I leaned over my baby and ran a finger across his face. "Naphtali. A big name for such a little boy. But you will grow into it."

Jacob lifted Naphtali to his lips and kissed his cheek. "Welcome to our family, Naphtali."

Changes

At the next annual sacrifice to Jehovah, Jacob thanked Jehovah for thirteen years of being in Harran and for his two youngest sons, Judah and Naphtali. Since Jacob came to Harran with the right to sacrifice, we enjoyed the opportunity to worship Jehovah in this holy rite. No one here had offered sacrifice in the years since Abraham left. My gratitude that I could take part in this sacred worship filled me with gratitude.

Laban strutted through the crowd, claiming all the children as his — including mine. I wanted to slap him. I would have if I were a man.

Leah saw me clenching my fists and put an arm around me. "Do not allow Father to distress you. Your sons know who their mother is. What does it matter if others think differently?"

One more year until we would become free of Laban. After that, Laban could not force us to stay in Harran. I looked forward to our leaving.

That evening, we made plans to begin our preparations to leave. We had much to prepare, but with Jehovah's help, we would be ready when it was time to go.

Although Reuben, at only six, was young to leave her side, Leah agreed to allow Jacob to take Reuben with him to care for the animals.

Jacob frowned as he explained to Leah and me, as mothers to his sons. "I would allow Reuben two more years at his mother's side, but we have not the time to let him grow. I need to enlarge my flocks. I will hire herders soon, but like your father when I arrived in Harran, I require a son from our family to work with the herders. The animals must learn to love and follow our sons."

I put an arm around Leah, understanding her concern.

In the next weeks, Leah and Rachel taught me to weave. I had helped Rachel set up her loom, so stringing the warp threads caused me little trouble.

Weaving the weft over and under and keeping it tight gave me greater problems. It surprised me when Rachel encouraged and praised my work. My first attempt at weaving would make fabric for a small, cool summer tent.

***

Two months after we made plans to leave Harran, Zilpah came into my chamber. Her lips pressed together in a slight grimace. She opened and closed her mouth and pulled on her ear.

"You look like you have a problem," I said, looking up from feeding Naphtali.

She opened and closed her mouth a few times, unable to make any sound. She paced in front of me, holding up a finger. At last, she worked her jaws enough to speak. "How did you resolve your mind?"

I crunched my eyebrows together. "What do you mean?"

"How did you accept Jacob when Rachel gave you to him?"

I gazed into her eyes, seeing into her heart. "Leah asked you to become Jacob's concubine." Why would Leah ask this of my friend? She did not suffer from barrenness as Rachel did. There had to be a reason I could not see. But we would become closer friends again.

Tears filled her eyes as she nodded.

I patted the seat beside me, and she moved closer so I could put my arm around her shoulders. "Jacob is a good man who will understand you. He will treat you with kindness and respect."

"But how do I overcome my anger and hurt?" she wailed. "Leah knew I did not want this. Ever."

I patted her back as I often patted Naphtali when he cried. "Women seldom have a choice in marriage. Only Rachel wanted Jacob, and he chose her. None of the rest of us who came to this house had a choice. Laban forced Jacob to marry Leah. Rachel forced me. Now Leah has asked you to become Jacob's concubine as well. I learned I could accept him with grace, or fight him. Jacob is not one to fight. He is too kind." I grinned at Zilpah. "Laban could have given us to fat, lazy drunks. Instead, we are given to a man of God."

Perhaps Jehovah had a hand in this, *as He did with me.*

Zilpah sniffed back her tears. A small smile graced her face. "It could have been worse. Laban could have given me to one of his sons as a concubine. Can you imagine being a concubine to his sons, Shelomiy or Chayim?"

The thought sent shivers through me. "Better Jacob than one of those spoiled men-children." Naphtali finished eating and lay back in my arms, sleeping. A satisfied, milky smile filled his little face. How I loved him. I would not have him or Dan if I were not Jacob's concubine. I moved him onto my shoulder and patted his back.

Zilpah wiped her face. "Leah will make the announcement on the Sabbath. She told me to wear my best dress. She wants me beautiful for Jacob."

I nodded as I rocked my baby. "She treats you better than Rachel treated me. Rachel wanted me in an old, unflattering dress. Have you chosen a dress yet?"

She sighed. "Not yet."

"Choosing a dress is of little importance compared to the changes coming for you." I laid my sleeping Naphtali in his basket and asked Orna to look in on him before we plodded down the stairs to choose her most beautiful dress. Talking of dresses would take her thoughts from the coming change in Zilpah's life. I helped her choose a beautiful blue dress. I offered to make her a circlet of flowers for her hair, but she, like me, did not want the people there focusing on flowers on her head instead of worshipping Jehovah.

"What if Leah changes her mind?" Zilpah's smile wavered.

I pushed a stray strand of hair from my friend's face. "I hoped Rachel would change her mind, too. She did not. I doubt Leah will. I am happy now. My sons bring me joy I did not have while I was alone. You will be happy someday too. Maybe not today or on the Sabbath, but someday, perhaps years from now, you will remember this conversation and tell me I am right." I smiled, trying to cheer her.

The next Sabbath, I had a circlet of flowers for her head in a basket at my feet. When the sermon ended and the teacher asked about questions or announcements, Leah stood and strode to the front. I opened my basket and lifted out the circlet and set it on Zilpah's head.

"You did not have to do that," she whispered.

"No. But you need someone to make you feel special."

After accepting Zilpah, Jacob led her out of the sanctuary. I remembered my first days with him and hoped Zilpah would return a happy woman.

While she was gone, Leah assigned Pili as her maidservant and Didi to serve Zilpah.

We sat working together in the weaving chamber. Since Jacob made me a loom, there was less space in the room. I seldom entered when both Leah and Rachel were weaving. But that day, Leah invited me to join them.

"I expect Jacob will hire more maidservants now," Leah said. "We will need someone to be our cook. If you know young women who would work for us, please give me their names."

I thought of the young women who sat together in the sanctuary on the Sabbath. One or two of them may work.

The morning I expected Jacob to bring Zilpah home, I went to the kitchen early for food while my little ones slept. Zilpah sat scooping grains from a bowl.

"You returned early?" I said, lifting my eyebrows in silent question.

"You were correct. Jacob is a gentle and sensitive man. I will find joy with him."

I nodded and dished up a bowl of grains. "It is hard for others to make these choices for us, but this choice is not terrible."

She grinned. "It could have been much worse."

We giggled over our grains.

Pili entered to get a tray of food for Leah. "What are you two giggling about?"

I glanced at Zilpah and giggled again. "Private matter."

Pili scooped grains into a bowl and set it on a tray.

"Who are you taking food to?" Zilpah asked.

"Leah. I am her new maidservant. You will be busy with other things now."

Zilpah's eyes opened wide.

I elbowed her in the side. "Remember when I left? I came home to find Leah had given Nita to Rachel as her maidservant. Your status has changed. You cannot be Jacob's concubine and serve Leah as her maidservant."

Zilpah congratulated Pili before she lifted the tray and left the kitchen.

I remembered the day I returned home with Jacob. I faced Rachel's wrath, then Leah changed everything for me. I suspected it would be easier for Zilpah. Leah would have thought through all those changes before she asked Zilpah. What a blessing for my friend. Leah had not demanded her to give in. She had asked her. I would explore my feelings about it later.

"Expect Leah to discuss your change of status," I added. "It takes time to learn."

Later that day, Zilpah invited me to help her pack her possessions into baskets and move them to her new chamber near mine.

Didi entered as we emptied the baskets. "Allow me to put your possessions away so I will know where to find them."

We sat together while Didi arranged Zilpah's possessions, giving her directions.

"What chores did you lose?" I asked.

"Lose?" Her eyebrow quirked up.

"Your status changed. I am no longer required to help with washing the clothing, although I wash my own bloody cloths. What did Leah take from you?"

"Oh, that. I am no longer required to help with cleaning the clothing, either. Nor am I expected, or allowed, to prepare the meals." Zilpah's chin dipped down.

I touched her arm. "You enjoy cooking more than I do."

"I do. You still have your healing. It gives you purpose beyond your family. I was the cook. I planned the meals and cooked most of them. What do I have now?" She closed her eyes and took a deep breath.

"Did you tell Leah?"

"I tried. She did not want to hear. She says we need someone like Ada to do the cooking. I did that. I supervised the other maidservants when I did not cook." She stared up at me, her voice thickening with emotion. "Now what do I do?"

"You will learn to accept your new status, higher than the other servants, but not as high as Rachel and Leah."

"And what do I do with my time? What will I become?"

I shrugged. "You will find your place. You will see."

***

In the next weeks, Zilpah bloomed. She supported every woman in the household. I found her beside Nita, holding her bloody hand while they waited for me after Nita had accidentally sliced a finger. She comforted Orna when her grandmother died, and Orna could only spend a day with her mother. Zilpah laughed at our jokes and cried with us in our sorrows. She worked beside us and encouraged us.

Although a new young woman took over the cooking, Leah allowed Zilpah to continue planning our meals. I taught her to tend the bees I had enticed into our garden and to prepare the honey for eating and healing. She also joined us in the big outdoor weaving tent Jacob had set up for us to weave tent fabric in, learning to weave faster than me. She no longer came to me to complain in the privacy of our chambers.

Zilpah missed her moon time the first month after becoming Jacob's concubine. I examined her after four months.

"Your child is growing well," I said as she sat up.

"He has treated me well. He has caused me little nausea."

I raised an eyebrow. "He?"

"Jacob believes we will have a son. Has he ever been wrong?"

I sat on the stool in front of her dressing table. "I have not heard of it, but Leah has not shared every time."

We talked about other things, then I said, "You found your place."

Her eyebrows lifted.

"You are a healer of souls. I have watched you bring comfort and joy to each of us, even Rachel and Leah."

"I try to help where I can," she said, pushing a lock of hair off her face.

"It shows. We lean on you to heal our hearts as others depend on me to heal their injuries." I stood and put a hand on her shoulder. "And now, you increase the size of the family."

"And give Leah another child."

"She is busy enough with her four sons," I said. "She will not claim your son as Rachel has claimed my sons."

"I pray she does not."

About nine months after Jacob led Zilpah from the sanctuary as his new concubine, I helped her give birth to a son. As Orna had helped Zilpah when I gave birth to Naphtali, Leah entered the chamber and assisted me without question.

"It is good for me to do this," Leah said. "I experienced it only from my side. I will know more about your efforts."

Jacob stayed with Zilpah, giving her support and encouragement. I swallowed my frustration that he had not been with me for Dan's birth. I could have told him about his coming child before he left the house. I learned the hard way. I had chosen pride over his attentive support.

With a weary smile, Zilpah held her son in her arms, Jacob sitting next to her. "What will you name our son, Leah?" she asked.

Leah wiped her hands and walked closer to the bed. "You are certain of this?" she asked.

At Zilpah's nod, she answered, "Jehovah has blessed us. A troop comes. His name is Gad."

Zilpah kissed his little head. "Welcome to our family, Gad."

A twinge of grief for my chosen sister pinched my heart. I knew she would have wanted to name her son as I wished to name my sons. But we would not have our sons without our mistresses.

***

Soon after Gad's birth, Jacob offered his fourteenth sacrifice and gave thanks for his large family. Of greater importance, he had completed his fourteen years serving Laban and became a free man at last.

As usual, Ada served the feast that followed. I brought my sons to show her, as I had done since their births.

"They are growing," Ada said. Her smile warmed me.

"I thank you for teaching me. You were the mother I needed ..." I swallowed the lump filling my throat.

She hugged me. "I have loved you since you came to my kitchen, a scrawny girl who knew how to clean tubers."

I laughed away my tears. "I knew how to help you. I would not know how to love my sons without you."

She gave me another hug. "Do not forget me."

I would not.

Laban did not want to give up the servant who had increased his wealth. He and Jacob conversed near the end of the celebration, their expressions intense.

Rachel stood with us, waiting for the men. She shuddered. "Father will insist on something we do not want."

That evening, when our sons were sleeping, Jacob called us to counsel with him. He sucked in a deep breath before speaking. "You know I planned to return home now."

The four of us nodded.

"Will we leave then?" Rachel asked.

Jacob frowned. "We cannot. Laban insists none of the flocks are mine, says he gave me only the older ewes to feed my family. None of the animals are mine to increase my wealth." Jacob snorted. "He forgets the many orphans I saved over the years, the orphans he gave me since the first year I worked for him. Laban would have no wealth without my help."

Leah tugged on her braid. "What are you going to do?"

I leaned forward, my heart thudding. I never trusted Laban, and this did not surprise me.

"I reminded Laban of his increased flocks, the many saved orphans his sons and herders ignored, and his promise that more than half of those orphans would be mine. His flocks have increased because I cared for them."

Laban always takes more than his share.

"What will Father give us?" Rachel asked.

Jacob leaned back in his seat. "I did not ask Laban to *give* us anything. Rather, I suggested that I keep all the colored animals as payment for my continued care of his animals."

"Few animals are colored," I said, then slapped my hand over my mouth. I still struggled to believe I could voice my concerns and opinions.

"Normally. The animals he agreed would be mine were both colored and white," Jacob agreed. "However, Laban's flocks have more colored animals than he suspects. I will separate them from his as my payment for continuing to work for him. Jehovah will bless us."

"Father will keep your flocks if you do not separate them." Rachel leaned toward Jacob, her eyebrows drew together.

I glanced at Zilpah, who nodded. We knew Laban's avarice.

"Years ago, I suggested to Laban we should separate our flocks when I first took half the orphan lambs." Jacob shrugged. "He did not agree. Now he claims them as his. I will move my animals away from his."

Jacob's sigh filled the room. "If he finds any unmarked animals among my flocks, he will accuse me of stealing them although many of my animals are white. I must lose those."

"But those are yours," Zilpah cried.

Leah gasped. "Would he search your flocks for stolen animals?"

"He would." Jacob nodded. "Unless they are newborn animals, he will claim them. I will not take any belonging to Laban. Jehovah will bless us." He scratched the back of his neck. "I need to return to my father and beg his forgiveness."

"Be careful," Rachel said. "Father will change the terms."

"He has many times already." Jacob gazed for a moment at us. "I will work longer hours as I tend my flocks and Laban's. I have trained his herders well, but when the young come, I will attend to both my animals and his. Be prepared."

"Simeon is almost old enough to help ..." Leah whispered.

"He asked my permission to help today." Jacob chewed on his lip, gazing at Leah. "Will you allow it?"

Leah's nod was slight and hesitant.

"Good, for I said he could. He will go with Reuben and me in the morning."

"You agreed without asking me first?" Leah lost her usual calm. Her eyes opened wide and her voice lifted. "I did not expect you to take him ... tomorrow?"

Jacob reminded her of our need to have sons with the herds to love and protect them. I ducked my head, grateful that my sons were still too young for his needs.

He took Leah and Rachel's hands, then gazed at me and Zilpah. "Our wealth will increase, and we will go home."

Your home is mine, for it is the only home I have had since Mama took me to Laban.

"Will you have enough herders?" Zilpah asked.

Jacob ran his hand through his hair. "I have some, but will hire more as my herds increase. When I have larger herds, we will return to Canaan."

Jacob rose. "But now I must go divide the flocks while there is enough light to do it. Tomorrow we will repair our paddocks."

He embraced each of us and left the house.

Simeon came home with injuries from the cattle. They bumped into him, leaving bruises on his arms and back. When one bruise healed, another animal would cause another.

Leah entered the kitchen while I tended his wounds. "What are you doing to be bruised?" she asked.

I rubbed an ointment into his bruise.

"The big bulls like to bump into me when we feed them. They must not see me," the boy said. "I am growing. Soon they will know I am there and stop bumping me."

"Can you not see them coming and stay out of their way?" I asked.

"They crowd in on me." Simeon's face had grown darker from working outside. "They are funny. I try to avoid them."

"I would be happier if you would avoid the bruises they leave," Leah said, tousling his hair.

Simeon ducked his head. "Yes, Mother. But they are nice guys."

"Nice?" Leah cried.

"How can you call them nice when they bump into you?" I asked.

"They rub against me, looking for affection," the boy said with a grin. "How can you not love big animals who want attention?"

Over Simeon's head, I shook my head and lifted my eyebrows at his mother.

Her knowing grin reminded me of our pride and love for our sons. "What are we to do with you, Simeon?"

"Love me like I love the big bulls," he said.

Leah and I laughed.

"We love you," Leah said.

"Do not let them step on you, though," I said.

"They will not," Simeon said, pulling down his tunic and running off to play with Levi and Judah.

"It must be hard to allow him to go among those big animals." I set my ointment back in the healing basket.

"Jacob gave him a father's blessing of protection. I must trust Jacob and Jehovah."

I remembered each time Jacob had placed his hands on my head before my children were born. Because of those blessings, I felt Jehovah's presence. Perhaps Jacob's blessings had prevented problems with all the births of our children.

As each son reached six years of age, Jacob took him to work with the animals. He would need their help when at last we left Harran. I had to believe Jehovah would lead us from Harran.

***

Within the year, Zilpah carried another child. Rachel learned of it and enticed Jacob to her sleeping pallet most nights. With four women, it was harder for Jacob to come to mine. Deep within me, I knew he would tire of me. Papa did. Mama did. I lose those I love.

Before Zilpah gave birth to her second son, whom Leah named Asher, Leah was big with another child. She named her fifth son Issachar. Between Leah, Zilpah, and me, we had nine noisy sons living in our home. It was loud and happy. Leah hired another cook to help fill their empty stomachs.

I missed Jacob coming to my chamber as often but did not miss the sickness that came with carrying a child. Still, he showed me the same love as he had from the beginning. It seemed Jehovah had closed my womb. I was happy with my two sons.

In the following years, Leah gave birth to another son, Zebulun. Shortly after Jacob offered his eighteenth sacrifice, Leah conceived another child, her seventh, a little girl she named Dinah.

Then one morning while we ate our morning meal, Rachel leapt from her seat and rushed out the door without warning.

I followed her out in time to see her lose everything she had eaten.

When her stomach settled enough for her to stand again, I helped her wipe her mouth. I hesitantly asked, "Are you —?"

"I hope this is a miracle from Jehovah."

I handed her a cup of cool water from the bucket we kept outside the kitchen door. "When did you last have your moon time?"

She sipped the water. "Two months ago." A silly grin filled her face.

I smiled too. "Does Jacob know?"

"I have not spoken to him about this, fearing my sickness is imaginary." Rachel shrugged.

"He will know. He always knows."

"How?"

It was my turn to shrug. "He always does."

Perhaps it was her age or her body. Whatever the cause, she spent six months on her pallet, too sick to join the rest of the family.

Jacob calmed my concerns. "Jehovah would not have filled her womb with a child to take it from us," he said.

I assessed Rachel each day to ensure she ate something, even if it was a clear soup, and the baby grew. She stayed busy, spinning or writing the story of her life. Many days Leah sat with her.

"Why write your story now?" I asked. "You are young and have much to look forward to. Your child —"

"My son."

"Your son will need you to teach and love him."

"Perhaps he will appreciate my life story. I heard our ancient mothers wrote their stories. I would like to read them. Besides, writing gives me something to consider besides my sick stomach."

She finally left her sleeping pallet in her eighth month. We joyfully welcomed her back into our family circle.

Jacob had asked about our preparations to move many times. At last, we reported we could leave at any time.

"I would like to give birth before we leave," Rachel said.

Three weeks later, Jacob ran into my chamber asking me to help Rachel. With mine and Zilpah's help, she gave birth to a son.

After his birth, Jacob asked, "What will you name our son?"

I stopped to listen.

Rachel lifted her wonder-filled gaze from her babe. "Jehovah has taken away my reproach. His name is Joseph."

Joseph ended her jealousy as well.

Dispute

Jacob had worked for Laban for almost twenty years when he warned us during the evening family time we would soon leave Harran. I would miss my brother, who still worked for Laban, and Ada too. I would not miss Laban.

Laban had done little to protect me or his other maids. He took me in when Mama needed a home for me, but his selfish, grasping ways had caused problems for my mistress and me. Although I had lived in Harran all my life, I was ready to move on, get far away from Laban's controlling ways, and meet Jacob's parents. He spoke only of their love for him and Jehovah. Perhaps I could finally find safety and my place with them.

After the next Sabbath meeting, Rachel overheard a conversation. She reported it to us.

"Chayim and Gera, stood in the back of the sanctuary, complaining to their friends. I sat near them, not trying to hear. They believe you have taken more animals than Laban agreed were yours. They believe you stole their inheritance. Jacob, they plan to 'teach you a lesson.' I fear for your safety."

Jacob nodded as Rachel shared the tale. "I will take this to Jehovah. But you should all begin packing now. I expect He will tell me to leave before your brothers can harm me."

We pulled baskets from storage, cleaned them, then filled them with our possessions. We packed everything, ready to leave when Jacob called. Jacob's men servants carried many of our baskets and trunks to the field farthest away from our home, near the camels.

Three mornings after the Sabbath, Jacob sent a message calling us to meet him in the far field. Men rushed to take away our last baskets while we followed the messenger.

At eight, Naphtali had been working with the sheep with his brothers for nearly two years. He stood with Dan and the other five brothers when we arrived. I wanted to run to embrace them, but they stood still, watching.

Men carted the last of our possessions to the waiting camels. They loaded baskets and trunks onto donkeys and the many camels, including the camels with saddles waiting to carry us, and donkeys saddled to carry men servants. Our maidservants directed the men in placing our possessions. I smiled as they enforced their will on the men.

Jacob stood waiting for us at the edge of the throng of men and animals. Besides all the camels needed to transport us and our possessions, herds of sheep, goats, cattle, and horses milled around us filling the air with dust and noise. Although aware of the tumult, Jacob stood in a pool of stillness.

Jacob turned his gaze from the loading to the four of his women, waiting for his word. "Your father's love for me, what little there ever was, has departed," he said. "He no longer considers me his son, the husband of his beloved daughters."

Leah snorted.

"He considers me a servant, nothing more." Jacob clenched and unclenched his hands. "Jehovah, the God of my father, has been with me as I served Laban with honor for twenty years. Jehovah did not allow him to hurt me."

Laban considered everyone to be *less than himself. I only saw him condescend to treat Avagail with some kindness. He regarded others, especially his daughters and their husband as servants or worse. Since before coming to his home, I knew of his wickedness. He proved it many times as his sons mistreated the maids. I will gladly leave him far behind.*

Jacob brushed his hands together, as if wiping away all those years under Laban's rule. He recounted the changes in the agreement between himself and Laban. "Each time, Jehovah blessed me."

We heard these complaints many times over the past years. Jacob needed to explain to us and himself the righteousness of leaving without Laban's blessing.

I looked into his face. His beard had grayed, his smooth face wrinkled. Life under Laban's harsh rule had aged him.

He continued. "An angel came to me, commanding me to leave this land and return to the land of my father."

I sighed. *At last.*

Jacob's gaze found Rachel, then Leah. "What will you do? Will you go with me or stay with your father?"

A ferocious look filled Leah's face. "Father took everything from me. There is nothing here for us. My children and I honor you and will always follow you as you serve Jehovah."

"Nothing here for us," Rachel agreed, squeezing Joseph close. "We are strangers to Father, not his daughters. He sold us. We have nothing from him. I will do as Jehovah commanded. I have only desired to love and be with you."

Jacob's shoulders rolled back and he stood taller, as if some of the heavy weight on them had lifted.

Jacob turned to Zilpah and me. "What will you do? Will you go with me?"

"Where else would we go?" I asked. "Laban gave us as your wives' maidservants and slaves. My sons and I are grateful to be part of your family. I happily choose to go with you."

"There is nothing to keep us here," Zilpah agreed, lifting her head high. "Our families no longer count us as daughters and sisters. My sons and I are honored to be yours. We will go with you."

"We go with you, our husband and father of our sons," I said with a firm nod.

Jacob swept his hands out. "Time to leave."

He called his camel drivers to bring our camels to us and settle to their knees. He helped each of us onto the animals. All his sons, including little Asher, rode camels. Leah's Zebulon rode with her and her daughter, Dinah. Rachel held Joseph close.

I settled onto the saddle, rocking forward and then back as the camel rose in its awkward way.

Jacob dropped his raised hand, signaling our escape from Harran and Laban.

Our sons cheered at Jacob's signal.

I lurched forward, beginning the long trek toward Canaan. Excitement rumbled in my stomach. At last, we left the place where I lost my freedom. I looked forward to Cannan and meeting Jacob's family.

We crossed the Euphrates River the next day. Rather than the fast-moving water I expected, we found a slow, lumbering river at the ford. Jacob led his family and the others across and took us down the trail that opened into a clearing large enough for us and our animals, where we dismounted to rest. The older boys went back with Jacob to lead the animals across the water.

The younger sons begged to join them, but Jacob warned the younger sons that he needed them to watch over their mothers. They stood near us, with their shepherds' crooks watching in every direction. I wanted to laugh, but our young sons' fierce expression prevented the eruption of laughter.

Jacob and the others brought the flocks across the ford faster than I expected, losing no animals. Jacob gave the herders and flocks a brief rest, then we mounted our camels and were off once more, with the broad elevated, darkly shadowed green of Mount Gilead as our guide.

"Why do you look behind us, Zilpah?" I asked.

"Do you not fear Laban will follow and force us to return to Harran?"

I bit the inside of my lip. "I suspect he will try, but we are beyond the land of Harran. He has no control over us here. Besides, Jehovah is with us. He commanded us to leave. We will be safe. Jacob promised."

She swallowed hard before nodding. "Yes. Jehovah is with us."

"We will be safe." I reached across the space between our camels and touched her arm. "Do not fear."

The camels swayed us apart, and my hand no longer touched hers. I smiled encouragement to her.

She continued to search the dusty trail behind us. When I noticed, she shrugged. She had suffered longer in Laban's home and had more reason to dislike him than me.

By mid-morning on the seventh day out of Harran, we reached the base of Mount Gilead. Rolling foothills rose in soft mounds behind us, dry and golden. A few acacias, oak, and terebinth trees provided us with scattered shade.

Jacob set a guard, while the herders set up brush enclosures for the animals. Men servants set up tents, and women lit fires to prepare a meal.

A shout from the guards turned us to stare back along the trail. A cloud of dust streamed above it.

"Laban," Zilpah growled.

I moved to stand beside her and took her arm. "Will he force us to return to Harran?"

Her stern confidence surprised me. "Not me. I will not return unless Jacob commands it. We are his concubines. He is our lord and master."

I swallowed the fear that filled my throat, remembering the words we had shared earlier. *Jehovah will bless us. Laban has no right to force us to return.*

Laban, his three sons, and his men emerged from the dust, racing toward our camp.

"Jehovah, bless us," Zilpah prayed.

"Amen," I agreed.

Rachel and Leah edged closer. Jacob strode to our little knot of women. "Do not fear. Jehovah is with us," he comforted. "Take the young children away from the horses' milling feet and stay in your tents until I have soothed Laban's anger. You will be safe. All will be well."

Dan and Naphtali joined the older boys, ranging behind their father as we took our littlest children to the tents. Zilpah's sons dragged their feet in the dirt, reluctant to follow her, so I grabbed Asher and carried him to his Mama's tent.

When we had the little ones settled with their mamas inside their tents, I stood just inside my tent to watch.

Laban and his men arrived, racing toward Jacob and our sons until I feared they would overrun our men. I covered my mouth to muffle a cry and heard a quickly silenced scream from another tent.

Laban's stallion reared near Jacob, its front hooves pawing the air. Laban fought to calm his horse. He had grown heavyset in the twenty years Jacob worked his fields and herded his flocks.

With a hand on my chest, I calmed my racing heart. To my surprise, the boys stood their ground firmly behind their father.

Laban dismounted. His wealth and excess of rich food showed in the folds of his face. He stood with his feet spread wide, his whip idly tapping his leg as he stepped close to Jacob.

Jacob stood a head taller than Laban. His muscles rippled beneath his loose robe. He had nothing to fear from this puffed-up, selfish man, especially with Jehovah on Jacob's side. Jacob's hands settled on his hips, mirroring Laban, as he waited for Laban's men to alight and arrange themselves in a semicircle behind their master.

The air crackled with tension. Men and boys stood stiff, with narrowed eyes and flushed skin. They deliberately lowered their heads to stare at the men in the other group. Jaws were set, arms were crossed, and all stood in a wide stance.

"Why have you stolen away without warning?" Laban bellowed. "Did you also take my daughters as captives?"

I shuddered in the safety of my tent.

Jacob responded in a low, controlled voice. "Your daughters, my wives, came with me willingly. I left Harran at Jehovah's command."

Laban's men flicked their eyes away from their master toward Jacob before returning to Laban. Did they show respect for Jacob or wait for a signal to attack?

Laban raged on. "I would have sent you away with a feast and songs. You did not allow me to kiss my daughters and grandchildren. I would have offered you a blessing."

I doubt that.

Jacob sucked in a breath to speak, but Laban continued to shout.

"You did a foolish thing." Laban's bluster sounded whiny.

Jacob interrupted Laban's tirade. "I left without giving notice for a reason."

"You left on a day you knew I would not see."

"Yes, for you would have prevented my leaving with some false reason or another, as you have so many times in the past. Since I came to Harran, you have known my intent to return home. Yet each time I brought it up, you found a reason to keep me. I return home now."

Laban stomped his foot. "Bah. I would have given a feast for you."

"When did you care enough to celebrate in our honor?"

Never!

"Every year —"

"I offered sacrifice and you allowed it, joining in our celebration. My wives and the other women provided the food. When did you roast a ram or bull for us? Never." Jacob's control slipped, and he became strident.

Laban shuffled back from Jacob's ire, then jutted out his chin and moved forward toward Jacob, who stood with heaving shoulders. "When did you ask for a feast?"

"Why should I, the husband of your two beloved daughters, need to request a feast?"

The two men reminded me of wildebeest in rut, prepared to fight as they stood nose to nose. Laban's fists clenched. Jacob stood with widely placed feet. Until Jacob heaved a sigh and lowered his voice. "It is past time for me to return to the home of my father. I must visit my mother once more."

I want to meet Isaac and Rebekah.

"I must take my place as Isaac's son in Canaan," Jacob continued. "I take my family with me as is my right. They choose to go." Jacob turned as if gathering his sons into widespread arms, then spun on his sandaled heel and stomped back to Laban. "I have become competition for your sons. I left before they could injure me as they planned."

"Injure you?" Laban turned to stare at his sons, who lifted their hands and shook their heads, hoping to show their innocence. Was it a ploy? Did Laban not know of his sons' continued venom toward Jacob and their view that he had taken what they thought was theirs? How could he not?

"I will deal with you at home," Laban growled, then turned back to Jacob. "They told me you had stolen my animals." His gaze rested on our many penned animals, and he tightened his fist. "You have many more than I expected."

"They all belong to me. Each time you changed my pay, Jehovah blessed me with more. If you had honestly remembered the covenants we made, you would know these are mine. Your animals are home, in your paddocks and fields."

All the animals here were speckled, striped, brown, or another variation. None were the white Laban claimed.

The two men argued about Laban's wealth until Jacob reminded him he had been forced to build new paddocks for all of Laban's animals.

Laban's fists relaxed. "Sons believe everything belonging to their father should be theirs." He chewed on his lip. "My sons think everything I have should be theirs, and none is yours. I shudder to consider what would happen to my daughters if I were forced to leave them in their care."

"Your daughters are mine, and I care for them." Jacob's intensity sent shivers down my spine. "I protect my wives and my children."

"I cannot hurt you, for the God of your fathers spoke to me last night." His face twisted.

How can he say the God of Jacob's fathers? Does he not believe in Jehovah?

"He warned me to take heed of the words I speak to you, whether good or bad. You have longed to return to the land of your father these many years." He nodded toward Jacob. "But why would you take the images of my gods?"

Laban has many images set out in his home. He said they were to prevent suspicion from the other residents of Harran when they visited. Jacob never does. Is Laban honorable in his belief in Jehovah?

Jacob dragged his hand through his hair. "I know nothing of your idols. Your images are not here. I serve only Jehovah." He swept his hands toward the tents. "Search our baggage. You will find nothing. If you do, the one who took them will die."

Silence echoed through the camp. *Jacob will kill the guilty one?* My heart thudded. *Please do not allow Laban to find those images!*

Jacob led Laban and his men toward Zilpah's tent. *Why her first? Did he not trust* her? *No,* she *is* the last *to join the family. I will be next.*

My gaze lit on the baskets and trunks stacked in disarray in my tent. I had not had time to sort and organize them. *Laban's men will not find his* images *here.*

Thumps from inside Zilpah's tent warned me they were not just pawing through the baskets. They had dumped them. I sucked in a breath. *No idols here.*

I peeked through my tent door to see Laban stomping out of Zilpah's tent. I moved farther into my tent, waiting.

Jacob led the others inside. "Bilhah, Laban believes someone took his god images. We must search your possessions."

"There are no images here. I did not take them," I said as I moved to the edge of the tent. My heart beat furiously as the men stepped closer to my baskets. *If someone put them there, would Jacob kill me?*

"I do not have your images," I cried. "Leave my possessions alone!"

Jacob stood beside me and held my hand. "If you did not take them, you are safe."

"I did not. They are not here," I moaned.

"Trust Jehovah," he murmured.

I sucked in slow breaths until my heart calmed. What had caused the fear?

"We found no images," Laban's man said, standing in the mess he and his men had made.

Laban gave me a curt nod and left my tent.

Before Jacob followed, he bent to kiss my cheek. "I knew you had nothing to fear."

I bent to bring order to my possessions, folding the clothing and replacing it in the trunks and baskets. Somehow, I found the one bowl my mother had given me unbroken. I held it near my chest and allowed the tears to fall.

Without completing the task, I wiped my tears and returned to my tent door as Jacob filed out of Rachel's tent behind the others. Confused frustration filled his face.

He must have searched Leah's tent while I ordered my possessions. *But what did Rachel do? I will learn* later.

Leah moved to stand outside her tent. She looked at Rachel and lifted her shoulder. Not her, not me or Zilpah. Who would have them?

Zilpah walked to stand with her in front of her tent. I wiped away my tears and joined them.

"Where are Laban's images?" I whispered.

Zilpah shrugged.

Rachel stepped from her tent and stood alone, watching.

No one spoke.

Jacob led Laban and the others away, looking like the dark sky in the middle of a storm. He stopped a distance from all the tents with his arms folded across his body, frowning at Laban. "Well?"

Laban cleared his throat. "You know I found no images."

"For twenty years now, I have lived with your mistrust and harsh treatment." Jacob's jaw tightened, and frustration filled his voice. "I cared for your animals. My family suffered while you grew fat."

Laban growled.

Jacob continued. "I did not sleep while waiting for the ewes and she-goats to bring forth their young. For what? To hear you complain when one ewe or she-goat succumbed to the rigors of birthing."

Jacob clamped his mouth shut and strode away before turning on his heel, turning back with tightness around his eyes and his nostrils flaring. "In twenty years, seven of those for Rachel, and you deceived me and gave me Leah. You forced me to work another seven years for Rachel. In the last six years, you changed my wages ten times! There is no fairness or justice in you."

Laban cleared his throat. Before he could respond, Jacob's frustration and anger spilled out. "If you had not feared Jehovah, you would have taken *everything* from me. Jehovah has seen my afflictions. He has seen my honest labor and rebuked you."

Laban moved forward, raising a hand to set on Jacob's arm, but he flinched away, refusing to accept Laban's touch.

"These are my daughters, and the children are mine," Laban said.

I am not your daughter. My sons are not yours!

Laban persisted. "All you see is mine." He dropped his voice. "What can I do today to these my daughters or their children?" He shrugged and lifted his hands. "Come. Let us make a covenant between us. Let it be a witness between you and me."

Jacob stomped away, then stepped back with less fervor to stand in front of Laban, then paced away once more. He picked up an off-white stone and carried it back to Laban. "This will be a pillar as a witness of our covenant of peace."

The two of them, with their sons and men, built a heap of white and gray stones. Would Laban keep this covenant? Would his sons? I struggled to believe.

While they worked, Leah beckoned Zilpah and me to join her. I wondered why Rachel did not join us, but as Leah instructed us and the other women to prepare a meal for the men to seal their covenant, I put Rachel out of my mind.

We served the men, then returned to sit in front of Leah's tent.

After eating, Laban stood and called on Jacob to make the stone heap a witness of their covenant of peace. They stood together, speaking of their covenant.

We rose early the next morning as Laban and his men prepared to leave. Laban took Leah and Rachel in his arms, kissing them, then kissed and blessed each of our children, even mine.

Laban was finally out of my life. I prayed to never see him or his sons again.

Esau

We traveled onward toward Canaan. Jacob hoped to meet his twin brother, Esau, and find forgiveness. After twenty years, his concern about Esau's welcome caused fervent prayers and shaky hands.

The open land and uninterrupted sky made me feel small at first. But after Laban's attempt to return his daughters to his control, the fresh air, freedom, and space lifted my heart. At night, Dan and Naphtali would lie beside me, whispering the stories of their adventures.

"A donkey stopped to stomp a serpent's head today." Dan's eager whisper sent chills down my back that night.

"A serpent? Was the donkey injured? Were you?" I considered the herbs I had brought with us, hoping there were enough for Dan's coming bruises.

"The donkey killed it before it could bite me or any of the others. They are smart. Levi's horse leapt away and reared. He had to fight it to regain control. The donkeys are never as unstable. I can trust them."

I thanked Jehovah for that. "I did not know we would have serpents to face on this journey."

Dan grunted. "They are vile creatures. Simeon killed one among the kine yesterday. We must remain watchful. I am grateful you ride high on the camels who plod along, uninterested in the serpents who slither away when they hear us coming."

"I will check my supply of herbs! I would not want to be short if a serpent bit one of us or our herders." I groaned. I had no experience in treating viper bites. I prayed they all would race away at the sound of our caravan. But two had not. Others may not escape. I shuddered.

Nights later, Naphtali took my hand. "The ewes carry little ones. Will Papa stop when the time comes for their birth?"

"Lambs?" I had not thought about young animals on the journey. Jacob had not considered them in his planning, or he had not told us of those plans. "I suspect he will stop. He has always loved the sheep and given them special attention during lambing time."

"I hope we arrive in Canaan before the lambs are born. I would not want to stand guard against wild animals during their birth."

"Wild animals?" My voice lifted above the soft whisper we usually used in our night visits, relieved Naphtali could not see my face pale.

Naphtali shushed me. "Mama, you know wild animals like baby animals."

I breathed deeply to clear the sudden fear. "I do. Have you seen wild animals on our trek?"

"I see their eyes following us, but Papa reminded me they do not like so many people. My sheep and I are safe with the others. If one attacks, I will hit it with my crook and stab it with my knife."

Although my heart raced, I kept my voice low and even. "That is brave of you. Be certain you do not leave the group. If a ewe wanders away, call a herder to help you get her. Two against a wild animal is safest."

His little boy voice filled with disgust. "I know, Mama. No one leaves the caravan alone."

I ran my fingers through his russet-colored hair and murmured. "Do not grow up too fast."

After passing the Jordan River, Jacob sent messengers in search of his brother. When they returned days later, lather covered the messengers' camels. When they neared Jacob, we urged our camels closer, wanting to hear what had happened with the messengers.

Before speaking, their leader took a long drink from the flask of water Jacob extended to him. He wiped the splashes from his beard. "We met your brother Esau and shared your message. He sent us ahead."

Jacob waited.

"Esau comes to meet you with four hundred men."

Jacob swallowed, and his face blanched. "Does he come to destroy me?" he whispered. "Does he still hate me after all these years?" He bent his head in silent prayer.

I added my prayers to his. Would Esau destroy us? Did Jehovah send us into this wilderness to be destroyed? I could not believe it was so.

Jacob called for Demas, his oldest and wisest servant since he had come to Harran.

Reuben waved to a small boy, who leapt on his donkey and sped toward the herds of animals in the back of our caravan.

The short, squat Demas ran as fast as he could at Jacob's call. Breathing hard from his run, concern filled his dark eyes.

"Esau comes," Jacob said. "I will not have him destroy everyone in my family and all my flocks. Divide the flocks into two parts. Leah and Zilpah with their children and one part will go with you to the west. I will take Rachel and Bilhah with the other half with me to the east. If he destroys one camp, the other will escape."

Separated from Zilpah? No! At least Dan will have Simeon's help with the bulls.

Demas bowed.

Fear rippled through me as I rode close to the other women, reaching for their hands. We shared our love and fears silently, not wanting Jacob's plans to be affected by our fears. Our quick embraces across the space between our camels said everything. None of us wanted the separation. But Jacob had spoken. We obeyed.

Reuben and Simeon went with Demas to divide the flocks. When they returned, Jacob directed Leah and Zilpah to take their children with Demas.

Zilpah's shudder sent another spark of fear through me as she waved. *Will I see her again? Will Esau destroy us? Surely he has overcome his anger in twenty years?*

Jacob called us to follow him east, away from the other half of his family and wealth. I missed the others as they rode away.

Rachel rode next to me and put her hand on my arm. "Jacob does what he believes to be right."

I nodded and swallowed hard. "Why does he fear his twin brother?"

"They argued before he left Canaan. Esau's threat to kill him sent Jacob to Harran, seeking refuge with his mother Rebekah's family. That was our family. My father took him in."

I remembered the day Jacob came to the house of Laban, who had welcomed Jacob with love and the expectation of the wealth Abraham had conveyed when he sent his servant to find a wife for Isaac — Rebekah.

But it did not happen. Jacob brought no jewels, gold chains, nor other wealth. All he brought was himself.

And now we rode, returning to his home, and Jacob still feared his brother's angry retribution, regardless of Jehovah's command.

We spent the night in prayer. Before I settled Dan and Naphtali for sleeping, Dan whispered, "Would Jehovah allow Uncle Esau to hurt us?"

Naphtali gripped my hand. "Why would Jehovah send us into the desert if Uncle Esau will hurt us?"

"Jehovah would not send us here to be hurt by Esau. We must trust Jehovah."

"Mama?" Naphtali's young voice quivered. "Can we pray? I miss Reuben and the others."

"Can we, Mama? We must pray for the other half of our family." Dan's yearning matched mine.

We knelt on our blankets and raised our hands in prayer to Jehovah.

My sons lay on their blankets and slept. They trusted Jehovah.

I joined Rachel in prayer throughout the night. Did we trust Jehovah as my young sons did?

The next morning, Jacob repented of dividing his family and flocks and gathered us again into one camp. I clung to Zilpah in relief when she returned, then hugged Leah tight. Tears ran down our faces. Our separation had hurt as if an arm had been torn from me. Their return made me whole once more.

Our sons cheered when they saw the others. They bumped into each other, slapping backs and punching shoulders. Joy filled us all. We would face this together. I determined to be brave and trust Jehovah as my sons did.

Jacob divided small groups of sheep, goats, cattle, horses, donkeys, and camels and sent them as gifts to his brother. Naphtali bit his lip, refusing to cry when the herders took his favorite lamb.

Dan put an arm around his younger brother. "It hurts when we lose our friends, but others will replace them. Trust Jehovah.

Love for my sons overwhelmed me. All my tears caused a headache. I reached for my water jug to stop it.

The next morning, we woke to see Esau and his men riding toward us in the distance.

Jacob dressed in his best blue tunic, worn beneath a dark blue robe, covering his broad shoulders. His light brown hair had darkened with thin streaks of gray, hanging in long curls down his back. His intelligent blue eyes shone intensely from his tanned face. White now streaked his brown beard, flowing down his chest.

We had all dressed in our best clothing, wearing Jacob's dark blue, prepared for Esau's arrival. I prayed Esau had forgotten the insults to his pride and would welcome his brother.

"I will send each of you ahead to gain Esau's forgiveness," Jacob said. "You will go with your sons. Zilpah, then Bilhah, Leah, and Rachel will follow with their children." He looked at each of us, holding our eyes with his love.

I trusted Jacob and I trusted Jehovah. Jacob would not send us to greet his twin if he feared for our safety. Certainly Esau had forgiven Jacob, or Jehovah would not have brought us here.

"I will follow last. Perhaps your beauty and gentleness will soften Esau's heart, and he will welcome me home." He dropped his eyes. "I pray he welcomes me home."

Our beauty. He thinks of each of us as beautiful. His love for us is amazing. My fear diminished.

I glanced toward Zilpah, who visibly swallowed and gathered little Gad and Asher close. She stepped forward. Gad threw his shoulders back. Asher tagged along beside his mother, holding her hand.

I signaled to Dan and Naphtali, who quickly joined me. We stood waiting until Jacob nodded toward us to begin our march. Dan's dark hair and Naphtali's russet hair gleamed in the sunlight. My sons thrust out their chests, unwilling to let the others see any fear.

My heart fluttered within me, keeping the same pace as Zilpah, who marched in front of me. A gentle breeze caused our robes to sway. I clutched my tichel at my neck, as little Naphtali's hand trembled in mine. Was it his hand or mine that trembled? I prayed Esau had forgotten his enmity.

Tall camels rode toward us. Tinkling bells on their blankets and harnesses jingled. Hope for forgiveness whispered in my heart.

We followed Zilpah far enough behind that their dust did not choke us. We heard the shuffling of Leah and her children behind us. I prayed Jacob had made the correct decision and we would soften Esau's heart.

When the camels neared Zilpah and her young sons, the lead rider slid off his camel. A tall man like Jacob with red hair and beard curling behind his ears and down his chest. A rust-colored robe over a tan tunic fell past his knees, cloaking his broad shoulders. Eyes, much like Jacob's, but green rather than blue, sparkled from his windblown face. His broad smile brightened the light of hope.

Before Esau could reach Zilpah, Jacob raced past us, stopping briefly to bow seven times before he reached his brother.

Esau ran to meet Jacob, lifted his brother from kneeling, then threw his arms around him.

"Jacob, my brother," Esau wept. "I have missed you."

"And I have missed you," Jacob cried.

Oh, to greet my brothers with such joy once more. I will never see them again. Jacob and Esau's joy is bittersweet.

When at last they separated, Esau swept his hand toward us, Jacob's women and children, now standing in a little knot, tears moistening our eyes. Jehovah had answered our prayers. Esau had forgiven Jacob.

Their joy of their reunion spread to me and my sons. I hugged Naphtali and gripped Dan's hand. We were safe. Esau had accepted Jacob.

"Who are these?" Esau asked.

Jacob cleared his throat. "These are the children whom Jehovah graciously gave to your servant."

He beckoned us to step forward. Zilpah, with Gad and Asher, arrived first, bowing low before Esau, who lifted her up and kissed her cheeks and spoke kind words to her sons.

I followed. My concern became rejoicing as I sank into a low bow. Esau lifted me from my knees and kissed my cheeks, smelling of camels, dung, and the sweat from his long ride. My nose twitched. His red hair, redder than my Naphtali's russet, tickled. He told my sons they had grown strong and handsome like their father. Esau's smile warmed me. I wondered what our lives would have been like if he had come to Harran with Jacob. Would Rachel have desired Esau or Jacob?

Next, Leah stepped forward with her six sons and Dinah. She too bowed, and Esau lifted her. He clapped his hands across the boys' backs, kissed her on the cheeks and Dinah on the forehead. He spoke to each of her sons, who responded with a grin. Reuben, as the oldest, stood straight, glowing in his uncle's praise.

Last, Rachel reached Esau, bowing low. He lifted her as he had lifted the rest of us, and kissed her cheeks, admired her beauty, and tickled baby Joseph until he smiled.

At last, Esau turned to Jacob. "You are blessed with a beautiful family. Jehovah has blessed you with a large posterity. But what did you mean by sending those animals to me?"

Jacob ran a hand through his hair. "I sent them to find grace with you, my lord."

Esau sent his red, curly hair shaking. "I am not your lord. I am your brother. Jehovah has blessed me. I have enough without your gifts. Keep the animals."

How like Jacob he is. Some of our sons have the same color hair and eyes.

Jacob's brown head shook in refusal. "If I have found grace in your sight, receive my gifts. I have seen your face as if I had seen the face of Jehovah, and you are happy to see me. Take my blessings, I beg of you, because Jehovah has blessed me with an abundance and enough."

The brothers argued, each wanting the best for his brother.

"I will lead the way home." Esau said. "We will soon be with our father. Joy will fill him to see you once more."

"And mother? What of mother?" Jacob reached for his brother's hand.

"Mother watched for your return these many years, yearning to see your face." His face darkened as he ducked his head and frowned. "We lost her only last month to a sickness. Her last words were of you."

Jacob's joy collapsed. His lips trembled, and he pressed them closed. His hands shook. "Last month?" he asked, his voice cracking. "I missed her?" He struggled to find his breath.

I will never meet Rebekah. Never hear her stories. Never know about Jacob's childhood from her. The loss brought more tears to my eyes.

Esau wrapped his big arms around his brother once more. Their tears mingled. "She sent messages to Harran, seeking news of you. But the messengers did not return with news. She prayed you still lived, but the illness overtook her. Had you returned a month ago, her joy would have revived her."

Laban! He refused the messengers.

Sobs shook Jacob. "I should have left earlier."

If only Laban had agreed to let us leave last year. We would have known Jacob's beloved mother.

"You could not have known of our mother's illness. Her sickness came suddenly. You did not know." Love filled Esau's words.

"The Spirit warned me to leave earlier," Jacob sobbed. "I desired to avoid a confrontation with Laban. Had I not shirked the disagreement, I would have arrived to kiss her one last time, to introduce my children to her, to let her know we obey Jehovah's commands."

Esau patted Jacob's back, repeating the words, "You could not have known."

"I did not listen. In my unwillingness to argue with Laban, I lost my last opportunity to kiss my sweet mother's face."

Laban. Always Laban. He can hurt us no more.

Esau comforted his brother until Jacob finally wiped the tears from his face. "I am blessed to find you here welcoming me home. I should not ask for more, except ..." His shoulders shuddered.

A gentle argument ensued between the brothers about Jacob riding behind Esau and his men. Esau could not convince Jacob to change his mind to go with him, nor accept Esau's men as our guards. With another enthusiastic embrace and many tears, Esau leapt onto his camel, signaled his men, and rode away with shouts of joy.

If I could not meet Rebekah, I looked forward to meeting Isaac.

Bear Attack

We traveled more slowly than Esau's wild ride, protecting our young children and young animals from the hasty ride. Rather than follow Esau's trail to Mamre, we settled in Succoth, within Esau's land where they guarded the animals giving birth.

Jacob could not introduce his wives and family to his mother. His grief prevented our continued travel, though we were close to Mamre and his father. We had many more animals than the land could handle in the land Esau claimed. Jacob feared they would be a burden on Isaac's land.

He built a house big enough for all his family, and huge brush pens for all the animals, near the river. His sons and hired herders spread out among them, watching the animals. Dan and Naphtali took their turns during the day, and at night as they grew older.

When we had settled, Jacob announced he would leave us to visit his father.

"Why did you wait so long? Do you not miss him?"

"You needed a safe home before I could leave you." His face softened as he looked at me and the others of his women. Then he licked his lips. "Father loves Esau more than he loves me. Mother shielded me from the arguments, doing all she could to help me succeed. She loved me as Father loves Esau."

"I am grateful Papa loves each of us," Dan murmured to me.

"We would have been safe in our tents," Reuben argued.

"The men of this land need to know me, know I will protect my family, and know I will take vengeance on any who would consider harming you. They know that with our home and protected animals in their pens.

We have struggled enough! We do not need the surrounding men to attack.

"When Father promised Esau his blessing for a bowl of venison stew, even after Esau sold the birthright to me, Mother helped me deceive him." Jacob inhaled. "Then, when Esau learned of his loss, he thought to take my life."

Jacob has lived on both sides of deceit. No wonder he was concerned about Jehovah's love.

"Mother heard of Esau's plan and warned me to leave. She suggested to Father that I should go at last to Harran to find Laban. They hoped he had a righteous daughter for me to marry."

"Two daughters," Judah murmured.

"Yes." Jacob turned to him. "And I am grateful for both of them." His eyes found Rachel and Leah, "And their maidservants." He found Zilpah and me, his warm blue eyes expressing love."

How did I deserve this loving man?

The next morning he left us to visit his father, taking a few men servants as escorts, leaving most of them behind to protect us in his absence. Thc older sons complained, wanting to meet Isaac, but Jacob would not take them.

As I kissed Jacob goodbye before he left, I wrapped my arms around him and thanked him for leaving my sons behind with me.

His reply gladdened my soul. "You and your sons will be safe here. I will return soon with a message from my father."

Jacob returned within the month, joyously exclaiming that his father loved him. "Father welcomed me with open arms and showered me with his love. He missed me almost as much as he misses Mother."

His gaze lifted to search the eyes of each of his sons. "Father loves me, but he agrees. Our sons need to be stronger before we return to live near him. The men of nearby lands would fear our added numbers and may attack in our weakness."

His older sons disagreed, but Jacob remained firm. "Your younger brothers must grow and become strong. Then we can move to your grandfather's land and prove our strength to the Canaanites."

We lived there while our sons grew older and stronger and worked with the animals and in the fields.

One day in the third year of living in Sucoth, Simeon, Judah, and Gad carried Naphtali home between them on a robe, shouting for help.

Leah met them near the door. I hurried in to see why they shouted. The brothers stepped back, revealing my son. A little cry escaped my lips.

My heart beat wildly seeing Naphtali covered in blood. "What happened?" I stammered. *Jehovah bless my son!*

Naphtali lay still, overcome by the pain of his injuries. I touched his neck, searching for the beat of his heart. I felt a weak thump. He still lived, praise Jehovah.

"A bear," Gad groaned and shook his head. "We shouted at it, waving our shepherds' crooks, to chase it away. But it focused on Naphtali."

I ran for my healing supplies, shaking so hard I struggled to hold my basket. They had laid Naphtali on a table in the sitting area, rolling him onto his stomach.

"A sow bear got him," Judah murmured when I returned.

Our gasps echoed when they peeled back the ragged robe covering Naphtali. Blood covered his back, filling the deep gouges.

"Thank you for bringing him here so fast. With Jehovah's help, I may keep him alive." I glanced up at the brothers and offered them a slight smile. "How did this happen?"

"Naphtali searched for a lost ewe, big with her young," Simeon said. "Ewes will wander away just before they lamb, silly animals." He swallowed. "He found her in a thicket."

I fought back tears. *I cannot sob now. I must save my son.*

Orna brought an urn of warm water, a bowl, and clean cloths.

"I need my needles and thread," I said.

She nodded, poured water into the bowl, and I dropped herbs into the water and swirled them around, then rushed from the room.

I dipped a clean cloth into the mixture and mopped the blood from my son's back, listening to Simeon's narration.

"Naphtali loves his sheep. The ewe delivered twins and refused to leave the thicket. He scooped one lamb into his arms and turned to call Reuben when the sow bear and her cubs ambled past the thicket."

I gasped. *Not bear cubs!*

Blood poured from his injuries. Leah grabbed a towel and pressed it against Naphtali's back, seeking to stem the flow. I handed her another cloth. "Press here," I pointed to his shoulders. "We must slow the bleeding."

Orna found the needles and threaded them. While Leah pressed on the bleeding scratches, I stitched the deepest ones.

Leah nodded to Simeon to continue his story.

"Without knowing it, Naphtali backed into a cub. The cub squalled, and the sow turned on him."

I inhaled but continued to stitch. Naphtali's life depended on me.

"He ran toward me," Simeon continued, "luring the sow from the ewe and the other lamb, but the sow ran faster. She jumped onto his back, raking it with her claws."

I shuddered. Jehovah, *guide my hands.*

"I feared she would never let go," Judah whispered, his voice cracking. I glanced up to see if tears flowed. They did, from all three brothers.

"Then she roared, gave a last swipe, and ambled toward her young, gathering them close before they wandered away, uncaring of the damage she had done to Naphtali. And before you ask, he tossed the lamb to Reuben as he fell."

"The ewe and her lambs are safe then?" I asked, glancing from Naphtali to Simeon. Naphtali would ask when he woke. But my concern was for my son. I tied a knot and continued stitching. I had to close the wounds and stop the bleeding.

Simeon looked up at me. "They are. Reuben dragged the ewe and her other lamb out and carried them back to the flock." His eyes dropped back to my hands.

I dabbed the blood away and added more stitches.

"So you brought him here?" Leah asked.

"He was hurt too badly for us to help him there. We used my robe to bring him home."

"This is your robe?" Leah asked.

At Simeon's nod, Leah shook her head. "Your robe is bloody and ruined. I am grateful you used it to bring your brother home."

"Mother!" Simeon cried. "We had to get Naphtali home to Mama Bilhah fast."

"It is good that you did," I said, biting my lip. "He may not have survived."

"Will he survive with your help?" Leah asked. "Poor Naphtali. Your healing skills bless us, Bilhah. We would have no hope without them. I pray Jehovah directs you."

Gad watched with his lower lip between his teeth. "We all pray."

I continued to stitch, praying the bleeding would stop and my son would live.

***

With Leah's help and his brother's prayers, it took hours to stitch the worst of the gouges together. I cleaned Naphtali's back and ladled honey across it to seal and heal the injury. I prayed I had washed all the dirt away. In all my ministrations, my son never cried out, sleeping through the pain. Jehovah blessed him.

Although I washed the injuries with a solution that fought the sickness, the bear had filthy claws and pressed strands of Naphtali's tunic into them. Over the following days, sickness caused him to toss and turn in his sleep as his body fought off the sickness.

Only when he finally woke did he cry out in pain, but he bit back the cry. Until he healed, I sat beside my son, murmuring words of love, hope, and encouragement. Leah often joined me at Naphtali's side, mopping his forehead with a cool cloth and allowing me to rest.

Later, I washed the injury with a weaker solution and soothed ointments on the scabs, hoping to heal them enough to avoid scars that would hinder his movement.

He lay face down for three weeks until the worst of his injuries had healed. I gave him a concoction to help him sleep through the pain. When Naphtali could lie on his back once more, no longer sleeping through the day and night, he worried about the scars affecting his ability to care for his sheep.

And then he complained, "Women will not want me with these scars."

Women? You are but twelve! When did you begin to think about women? You have years to worry about their acceptance.

With a small chuckle, I said, "They are proof of your courage." I tried to offer encouragement. "Few men will save a lamb while a sow bear attacks them."

He squeezed his eyes together and grinned. "Will women like my story?" he asked. His eyes twinkled above his grin. He reminded me of Avdon. How I missed my brother.

"Women will know you will protect them even from bears," I said with a chuckle.

"Do not heal all the scars, then," he said.

"I would not if I could. But you want them to heal so they do not pull when you stretch your back."

Naphtali considered that. "I would not want it to slow the swing of my sword or stop the speed of my spear. Heal those if you can, please, Mother."

When he returned to his place beside his father and brothers, he did so proud of the scars raking his back.

Two years later, Naphtali brought me a gift. When I unfolded it, I found the tanned hide of a brown bear.

I looked up from the hide. "Is this —?"

He grinned. "The skin of the bear that attacked me? Yes. I found her. Her cubs have grown and no longer need her. I waited, for I knew you would care about the cubs. I tanned it for you for saving my life."

I buried my face in the soft fur. "This will keep me warm on cold nights."

Naphtali's grin slipped. "You have too many nights alone."

"Your father is a good man. He makes me happy. I am happy to be his concubine. I thank you for this bearskin. It will keep me warm when I snuggle under it."

On one of Esau's frequent visits, he pounded Naphtali on the back and told him how the women would love to hear the story.

***

We had lived in Succoth for seven years when Joseph was eight. Jacob had insisted he take Joseph to work with the sheep, protected by his brothers for a year. Although Rachel tried to keep him close, she had to give in to Jacob.

On the evening of Joseph's third day working with his father and brothers, Rachel shared her concerns. "I have only one child," she cried. "I cannot lose Joseph to the lions or wolves!"

"But the sheep love me, Mother." Joseph took Rachel's hand. His excitement spread through the room. "I do not grow tired. They and my brothers look out for me."

Jacob reassured her, telling her he kept the boy near him or one of the older boys for protection. Joseph considered himself a man, as the other sons had when they joined their father tending the sheep, but Rachel feared. I asked Dan and Naphtali to protect their beloved brother.

Jacob and the older boys stayed with Joseph, protecting him. Still, Rachel did all she could to protect him from danger, or from doing anything that might look dangerous.

After two years of this, Dan grumbled about it to me. "Joseph is no longer the baby Mother Rachel believes. Why can she not see he is a man?"

"As her only child, Mama Rachel fears for Joseph." I tried to soothe my son's concerns. "She waited many years for him. She fears she will lose him."

Dan grimaced. "She will lose him if she does not allow him to become a man. Does she not understand Jehovah protects him, as He protects Naphtali and me?" He stared at his feet, then looked up. "Even as He allowed the bear to attack Naphtali."

"His protection came as he directed your brothers to rush him home and my hands to stitch him up. I pray Jehovah continues to protect each of you."

A few months later, Naphtali came to me, complaining that Rachel did not allow Joseph to become a man. "All the animals love him. His gentleness draws them to him. Each comes when Joseph calls." Naphtali shook his head. "I would like the camels to come when I call."

"Mother Rachel will recognize he is a man soon. You continue to watch out for wild animals."

Naphtali shuddered. "They come looking for easy food, but we keep them away. Joseph is safe."

"Thank you, son. Keep him that way."

When Naphtali left me, I shook my head. What could I say to help Rachel accept her son's growth? It would be difficult, for she had never fully recovered from Joseph's birth. She had started her life story during the days she waited for his birth. She now returned to that task. She clung to her son as she clung to life.

Dinah

After twelve years living in Succoth, where Rueben and Simeon found wives from among Esau's daughters, we moved to live outside of Shalem, where we pitched our tents. Jacob took his older sons into the city and purchased a parcel of land from Hamor, a Hivite leader, paying him one hundred pieces of money. Jacob knew some of his sons required wives and hoped to find righteous women among these Hivite people. More importantly, he knew we needed the opportunity to add to our small provisions from the local market.

We set up our tents in a small family village of ten tents, with tents for each wife and tents for the unmarried sons to share. Along the outside, our men and women servants set up their smaller tents. We soon settled in.

I was happy to be near a city once more, even a small city like Shalem. It had markets and other women we could visit. I purchased the herbs I could not grow for my healing treatments. Zilpah found new food, some brought on camels from faraway lands. We sold our extra skeins of wool and purchased cotton there.

Dinah found the friends she had missed during the years of our travels. Young women befriended her when she visited the markets with her mother. At thirteen, she had become as beautiful as her mother, and Jacob always assigned guards to her when she left home. All eleven of her brothers were protective of her, but they spent much of their days in the fields and with the animals.

During that time, Rachel came to me, struggling with nausea once more. After an examination, I asked, "When was your last moon time?"

She rubbed her forehead, considering the question. "Since before we left Succoth. Two months? I thought it had stopped because of my age."

I chuckled. "No, Rachel. You are carrying a child."

"At my age?" she cried.

"Remember Sarah?" I asked. "She waited almost a hundred years, and her womb had dried. Yours has not."

"At last! Praise Jehovah. He is trusting me with another child." She smiled through her tears.

Once more, the sickness kept her close to her sleeping pallet, struggling to carry this child until time for its birth.

One late afternoon five months later, after our sons had left the camp with Jacob to help him with the birthing of camels. I sorted herbs for my healing remedies. As I worked, Leah's sobs penetrated my tent and thoughts. With concern, I pushed away from the table to investigate.

Rachel was sending a messenger off on his donkey as I pushed my tent door open. *Why is she up?*

"Did I hear Leah sobbing?" I asked Rachel.

She waved toward her tent with a nod. "She is in my tent." She turned to walk back to it.

My muscles tightened. "Why is she sobbing?"

I followed Rachel toward her tent.

"Dinah did not return from Shalem," she said with tears in her voice.

I gasped. "Where would she be?"

Before Rachel could answer, Zilpah strode toward us. "Did you say Dinah did not come home? Were her guards not with her?"

Rachel opened her tent door and invited us in. "She did not return from her friend's home in Shechem. Her guards could not find her."

"Has someone sent for Jacob?" Worry filled Zilpah's eyes.

Rachel nodded. "I just sent a messenger."

Leah sobbed, crumpled in the middle of the floor, with shaking breath, her hands covering her face. Zilpah and I rushed to kneel beside her. We rubbed her back and spoke words of assurance.

"Jacob will come soon." Rachel moved uncomfortably back to her seat, her hand covering her unborn child. "The boy sped away as fast as his donkey would carry him."

Leah's head bobbed, but her sobs did not slow. We all loved Dinah. As the only daughter among us, we doted on her. What could have happened to her? *Why would she be gone?*

Eventually, Leah's sobs slowed. We all moved to more comfortable seats. Zilpah stayed beside her, holding her hand.

Rachel laid on her pallet, too weak to sit.

I found a warm, damp cloth to wash Leah's face.

Nita brought us tea and cakes, and we settled in to wait for Jacob. The camel barns were on the far side of the fields.

We shared stories of Dinah, some serious, some funny. We giggled at the funny ones, even Leah. Some tales caused us to shake our heads. As we waited, the sun set, our heads drooped, and we drowsed on our hands.

Finally, near dawn, a shout from outside roused us. Our men had returned. We rushed out the tent door to meet them. Leah fell into Jacob's arms, sobbing her fears for their daughter.

Dan and Naphtali came to stand by me. "What has Dinah done this time?" Dan asked.

"She went to visit friends in Shalem yesterday morning," I murmured. "When her guards returned to get her, they could not find her."

"Did they go to all her friends' homes?" Naphtali asked, his brows lowered.

I shrugged. "They told Leah they did. I suspect they returned to the city, searching for her."

"She should not have gone to Shalem," Dan whispered.

"Why?" I asked. "She needs female friendship from others her age. We have no young women for her to gossip and share dreams with."

"What can they give her?" Naphtali asked. "They do not worship Jehovah. The men of Shalem do not honor Him. There is nothing there for her."

"You would not understand," I murmured. "You have always had the friendship and support of your brothers. Women need women friends."

"What friends have you had?" Naphtali asked.

"Zilpah, Leah, Rachel, and the other maidservants."

Dan grunted. "Dinah should have accepted the friendship of these same women."

"We are all old, like her mother," I said.

"I hope she learns something from this," Dan said.

I hoped she would. I feared the young women from Shalem had not treated her well. I prayed for her safety.

***

My heart broke for Leah as Jacob led her to her tent to comfort her. I mixed a weak sleeping remedy for her. She needed to sleep for a while, but not all day. I took it to her tent and gave it to Jacob for her.

Then I stumbled to my pallet. I had been up most of the night too. My nodding sleep on my fist provided little rest. The sounds of the camp muted when I closed my tent behind me.

Dan and Naphtali were men living together in a tent with Gad and Asher. I had learned to enjoy the peace of my tent. Most nights I only heard the sounds of guards protecting us.

On this day, although I expected to hear the sounds of people performing their daily activities, I heard nothing.

I slept fitfully. Fears for Dinah filled my dreams until I dragged myself from sleep. I washed, dressed, brushed my hair, and pushed through my tent door with a prayer. *Please, Jehovah, bring Dinah home to us. Protect her.*

I wandered to the cooking tent, hoping food would be available. Orna appeared at my elbow. "I thought you would wake up hungry. Sit. I will bring you a bowl of grains and a cup of tea."

I nodded my thanks and sat near a low table, my head drooping on my hand.

Orna brought the food. The fragrance and warmth of the food woke me.

I signaled for her to sit with me. "Is there word of Dinah yet?"

"Not yet. The sons grumbled about it, but Jacob sent them to work in the fields. Some wanted to ride to Shalem and tear the homes of Dinah's friends apart until they found her. Jacob refused, seeking to maintain a good relationship with his neighbors. He would not leap to unfounded conclusions."

A shout echoed through the camp, warning us of visitors. I swallowed the grains and stepped out to watch Jacob greet them.

"Jacob will want to offer them food," I said. "Are tea and cakes available?"

Orna nodded. "Enough for those men."

Tall, dark, haughty men, dressed in bright colors, dismounted from their earthy-smelling, pawing horses, followed by their many men servants. I felt darkness from them and shivered. *Jehovah, protect us. Protect Jacob.*

Jacob stepped forward to greet them. His measured steps thudded across the hard-packed earth, although between helping camels give birth and Dinah's disappearance, he had not slept the night before. He welcomed the two men, obviously father and son. Their men sat in a circle behind them.

Rachel joined us as we stacked cakes on trays, insisting she help serve the men. She took a tray to serve Jacob and his guests. I stood back, watching them sit on Jacob's rug beneath the feathery leaves of the terebinth tree. Reuben and Simeon's wives edged closer until I waved to invite them to join us.

As always, Jacob treated his guests with courtesy, graciously inviting them to eat the cakes and tea, waiting to hear their requests.

Rachel withdrew after setting the cakes in front of the men.

When the men had eaten, Jacob asked, "How can I help you, Hamor?"

Hamor. The one from whom Jacob purchased the land where we live. The younger man must be his son.

Hamor set his cup down and inhaled. "My son, Shechem, desires your maid to be his wife."

They have Dinah!

"Dinah is a beautiful young woman and precious to us," Jacob restrained himself. He knew they had her. "We have not seen her since yesterday. Is she safe?"

"She is well," Hamor said, glancing at his son.

Was that a warning? He knows where Dinah is.

Leah peered toward Jacob and his guests through her tent door.

Jacob had to be seething. This man and his son know where our Dinah is. How can he show such calm?

"Hamor, you have been good to me," Jacob said, smoothing his face. "But I must have my daughter returned from Shalem before I could ever consider giving her to your son, or anyone."

Hamor touched his son's shoulder. "Shechem loves your daughter and refuses to give her up."

What have they done to her?

Leah stepped from her tent and leaned against her tent pole, swaying. Was it from fatigue or emotion? I moved toward her. She would need my support. But tromping feet caused me to look the other way. All our sons marched from the fields toward their father and his visitors.

Rachel stepped next to Leah, and we edged closer toward the men, needing to hear their discussion.

Our sons ranged around the visitors, with Simeon, Reuben, and Levi closest to their father.

"Where is our sister?" Simeon demanded with a flushed face, widespread legs, and a piercing look. Always protective of Dinah, it did not surprise me he spoke for her.

"Shechem has kept her safe," Hamor said.

Shechem sat with crossed arms, his chin thrust out, and inhaled deeply.

Safe? Safe from what?

"Is she safe?" Reuben asked. His lip curled, his eyebrows furrowed, and his nose wrinkled. "Why would Shechem keep her safe?"

I wanted to hug him for his bold question.

Hamor pushed himself to sit taller, unwilling to allow these young men to intimidate him. With a warning glance at his son, he said, " My son loves your daughter. He asked me to get your permission to marry her." He cleared his throat. "He said she was wonderful last night."

Shechem clenched his fists and stirred.

Jacob stood with clenched fists. All eleven of his sons stepped closer. I feared they would take Shechem's life. Hamor and Shechem stood along with their men. Fists raised. Swords sounded in sheaths.

"He has her," Zilpah whispered in my ear frantically. "And he used her."

Our sons rumbled in the background. Jacob, his face red with rage, unclenched his fists and raised his hands, palms up and forward, to still the men's voices. "She *was wonderful* last night?" he grated. "Did he defile my daughter?"

Shechem swallowed and worked to smooth his face.

Our young men grumbled even louder. They would have shouted obscenities and drawn their swords in battle against our visitors if Jacob's control over them were not so great. Their righteous anger evident for all to see.

Dan stood across from me, his hand on his sword, his jaw tight. If Jacob had given the word, they would attack the men of Shechem. But Jacob was a man of peace. He would not attack visitors, even for this.

"Did he defile Dinah?" Jacob's voice softened, yet he filled it with greater danger.

Hamor stuttered, "N-no ... No. I do not believe he did."

Shechem glared at his father and set his left hand on his hip, the right hovered near his sword.

Jacob's face tightened and turned to Shechem, his voice calm and dangerous. Peril exuded from him. "Did you defile my daughter or not?"

Hamor spoke before Shechem could answer. "He may have. He should not have." His face had lost much of its swarthy color. "He made a mistake, overcome by your daughter's beauty and charm. But now he desires to redeem that mistake. He desires to marry her."

I inched closer. I would thump him if given the chance.

But Zilpah whispered, "Jacob will resolve this with Jehovah's help." She gripped my upper arm.

I swayed forward, wanting to choke the son and his father, but waited, willing to see what Jacob would do.

Our sons shouted angry complaints at the defilement of their sister, and I joined in soft approval of their wrath against Shechem's treatment of their sister.

Hamor's voice rose above the shouting of our sons, addressing Jacob. "My son longs for your daughter. I pray you agree to give her to him as his wife." He stared around at Dinah's brothers. "Make marriages with the women of our city. Dwell with us in our land. Trade with us. Become wealthy."

"How much more wealth do we need?" Leah whispered.

What wealth can compare to a safe, undefiled daughter? *You have taken that from us.*

A sudden silence filled the clearing, perhaps from a silent signal from Jacob and Hamor.

Shechem spoke into the silence before his father could prevent him. "Let me find grace with you Jacob and your sons, Dinah's brothers." He did not turn to look at the mob of brothers but held Jacob's eyes with his. "Whatever you ask, I will give it. Ask of me what you desire for a dowry and gift for her hand. I will give it. But give me the damsel to be my wife." Pleading filled his eyes.

What could he give Jacob for the defilement of a daughter? *Not even the fourteen years required by Laban would compensate.*

"Now he asks," Leah choked, "after defiling her."

"Listen," Zilpah whispered.

Simeon glanced at his ten brothers, receiving a nod from them. He stepped close to Jacob while keeping his hard stare on Hamor and Shechem. "We cannot allow this. It is a sin to give our sister to an uncircumcised man, one who has not made covenants with Jehovah."

Everyone held their breath. Jacob stood with a clenched jaw, silent, allowing Simeon to speak.

I held my breath, unsure of his demand, but proud of him for insisting Shechem become one of us, accepting Jehovah's covenant.

Simeon broke the silence, not asking his father's permission. "We will consent to this marriage if you become like us, making a covenant with Jehovah. But only if every man of Shalem accepts the covenant and the circumcision, will we give our sister to you, defiled as she is."

An angry murmur surged from his brothers.

Shechem's face blanched. Even Hitites had heard of Jehovah's covenant.

Jacob relaxed his fists. Perhaps he had considered a similar demand?

"We will take your daughters as our wives," Simeon continued. "We will dwell with you and become one with you."

No one spoke as Hamor and Shechem gaped at each other.

Simeon's words echoed through the camp. "But if you will not do as we *demand*, accept circumcision and make covenants with our God, we will seize our sister and leave this cursed land."

Shechem grinned.

He thinks he has our approval.

But Hamor swallowed over and over. "We must speak to the men of our city," Hamor said. "We cannot make an agreement including all the men of the city without their approval. We need time to discuss this with them."

I shuddered. *When will we get our sweet Dinah back? Simeon, demand they give her back.*

Simeon sneered. "You have three days? No more."

How can he say such a thing? *These men must* pay *for what they did to Dinah.*

"But our sister may not remain in your home to be defiled again. Send her home, or to her friend Ismet's house, where she will be protected and find safety." Simeon's gaze fell on the defiler. "Do not defile her again."

I shivered at the threat in his voice.

But Shechem did not. Before he could speak again, Hamor spoke. "She will go to Ismet's home. Three days will be enough to make our decision. We will advise you when the decision is made and the date of the rite."

Simeon's sharp nod said it all. That was all the time they had.

Hamor, Shechem, and their men prepared to leave. Jacob stood with them. Hamor took Jacob's hand and shook it, accepting the conditions set.

Our sons glared at the visiting men, who turned their backs to us, harsh words filling their lips. These men failed to understand the danger they faced.

Hamor murmured, loud enough for all to hear, "Do not fear, son. The men of our city desire to trade with this man to increase their wealth. The maid is yours."

Hah! They will not give Dinah to you.

Vengeance

Three days later, Hamor returned with the news of Shalem's agreement to Simeon's demand. They would perform the circumcision in two days. I served him cakes and stood near during the discussion.

Once again, Simeon warned him against changing the date. Jacob suggested he could oversee the rite, but Hamor refused. "Our priests know the rite."

"Do they know the covenants?" Levi asked.

"We will manage," Hamor said with a shrug.

"And Dinah?" Jacob asked. "Is she safely with Ismet? My guards have gone to her house to bring her home. Ismet's father would not answer the door."

Hamor nodded. "Yes, we took her there when we returned from your camp."

Did you? I doubt that. I suspect she continues to be a prisoner *in your home.*

We waited two days, praying for Dinah, and wondered when Dinah would come home. *Will they allow her to prepare for her wedding? How can she wed the man who defiled her? I pray she does not care for the man who defiled her.*

For three days after the circumcision rite, Dinah remained in Shalem. Before midday, Dan and Naphtali stopped by my healing tent.

"Simeon and Levi are missing," Dan said.

"We fear they have done something they will regret," Naphtali added.

Something they would regret? "What would they do?" I feared they had done something dangerous.

Naphtali cleared his throat and wrinkled his brow. "Anything. Shalem's men are weak from their circumcisions. We must find our brothers and sister."

"I will prepare." I feared our sons would return injured.

All the remaining sons rode down the trail toward Shalem.

I spent the next hours preparing poultices and tinctures inside, then rolling bandages in front of my tent. My deep concern for our sons made my stomach sick. I feared our sons would return injured.

Simeon and Levi returned first, bringing Dinah with them, all three splattered in blood and gore. Leah hurried from her tent at Levi's call and took Dinah into her tent. I stopped Levi and Simeon.

"Were you hurt? You are covered in blood."

Simeon smirked. "We are not injured. Do not fear. None of our brothers will have injuries. We go back to help them."

They mounted their horses and raced off toward Shalem.

What was happening? What had these two sons done? Where was Jacob? How did they do something horrible like this without him knowing? I chewed on my lip. This would cause problems between us and Shalem.

I tried to enter Leah's tent to examine Dinah, but she refused.

I returned to sitting in front of my tent, filled with dread. The blood on Dinah and her brothers still concerned me. What had Levi and Simeon done? Had Dan and Naphtali joined them? I returned to rolling bandages, offering prayers for their safety.

Rachel paced around the camp, pausing, then pacing again, unable to settle. I encouraged her to sit with me and drink some tea to calm herself, but she could not stay seated. I feared for her coming child. She would sit briefly, then leap to her feet and pace toward the head of the trail once more. "Where are you, Joseph?" she repeated.

Zilpah joined me. She grabbed a bandage and rolled it, setting it in a basket, ready to be used.

"Will you need these?" she asked.

I shrugged. "Levi says no, but what else can I do while I wait?"

"I pray Levi is correct, but what caused the blood on them?"

I shook my head, unable to speak. I had done all I could to be ready to heal any injury, so Zilpah and I threaded needles for stitching injuries as we sat beneath the terebinth tree. Rachel found her way to us, but could not sit or stand still, so intense was her turmoil.

Simeon's wife first joined us, silently helping to roll bandages. Then Reuben's wife came to sit with us. The two wives of our sons tucked the needles into a cloth to keep them clean.

I frequently lifted my head to stare down the trail, seeking evidence of our sons. At last, a faint dust cloud appeared over the trail. Zilpah and I joined Rachel to gaze down the trail and wait for answers.

The cloud of dust increased.

"What causes all the dust?" Zilpah asked.

"All our sons would not create that much dust," I said. A shiver of fear raced down my spine. *Are the men of Shalem coming to attack us? But Levi said our sons would not be injured.*

The cloud advanced toward us. Eventually, the upright shapes of people appeared. Too many to be our sons, and small ones among the taller ones.

Whining children and sobbing women moved slowly toward us and into the center of our camp, filling the open space in front of our tents with din. None paid much attention to us, the women whose home they had invaded. I led Rachel away and stood with her and Zilpah in front of her tent.

The large group of over a hundred women and children came to a halt, clinging to each other or soothing weeping children who collapsed at their feet. Their voices rose in protest and grief, complaining that our sons had destroyed their men and their homes.

"Why would they kill our men and burn our homes?"

"What will happen to us now?"

"They killed my husband and older sons.

"Why did they blame every man in Shalem? My men did nothing," they cried, among other complaints.

Leah and Dinah stepped out of their tent and joined us as we watched the milling women and children who stood in knots around us. The young women who were once Dinah's friends stomped past us with stiff backs and angry eyes. Ismet stepped forward and spat at Dinah's feet.

"Is she not your friend?" Rachel asked, disgust showing in her body and voice.

"Not now," Dinah answered in a strained voice.

She had washed and changed her clothing, but bleakness surrounded her. Her muscles twitched as she clenched and unclenched her fists.

Dinah will need much love to overcome her experience.

"What will Father do about this?" she asked through clenched jaws.

"I do not know," Leah said, gripping her crossed arms in front of her.

"Nothing good," I murmured.

Dan and Gad rode into sight behind the crowd of women.

Behind them, animals from Shalem complained as Naphtali, along with three brothers, and Jacob's herders pushed them past the camp toward the animal pens.

Behind them, clouds of smoke rose above the city. *What happened?*

I saw no injuries, but some women or children may have been injured. They would need food and shelter. I walked through them, asking about injuries. Some women had cuts on their hands or arms. I led them to the healing tent set up near mine, grateful to have prepared for injuries.

The women accepted my help, grumbling in low tones, unwilling to answer my questions. None complained. They stared forward, unspeaking. Their grief or anger kept them mute. When I asked about their injuries, their eyes flashed, and they bristled.

"We did not start this," I wanted to shout. "It was your men, your leaders who took our daughter and defiled her. You could have stopped it. Someone among you could have stopped it."

But, like them, I kept my frustrations inside and sought to treat them with kindness. These women had not hurt our Dinah. Hamor and Shechem had.

When I completed the bandaging, our maids showed them where to wash and gave them herb tea. They nodded and walked away to join the others.

Zilpah directed other maids to fill huge cauldrons with stew, while others mixed flatbread.

My stomach churned. What would Jacob do with all these people? Where was he?

***

Dan and Naphtali found me when I returned to my tent to change.

I scanned their bodies for signs of injury.

“We are well,” Naphtali said, gently lifting my hands away from his arms.

“We have no injuries,” Dan agreed. “The struggle ended before we arrived.”

“Before you arrived?”

Dan looked at his feet. “No man stood against us.”

“None of their men?”

Naphtali glanced at his brother. A silent message passed between them.

“Naphtali? Dan? What happened?”

Naphtali sighed. "You will hear. We cannot keep the horror of Shalem's last day from you."

"Last day?" I yelped. *The smoke.* "You burned the city. Why?"

Dan led me to my cushion. Together, he and Naphtali shared what they found when they arrived in Shalem. They watched me close as they shared the horrors they found, waiting for me to be sick. They forgot I had served as a healer for many years, seeing terrible things. My concerns were for the women and children who now sat in huddled groups. I had learned to love those who had sold me herbs in the market.

Their description of the deaths of all Shalem's men made me ill, but I did not allow it to show.

"We brought all the women and children here," Dan said, ending his story. "There were no men left to protect them."

"Some women tried to defend their men. They failed." Naphtali stared at his lap and twisted his hands together. "We brought their wealth and animals with us. Then we burned the city. There were too many for us to bury."

I closed my eyes. How could these two young men, our sons, have done this? How could the others have helped? What would happen to them? How would Dinah recover from the abuse? What about Leah, Simeon, and Levi? How would Jacob and Jehovah recompense them for this horror?

Solutions

When I returned to my healing tent, a few women who had concealed their injuries earlier waited for me. I bandaged their wounds and gave them the treatments that would help them heal.

As I walked through their encampment, I discovered many who had not brought blankets. I gathered all the extra blankets I could find to give to those in need.

For a time, Zilpah joined me in giving out blankets. When I searched for more in my tent, she scratched on my door. "Jacob is back. He has called a meeting at Rachel's tent."

"Does he know what happened?"

"Not much. That is the purpose of our meeting. Asher says Jacob wants to hear what happened from each of us." She left to tell the others.

I found one last blanket and took it to a woman who needed to cover her daughter, then hurried on to Rachel's tent. I arrived with Leah and Dinah. We entered and sat on cushions Rachel had scattered on her floor. *Did she expect us? Usually, he would go to Leah's tent, but she and Dinah were recovering.*

Leah and Dinah entered and found a cushion. Joseph, Asher, and Naphtali entered next. Naphtali grimaced at the others and came to sit beside me. The others entered, finding seats near their mothers. Dan sat on the other side of me, squeezing my hand briefly. Reuben found a place near Leah and Dinah with his wife. Simeon came with his wife, Levi tagging behind and sitting beside his brother.

Jacob entered last, staring around. He nodded toward his wives and concubines and his son's wives as he passed us, then opened his arms to Dinah. She rushed to him and accepted his embrace and soft words of comfort. When she sat next to Leah once more, he stepped to the seat beside Rachel's sleeping pallet and sat.

Only Dinah's soft sobs filled the tent. Everyone else gazed at Jacob, who took Rachel's hand. Leah's nervous smiles reflected our mood.

None of Jacob's sons smiled. Simeon and Levi focused on a spot behind Jacob's shoulder, unwilling to meet his eyes. Most of the others met his eyes, then stared at something in their laps. Even Dan and Naphtali shared an anxious unwillingness to meet their father's eyes.

"What happened here today?" Jacob finally asked. "Why are women and children gathered around fires in our camp?"

No one responded.

I glanced at Levi and Simeon, sitting near Leah. Although they sat with stiff, straight backs, they refused to look at Jacob. Soon, everyone looked at the two young men.

"Reuben?" Jacob asked. "What is this all about?"

I flinched. I expected him to ask Simeon or Levi.

Reuben shifted on his cushion. "We brought the women and children of Shalem here to protect them. No men are left there."

Jacob's eyebrows lifted. "No men to protect their women and children? What of Hamor? Shechem? The men who sit at the gates? Where did they all go?"

Reuben bit his lip and stared at his hands in his lap.

"Reuben?" Jacob said in a low, dangerous voice.

Reuben looked up. "Dead. Ask Simeon and Levi what happened." He gazed once more at his hands.

"Simeon? Levi?" Dismay filled the question. "What did you do?"

They continued to stare past Jacob's shoulder until he growled their names once more. Simeon glanced at Levi and set his wife's hand in her lap. "Should we allow those men to treat our sister as a harlot?"

That is his justification?

"What did you do?" Jacob deepened his growl, causing me to shudder.

"You did nothing," Levi spat at his father. "You allowed them to keep Dinah. You knew where she was. You knew Shechem held her, defiled her, and treated her as a harlot. We would not allow that."

"You did not trust me to resolve the problem?" Jacob asked.

Levi and Simeon shifted.

"Simeon?" Jacob demanded an answer.

"You said nothing when we insisted their men make covenants and accept circumcision," Simeon retorted.

"I had plans, but you did not give me an opportunity to implement them. You demanded their circumcisions. They would be sore today, three days after the rite. I intended to meet with them tomorrow, demand Dinah and concessions, when they could think about something more than their injuries."

"What plans did you have?" Levi demanded, almost shouting.

"We will keep our voices low. We do not share family problems with servants and do not need those camped outside to hear."

Levi clamped his mouth on his loud retort and sat back, staring at his father.

"It does not matter what plans I had to resolve this. You took away my right of vengeance. What did you do?"

Simeon glanced at Levi, then spoke again, puffing his chest out. "We waited until today, when those men would have no way to protect themselves."

I tore my gaze from Levi to look at Jacob's impassive face. *What will you do to them?*

"We took our vengeance on them and stopped a greater danger," Levi bragged. His knees bounced on the rug. "They planned to take more than Dinah. They wanted all our women and animals. They planned to overcome us during the night and kill you and your sons." He paused and looked at Leah. "Mother, you and Mother

Rachel, Mother Bilhah, and Mother Zilpah, my wife, and Reuben's, all would become servants or slaves to them. All our menservants and maidservants would become their slaves. We could not allow that."

I shuddered at the thought.

"What made you think the men of Shalem would do such a thing?" Jacob growled.

"I have a woman friend among their people, Najeem. She warned me of their plans." Levi sat taller and stared at his father.

"When?"

"After Shechem took Dinah."

"You knew when Hamor came seeking Dinah's hand? And you did not tell me? Why?"

"I had planned to tell you that day. You sat with our enemy before I could share with you." Levi's eyes begged his father to understand.

"And your suggestion that they all become like us?" Jacob's eyes shifted to Simeon.

Simeon blew out a breath. "It was a ploy. We could not overwhelm them in their strength. But we could take out our vengeance on them while they suffered."

Jacob's thick eyebrows drew together, becoming one. "Why did you not share with me after Hamor and Shechem left our camp? Why did you not allow me to decide?"

"Would you have killed them all as we did?" Levi demanded. "We two, Simeon and I, went to Shalem, killing every man. All their men are dead because we took our vengeance on them. Would you have gone with us? Would you have taken our brothers?"

Jacob leaned forward. "You destroyed them all? You took away my right of vengeance." He shook his head. "No. You make me stink in this land and all the lands around. Many men live in those lands. We are few compared to the hundreds who will descend on us, killing us and taking our women as slaves, because you claimed vengeance, murdering ..." The word hung above us all. "Yes, murdered all their men. Can we stand against their hundreds and live as they come against us to find recompense for the slaughter of their neighbors and families?"

Hundreds of men attacking us? No!

Simeon's head fell to his chest. "We did not consider the men of other lands. Perhaps we expected them to understand our right to defend our sister's purity."

"Would you have us allow Shechem and Hamor to treat our sister as a harlot?" Levi cried.

Jacob looked at Dinah. "We will discuss this alone. You have much to tell me."

She bowed her head. "Yes, Father."

What had Jacob heard about Dinah?

"What do we do now, Father?" Reuben asked. "We brought Shechem's women and children here to protect them from wild animals and marauding men. They and their animals would not be safe there. What do we do with them now?"

Jacob dropped his head into his hands and shuddered, then turned to Zilpah. "Discuss this with the women of Shalem. Give them a choice. Take Rachel if she is well enough to walk a distance." Shaking his head, he turned back to Levi and Simeon. "You have made enemies of these women and children. They will not see your bringing them here as a blessing. You took them as plunder. You claimed their wealth. What more can they think?" He stared at Simeon, Levi, and then the other sons.

"Simeon and Levi brought that wealth here," Judah said.

"And you others are as guilty as Simeon and Levi." Jacob turned his stare toward Judah.

"We did not kill any of those men!" Naphtali cried.

"But you willingly accepted the plunder. You brought their animals to our paddocks."

"To protect them," Reuben said.

Every son stared at their father. Jacob shook his head and rubbed his eyes.

"You have made me stink. I must go speak to Jehovah to learn what to do about this stench." Jacob stood.

"You have not eaten your evening meal," Zilpah said.

"Nor will I eat until I receive an answer from Jehovah." Jacob gazed at each of his wives and concubines. "Are all the women and children from Shalem cared for? Did any receive any injuries?" He turned toward me.

"I walked among them, searching for any injured," I said. "I cared for those I found. I suspect more will come to the healing tent tomorrow for assistance. They did not trust me. None would speak to me."

Jacob nodded.

"I fed them," Zilpah added. "Their children have eaten, and we provided blankets for those with none."

"They are confused," I added. "I will do what I can for them."

"Go tomorrow and find their leaders," Jacob said, nodding to Zilpah, then to Rachel. "Talk to them. Learn what they want us to do with them. We will give them what they desire if we can. Do they desire we leave them here, take them to family in other lands, or take them with us? We must know what they want by tomorrow."

Rachel nodded. "We will ask them."

If they answer.

***

I returned to the healing tent the next morning. As I expected, women waited for my help.

"What will you do with us?" one asked.

I gazed into her eyes. "What would you like us to do for you?"

She bit back her anger. "You cannot bring our men back." She huffed. "I have visited with others." She flicked her eyes toward the open tent door. "Most are grateful for the protection your men provide. I heard the lions out there last night." She shuddered. "We would not have survived against them, or the roving men seeking women to defile. We are safe here. No one attacked us."

I shuddered at the thought. "Our men know better than to attack women. Their father, Jacob, will not allow harm to come to you within our community."

"We will gladly offer ourselves to you to be your maidservants in return for your protection. Some of our women are already helping in the cooking tents. I would join them, but my daughter is too young to be near the fires."

"We will find something for you to do," I said.

Throughout the day, the women gathered in small groups, speaking in low tones. Sometimes their voices lifted until others hushed them. The young women were among the angriest.

I watched for Jacob's return all that day. He did not stride across the fields toward our tents until the next morning, a thoughtful frown on his face.

Joseph stepped into my healing tent, telling me of Jacob's return and requesting that we meet in his mother's tent once more.

I finished bandaging a woman's burned hand and excused myself to stride to Rachel's tent, where I found a place next to my sons. I was last to enter and sit in silence, as the others did, waiting for Jacob to lift his head and share with us what he learned from Jehovah.

"Father," Joseph murmured. "Everyone has gathered. We are all here, waiting for you to share with us what Jehovah wants us to do."

Jacob nodded and took his time lifting his head. "Jehovah spoke to me once more." His gaze focused on Simeon and Levi. "You caused us and others many problems, pains, and sorrows. It will take time and great repentance, but Jehovah has an answer for that."

Simeon and Levi cleared their throats, as if preparing to answer.

Jacob spoke before they could. "We have much to do." He turned to Rachel. "What do the women of Shalem desire?"

Will she have the same answer I would give?

"Zilpah and I found Noora, Hamor's wife, whom the others recognize as their leader." Rachel glanced at Zilpah, who nodded for her to continue. "Most desire to stay with us. They will become our servants if you will teach their young sons to herd and care for the animals."

They had.

Jacob nodded. "That is good. With so many more animals, we will require their help." He gazed around the circle, peering into our eyes. "We travel to Bethel to sacrifice, then on to Mamre and my father. Too many in the lands surrounding us are angry. We are no longer safe here."

Because Simeon and Levi took vengeance.

The two sons swallowed and bent forward, their shoulders caving in.

"Jehovah commanded us to put away all the strange gods among us and become clean. We will go up to Bethel. There, I will make an altar to Jehovah, who answered me on my day of distress and has been with me since."

A murmur filled the tent. Laban had gone through all our baskets looking for his images. Certainly, everyone here would have disposed of any not belonging to him. Or had some purchased images in Shechem?

"My instructions are for all who live among us," Jacob added. "Reuben, gather our guests. Bring all our maidservants and menservants. Naphtali, go call in the herders. Tell them to enclose the animals in the paddocks for safety. They must hear this command

— Jehovah's will — from me. We can stay here no longer. We must leave tomorrow before the men of other lands come to fight against us."

Reuben stood and walked out. Naphtali followed. The rest filed out behind them.

Naphtali mounted a horse and rode toward the far fields and paddocks to tell the herders to come.

The women of Shalem brought their children close, staying a distance from Jacob. Our maidservants and menservants found places behind them. Soon, herders rode in from the far fields.

When Naphtali returned and nodded to his father that all from the fields were here, Jacob climbed up on a log so all could hear him.

"We are no longer safe here," he said. He nodded to Shalem's women. "Men from other lands will hear of your losses and come seeking your wealth, your women, your children, and your animals." He glanced at Rachel, who stood on the ground beside his table. "Rachel tells me you choose to stay with us. We will include you in our community."

He stared into the crowd of women and children, taking time to look into the eyes of the women. Many, whose expressions had been angry as they gathered, now softened under his gaze.

"We leave here in the morning. Today we must prepare. Go through your belongings. Bring all your strange gods, your images of gods you once worshiped. They must stay here. We must become clean of this evil. Prepare to come before our God, even Jehovah, who will save and protect us."

Murmurs filled the crowd.

"When do we receive our assignments?" Noora asked. I had seen her with many of the injured. They had identified her as their leader.

"Soon. Perhaps on the coming ride. Your sons will learn to herd and care for animals. We will protect you as you become one with us."

Jacob spoke to the herders, menservants, and women servants, telling them how to prepare to come before Jehovah.

The crowd dispersed, moving toward tents and campfires. Many chattered together, discussing the move. For most of us of Jacob's family and servants, the move was not unusual. We had moved before.

I went to the healing tent, packed my supplies, and cared for last-minute injuries. Aqeela entered as I set jugs of healing solutions into a basket, tucking bandages around them for protection.

"Mistress Bilhah?" she asked. Her wariness caused me to turn.

"Are you in need of healing?"

"No, mistress. I have some training in healing. Can I work with you?"

I glanced up, surprised. "I have no time to test your skills and abilities. But I will be happy to have you help me pack this tent. I will test you as we travel."

Aqeela nodded and found a basket and filled it with dried herbs. Soon we had everything prepared for the move.

"I will stay here with your baskets and trunks," she offered. "You must have a tent full of possessions you need to prepare to move."

I nodded and glanced around for someone else to look after my healing supplies, although I had no reason to distrust her.

"I will keep others away. No one will touch them except your men when they are ready to load them onto the camels."

I bit my lip. I had to pack my tent. Nurit passed the healing tent. "Have you packed everything already?"

"I have with Aqeela's help. Would you stay here with her to ensure all is well when the men come to pack it?"

Nurit grinned. "Aqeela is a good woman. I will stay with her. Orna has started packing your possessions."

"Thank you." I turned to Aqeela. "I apologize. I do not know you well enough to trust or mistrust you. I do not want to cause hurt feelings, only protect my healing supplies."

I will not have time to make more *if I could find the correct herbs.*

I hurried to my tent and found Orna working to fill trunks and baskets with my possessions. Before the sun rose, both tents were ready for the men to load them onto camels.

The night before, I prayed, begging Jehovah to give Jacob the best solution to our problem. When he spoke of his answer, I knew Jehovah had answered my prayers. I knew we were to leave this land. Still, I worried about the coming journey. It was a terrible time for Rachel to travel with her poor health and coming child. Worse, I feared the hundreds of men who threatened to take our lives in retribution for the men of Shechem.

Oh, Simeon and Levi. Why did you not consider them?

Journey to Bethel

We traveled toward Bethel, fearing an attack from the men of the surrounding lands. Jacob assigned Simeon and Levi to follow at the back of our company to ensure we lost no animals and no armies raced to attack us from the back as a consequence of their rash actions.

As a concubine, I rode toward the front along the dusty trail. I looked into the dry hills, searching for the men who would attack us. Everyone kept their heads moving, watching for angry armies, looking into every dry wadi, every fold in the hills, wondering when those angry and greedy men would assail us.

Simeon and Levi returned each evening coughing and covered with dust. The other sons did not get off much better. They had received dirty, hard assignments as well. All the sons joined the guard each night, watching for an attack. Only Jacob and his guards rode at the front, out of the dirt and dust kicked up by the animals.

I pulled a scarf from the bag behind my saddle early on the first day and wrapped it around my face to protect it from the dust. The women who rode near me did the same. The servant women and the women of Shalem saw our scarves and followed our example for themselves and their young children.

The first night, as the sons came for food, hacking up the dust of the day from their throats, I warned them to wrap a scarf or something across their mouths and noses to keep the dust out. "You will be sick and miserable if you do not."

"Wear something across your face," Jacob added from beside the campfire. "We need you alert and healthy if we are assaulted . We do not know when or where the men of these lands will come upon us."

The young sons of Shalem's women received scarves from our herders and had not suffered as our sons did.

Only Levi refused. He came to my healing tent after two days of travel, asking for help. I mixed him a tea to clear out the dust, leaving out the honey. He could drink the bitter tea.

"Maybe you will listen and wear a scarf to protect you when you are told," I said when he complained.

Simeon and Joseph laughed. Levi ducked his head and grumbled. After that, he wore a cloth across his face.

Leah and I took turns riding with Rachel, covering our faces to keep the dry, gritty dust out. Rachel's health had worsened during the week of our struggle to regain Dinah from her defilers. I feared for her unborn child. It was still too early for his birth, and Rachel was no longer young. I kept my concern about her health from her.

While I examined Rachel in her tent while we waited for Dinah's return, she admitted her fears to me. "I fear I will not survive the birth of this child."

"You will give birth to and raise this son." I hoped Jehovah would support my confidence.

Now, as she slumped in her camel's saddle, I feared for her. Though her nausea had improved before Dinah's defilement, it now returned worse than ever. She ate so little I worried about her child and her life. How could he grow? I nudged my camel forward, allowing Leah to fall back.

When my camel plodded along next to Rachel's, she lifted her head. I expected her to moan. Instead, she surprised me.

"Bilhah, I need to apologize," she said, her voice low and filled with misery.

"Apologize? Why would you need to apologize?" I lifted my eyebrows. I could think of nothing requiring her apology.

"I forced you to become Jacob's concubine, forced you to give him children in my place. I wanted children so desperately, I would not listen to your pleas." She drew in a ragged breath.

Before I could speak, she held a hand up and continued. "I apologize for not listening to your needs and forcing you to become Jacob's concubine rather than asking him to find you a husband. I wanted Jacob as my husband, with no other wives, but Father decided differently."

She suppressed a sob, and I set a hand on her arm.

"And then I forced you to become part of our family, making three and then four of us competing for his attention. All I wanted was Jacob's attention. I was selfish. I could never have it all. I never will." She stared at me, her eyes begging forgiveness.

I swallowed. "I was angry the first days after you insisted. I wanted a man who loved me, who wanted me, and only me. Jacob did not want me. He loved you then, as he loves you now."

"He loves you now as well." Rachel massaged her bulging stomach. "I see it in the way he treats you. I understand now and honor you and him for your obedience to me."

"Jacob is an honorable man. I knew he was when he accepted Leah and agreed to work another seven years for you. He treated Leah as a woman he cared for. When I set my anger aside and considered him, I knew he would treat me well." My face warmed. My experience with Jehovah's whispering was too sacred to share. "And he treated me well, especially those first nights. I know now that Jehovah had a plan for me and you. Your children will be a blessing to you and Jacob. Jehovah has blessed me."

Rachel smiled and cleared her throat. "There is more. I apologize for claiming your sons. That was unfair of me. You suffered through the nausea and childbirth. I had no right to claim your children." Her lips pressed together in a slight grimace, and touched her stomach once more.

I sank into my memories for a moment, then looked up and smiled. "Yes. But you did what you needed to do. I forgave you long ago. My Dan and Naphtali know I am their mother. You treated them well, and they enjoyed the time you spent with them and the help you gave them. It was good for our sons to grow up together as brothers with four mothers who loved and cared for them." I leaned across the space between our camels and touched her arm. "Now you must relax and care for yourself and your coming child."

Tears welled up in her eyes. "How can you be so forgiving?"

Our camels separated, walking around a boulder.

"I grew to love you when we were girls and your mother assigned me to be your maidservant. I felt your pain when Laban forced you to wait those years for Jacob, and after. Then you suffered as Leah had children and you could not." I stared into her eyes, hoping she would feel my sincerity. "I saw your need and expected you to call on me. I did not expect it to be as fulfilling as it became. But I gained sisters who love me now. Perhaps not sisters born of the same mother, but sisters who live together, sharing the same man."

The camels came close again, and Rachel's hand found mine and grasped it. "I do love you, Bilhah. I have learned to appreciate the love we share."

I gripped her hand. "That is why I forgave you years ago. I loved you when we were girls. I will always love you."

We released our hands and rode together, lost in our thoughts. I did not need Rachel to apologize, because I had forgiven her long ago. Still, her words healed the last of the pain I carried.

Then Rachel cried out, shifting in her saddle. "Oh! Ow!"

"What is it?" I urged my camel closer.

She shook her head. "A sharper cramp caused Benoni to move within me. It hurt."

She had called the babe Benoni before, a name meaning 'son of sorrow'. I prayed there would be no sorrow for her or her child.

"Riding is not good for you."

"Jacob stops earlier to help me. We will stop again soon," Rachel said with a sigh.

"I hope it is before your child pushes himself out." I prayed she would keep this child within her until after we reached our destination.

Not long after that, Leah took my place and I fell back in the line.

Noora rode from behind and urged her camel to plod next to mine. She had brushed her fine clothing of a city leader's wife, but it carried the dust of the journey. She frowned. "I am concerned about Rachel. She does not look good."

"As am I." I kept my gaze on Rachel. "I do not know if I have the experience to help her if the child comes early or if it is a difficult birth. I have never helped a woman so ... so old, and fear she will have problems."

Noora nodded. "You are an excellent healer. You did well with my women. I could not help them, for I left all my healing supplies behind. Your young men burned them."

Surprised, I looked at Noora. "You are a healer?"

She nodded. "I am."

My camel walked around a bush growing in the trail. When I returned to Noora's side, I asked, "Did you help deliver the children of your village?"

"All but my own children."

"Have you aided in difficult deliveries?" I glanced into her eyes, searching for the truth before looking forward again.

"Just last month I saved the life of a mother and child. The mother was younger than your Rachel, but her babe struggled to survive within the womb."

"Rachel's first child caused some problems. Her sickness lasted much longer than usual." I glanced up to see how well she rode. It looked like she slept. "This time, she is older and has struggled to eat. Worse, though I have not shared this with her, the child is not lying properly. I do not know how I can deliver him and keep them both alive."

I had not shared my fears with anyone else, and speaking the words to another who knew the responsibility helped relieve them.

"That is serious," Noora said. She grimaced in thought. "I have delivered a few children with this problem, and my mother, also a healer, delivered some. It is a dangerous time for both mother and child."

"Will you help me when it is time for Rachel to deliver?"

Noora chewed on her lip and inhaled. "I rode forward to offer my help. If we lose her or her child, will your people blame me?"

"It will be a difficult birth. I will explain to the family how challenging it may be. I will be there with you. If they blame you, they will have to blame me as well."

"Then I will help you." She slapped her camel on the side.

With her slap, I waited for the camel to run as horses would, but it continued to plod forward.

"Shall we visit her now?" Noora asked.

Stepping out of line to ride forward to Rachel, we urged our camels to plod a little faster.

"Rachel," I said, touching her arm.

She shook herself and opened her eyes.

"Are you well?"

"For now," she mumbled, closing her eyes and grimacing.

Noora glanced at me with eyebrows raised.

I nodded.

"Nausea?" I asked.

"The swaying with every step ..." Her voice drifted off.

"Swaying would not help," Noora muttered.

"Rachel, do you remember Noora?"

She opened her eyes and squinted across to Noora. "Yes. I remember you. You are the leader of the women from Shalem."

"I was. Now that is you," Noora said.

"No, not me." Rachel gave a small shake of her head. "Leah has always been the first wife and the one with responsibility for our home and women. If you need something, go to her. She will be more available now Dinah is back with us."

"I see her visiting with the women. Is that why?"

"Yes," I said. "Even as we travel and live in tents, Leah is responsible for us." I smiled at Noora. "Rachel, Noora is a healer. She has helped many more women give birth than I. Most of my experience comes from the ten children in our family."

"There are ten?" Noora asked.

"Twelve, but I needed help with my two."

The three of us giggled.

"Rachel," I said. "I asked Noora to help me when your time comes."

"And you agreed?" Rachel asked, her face twisting in her sickness.

"I offered," Noora replied. "I see you are not well, and that makes delivery difficult."

"I feared so."

I glanced at Noora, and she frowned.

"You will be well," I said. "Jehovah is with you."

"And He holds my life in His hands. I pray He allows me to live to raise my son."

I set my hand on her arm. "I pray He does. Your son needs you, and we do not want to live without you."

Rachel's hand covered her stomach. "If I do not live, he will still have three other mothers. Teach him well. Tell him I wanted him. I will give my life for his."

"I hope you do not have to," Noora said. "Do you mind if I examine you this evening? I can be more prepared if I know what to expect."

Rachel nodded, grimacing.

"Sleep if you can stay on your camel," Noora said.

"I will not fall. Jacob has secured me to my saddle." She closed her eyes. "Yes. I will sleep."

Noora and I slowed our camels and fell back in line behind her, discussing the needed herbs, salves, and remedies. It did not take long for us to become friends.

***

That evening, Noora and I went together to examine Rachel. She had eaten the thin soup Zilpah prepared especially for her, filled with nourishment. When we entered Rachel's tent, she lay back, rubbing her stomach.

In turn, we ran our hands across where the babe lay. I felt the child's body laying sideways, in the wrong position for his birth.

I glanced at Noora. She nodded.

"Your child seems to be comfortable like that," Noora said.

"It is not comfortable for me," Rachel moaned. "He kicks me here." She pointed at one side of her stomach, "And here." She pointed to the other side of her stomach.

"He is stretching," Noora soothed.

"But should he not be preparing for birth? Joseph never stretched across my body near the time of his birth."

Noora and I shared a worry as we looked at each other.

"What is the problem?" Rachel asked. "I see it in your eyes."

"He is not in the proper place for birth," Noora said. "Perhaps we can turn him. But it will hurt."

"Can we wait until after we reach Bethel?" I asked. "Jacob will stay an extra day there to offer a sacrifice to Jehovah. With Rachel's difficulty, he will ask for extra blessings."

"Can we convince him to rest before we reach Bethel?" Noora asked.

"The Sabbath is soon," Rachel said. "He will stop to celebrate the Sabbath. Can I wait that long?"

Noora chewed on her lip. "Possibly."

When we were alone, Noora shook her head. "I fear for her life. It will be difficult to turn the babe."

"I have never needed to turn a child within the womb. I am grateful you are here to help."

"Rachel's child will have to be turned more than any I have needed to reposition. It will hurt her."

"She is tough." I glanced toward her tent. "But she has never been this weak."

"Between her weakness and the baby's position, I fear for her," Noora said.

"We must tell Jacob."

I led her to where Jacob sat, discussing the next day's travel with his sons. I stood at the edge of the clearing, waiting for him to notice me.

He soon glanced up and saw me, then stood and joined us.

"Bilhah, have you been to care for Rachel?"

"I have," I said. "I took Noora with me. She served as Shalem's healer, helping their women give birth. She agreed to help me with Rachel."

"Is it dangerous for Rachel?" Jacob lowered his voice, his love and concern for Rachel showing on his face. He stared into Noora's eyes. I suspected he wondered how he could trust this woman, the wife of the man who had betrayed him, with his beloved wife's life.

Noora chewed on her lip, then nodded.

"Trust Noora Jacob. I do. We have discussed the problem, and she has had more experience with Rachel's difficulty. I trust her."

He nodded. "Tell me your concerns, Noora."

She swallowed. “I fear her life is in the hands of your God. If we cannot move her child, I do not know if we can save her. I am uncertain, but perhaps we can save the babe.”

Jacob groaned and dropped his head into his hands.

Our sons, watching us with their father, rumbled in their concern.

“What can I do?” Jacob asked. “How can I save them both?”

I put my arms around him, and he pulled me close. “Bilhah, I will depend on you to help my son come into this life and to save Rachel,” he sobbed. “Can you do that?”

“I do not know,” I mumbled through my tears. “I have not the skills. I pray Noora does, but if not, we cannot blame her.”

He looked over my shoulder at Noora. “Do your best, I beg of you, Noora. I need Rachel and my son to live.”

“Call on your God, Jacob. This is in His hands.”

Jacob moved my arms from around him and took Noora’s hand. “I promise you, Noora, if you do your best to save them both, I will not blame you if you fail. I will pray to Jehovah.”

Later, I saw Jacob slip into Rachel’s tent. I suspected he knelt beside his beloved wife and called on Jehovah’s blessings.

Benjamin

The next day, Rachel slumped over her camel, unable to sit up. Leah and I hurried toward her, but Leah's camel arrived first. She touched Rachel's forehead. "You burn."

Her words seared through me. She would already struggle to give birth to this 'child of her sorrow.' Burning would not help her at all.

Leah did not signal for me to come closer, but I watched her closely from a short distance away.

When Jacob called a halt for the night, Tzevi, the head manservant, hurried to raise Rachel's tent. As soon as he could, Jacob carried her to rest inside. Later that night, he once again slipped inside her tent.

Each morning, Rachel's tent came down last, after everything else was ready to go. Jacob carried her to her waiting camel and secured her on the saddle. I rode beside her, fearing for her and her child. She sagged against the ties that held her on the camel and waved away the water and food I offered. She could not continue like this.

Jacob brought his camel to a stop early on the fourth afternoon. I gazed around at the desert spot, confused.

"This is Bethel," he said. "We have arrived."

I stared, seeing only desolation, an empty space along a narrow trail through the desert.

"Arrived?" Leah asked.

"Yes. This sacred place is where Jehovah came to me, promising me the blessings of Abraham the night after I fled Esau's anger."

Not much to this place, but if this is where Jacob plans to stop, I am grateful. Rachel can rest.

When Tzevi and his men had prepared Rachel's tent, Jacob carried her in with a tenderness he did not often share with me.

When he had her settled, he took his sons to collect stones to build an altar.

"Will she survive?" Dan asked me after helping.

I shrugged. "She is in Jehovah's hands."

"What can we do?" Dan shuffled his feet.

I inhaled a tight breath. What could anyone do for Rachel? "Pray? Fast? Call on Jehovah, for only He can save her." I hope with His help, Noora and I can keep both Rachel and her child alive. My heart was breaking.

"Then we will fast," he said. "I will speak to the others. You are busy caring for Mother Rachel. If I can do anything more, let me know."

"You are a gentle, religious man like your father." I smiled and touched his face.

That evening, it surprised me to see only children come for food. Everyone else, members of our family and household, as well as those new ones added from Shalem, refused to eat. All were fasting for Rachel and her unborn baby's health.

On that high ridge, surrounded by rocks, we knelt together on rugs in the dust to pray, as Jacob led us, beseeching Jehovah for Rachel's life.

After midmorning the next day, Jacob and Reuben carried Rachel to a blanket prepared for her to observe the sacred rite of sacrifice. Leah and Dinah sat on either side of her, helping her sit upright, offering her cool water. I sat with Zilpah beside them.

Once again, during the sacred ritual, a tingle ran through my body from my toes to my head, and a warmth filled my soul. Jehovah had accepted our offering.

Jacob offered thanks for our protection and gave a portion of the sacrificial lamb to Zilpah to add to the meal she and her cooks prepared for us.

Rachel insisted on sitting with us at the sacrificial feast, although she ate little.

Before the feast ended, Joseph and Naphtali helped her to bed.

When Noora and I entered her tent, I knelt next to her and brushed the hair off her face. "We need to move your child," I murmured into her ear.

Her eyes opened a slit. "Move him?"

"He is not lying in the right position to be born."

She moaned. "I remember. I hoped he would move on his own."

Noora knelt beside Rachel. "It may hurt, for I will have to push on your stomach to move him."

"Will that make it easier for me to give birth to him?"

"If he stays put."

She brought her hands to her face and groaned. "Do what you must. Benoni must have a safe delivery."

We worked with him, pushing on him from the outside, me on one side and Noora on the other, until the child moved his head down. Rachel's grimaces and soft groans were her only complaints.

"Sleep now," Noora said. "You need to rest."

Noora and I spoke in my tent later. "Children like these are difficult to help bring into the world. They get comfortable and do not like to stay in the proper position for birth. If he moves ..." She chewed on her lip. "I do not know if I can save Rachel. We do not have a way to save them both."

"What do you expect?" My shoulders slumped, and I stared at nothing.

"If he stays where we put him, the birth should not be as difficult as we expect. If not ..." She huffed out her breath. "If not, we will lose one or both of them."

After Noora left my tent, I sat weeping. The tears dripped between my fingers, held to my face. How would we live without Rachel? How would she live without Benoni?

On the Sabbath the next day, we rested. I prayed the rest would help heal the sickness within Rachel's body before Benoni's birth.

I sat outside my tent, listening to Rachel moan.*What can I do to help her and Benoni live?*

'Do your best,' a soft voice murmured in my ear. *'Rachel is in My hands. If I take her home, it is My choice. Save the child.'* A tear slid down my face.

Jacob slipped into Rachel's tent once more.

We had stopped only long enough for Jacob to offer sacrifice and worship. Jacob wanted to push on to Mamre. "Perhaps the healer there can help you save Rachel."

On the trail the next morning, Rachel cried out. Leah rushed forward to help. Noora and I were close behind.

"Benoni comes," she moaned. "The pains are harsh."

Her words sent shivers through me. *Not here! Not now!*

Leah rushed forward to stop the caravan while Noora and I moved our camels to either side of her. Noora touched her forehead and gazed at me. Her eyes warned me of the burning I also felt when I touched her body.

I inhaled, mustering all the calm I could find within me before saying to Rachel, "Your Benoni wants to be born. It is time."

"Take care of him. He will need you to tell him how much I loved him, how much I wanted him," Rachel murmured through her moans.

"You can tell him."

"I fear not."

Jacob shouted at Tzevi to prepare Rachel's tent and hurried to her side. I moved away, giving him space to order the camel to kneel and lift her from the saddle.

***

Noora and I followed Jacob and Rachel into the tent. He laid her on the pallet with the gentleness I had learned to expect from him.

She had waited until almost too late. Benoni wanted to come into the world now.

Jacob helped strip off Rachel's clothing. Aqeela came in long enough for Noora to send her for both hot and cool water. We needed to cool her body and to have clean water to wash in.

Noora examined Rachel.

"Can you save them?" Jacob asked. "Please save them." I have never seen a man filled with such agony. Cords stood out on his neck, his shoulders curved forward, and his face had lost all color.

"I can save the child. Saving the mother is in your God's hands." Noora shook her head.

"The babe stayed in the right position," she murmured. "He and his mother may both live."

But Rachel's moans softened, her head fell to the side, and she became too weak to push out her child.

Jacob sat beside Rachel until she no longer responded to him. "Rachel, my love. You must waken. You must push our child into the world. Please Rachel. Please, Jehovah, bless my wife."

He dabbed a damp cloth on her head as he had with each of the rest of us, murmuring prayers and pleas to Rachel and Jehovah.

Noora commanded me to help her push on the top of Rachel's stomach with each squeezing pain. "The child needs out now!"

The time it took for the child to move through Rachel's body to be born felt like forever. Sweat dripped off my face. The stench of blood and fear overwhelmed me. I was aware only of pushing out Rachel's child.

Push. Push. Rest. Rest. Push. Push. She no longer responded!

"He comes," Noora called. "Keep pushing."

Push. Push. Rest. Rest. Push.

The child moved down. At last, he was out.

"He is here!" Noora cried. "Jacob, Rachel, you have a son."

She handed me the baby boy, and I rubbed his back. His robust cry filled the tent.

The babe lives!

Jacob leaned toward Rachel. "We have a son. Rachel." He touched her. "Rachel? Rachel?"

Noora leaned forward with one blood-covered hand and felt for Rachel's heartbeat. She moved her hand to another place on her neck, seeking the heartbeat elsewhere.

She glanced up at Jacob and shook her head. "She is gone."

"Gone? My Rachel is gone? Nooo!" His howl caused my stomach to clench.

Leah rushed in. She must have stood just outside the tent door.

Jacob slipped his arms beneath Rachel's thin shoulders and pulled her to him. "No, Rachel! Do not leave me. How will we get along without you? How will I raise our son alone? Do not go! Rachel. Oh, Rachel. What has happened?" he keened.

Little Benoni's wails joined those of his father's.

I rocked the babe, trying to soothe him. Tears streamed down my face, my pain for Jacob, for Benoni, and for me. I had never seen such sorrow.

"She was not strong enough," Noora whispered. "I saved the baby. I could not save his mother. I tried. I am so sorry."

Eventually, Jacob allowed Rachel's body to lie on the pallet and took the babe from my arms, clutching him to his breast. "Oh, baby. What will we do with you? How will we feed you?" Tears streamed down his face onto the blanket covering his newborn son.

"Rachel called him Benoni." Leah had stood in silence since she entered, but her face showed her grief.

Jacob lifted his head and stared at her, his lips trembling. "Son of my sorrow?" He shook his head. "No. I will not remember his birth with sorrow for the rest of our lives. His name is Benjamin, son of my right hand. He will stand beside me always." He ducked his head into the bundle of baby and sobbed.

Benjamin's squall increased, needing to suckle and a mother's calm, loving touch.

"How will we feed him?" Leah asked.

Noora wiped the blood from her hands. "Haala gave birth a month ago. She has an abundance of milk. I will ask her to share with this poor, motherless child." She dropped the bloody towel and strode from the tent.

Sooner than I expected, she pushed the tent door aside again. A young woman stood with Noora. "This is Haala. She sat outside the tent, waiting for your call. Your God warned her to be ready to act as nursemaid for your child."

The young woman, Haala, knelt next to Jacob. "Your son is hungry. He needs food to stay strong. I will feed him with my son. He will live to honor his mother. May I take him?"

She took care to avoid looking at Rachel's body lying on the bed.

Jacob resisted, but Benjamin's increased wail encouraged him to dry his tears on the blanket and hand Benjamin to Haala. "Bring him back to me after he eats, if you would."

The young mother tucked the baby close, soothing him, and left the tent.

Jacob stood with his shoulders drooping, his head hanging, and his chest caved in. He seemed to shrink in front of us. Only his soft sobs filled the silence of Haala's leaving.

Now what do I do?

I searched Noora's face, seeing the guilt on her face that I felt as well.

"I tried to save her," she said. "I tried."

"Jehovah needed her home," Jacob mumbled. "You did all you could. There is no blame for you."

Leah wiped her tears on her sleeve. "She is at rest with Jehovah. Blessed is the Lamb of God."

Jacob took Leah in his arms and wept on her shoulder. I put my arms around them, and his arm slipped around me.

Noora gently said. "I have much to do to prepare her body. Go mourn together."

I wiped away the tears from my face with my arm. "I will stay. She was my mistress. I have a responsibility to her." I bent to touch Rachel's arm. "I loved her."

"I will find a cave," Jacob murmured. "It would not do for wild animals to desecrate her body."

Not caring about his bloodied hands and face, Jacob's step faltered as he found his way out of the tent, calling to Joseph.

***

Men set up our tents once more, leaving an open space in the middle as we always had when we stopped in our travels. Jacob and Joseph found a cave in the foothills of the small valley above Bethel. Once Noora and I finished preparing Rachel's body, Joseph and Jacob brought her outside. They carried her to the center of our circle of mourners and set her on a soft pile of branches.

Where did they find branches?

Then I saw the trees and flowers growing all around. A fresh breeze lifted my hair.

I shook my head. *Where did this greenery come from? In my rush to help Rachel, I did not notice my surroundings.*

We found our places around Rachel and sat sorrowing. Reuben shared his memories. "Mother Rachel cared deeply about us, even when she tried to pretend she did not. She often gave me sweets when Mother would not." He glanced toward Leah.

"The important thing to remember, however," Reuben continued, "is that Mother Rachel loved Jehovah. He allowed her to have two sons. Joseph and now Benjamin. Jehovah is great. He loves her enough to take her home. May we live so we can be with her once more."

Others spoke of her love for them, then we followed Joseph and Jacob as they carried her up the hill to the cave. They set her inside, then closed the opening with stones to protect her body from wild animals.

Leah, Jacob, Zilpah, and I stood with our arms around each other, sobbing over the loss of our sister until the sun set.

"Father," Naphtali said from behind us. "If we do not leave soon, we cannot see the path."

Jacob looked up and shook himself as if coming to himself.

With heavy hearts, we turned our feet back to the valley and our tents.

I would miss my mistress every day. We had been together since we were ten. I had served her and loved her all these years. Now she was gone.

Because Jacob took me as his concubine, I did not have to consider where I would go now Rachel was gone, unlike her maidservants, who did not know whom they would serve. Leah would need to reassign them. Perhaps they would find husbands among the herders, or other menservants among us.

Before going to my sleeping pallet, I went through my supply of herbs and other remedies to be certain we would have enough. I did not know who would require them next.

We took our time preparing to travel the next morning. No one wanted to leave Rachel alone in the desolate cave. As we gathered our possessions, Jacob called us together. "I need to share something with you. In the night after our sacrifice, I communed with Jehovah. After He confirmed promises given to me earlier, he changed my name. I am now to be called Israel."

Jehovah changed his name as He changed Abram's. Jacob truly is a righteous man. As I told him years ago, Jehovah loves him.

The crowd around him buzzed like bees.

He allowed us to buzz. When it calmed, he raised his hands to regain our attention. "You may continue to call me Jacob, or you may use Israel. I will answer to both. But now we must be on our way. My father is not well. I need to be there in Mamre with him."

Jehovah must have warned Jacob of his father's health.

We mounted our camels and rode south once more, expecting another long day. As we left the valley, I turned to gaze at the cave holding my friend and mistress. I brought my hand to my heart to honor her, then turned my face toward the future. What would it bring?

Mamre

The next day, when it was my turn, I carried Benjamin close to my heart, inhaling his newborn scent, as we rode that day. I glanced down once to see his dark eyes looking up at me.

"You have a rough life ahead of you with your mother gone, little one," I murmured. "But we will love and care for you as if we were your mother. You will have three mothers to love you, three to watch you grow, and three to ensure you live an honorable life."

He blinked as if he understood my words. I cradled him in my arms and murmured to him stories of his mother, his father, his brothers, and about our journey, speaking for me as much as for him. "I lost my family early, but I survived, as you will. Your papa is broken today, but he will overcome it, as he has overcome all his problems, with Jehovah's grace. I promise you, little one, I will no longer fear losing my family. I will do all I can to help your papa and keep what is left of our family together."

Haala was always close by, ready to feed him when he fussed. She seemed to know when this child, this son of ours, was hungry. I thought back to the days when I fed my newborns, remembering my need for them to wake and eat. It must be the same for her.

We traveled through rough and beautiful hills. Small flowers grew along the trail, their bright colors contrasting against the dusty golden-brown of the hills. I marveled at the trees growing from rocky crags where none should grow. Huge bushes sometimes blocked our path, and the clomping camels stepped around them, sometimes grabbing a bite of their greenery.

Long before I expected, Jacob, er, Israel, rode past, directing us to a wide space in the trail near a trickling stream where we were to camp.

"Why so early?" I asked.

"It is better to arrive in Mamre in the morning. We are close. We can prepare to meet my father here and enter clean."

I nodded my understanding. I wanted to be clean and presentable when meeting Isaac, the great prophet of Jehovah.

Men put up tents and the camp settled into our usual routines. We warmed pots of water over fires, taking them inside to bathe and wash our hair. It felt delicious to be clean again, with no sand scratching my body, no dirt in my clothes or under my nails.

Dan and Naphtali stopped by my tent to show me they had washed themselves in the stream and spoke excitedly about meeting their grandfather. We all looked forward to meeting Jacob's father at last.

Israel insisted we enter Mamre as a joyful people returning home, not as an unwelcome runaway son slinking back to ask forgiveness. I looked back at our line of travelers as we plodded over the last hill. We almost shone. The herders had even cleaned the camels.

I searched ahead for a village like Harran or Shalem. Instead, bright, colorful tents, much like ours, scattered in ordered chaos throughout the space as though someone had plopped them wherever they fit. Smells of cooking grains and roasting mutton wafted toward us. My stomach gurgled. Vegetable and flower gardens surrounded the tents, connected to each other by wide, graveled paths. A wide avenue led toward the largest tent in the center, with an enormous green canopy of a terebinth tree growing in front of the tent.

Israel led us to the edge of the village and ordered our servants to dismount and set up the tents while we, Jacob's family, rode up the wide avenue.

The oldest man I had ever seen sat beneath the terebinth tree on a colorful blanket, the colors of the sunset. White hair hung past his shriveled face onto his shoulders. Another blanket draped around his shoulders, with knees and elbows sharply poking out. His pale blue, nearly white eyes gazed in our direction, more closed than open. He leaned slightly forward, listening to what he could not see.

Israel commanded his camel to kneel, and ours followed. Israel helped Leah off her camel, for she carried Benjamin. Dan helped me off my camel, and together with Naphtali, we joined the rest of the family, ranging behind Israel in our sub-family groups while a camel herder took away our camels.

A servant helped the ancient man stand, whispering in his ear, as Israel led us toward him. When we came near, Israel fell to his knees. The rest of the family followed, kneeling before this great, ancient man.

His eyes, once piercing, gazed toward each of us with intelligence much like Israel's. "Jacob! Jacob, my son!" he cried with a voice stronger than I thought could come from one so old. "I heard you were coming. It is past time you brought your family to meet me."

Israel stood, then kissed his father's cheeks. "Father, may I introduce my family?"

He beckoned Leah forward and introduced her.

"Oh, ho," Isaac cried. "The one Laban insisted you marry first."

I giggled at his merry voice.

"I am the ugly sister. Jacob wanted my beautiful younger sister. Father could not entice another man to marry me, so he disguised me as Rachel and married me to your son. I expected to be turned out, but Jacob has always been kind to me."

Isaac kissed her cheek and murmured something in her ear. She blushed.

He lifted his head and gazed around. "Where is Rachel? I do not see her."

He could not see her with blind eyes. He must have sensed her loss.

Israel swallowed. Sorrow filled his face. "Jehovah took her home. She did not survive the birth of her second son, Benjamin."

Isaac wound his thin, stringy arms around his son, and they wept. After some time, they separated, wiping their eyes.

"And the babe?" Isaac asked. "Did he live?"

Leah unwrapped Benjamin from his blankets and held him up for his grandfather to touch. "This is Benjamin, your youngest grandson, born two days ago."

Isaac touched his small face. "He will be a blessing to your family."

Even at his ancient age, Isaac's prophetic declarations warmed my heart. Jehovah continued to bless him.

Israel insisted his father sit again before introducing the rest of the family, beginning with Reuben and Leah's other sons and then Dinah. Then he called Joseph forward.

"This is Rachel's first son, Joseph."

Joseph took his ancient grandfather's hand and bent over it.

"Jehovah will bless you and your family through you," Isaac murmured.

Once again, I felt the comforting promise of Isaac's prophetic words. *What will Joseph do to bless the family?*

Joseph stepped back, and Israel introduced me.

I stepped forward, anxious to meet this honored man.

"This is Bilhah. She was Rachel's maidservant until she insisted I take Bilhah as a concubine to provide Rachel with sons. Bilhah gave me Dan and Naphtali."

I bent low.

"A beautiful woman who gave me handsome grandsons. I welcome you." Isaac spoke as if he could see me. Perhaps his prophetic vision opened his soul to me. He pulled me close, kissing my cheek. "How do you stay busy?"

"I have served the family as a healer. My mother was a healer who taught me as much as one can teach a girl of ten."

"You delivered little Benjamin?" Isaac asked, turning his head toward the babe.

"I did, but Rachel was so sick I needed help. We were blessed to have Noora join us. She knew how to save the babe, although we could not save the mother." I gulped down my tears. "I loved Rachel."

Isaac patted my hand. "You did all you could. Jehovah needed her home."

I nodded. Somehow his comfort broke through my pain. My tears spilled down my face. I kissed Isaac's cheek.

I stepped away, wiping away my tears as Israel introduced Zilpah and her sons, Gad and Asher, explaining how Leah had given her maidservant to him as a concubine.

"Four beautiful women," Isaac said, sighing. "You are blessed. How do you cope with them?" His teasing chuckle warmed me. I glanced at Leah and Zilpah. We all had bemused smiles.

"They are a blessing to me. They seldom argue and get along well. We have a happy family." Israel smiled at each of us. I felt his love.

Isaac called a servant to prepare a feast. The man ran off to pass on the order to slaughter a steer and a ram and give directions to the cooks.

We sat in a loose circle around Isaac and visited with him until Benjamin fussed. Haala appeared and took him from Leah.

Not long after, our sons excused themselves to settle their animals. Zilpah lifted an eyebrow in my direction. I agreed with her cue that it was time for us to leave. She had a meal to prepare, and I had injured to see to. We excused ourselves as well, promising to return for the feast.

As we reached our tents, we heard a shout. Esau raced a black stallion up the avenue toward Isaac, followed by three women and many men. I supposed the women were wives. How many of the men were sons? How many were servants? "How did he know when we would arrive? It is good he came. They need to spend time together."

I turned to seek those women from Shalem whose injuries still required my attention.

A servant passed on Esau's declaration that the men we feared on our travels had, with Jehovah's help, hidden in their homes, fearing our small band would destroy them. I smiled at the thought and the truth of Shalem's destruction.

I no longer had to fear a marauding army, but where would we live? Would Isaac invite us to join his community? I prayed we had reached the end of our journey.

Isaac Weakens

Esau had brought his wives and sons with him, making the feast loud and joyful. He told us he lived less than a week's ride from his father. He had heard from his servants of our troubles in Shechem and expected us to arrive sometime soon.

At the feast, we sat with Isaac. He fell into quiet contemplation when others were laughing and joking.

I stood to retrieve something and walked behind him. "Are you well, Father Isaac?"

He took my hand. "Well enough. I have lived many years, waiting to once more have my sons and grandchildren together again and happy. I thank you for your concern."

I gazed into his softly clouded eyes. Deep lines surrounded his mouth and eyes. He was not well. "If you need my help as a healer, send for me."

Isaac smiled. "I will. I hope my life will end sooner than later. I am ready to join my Rebekah. I grow tired of this life."

"You have lived many years."

"One hundred eighty." Isaac grinned. "Not as many as my father. Certainly not as many as our Grandfather Noah. But it is enough."

I kissed his dry cheek. "Call me if you need me."

He smiled and nodded.

It did not surprise me when, early the next morning, a messenger scratched on my door. "Isaac is asking for you and your healer friend, Noora, to come. He is failing fast."

"I will come as soon as I have dressed." I pulled on my dress, grabbed my basket of healing supplies, and hurried out the door, tying the ties on my dress. I tucked the tichel I wore more often since moving to Shechem over my hair as I hurried toward the tent Noora shared with other women from Shalem and scratched on their door.

A young woman pulled the door back enough to peep out. "What do you need so early?"

"I need Noora," I said. "We have been asked to assist one who is ill."

Noora nudged the young woman aside. "I expected this." She stepped through the door, her basket of healing supplies in her hand. We raced past the recently erected tents and past the colorful tents forming Mamre toward the terebinth tree.

I expected to find Isaac in the biggest, colorful tent, but the messenger stood outside a smaller tent, waving to us.

"In here," he said.

We entered and found Isaac on a pallet. Israel and Esau knelt next to him.

We examined the ancient man, who seemed to have failed overnight. His eyes flickered open, sensing our presence. "You came."

"I said I would come," I whispered.

"Ease me home. I do not want to stay any longer." His voice had lost all strength.

"Are you certain?"

He nodded. His unseeing eyes begged understanding.

"As you wish," I said.

We did what we could to comfort him and help him rest, but his time was coming.

Israel and Esau sent messengers to their families, asking them to come pay their final respects to their grandfather. Soon Leah entered with a cry. She rushed to kneel beside Israel.

Noora and I moved beside the tent wall, waiting to be needed.

"Isaac," Leah cried.

He opened his eyes as if to peer into her eyes. "Ah, Leah, my Rebekah's image. You have come."

She took his hand in hers. "You cannot leave us yet. I have not had time to know you."

"But you have met me, and I see my love in you," he whispered in a weak voice. "Care for my Israel. He will need your love and support in the coming years."

She glanced toward Israel, tears spilling off her cheeks onto Isaac's hands.

"Do not weep, dear Leah," Isaac's voice strengthened. "You know me through my son. I will be with you both in the coming years. Jehovah bless you both." He gasped and lay back, unable to say more.

Zilpah, our sons, and Esau's family entered soon after, each kneeling around Isaac's pallet. Isaac never spoke again.

Noora and I stepped forward and examined him again. His eyes showed no light, his heartbeat slowed, and his breathing became shallow.

But he struggled, fighting to breathe. He shuddered and inhaled again. Those on their knees sat back on their heels, finding a comfortable place to wait.

Isaac's breathing dropped twice more, then he gasped another breath, not ready to leave us. Israel laid his hands on Isaac's head and called on Jehovah to release his father and take him home.

Isaac's ragged, thin breaths slowed again, and then stopped. Noora slipped between Esau and Isaac. I moved next to his head on Israel's side. When no more shuddering breaths returned, we set our hands against his neck and wrist, searching for the beat of life.

I glanced into her eyes. Her head twitched. I closed my eyes and bowed my head.

"He is gone," she whispered.

I swallowed the tears that filled my eyes. I had too much to do now to weep.

"Jehovah has taken our father home," Israel said.

"May Jehovah bless him and us," Esau said.

One of Isaac's servants pushed through the family and set her fingers on his neck. After waiting a bit, she nodded. "He is gone. I will prepare him."

"No," Israel said before I could argue. "Esau and I will complete that task. We are his sons. It is our right."

"We will take him to Machpelah, where we laid Mother with Grandmother and Grandfather," Esau said.

At Israel's nod, Esau sent his sons with ours to prepare traveling tents and a wagon to carry the lamb to use as sacrifice. We women followed them, leaving Israel and Esau to complete their sad task of preparing their father for burial.

As I stepped out of the tent, I breathed in deeply, absorbing the fresh air of a world with both death and birth — often days apart. I glanced at the sun, which had moved past midday.

Noora came to stand by my side. "I will go let the others know," she murmured and left us, Esau and Israel's women.

We sat beneath the terebinth tree, enjoying the faint lemon scent mixed with a bitter, medicinal aroma.

We sat there, still at first, each of us absorbed in our own sorrow and memories. Then we shared stories of our husbands, laughing softly at their similarities. Although they had spent years apart, they had similar quirks and reacted the same to comparable challenges.

"I do not know what Esau would have done if my father had insisted he marry my sister first, though," Adah, Esau's second wife, a short woman who smiled often, shook her head.

"He would have turned her away." Aholibimah, his third wife, brushed back her long dark hair from her face.

"My father, Ishmael, would not have accepted a woman he had not chosen." Bashemath, Esau's tall, willowy first wife, said. "Your Jacob is an amazing man."

"I expected him to send me away," Leah admitted. "When he did not, I knew he was special. Although I knew of his kind nature in the seven years he worked to earn Rachel, I did not know how he would react to Father's deceit."

Maidservants brought trays of food for us. We nibbled, but could not enjoy the food.

After a time, people from Mamre, our camp, and Esau's servants filtered in, finding seats beneath the broad canopy of the pungent terebinth tree, giving us space to grieve in private.

Before sunset, Dan and his brothers returned with Esau's sons. All was ready to transport their grandfather. They sat with us, waiting.

The crowd grew until most of those living in or visiting Mamre filled the space under the tree and spread beyond. With muted voices, we waited for Israel and Esau to bring Isaac's body out.

At last, Israel and Esau stepped through the tent door, carrying the pallet with Isaac's body resting on it between them. The crowd silenced and stood, honoring Isaac, our leader and patriarch. Tears flowed unheeded down our faces. I did not want to cry in front of Esau's wives, but could no longer swallow my sorrow and allowed them to fall.

Esau and Israel shared memories of their beloved father, reminding us of his great love for and obedience to Jehovah. When they finished, Esau and Israel lifted the pallet once more and carried Isaac's body between them as they began the long hike to Machpelah.

The sun set, taking with it the light we needed to travel along the unknown, rocky trail.

Our sons carried torches ahead and behind us, lighting the way for us and the animals marching toward the sacred cave of Machpelah. We traveled through the night, arriving as the sun rose above the entrance.

I dropped to the dirt to rest, weary from our time with Isaac and the ensuing trek. However, my worry was not for myself. My concern was for Israel. He had suffered so much loss in such a short time.

In the dark, the place looked drab, a rocky mountain.

We dozed as we waited for Israel and Esau and their sons to remove the stones blocking the cave's mouth. They finished as the sun shone on the entrance.

The cave opened in the rough mountain slope, no longer drab. Esau and Ishmael lifted Isaac's body, still wrapped in his colorful blanket, and carried him inside and placed him on the shelf beside Rebekah. Isaac's two sons stood near the entrance, with their women standing nearby, as those who came with us passed by his body, bending to speak their farewells in his ear or to share a memory with him. Isaac's family passed him last. Each of us spoke soft words of love and honor to him.

"Thank you for trusting me and thinking me beautiful. Few men have," I whispered to him. I could not prevent a tear from rolling down my cheek onto his face.

After the wives and children stepped past, we waited outside the mouth of the cave for Esau and Israel. When they came out, we each set a stone in the doorway before our sons completed the task, setting the stones to cover the entrance and protect Isaac and Rebekah from wild animals and scavenging men.

I was blessed to know Isaac, even for a short time. I saw him in Israel and loved him. His soft voice and gentle touch let me know of his love. If only Laban had allowed us to leave before Rebekah's death. What would our life have been like to have known them both longer? I would never know.

We rested while Israel rebuilt the altar, fallen apart from disuse, and prepared for the sacrifice, then sat in silence during the rite. I suspect Esau and his family remembered their beloved Father Isaac. My thoughts centered on his love for us in the short time we were with him and the tender memories I had gained.

Rather than sleeping in the traveling tents we had brought, we mounted the horses that had trailed behind us on our journey and rode back to Mamre, where a feast awaited.

We did not laugh and dance during this feast as we had only nights before. Instead, we celebrated Isaac's life, listening to stories, both serious and humorous, about the man they loved. I learned much.

As the feast continued into the night, men and women made their way to pledge their support and allegiance to Israel.

Had Isaac waited all these years for Israel to return, ready to take upon himself the responsibilities of the priesthood and the village of Mamre? I thanked Jehovah for the opportunity to meet him.

***

The next day, Israel and Esau spent hours together discussing what to do next. As they met, we, their six wives, cleaned and aired the tent.

I gazed at the small, dark interior. "Why would Isaac live in this when a bigger one stands empty over there?"

"The big one is the tent he shared with Rebekah," Bashemath said. "He could not bear to stay there, where they had spent their lives together."

"I wondered," Leah said. "This is smaller than I expected."

"The big tent belonged to Rebekah. Abraham left it for Jacob's wife, if he ever brought her home," Adah said.

"He moved into this travel tent and claimed it as his own," Aholibamah said.

We soon had the small tent cleaned, opened the door, and lifted the flaps to allow in fresh, cleansing air. Then Bashemath took Leah to the big tent once belonging to Rebekah.

While the others sat in the shade of Leah's tent in which she had lived for the past months, I went to examine my patients. Most were now healed, although two still suffered from broken arms.

I did not know what I would do in Mamre. Surely, a healer had blessed the lives of these people. And Noora had more experience than me. We had few injuries or sicknesses in the years we had lived together. I doubted any would need my healing services. What would I do?

I joined the other women in the shade of Leah's tent awning, visiting and sharing stories. We ate the tea and cakes Dida brought.

When evening came, Esau and Israel joined us. Maidservants brought us a small meal, most left from the previous nights of feasting.

"Will you take the tent Father and Mother lived in?" Esau asked.

"Their tent?" Israel glanced up toward his mother's tent. "Is it still livable?"

"We went in it today," Bashemath said. "It looks like a maidservant kept it clean and aired in the years since Rebekah's death."

"Perhaps," Israel glanced at Leah. "We shall see."

Leah will receive the honor she has deserved all these years.

Near the end of the evening, Esau leaned toward Israel. "We will leave tomorrow. It has been wonderful to spend this time with you."

"Visit often." Israel set his hand on his brother's shoulder. "Father stayed here many years. I hope to stay as long as he did."

"I will know where to find you now you have returned to Canaan." Esau took the last honey cake.

Israel leaned back and placed his hands on his stomach. "I do not plan to leave Canaan again unless Jehovah commands it."

"We will continue to live in Seir. Canaan is a rich land, but there is not room for both our families and flocks." He wiped his hands on a cloth. "I will miss you, but it is best for us to separate our men and flocks. Your sons will be kings of these lands, as mine will be kings of our lands."

"I will welcome your next visit," Israel said.

The brothers embraced. We women hugged as well. We were now friends, sisters by marriage.

We bid them goodbye early the next morning.

Before they disappeared over the crest of the hill, Sachia, Isaac's head maidservant, touched Israel's arm to get his attention. "Will you need help to move your possessions into the big tent?"

"The big tent?" He shifted his head to face her.

"The big tent your grandmother gave to your mother. It belongs to your wife now." She turned to Leah. "Will you need our help?"

I smiled. *They recognize Leah as Israel's wife.*

She nodded. "Yes, Sachia. I would appreciate your help."

"I will return with help soon," Sachia said, turning to stride back into the main camp.

"You will live in that tent?" Zilpah asked.

"Have you been in it?" Leah asked. "It is nicer than Mother's home in Harran. If I am to help Israel lead the people of Mamre, I must accept the gift of the tent."

Will Israel leave Zilpah and me on the edge *of the village?*

"Bilhah, you and Zilpah are part of our family," Israel said. "We will move your tents close to the big tent." He must have heard my thoughts again.

"And our sons?" Leah asked, rocking on her feet, anxious to get to her tent. "They will not want to live close to us. Those without will soon have wives and children of their own."

"Benjamin and Joseph will need to stay closer for a time," Zilpah said, rocking baby Benjamin. "I will continue to keep Benjamin with me."

"I can —" Leah said.

"No," Israel interrupted her. "Joseph is too old to be living in a mother's tent. I will give him Isaac's tent. You cleaned it yesterday. It is the right size for a young man."

"Thirteen is too young to be alone with his brothers!" I cried.

"He will have a tent, but it will stay close to ours. He is not ready to live among the other young men."

We separated to pack our belongings yet again.

In the next few days, Israel moved some of Mamre's tents around, making room for Zilpah and me to have our tents near Leah's, whose old tent went to Noora. She shared with some of the older women.

Our tents enlarged the community to almost double, with close to 250 tents. We soon became part of Mamre, and I soon made many friends. I continued to consider my place in our new home. I doubted they would need my skills as a healer with two others with more experience, Lael and Noora. I learned to love the rocky land and the people who lived in it.

Dreams

In the next months and years, I learned to enjoy a more settled life, not running to every emergency, although our herders often came to me first. After Dan and Naphtali married lovely young women, their wives called on me.

As their other brothers had done, my sons chose beautiful young women. They now had homes and wealth enough to support families.

Dan married Miriam, a lithe, tall, young woman with piercing blue eyes and burnished brown hair. Naphtali had spent time with one of the young women from Shalem, but he listened to the promises of his papa, and instead found a loving young woman, Avri, from among the people of Mamre, who loved and served Jehovah. Avri came up to Naphtali's chin. He loved to tuck her under his arm to protect her.

Each of these young women was kind and loving, offering me the love I had missed over the years. They became my heart daughters, and I loved my grandchildren.

I enjoyed watching Leah become a leader of women. She had experience from our days in Harran without knowing it. She taught the women of Mamre to accept the whisperings from Jehovah and consider the needs of others, not just their own. She encouraged us to work together, to care for one another, and to give other women the support they needed. We became unified in our love for each other and Jehovah.

I had hoped our sons would learn the same lessons. They did not.

As Joseph grew, Dan and Naphtali came to me more often, complaining of Israel's love for Rachel's son.

"Father does not send him into the wilderness with the flocks as he sent us when we were younger," Dan complained. "Joseph seldom leaves Mamre."

"He is not seventeen yet," I said, trying to help them understand their father's protection of their younger brother.

"When I was seventeen," Naphtali said, "I fought a bear."

I shuddered at the memory. "Joseph is Rachel's son. Israel remembers and protects her son."

"And he loved her more than any of the other wives, her sons more than the rest of us," Dan said, heat filling his voice.

I nodded. "I knew from the beginning he loved Rachel. I was her maidservant during the years she waited for permission to marry Jacob. She was heartbroken when Laban married Leah to Jacob first."

"We have heard those stories. Father should love all of his wives," Naphtali said with a growl.

"And all of us," Dan added.

"Israel loves me. He loves and cares for all his sons. We knew his greatest love was for Rachel from the beginning. You will be happier when you accept it as well."

"He loves Leah now, and everyone here knows it," Dan said, becoming thoughtful.

I hoped their animosity would lessen. "And in the years since Rachel gave me to Jacob, he has shown me love. I have no reason to complain or for envy."

My sons left, mollified.

Mollified until Israel gave Joseph a special coat, signifying his birthright. Reuben had sinned and lost the birthright. Everyone knew about the birthright change and the reasons it went to Joseph, yet the special coat caused bitterness between the brothers and Joseph. Gentle teasing became venomous. They took every opportunity to trip him or cause him to look clumsy. Their dislike became hatred.

Then Joseph had dreams.

Everyone dreams, but we seldom share them with the family as if they were truth or visions from Jehovah.

Joseph did.

"He dreamed we were binding sheaves from the field," Dan told me one day while I folded my cleaned clothing. "It is not unusual for him to bind the sheaves, but his dream changed. His sheaf stood up while the other sheaves bowed down to him."

"Can you believe the nonsense?" Naphtali added. "What would make him believe we, his older brothers, will ever bow down to him?"

"We will not," Dan said with a snort. "We are his older brothers. He insists the dream came from Jehovah."

I shook my head. "He may have dreamed that, but to believe it will happen?" Although I struggled to believe his dream, I wondered at his surety. Had Jehovah blessed Joseph as He blessed his father?

"Joseph believes it will." Naphtali grunted. "We shall see."

"It is but a dream, and he is young and proud. Give him grace." I prayed the bitterness between the brothers would end.

I thought they had abandoned their hatred and sought to treat Joseph better until he had another dream.

My sons came to me in my garden the afternoon after Joseph shared his dream with them. "He dreamed the sun, the moon, and eleven stars bowed down to him." Naphtali stood stiff, as if to prove his unwillingness to bow to his brother.

I gasped in surprise. His dreams had changed, now including his father and ... mother. "All bow to him? Does this mean his father, mothers, and all his brothers?" But which one of his mothers did the moon represent? I rose from my knees.

"It sounds as Joseph believes. Do you believe him?" Dan demanded. Hostility rasped his voice and twisted his face, causing me to groan within.

"I believe he may have dreamed such a thing." The hatred on my son's faces at my words caused me to shudder. "But it is only a dream." *I pray it is only a dream.*

"Then why does he talk about it like it is a warning for all of us?" Naphtali asked.

"He never stops," Dan added. "It makes me angry."

"He is a lad. He will learn." I touched each of my son's faces, seeking to soothe away their hostility.

I hoped Joseph would learn and planned to take him aside to warn him. But I did not get a chance.

The older sons took the flocks to Shechem, where better food for the animals grew. They did not return for weeks, and their wives became concerned. I did not fear for their safety. They were together and would protect each other.

Joseph begged his father to allow him to prove himself a man to his brothers.

"Let me go ensure they are well. I can go alone," Joseph begged.

"Alone?" Israel asked.

"I need to prove to myself and my brothers that I can. Let me go, please."

Israel refused for three days. When our sons still did not return, he gave in and sent Joseph in search of them.

We prayed often for Joseph and his brothers, fearing something had happened.

At last, Reuben, Dan, and the other eight brothers returned, leaving their flocks with herders. They found us sitting beneath the terebinth tree, praying.

Israel leapt to his feet when his sons appeared on the path to the tree."Have you seen Joseph? Have you seen your brother?"

Reuben bowed his head. "We left Shechem and went on to Dotham. He did not come while we were there. But as we returned to Shechem, we found this." He brought a package from behind his back and unwrapped a bloody, torn coat, much like the one Israel had gifted Joseph. "It looks like ... Is it Joseph's coat? It looks like a lion attacked him."

Israel took the coat and buried his face in it, clutching it to his breast, his shoulders heaving. "Joseph. Oh, Joseph!" he wept. "Why did I not listen? Why did I send you alone to find your brothers? What happened to your sling, your staff? How did a lion take you? Oh, Joseph." He fell on his face, weeping.

All the family tried to comfort him, but Israel would not be comforted. "I shall go to my grave mourning my son as my father mourned me," he sobbed.

He stumbled into Leah's tent and fell on their pallet, weeping.

I gazed at my sons. They knew something. But they never shared.

I no longer feared abandonment. Now I must keep what was left of my family together.

***

In the next years, Miriam gave Dan a son and three daughters, while Arvi gave Naphtali four sons and two daughters. I loved and doted on these grandsons, staying busy.

Within a few years, Leah complained of excessive thirst. She slipped away often to relieve herself, and admitted, when I asked, of rising often during the night. I worried about her health and begged Zilpah to give her healthy food.

We did all we could to help Leah, but she lost weight. She refused to rest, claiming she needed to help the women of Mamre.

Fatigue set in. I watched her with her grandsons, bouncing them on her knee, then setting them down to play, which was not unusual. But she would slump back and close her eyes, exhausted from the slight effort of playing with grandchildren.

Israel noticed and prayed, begging Jehovah to protect his beloved wife. She would become healthier for a time, then sank into exhaustion, never to recover. My worry increased.

I consulted with Noora and Lael, Mamre's healer, seeking assistance in caring for my friend and sister-wife. We gave Leah potions and draughts. Some helped her temporarily, but none healed her.

Then Zilpah complained of dizziness and difficulty breathing. Both my sister-wives were ill. I watered my pillow many nights and spent hours on my knees, praying for Jehovah's help to heal them and for His blessings on them.

With Rachel gone and Leah and Zilpah sick, I approached Israel outside Leah's tent for a stack of vellum, a pen, and ink.

He stared at me. "Do you plan to write the story of your life?"

"Yes. How did you know?" My shoulders slumped.

"Rachel did before her death. Leah and Zilpah asked for vellum, pen, and ink in the last few months. Now you." He tugged on his hair as the skin bunched around his eyes. "Will you leave me as well?"

"I did not know Leah and Zilpah were writing their stories." I shrugged. I did not want to cause him more worry. "I saw Rachel write hers. And like her, my sons need to know about my life. If I do not write it, how will they know? How will their children remember me?"

"As Rachel said. But she was ill. Are you?" Israel leaned forward, putting his arms around me.

I shook my head. "No. I am not ill, but I grow older."

"And tell me," Israel stepped back to gaze into my eyes. "Do I need to fear for Leah and Zilpah?" He gazed into my eyes, his as piercing blue as when I first led him to a chamber in Laban's home.

I returned his gaze and chewed on my lip, seeking the correct words. He deserved the truth. "I fear you may. They decline regardless of all the healing remedies we have given them. I spend many nights in prayer for them."

He nodded. "I, too, have spent many hours in prayer for them." He stretched his hand out and took mine. "Do not become ill. I need you to live."

"You need Leah to live," I said. "She is your wife. I am but a concubine."

"Yes, I need Leah to live, but I fear she will not. Take care of yourself. I need you. Since Rachel's death, you have soothed my fears and tenderly watched over me and the others. Each night I offer gratitude to Jehovah that you came into my life to love me. I love you more every day. "

Tears blurred my eyes as I nodded. Israel had not spoken like this of his love for me in a long time.

I renewed my efforts to return Leah and Zilpah's health.

But I failed. Zilpah cried out one day and clutched her stomach. "It is only a stomach problem," she said when I ran to help her.

"Only a stomach problem?" I asked. "When does a stomach problem cause so much sweating?" I held her elbow and walked with her to her tent.

"It is a hot day," she argued as she lay on her pallet.

"Lie on your side. Perhaps that will help." I smoothed back her dark hair, now sprinkled with gray. "I will get more cool water."

I hurried to dip cool water into a bowl and grabbed a cloth before returning to Zilpah's tent.

She lay still on her pallet. I thought she slept and dipped the cloth into the bowl of water. I wrung the water out and put the cloth on her forehead. Her eyes did not move.

"Zilpah?" I whispered.

I moved my fingers to her wrist, searching for the beat of her heart.

Nothing.

I felt her neck.

No heartbeat.

"Zilpah!" I cried. Perhaps it was a scream. "No, Zilpah. Do not leave me!"

Israel rushed into the tent, carrying Leah.

"What happened?" Israel lifted his eyebrows.

"She is gone," I whispered. "I have lost my sister."

"No!" Israel fell to his knees and took her hand, weeping. Leah knelt beside him, sobbing and repeating Zilpah's name.

Gad and Asher darted into the tent.

"What is wrong with our mother?" Gad leaned over his mother and tenderly touched her cheek.

I swallowed and swallowed again. A lump had filled my throat, stilling my voice. "She —" I swallowed once more. "She is gone. She complained of a sick stomach. I helped her to her pallet. Her face was covered in sweat. I left for a bowl of water and a cloth." My tight, sorrowing voice a higher pitch. I pointed at the bowl. "When I returned, she was gone."

"Jehovah took her home to keep Rachel company," Israel said, lifting his head.

Gad and Asher fell to their knees, tears flowing. I started to step away, but Israel grasped my wrist and pulled me to kneel beside him.

"She is your sister. You have a right to mourn with us."

I could no longer hold back my tears and sobbed until I had none left to cry.

That afternoon, Gad and Asher found a cave above Mamre, where we buried Zilpah. They did not want her taken farther away. My heart broke. Only Leah and I were left. I feared it would not be long until it was only me to keep our family together.

***

In the following year, Leah continued to struggle with thirst and weight loss. Then, she struggled with frequent infections, which did not heal. I used honey and other ointments and salves, but the infections took much longer to heal.

I increased my prayers, begging for help.

Jacob came to my tent one afternoon. “Leah is failing, not healing. What more can you do?”

“I pray every night for an answer to that question. Jehovah has not answered me. I rubbed her hands and feet, trying to warm them and stop the tingling. Nothing helps." I lifted my eyes heavenward. "Oh, Jehovah, help me help her. I cannot lose another sister.”

Israel put his arms around me. “You will find the answer if Jehovah desires her to heal.”

I sniffed and nodded. “I am a healer. Why can I not heal her?”

“She is in Jehovah’s hands,” Israel said, leaning his head on mine, and wept with me.

Almost two months later, Leah could no longer rise from her sleeping pallet. She had become too weak.

“I need water,” she moaned. “I thirst.”

I poured her tea, hoping it would help her heal. Her hands were dry and rough.

Leah’s sons stayed with her, taking turns to sit and pray.

The wife of Jacob’s son, Tamar, came to warn me. "Leah struggled to see and has no vigor. My dog refuses to leave her."

I took my basket from the hook on a post and rummaged through it for my herbs and remedies. What more could I give her that would help? “Animals sense illness. They must smell it.”

I took the basket and went with Tamar to Leah’s tent. Israel was with her. Leah slept on the floor, protected by Tamar's big dog.

“She almost fell off her pallet. I had to help her lie on the floor.” He shook his head. “I am no longer strong enough to lift her.”

“Is she asleep?” Tamar asked.

He shrugged. “She is not awake.”

I touched Leah and called her name, but she did not move. I rubbed her wrists and patted her cheek. I worked with her for longer than I liked before she opened her eyes and mumbled, confused and unsure of where she was or what had happened.

I begged Leah to stay with us. "I cannot lose you too."

Israel gathered us in a small circle around Leah and prayed for her. She roused and appeared better for a few days, even sitting up in her bed and ruffling her grandsons' hair.

Then, one morning, she did not awaken. I sent a message to Israel and Leah's sons. They crowded into her sleeping area, taking turns holding her hand and speaking soft words to her.

Noora and Lael joined me, standing on either side of me near the tent wall.

"I fear she is leaving us," Noora whispered.

"She has blessed our lives," Lael said. "Jehovah will welcome her home."

I swallowed my tears past the lump in my throat. "I do not want to see her leave. I will sorely miss her."

After midday, she roused and gazed into the eyes of each son, then into Israel's eyes. "I will miss you," she whispered in a raspy voice.

"No!" her sons cried.

Israel took her hand in his. "I will miss you more. You have blessed my life. I did not recognize my love for you soon enough. You have been remarkable in your love and direction of the women you served. I love you, my beautiful wife. Remember that."

She nodded and closed her eyes.

"Tell Rachel I love her and Joseph. Be well, my love." Israel whispered.

Her sons wept, whispering tender memories of her to each other until Leah emitted a soft gasp and moved no more. Israel set his hand on her chest. Sensing no breath, he shook his head.

Lael hurried to lift her limp hand. She felt for a heartbeat.

None.

She moved her hand to Leah's throat.

She shook her head. "She has gone home."

I bit my lip, fighting back the tears.

Noora, Lael, and I stepped forward. "We will prepare her."

"No," Reuben and Judah cried. "She is our mother. We will prepare her."

"We will take her to the cave at Machpelah," Israel said. "We will bury her with Father and Mother, Abraham, and Sarah. When I die, bury me there as well."

Reuben nodded.

A low wagon carried Leah's body to Machpelah.

Israel kept me beside him as we walked, holding my hand and speaking softly to me.

When we arrived in Machpelah, Reuben and his brothers quickly opened the cave. Reuben and Israel lifted Leah's body from the wagon and, with gentle care, carried it in, setting it on an empty shelf. They stood back while everyone else filed past, whispering condolences to the sons and soft words to Leah.

When it was my turn, I stepped to her body and bent low. "I will miss you," I whispered. "You always treated me fairly. You helped me move into my new place with Jacob with grace. I thank you. I will strive to be as fair with the women of Mamre as you were." I touched her cold face and stepped away.

Israel wept, whispering words of love to her. "Forgive me for not seeing your worth in the early days. I love you," he sobbed.

He stepped back, and I led him out of the cave. We each set a stone in the opening, and then her sons completed the closure.

Before the sun set, Israel and Leah's sons restored the stones that had fallen from the altar, as we had not used it since Isaac's death. Then we watched Israel offer a sacrifice honoring Leah.

We spent the night there, singing songs and telling stories of Leah's life.

The next morning, we left her with Abraham, Sarah, Rebekah, and Isaac. I missed my sister. Only I was left to hold this family together.

Drought

Over twenty years had passed since the lions took Joseph. All our sons had families, including Benjamin. Israel still mourned Joseph and his deceased wives, but we found peace together, he and I, watching our family grow and learn.

Until drought came to Canaan. No part of our land received rain for months, and then into a second year. We had little seed left. If we ate the grain we had remaining in our storage pots, we would have none to plant. If we did not eat it, we would not live to plant. Our servants slipped away, seeking food elsewhere.

A messenger passed through Mamre. Israel asked if he had found anyone had food they would trade.

"All the lands in Canaan struggle. No rain has fallen to water their grains." He rolled his lips inward. "There is word from Egypt, however. The Pharoah's next in command, his Vizier, has filled their granaries, anticipating this drought."

"He has grain to sell or trade?" Israel kept his rheumy eyes on the messenger's.

The man nodded. "Only Egypt. You can purchase grain from him."

When the messenger left, our sons gathered around Israel. "We must go purchase food. Our children suffer already," Reuben paced in front of his father. "I cannot stay here when there is hope in Egypt."

Israel sent his sons, all but Benjamin, to purchase enough for us to live. While they traveled, we ate less, and our children and grandchildren grew thin. If the ruler did not allow our sons to purchase grain, we would lay ourselves in our graves and die.

Miriam prepared thin mush from some of the last grain. There was so little left, I did not know how it would keep our weakest alive until our sons returned.

One day, with no strength to move, we lay beneath the terebinth tree, which had lost most of its feathery leaves.

Naphtali's son, Guni, sat up slowly and pointed south. "Does that dust mark the return of our fathers?" He licked his dry lips. "Or is it another dust storm?"

Dust storms had teased us before, dashing hope that our sons had returned.

I pushed myself from my blanket to stand, leaning on my cane and staring into the cloud of dust. "It is not a dust storm. I see the shape of their donkeys." Too weak to do more, I waited for their return, barely mustering a small smile of relief.

Two grandsons helped Israel to his feet to stand beside me.

Our sons steadily appeared from the dust.

"Do you think our prayers are answered?" Israel murmured in my ear, not wanting the others to hear. "Has Jehovah answered our prayers? Do they bring food?"

I clung to the hope and waited. They moved so slowly.

Benjamin had risen from his blanket and hobbled to stand by us. Hunger had taken so much from him, his robe hung loosely from his shoulders.

As our sons came up the broad avenue toward our tent, I counted them. One, two, three ... nine. "Only nine sons!"

I looked into their drawn and sad faces — Reuben, Levi, Dan, Judah, Naphtali, Gad, Issachar, Asher, and Zebulon. Simeon? Where was Simeon?

As they dismounted, their wives and children struggled to meet them, embracing their husbands and fathers in tears. Simeon's family stood back, fear filling their faces. His wife visibly shook.

Benjamin moved amongst his brothers. "Where is Simeon?" Alarm filled his voice.

Naphtali and Dan embrace their wives. I missed them as much as their families had, and had feared for their safety. Dan led Miriam toward me, then Naphtali brought Arvi. Their wives waited while each son swept me off my feet in their delight of seeing me again. I wept with joy.

Reuben came to report to his father, and after embracing Israel and me, raised his arms to silence the noisy crowd. After everyone found a place to sit, he told his story.

"The Vizier, who is the lord and ruler of Egypt beside the Pharoah, sold us grain enough to feed our families for a year." He motioned to the donkeys standing with full sacks of grain on their backs.

Relief flooded through me. The donkeys carried full bags. *Food! We will live. Praise Jehovah!*

Dan squeezed my hand.

"But the Vizier spoke roughly to us and called us spies." Levi folded his arms tightly and pressed his lips together.

Reuben stared, and Levi ducked his head, allowing Reuben to continue the story.

"He called us spies, yes, but we told him we were not spies, just ten brothers, sons of our father. When he pressed for more information about our family, I answered that one brother is no longer with us, and the youngest stayed with our father in Canaan."

"And did he believe you?" Israel leaned closer to Reuben.

He shook his head, as did all the other sons. "He spoke through his servants, not knowing our language. I thought he believed me, but he stomped around demanding, 'I will know if you are honest men if you leave one of your brothers here with me and return with the younger brother. I will give you enough food for your households and send you away.'"

Israel inhaled deeply.

"We argued with him, telling him we could not bring our youngest brother, for our father could not withstand the loss of another son." Reuben hung his head. "But he insisted we comply. He pointed his stick at Simeon, and his guards took him." Tears dripped into Reuben's beard.

Benjamin sat with wide eyes and mouth slack. His wife gasped and shook her head.

"How could you leave your brother, knowing how I grieve for ... for Joseph?" Israel cried out, pulling his hair and staring at Reuben, then at each of the other sons. His face lost all the little color he had left.

They left Simeon behind? Our family could not withstand another loss. Not now. Our lives were too fragile. I feared for Israel's life. He had suffered too much loss. It may destroy him to lose Benjamin.

Reuben continued, "We knew it would break your heart to lose another son. We argued with the Vizier, telling him so. He would not relent. After we discussed the problem, we agreed to the Vizier's demands, knowing our families would not live without the food." He bowed his head. "We had no other choice."

Issachar could remain silent no longer and added, "And then, the Vizier, that wicked ruler, said through his interpreter, 'And bring your youngest brother to me. Then I will know you are not spies, but are honest men.'"

Benjamin gasped. "Why would he want me? I am nothing, only the youngest son."

My throat constricted. Why would the Vizier care so much about our family, and why would he want to hurt Israel? "Did Simeon agree to stay?" I glanced at Israel, knowing he needed the answer as well.

"No, he did not," Reuben said, glaring at Issachar. "The Vizier bound Simeon and warned us we should bring our youngest brother or he would know we are spies. He had his men load grain onto our donkeys and sent us away with a warning to return with Benjamin."

I stared south toward Egypt, wondering what would happen to Simeon.

Our sons went to their donkeys and opened their sacks of grain.

"Oh, no!" Dan cried.

The other eight brothers echoed his cry of surprised sorrow.

"What is it?" Israel moved slowly toward Dan.

"He will certainly believe we are not only spies but thieves, for look," Judah pulled a packet out of his bag of grain as well.

"What is it?" I asked, afraid I already knew.

"Our coins," Naphtali said with a sigh. He dumped the coins from his bag into his hand and counted. "Everything I took to pay for grain."

"And all I took," Zebulon moaned.

Each son counted the coins in the mouth of his bag. All they had taken to purchase grain was there.

Israel fell to his knees and pressed his forehead to the ground. "You have bereaved me of my children," he wept. "Joseph dead, Simeon gone, and now You will take my youngest, my Benjamin, for grain." His shaky hands pulled at his gray hair once more.

Benjamin stood near me. I murmured to him, "I fear the grief may bring your father to his sickbed. You are his last connection to Rachel, your mother. He cannot lose you too."

Too weak to rush, Ben shuffled to his father and patted his back as he whispered into his ear.

"No, father," Reuben knelt beside Israel. "Your sons are not gone. Joseph is with Jehovah, but Simeon is safe in Egypt with the Vizier. Let us return to Egypt with Benjamin. You can slay my two sons if I do not bring Benjamin back."

The women gasped. I put a hand to my chest. How would it help to soothe Israel's sorrow to slay his grandsons? I thought it absurd to offer such a drastic solution.

Over the next months, Israel would hear nothing of it. Though the brothers, including Benjamin, entreated him, seeking to change his mind, Israel would not budge. He would not allow Benjamin to go with his brothers to Egypt to ransom Simeon. "You brought back grain to feed us for another year. With Jehovah's blessings, we will have rain before the year ends."

The year dragged on. No rain fell. Thankfully, the grain from Egypt kept us alive.

By the end of the year, I no longer offered bread with meals. We had already slaughtered most of the animals we had used for food. Only a few thin donkeys survived. We had nothing to feed them.

Israel offered our last perfect ram in sacrifice and prayed for rain. But none came and the drought deepened. Once more, we would not survive if we did not receive help.

Because Israel saw the intense suffering among his grandchildren who began to waste away, he finally relented at a family council, as usual, beneath the drying terebinth tree. We implored Jehovah in prayer, but with no perfect rams left, Israel could not offer another sacrifice.

He leaned on his staff, his face gray from dust and hunger. "Go beg grain from Egypt, but do not take Benjamin, I pray."

Judah rose. He had shown the most compassion toward Israel since returning from Egypt.

Perhaps Judah can convince Israel to allow them to take Benjamin. Judah will protect his youngest brother.

Israel nodded for him to speak.

Judah cleared his throat. "The Visier solemnly insisted. We will not see his face nor receive any more grain if we do not bring our brother with us. I doubt we will see Simeon again. If you send Benjamin, we will go again to Egypt and buy more food." Judah pressed his fists to his lips and closed his eyes. "But if you will not send him, we will not go. The Vizier is fierce. His word is law. We will get nothing without Benjamin."

"Why do you deal so ill with me?" Israel cried. "If you had not told him of your younger brother, he would not demand him."

"The man asked us immediately about the state of our family," Asher said, standing. "He asked if our father was yet alive and whether we had a younger brother. His words were so kind at first. How were we to know he would call us spies and demand we bring our brother to him?"

"Father," Judah said, leaning forward, stretching out his hand. "Send the lad with me, and we will arise and go in the morning. For we must live, both we and our little ones. But without food from Egypt, we will all perish."

Judah placed his hand over his heart. "I will be the surety for him. I promise anything you require. If I do not bring him home to you, I will take the blame forever. You can take my life and the lives of my children."

Anything? Oh, *that the wicked Vizier will treat us kindly and return our sons. Our family has lost too many. Our family must* reunite.

A tear trickled down Israel's cheek. He bowed his head in defeat. "If it must be so, take the best we have from the land to trade. Take balm and honey, spices and myrrh. And take double the coins you took last time, for certainly it was an oversight. You must not appear as thieves or spies." Israel shook his head, ignoring the tears flooding down his face onto his robe. "And ... and..." His struggle was evident to all. He covered his eyes with one hand. "Take your brother, Benjamin. Rise now and go to Egypt. May our God, even Jehovah, give you mercy before the Vizier of Egypt, that he may send both Benjamin and Simeon home with you."

Benjamin rode away with his brothers on his donkey not long after. The brothers feared their father would change his mind once more.

We cried. I feared I would never see him again. He was our last connection to Rachel. What would Israel do if his sons returned without Benjamin? I did not want to find out.

Time passed, and once more we were forced to reduce the size of our meals. We watched and waited, praying for all our sons to return from Egypt.

Starving

We had little grain to feed our children. Already hungry when Israel finally sent Benjamin with his brothers for sufficient food to prevent deaths, the children lost all vitality. The lack of food affected each of us.

As the only healer left in Mamre, the weight of keeping everyone alive crushed my shoulders. How could I? I had dried all my herbs and made tinctures and salves of the ones I could.

I turned my attention to our food. The daughters of our heart, wives of our beloved sons, took on the responsibility of preparing meals, ensuring the little food we had would last until their husbands returned from Egypt. I took responsibility for portioning the small amount of grain and soup bones each day and encouraged foraging for anything we could add. Eventually, no one had the strength to forage.

We reduced portions for each person. Our older grandsons lost weight, no longer strong and muscular. Their arms became thin and weak, as did their mothers'. I struggled to move through the tents to care for the weak of our family. What more could I do to keep us alive and together?

Worst of all, Israel's sight dimmed.

"I see only shadows," he confided to me one night on our pallet. He lifted his head and turned toward me. "But the others are not to know. I can find my way about still, and my staff will hold me up."

I prayed every day, through the day. *How do I* restore *his sight? How do I keep my good husband alive? Please, Jehovah. Bring our sons home soon — with food.*

Even if our sons returned sooner than expected, there would be little or nothing left to eat. When our sons returned — if they returned.

Israel brought us together in prayer every morning and night, begging for our sons safety and for a softening of the Vizier's heart. If they did not return with grain, we would die.

With the responsibility to keep them all alive, I maintained a prayer in my heart. Every grandchild, each of their mothers, and especially Israel must live to see our sons again. I knew so well the importance of family, of retaining our togetherness. I suffered as a child. I would prevent any dissolution. Our strength came from our unity.

The wadis stayed dry, no longer flowing with life-giving rain. The trees had withered. All the wells had become shallow, offering us only brackish water. The springs we depended on for fresh water dribbled in a muddy trickle. The once fertile terraces on the hills above us shed their soil to the wind.

We moved slowly, covered in dust, unable to consider much more than the next meal.

Few of the women could perform any chores. Layers of dust settled on everything. No one had the strength to clear it away.

Children stopped playing, no longer strong enough to run or consider joining in their favorite games. They became listless and dazed, clinging to their mamas, not even crying for food. Their stomachs swelled, and their arms had little more than skin over bone.

I did all I could to help each member of our family. I could cry no more, for not enough moisture filled my eyes.

One by one, the children retired to their pallets, unable to rise. I moved from tent to tent, pallet to pallet, offering a sip of brackish water and a bit of a nasty tincture. Their mamas followed with small portions of thin soup.

When my strength lapsed, we moved the youngest children into our big tent where I could care for them more easily. Their mamas and older brothers and sisters slept in nearby tents or beneath the terebinth tree, where they could help when needed.

Israel moved through the tent among the children beside me, setting his gaunt and wrinkled hands on each grandchild's head to beg Jehovah to keep them alive until their fathers returned with food.

One evening, after many weeks of struggling and listening to our grandchildren's weak cries, Israel and I held each other in our sleeping area in the back of the big, colorful tent Rebekah had left for Jacob and his wife. We prayed and sorrowed in silence. We had too little water to waste it on tears.

"I should not have allowed Benjamin to go with his brothers," Israel moaned . "I have nothing left of Rachel."

"You have Benjamin's wife and children. But surely Jehovah will preserve his children. Do you not remember what Isaac said about Benjamin?"

"He will stand at my right hand." A small smile warmed Israel's face. "Father was a prophet. Surely he knew. But that Vizier, why would he insist Benjamin come to him?"

My head rocked on the pillow. "Jehovah must know something we do not."

"Perhaps. He promised me all the blessings of my father. But how can I receive those blessings when we are starving, and our sons are lost in Egypt?"

"I remember a time, years ago, when Rachel feared her father would never let her marry you. In those days, we had one thought: 'Trust Jehovah.'" I ran my fingers through his white hair. "Now is another time to trust Jehovah."

"Trust Jehovah." Israel kissed me. "We can do that. But how will you keep us alive until our sons return?"

"Me?"

"You are our healer."

I drew back. *Is this why Mama taught me to heal, why Jehovah gave me the gift? To save my family?* I trembled. *Jehovah always knows.*

"I will do all I can. I want nothing more than to save our family." I sat up on our pallet. "But I will need your help. Your prayers."

Israel ran his fingers up my back and caressed my shoulder, then tugged me back to lie beside him. "If this is Jehovah's will, we can do it."

I turned toward him. "I just pray Judah returns with Benjamin soon."

"And Simeon."

"Yes, Simeon. And soon. For we will not survive much longer without food."

Two mornings later, Miriam made a weak soup made up of an old bone we had used five times before and added the last of our grains.

"Enjoy." She ladled soup into Israel's bowl. "This is the last of the grain."

"Then give it to the children," Israel dumped his soup back into the pot. "I cannot eat when the children need food."

"You need to eat to live," Miriam said, scooping a small portion into my bowl.

"I will wait for Dan and the others to return." I dumped my soup back in. "The little ones need food more than me. Jehovah will help Israel and me survive, if it is His will."

Miriam shook her head. "You will not live long without food."

"Our sons will return soon." Israel touched his empty stomach.

Miriam tried to refill my bowl."Mother Bilhah, you cannot help the children live if you do not eat."

I pushed the ladle back. "No. I will wait until tomorrow."

"You are hardly strong enough now to keep our children alive. You must eat!" Miriam tried to pour the soup into my bowl."

"Maybe later. Feed the others first." I pushed her ladle back once more.

Miriam huffed and dumped the soup back into the pot. "It will be here for you later."

I slowly made my way through the tent, touching each grandchild, giving them a small sip of water, and speaking softly to each one.

"Is there rain yet?" Timna, Naphtali's littlest daughter, asked. What had once been soft curls was now thin, stringy hair. I missed her curls. "I have prayed for Jehovah to bless us."

"No rain yet, little one," Israel bent to lift the cup to her lips to drink. "Jehovah will hear your prayer and rescue us."

Do you believe He will?" Shillem, Timna's older brother, asked, his innocent eyes filled with hope.

Israel turned to help him drink. "Jehovah always listens to the prayers of His little ones. Have you prayed?"

"Not yet. Will you help me?" Shillem touched his grandpapa's hand.

Children throughout the tent took up the cry. "Help us pray, Grandpapa."

Israel and I slowly knelt and raised our hands. The children who could, dragged themselves to kneel in their beds and lifted their hands. The others, too weak to kneel, lifted their hands and repeated Israel's prayer.

After the prayer, Timna pushed herself up. "Papa will return soon." A glow filled her eyes. "Help me go wait for him from beneath the terebinth tree."

"Are you certain?" I tried to push her back down. "You are too weak."

As I helped Israel from his knees, Avri shuffled across the tent to little Timna's side. "I heard your voice. I have soup for you."

"I want to go wait for Papa." Timna lifted her little arms so her mama would lift her.

Avri turned her head towards me. "Will he come today?"

I lifted my shoulder in a slight shrug. "Timna has prayed. She believes they will come home today."

"Father Israel, do you believe it will be —?" Avri coughed and sipped some water. "Will it be today?"

Israel helped another grandchild drink. "Jehovah answers the prayers of His little ones. I believe they will come." His voice cracked.

"You need to eat, Father Israel." Arvi stepped toward him.

"No. I will eat again when our sons return." Israel helped another child to drink.

"I want to go out and wait for my papa," Ard, Benjamin's youngest son, said.

All the children took up the cry, seeking to sit beneath the terebinth tree and wait for their papas, many too weak to do more than squeak.

Arvi lifted her hands to quiet them. "Your mamas will be here soon. They bring you some soup. Eat. Then we will take you to sit under the terebinth tree. We will wait together."

Israel and I finished walking between the children, giving them small drinks. The other mamas with older children entered with soup. We helped them feed the children, then supported the little ones from the tent. It took some time, but we had nothing more to do. In the end, the children helped hold me up as much as I held them as we tottered toward the terebinth tree. Eventually, all the children, their mamas, Israel and I sat beneath the broad, empty limbs of protective and starving tree.

I glanced up at the blue sky between the dry branches. *Oh, Jehovah, bring our sons home before we die. We have* nothing *more to feed our children. We need the food they will bring.*

My stomach had stopped hurting in the previous days as I had eaten less. I stood to take water to a child, but fell back onto the rug. I had no strength to stand.

"Stay down, Mama Bilhah." Miriam put a hand on my shoulder. "His mama can give him water. You rest. Do you think Dan and the others will bring us food today?"

"Our children believe. How can I not? Jehovah honors the prayers of little children."

We stared down the long avenue and along the trail south toward Egypt, hoping to see the dust of their donkeys until our eyes stung.

The sun moved far across the sky toward the low western mountains, and most of us lay drowsing in the heat, too weak to sit. My prayers continued through the day. *Please, Jehovah, bring our sons home with food for their children.*

We grew too weak to return to our pallets in our tents. The women did not move to prepare more soup. There was nothing to make. If our sons, their husbands, did not return, we would not live to see it.

Our family could not end this way, not separated, not broken as it was. Certainly, Jehovah would bring them home in time.

Egypt

The sun slanted through the dry limbs of the terebinth tree. A child called out. "Papa comes. Look."

Pushing myself up onto my elbow, I looked south. A cloud rose along the trail to Egypt. But this cloud was much too big to be our sons and their donkeys.

Our sons' wives cried out in fear, thinking the Egyptians had come to take us as slaves.

"If the dust cloud brings Egyptians to take us into slavery," Zebulon's wife moaned, staring toward the oncoming cloud. "We can do little to stop them. We are too hungry and weak to protect ourselves. Few of us can stand anymore." She lowered her head. "Whoever it is must have learned our husbands are gone, leaving us defenseless."

I struggled to sit, then helped Israel. He called out with his dry, rough throat to calm the women. "Remember, dear daughters, our children prayed for their papas. Jehovah will not send enemies to attack us. Trust Jehovah."

I pushed myself to my feet and wobbled on my cane among them, speaking soft words to calm everyone. "Trust Jehovah. All will be well."

Israel used his staff to push himself to his feet. I struggled to return to his side to support him. We stood with arms threaded together, watching the cloud move toward us. The women and some younger children struggled to stand.

The cloud moved steadily upward. Oxen and donkeys appeared out of the dust. In earlier times, we would have sent grandsons on donkeys to investigate. But we had sent all our donkeys with our sons. Our grandsons had no strength to run to greet this caravan.

"What is that creaking?" I held onto Israel's arm.

He could only shake his head.

The smell of dust and animals accompanied the creaking. I thought the fragrance of grain filled the air as well. Did it? It did not smell or sound like enemies coming to capture us. A donkey brayed. A bull bellowed. A goat bleated. I could only stare in awe at the animals moving our way. And food!

Twelve huge wagons pulled by oxen appeared out of the dust with our sons riding beside a driver high on each seat.

"I see Benjamin!" Israel gripped my hand.

It trembled in his. "Our sons have returned."

"As the little ones said. How could their papas not come today? The children believed."

I shook my head and closed my eyes. "Our family will be together once more." I laid my head against his arm.

"I am grateful you stand with me. I love you," Israel whispered.

"And I love you. Jehovah has blessed us." My heart pounded in my chest. I still marveled at Israel's love.

The wagons turned up the broad avenue toward the terebinth tree and our family.

At last, the lead wagon came to a stop in front of us.

Benjamin leapt from the wagon and ran to Israel.

Israel dropped my hand and caught his youngest son in a tight embrace. "He allowed you to come home," he cried, his scratchy voice barely rising above the noise of the last wagons coming to a halt.

Benjamin's wife and children found the strength to come forward, leaning heavily on him. He supported them in his sturdy arms.

All our sons looked healthy and well fed as each wagon stopped. Sons jumped from the high seat and ran to his own wife and children, where he embraced them, then brought them to Israel and me near the trunk of the terebinth tree.

Judah arrived shortly after Benjamin. "He is alive!" Judah shouted, tears running down his cheeks.

All the other sons echoed his words. "He lives, Father! He is alive!"

I searched the growing crowd for Simeon and found him with his arms surrounding his wife. Alive! He had returned to us alive. I would sing if I had the strength. I silently praised Jehovah for bringing us back together, a complete family once more.

"Benjamin came to me already." Israel patted Benjamin on the back, but Benjamin stepped back, making space for his brothers to join us. "Praise Jehovah. Benjamin lives."

Simeon stepped forward, and Israel embraced him. "And you have returned as well. Praise Jehovah."

"Yes, Father," Judah took Israel's hands when Simeon stepped away. "Benjamin and Simeon are with us. But Joseph! Your son, Joseph, lives!" Judah had not smiled as wide since we lost Joseph.

Joseph? What does he mean? My body trembled, and I searched for Joseph to step out from behind the others.

"He is the Vizier, the governor of Egypt," Judah continued, puffing out his chest. "It is he who replaced our money, who kept Simeon, and insisted we bring Benjamin to him. He knew how hard it would be to send Benjamin, but he craved to see his brother after all these years. Joseph says it was Jehovah who took him to Egypt all those years ago to prepare him for this time. Jehovah took him there so he could provide us with food in our need and keep us alive in this terrible drought."

"Praise Jehovah!" I cried. Time seemed to slow. Could it be true? Joseph alive? They say he lives! I turned to Israel.

Tears ran down his face. He grasped Reuben, seeking confirmation of this miracle.

"It is true. And there are five more years of drought ahead." Reuben set his fist on his chest. "He and his Pharaoh sent wagons to bring you and all our household to Egypt to keep us alive until the drought has passed. They have land for us to settle on to provide for our needs. All because Joseph is our brother — and he lives!"

"His dream ..." I murmured.

"Came from Jehovah," Israel whispered. He stood taller than he had in many months.

A jolt of joy spread through my body. "We will survive this drought. All of us! We will all be together once more after more than twenty years, even Joseph." I wanted to climb into a wagon and turn it toward Egypt. I wanted to go to Joseph now, hold his hands, touch his face once more. Jehovah had blessed us beyond our dreams. He had heard my prayers. Our family would once more gather as one.

We celebrated late into the night, feasting lightly on the food our sons brought from Egypt, for we could not eat too much in our condition. Our children enjoyed the rich milk from the she-goats. Although too weak to dance when our sons arrived, our bodies strengthened enough to sing our praises to Jehovah.

My sweet grandchildren smiled once more. Each came to us whispering, "We trusted Jehovah."

I whispered back, "And he brought your papa back as you prayed."

Mothers smiled and hugged their husbands. All would be well at last.

Later that night, on our pallet in our tent once more, Israel woke me. "Jehovah spoke to me. He told me not to fear Egypt, for He will go with us and make a great nation of us. Then He will bring us out of Egypt. Joseph will touch my eyes, and I will see him once more. We will go to Egypt."

My loving Israel will see Joseph again. Joseph's touch will help him see clearly again. Praise Jehovah.

The next morning we gathered our possessions and packed them. When we had packed everything into the wagons,, including our collapsed and folded tents, our women, children, and eleven sons sat in the wagons sent by the Pharaoh. Israel knelt to offer a prayer for our protection on the journey.

We brought with us seventy men, sons and grandsons, and all their women to see Joseph in Egypt. The few servants who had not left earlier would travel with us.

Israel climbed into the lead wagon and sat beside me on a folded blanket to pad the hard wooden seat.

I scrutinized the now dusty and barren land that had once housed our family for more than twenty years. It could no longer give us the life we had once enjoyed. I turned to face the trail south, where our family would become complete once more. I softly praised Jehovah.

***

We rode through the dusty land of Canaan for many days. After sitting a short time, Israel and I weakly moved to lie between food at the bottom of the wagon bed. The food our sons brought from Egypt continued to help us regain our strength. As we neared the Nile and the courts of the Pharaoh, we sat upright on the wagon seat. Children ran beside the slow wagons, dancing and playing once more.

My heart sang. Soon we would see Joseph and Israel would regain the joy he had lost on that day so long ago when Reuben gave him a torn and bloodied coat. I shook myself. I did not want to remember that day. It no longer mattered. Joseph lived, and we would soon see him for ourselves.

The Nile trickled in a narrow stream between wide banks. The riverbed had cracked and dried. How could this land feed us and their people?

Joseph sent guards to lead us along the banks of the Nile. Two days later, we reached the gates of the enormous walls of Memphis. The city glittered. The gates opened wide to welcome us. More tall, strong guards, dressed in short leather half-tunics with weapons strapped across their backs, came forward to escort us through the noisy, busy streets. Blank stares and hostility greeted our procession. Did they believe we would take their food?

I had never been in such a vast and wealthy city, and had become accustomed to living in tents. The many vast buildings stood much larger than our humble Harran. I had to remind myself to close my mouth.

At last, our wagons arrived at the Pharaoh's enormous palace. Reuben hurried forward to help us onto the white stone street. Two tall men stood atop the palace steps, wearing long white kilts nearly reaching their heels, and only leather straps crossing in front and back over their naked upper bodies, glistening with oil. Black kohl lined their eyes. They stood in regal magnificence.

Israel gripped my hand as we climbed the low stairs. When we neared the men, Israel tugged me to kneel beside him, honoring the Pharoah.

The younger of the two men rushed down the steps and lifted Israel up. "No, you must never kneel to me. You are my father!" He embraced Israel.

Joseph! At last.

I glanced up at the other man, who nodded acceptance. I slowly stood beside Israel.

Joseph clasped Israel's arms. "Father, it is me, Joseph." He touched Israel's eyes.

"My son!" Israel stood taller, and tears streamed down his face. "I see your face at last. Jehovah has given me sight to see you. I thought you dead."

"No, Father. I am very much alive." He turned to me. "Mother Bilhah! I have missed you." He pulled me into an embrace. It surprised me how tall and strong he had grown. I marveled to once more embrace him. I held him tight as I imagined Rachel would have.

I touched his face. "It is really you. You live." Now tears streamed down my cheeks.

Joseph laughed away his tears. "I do."

He glanced back at the others who knelt below us on the stairs. "Reuben and Judah told me about Mother Leah and Mother Zilpah. I regret I was not there to tell them goodbye."

"They thought they would meet you with Jehovah," I said.

Joseph smiled a rueful smile. "No. Jehovah brought me here to Egypt."

"To interpret my dreams and prepare my land against this drought." The Pharaoh gently slapped Joseph's back.

"So I could bring you here and save you." Joseph's grin was balm to my weary soul.

We had all knelt to him — the sun, the moon, and the stars. We fulfilled his prophetic dream.

Joseph waved everyone to the top of the stairs, to stand on the great palace porch. He stood next to his father as he greeted each of his brothers, exclaiming at the beauty of their wives and daughters, and the strength of their sons.

Then he beckoned toward a small group of people who stood behind him, in the shadows of the portico. A beautiful woman with shining black hair came forward with two young men. "This is my wife, Asenath. These two boys are Ephriam and Manasseh. Boys, this is your grandfather and grandmother."

Israel kissed Asenath on the cheek, then turned to speak to the boys. I accepted Asenath's embrace. "You have handsome sons."

"Like their father."

I glanced at Joseph. "Yes, like their father."

I watched my sons together, all twelve of them with their father. Our family was finally together. The sun, the moon, and the stars, and we gladly bowed before Joseph.

May Jehovah bless our united family in Egypt.

To women who accept challenges
Even when they are difficult.

Acknowledgements

You read another book. I am grateful.

It took much longer than expected to write this book. I wrote it at the same time I wrote the other three books telling the stories of the wives of Jacob. My brain did not handle four books well. But the books are finished.

Many people have helped in the writing and publication of this book. Most importantly, I give thanks and appreciation to my husband, Jack, who sits patiently beside me while I ignore him and write.

Thanks also to my family: sons, daughter, grandchildren, and parents. They always support me. Even my aged parents who can no longer read, encourage me in my work. They bless my life.

My writing group has given me the support I needed during the time it has taken to write these books. My friend and supporter, Carol Malone, has been of special help.

I thank my editor, Ora Smith, for her careful editing and thoughtful comments and suggestions to make this a better book for your reading entertainment. Also, I thank my cover artist, Dar Albert, who has created a beautiful cover. I give both women my profound gratitude.

Thanks go to my AngelCAST team for the final read, finding the typos and last missed mistakes. Any more missed mistakes are my responsibility.

Finally, thank you to you, the reader, for choosing to read this book of fiction. I created it for you.

Book Club Questions

1. As Bilhah's family fell apart, she struggled. How did the loss of her father, brothers, mother, and sister affect the rest of her life? Who became her new family in Laban's home? How did they help her? Have you had others become your "heart sister" or "sister from another mother?" How has this helped you?
2. The maidservants gossiped about Laban's daughters, Rachel and Leah. What did they have to say about Rachel, Bilhah's new mistress? How did Bilhah respond to the other maidservants' gossip? Why would she? Have you seen this happen in your life? How would you respond to gossip about your friends?
3. After Rachel and Jacob waited seven years to marry, Laban forced Leah to marry Jacob first. What could Bilhah have done to help warn Jacob? Could she have left Laban's home? What could she have done to survive if she had run away? Would Laban have allowed that? Was Bilhah a victim of Laban's selfishness as much as Rachel, Leah, and Jacob?
4. As "neither wife nor maidservant," Bilhah struggled to find her place. How did this affect her relationship with Zilpah? How did they overcome this? Have you struggled to understand changes in your own or a friend's life? How could you resolve the challenge?
5. Bilhah's mama healed others and taught her as much as she could before taking her to serve Laban. How did this skill of healing others as a young girl change her life? How did it bring her closer to her family and Jehovah?
6. Dinah's experiences in Shalem changed everything for Jacob's women and families. How could they convince

Shalem's women to integrate into their community? How could they accept Bilhah's kindness under such difficult circumstances? Could you?

7. Bilhah lost her sister-wives to illness. In the end, Jacob had only Bilhah to lean on? How did her life prepare her to accept this? Did it surprise you?
8. Joseph's dreams infuriated his brothers and turned them on him. However, because of their treacheraous actions, he saved their family. In what ways do you think the brothers suffered, knowing they had captured Joseph before he went missing? How would it change their trust in Jehovah and their love for Joseph to find he was the Vizier who would save the family?
9. Rachel waited nearly 20 years after she married Jacob to have Joseph. What was Jehovah's purpose for this long wait? What do you think Benjamin's purpose was?

Did You Enjoy This Book?

If you did, will you do something for me?

I'm an independent author, publishing my books without the backing of a major publisher. That means no six-figure advances and no advertising budget. This makes it difficult to promote my novels and put them in places new readers can find them. But you can help me.

Honest reviews and genuine "word-of-mouth" advertising make all the difference. I'm not asking for one of those awful book reports I used to try not to sleep through, that you did in school. What will help me is if you would leave an honest star rating and a couple of sentences on the bookseller's site where you purchased this book. Or a brief review on your blog. Or tell your friends about it on your favorite social media sites.

Let people know what you liked about this book, and why they might like it, too. And if there was something you didn't like, you can say that, as well. Constructive criticism helps me write a better book next time.

But please. No spoilers!

Would You Like a Free Book?

If you have not yet agreed to receive my weekly newsletter, Angelique's Historical Fiction Reader, maybe now would be a great time to join. If you would like a short story about Eve assisting Adam, click here[1] to receive *Avenging Angel.*

If you want to read the short story about Shamgar, the healer who helped Ziva and Crites, click here[2] to receive *Damaged Healer.*

If you currently receive my weekly newsletter and did not receive one of these free books, let me know. I'll be happy to forward you a link for either book.

Angelique@AngeliqueCongerAuthor.com

Happy Reading,

Angelique

---

1. https://dl.bookfunnel.com/to6h2blg9y
2. https://dl.bookfunnel.com/ldg1thkpcj

Books by Angelique Conger

Ancient Matriarchs

Eve, First Matriarch

Into the Storms: Ganet, Wife of Seth

Finding Peace: Rebecca, Wife of Enos

Moving into Light: Zehira, Wife of Enoch

Out of Darkness: Imma, Wife of Noah

We Stood Beside Them: Other Wives of the Patriarchs

Lost Children of the Prophet

Lost Children of the Prophet

Captured Freedom

Abandoned Hope

Brotherly Havoc

Betrayed Trust

Convicted Deliverance

Trouble Escaped

Contrary Devotion

Impassioned Grief

Love Defied

Hidden Purpose

Concealed Innocence

Struggle for Limhah

Combating Cults

Fighting Foreign Armies

Defending Faith

Into Egypt

Out of Egypt

Discovery

Settlement

Enemies

Women of the Covenant

About the Author

Many would consider Angelique Conger's books Christian-focused, and they are, because they tell stories of women and events in the Bible. She writes of people who believe in Jehovah. However, though she's read the Bible and searched for more about these stories, not finding much to help, her imagination fills in the missing information, creating fascinating stories that keep readers wanting more..

Angelique Conger discovered the wonders of writing books later in her life. Books, however, have always been important to her. As a little girl in a small town, she received a library card of her own at the tender age of five, unusual in those days. She made good use of it.

Angelique reads a book, or three at once, much of the time. She reads most genres of books and, until a few years ago, only toyed with writing them. Since beginning her creative journey, she has spent hours each day learning the craft of writing and editing.

Angelique lives in Southern Nevada with her husband and two cats, who show love by sharing her pillow and sleeping at her feet. She enjoys visits from her grandchildren and their parents.

Don't miss out!

Visit the website below and you can sign up to receive emails whenever Angelique Conger publishes a new book. There's no charge and no obligation.

https://books2read.com/r/B-A-NFPH-FGVFJ

BOOKS 2 READ

Connecting independent readers to independent writers.

www.ingramcontent.com/pod-product-compliance
Lightning Source LLC
LaVergne TN
LVHW041108080826
845145LV00007B/1733

* 9 7 8 1 9 4 6 5 5 0 8 5 9 *